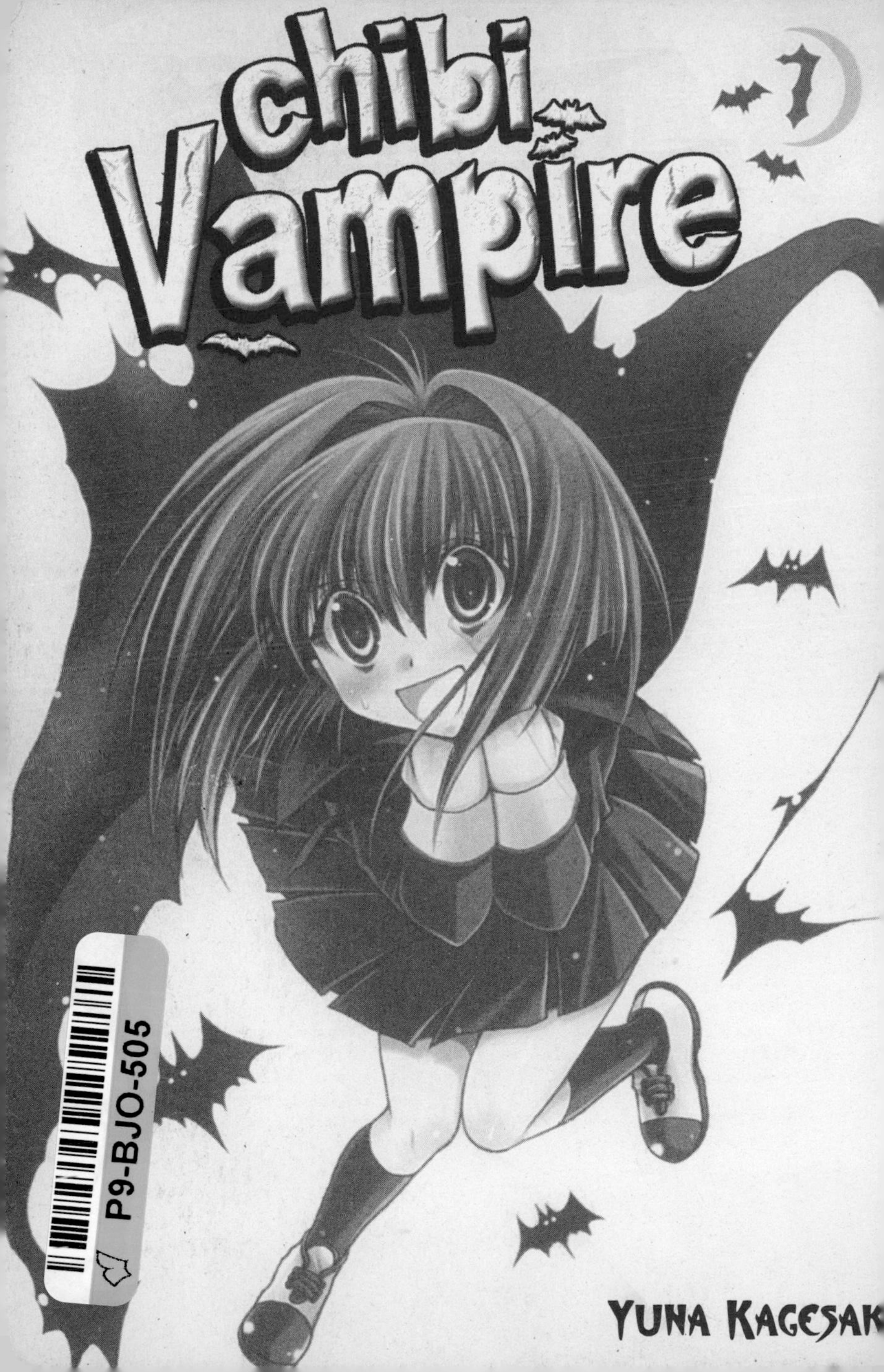
Chibi Vampire
7
YUNA KAGESAK

Chibi Vampire Volume 7
Created by Yuna Kagesaki

Translation - Alexis Kirsch
English Adaptation - Christine Boylan
Copy Editor - Nikhil Burman
Retouch and Lettering - Star Print Brokers
Production Artist - Mike Estacio
Graphic Designers - Fawn Lau & Colin Graham

Editor - Tim Beedle
Digital Imaging Manager - Chris Buford
Pre-Production Supervisor - Erika Terriquez
Production Manager - Elisabeth Brizzi
Managing Editor - Vy Nguyen
Creative Director - Anne Marie Horne
Editor-in-Chief - Rob Tokar
Publisher - Mike Kiley
President and C.O.O. - John Parker
C.E.O. and Chief Creative Officer - Stuart Levy

A  Manga

TOKYOPOP and 🐢 are trademarks or registered trademarks of TOKYOPOP Inc.

TOKYOPOP Inc.
5900 Wilshire Blvd. Suite 2000
Los Angeles, CA 90036

E-mail: info@TOKYOPOP.com
Come visit us online at www.TOKYOPOP.com

KARIN Volume 7 © 2005 YUNA KAGESAKI
First published in Japan in 2005 by FUJIMISHOBO CO., LTD.,
Tokyo. English translation rights arranged with KADOKAWA
SHOTEN PUBLISHING CO., LTD., Tokyo through TUTTLE-MORI
AGENCY, INC., Tokyo.
English text copyright © 2008 TOKYOPOP Inc.

ISBN: 978-1-59816-881-5

First TOKYOPOP printing: February 2008
10 9 8 7 6 5 4 3 2 1
Printed in the USA

Chibi Vampire

Volume 7

Created by

Yuna Kagesaki

TOKYOPOP®

HAMBURG // LONDON // LOS ANGELES // TOKYO

OUR STORY SO FAR...

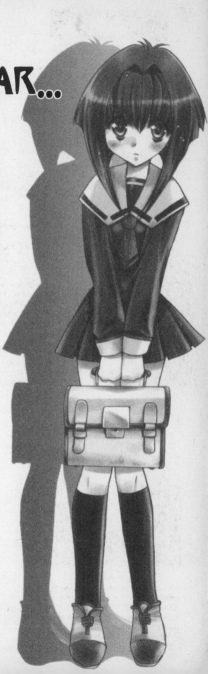

KARIN MAAKA ISN'T LIKE OTHER GIRLS. ONCE A MONTH, SHE EXPERIENCES PAIN, FATIGUE, HUNGER, IRRITABILITY—AND THEN SHE BLEEDS. FROM HER NOSE. KARIN IS A VAMPIRE, FROM A FAMILY OF VAMPIRES, BUT INSTEAD OF NEEDING TO DRINK BLOOD, SHE HAS AN EXCESS OF BLOOD THAT SHE MUST GIVE TO HER VICTIMS. IF DONE RIGHT, GIVING THIS BLOOD TO HER VICTIM CAN BE AN EXTREMELY POSITIVE THING. THE PROBLEM WITH THIS IS THAT KARIN NEVER SEEMS TO DO THINGS RIGHT...

KARIN IS HAVING A BIT OF BOY TROUBLE. KENTA USUI—THE HANDSOME NEW STUDENT AT HER SCHOOL AND WORK—IS A NICE ENOUGH GUY, BUT HE EXACERBATES KARIN'S PROBLEM. KARIN, YOU SEE, IS DRAWN TO PEOPLE WHO HAVE SUFFERED MISFORTUNE, AND KENTA HAS SUFFERED PLENTY OF IT. MAKING THINGS EVEN MORE COMPLICATED, IT'S BECOME CLEAR TO KARIN THAT SHE'S IN LOVE WITH KENTA... SOMETHING THAT CAN ONLY BRING TROUBLE. LOVE BETWEEN HUMANS AND VAMPIRES IS FROWNED UPON IN VAMPIRE SOCIETY, AND KARIN'S FAMILY HAS DECIDED THAT A RELATIONSHIP BETWEEN THEIR DAUGHTER AND A HUMAN BOY IS TOO DANGEROUS. THEY HAVE FORBIDDEN KENTA FROM EVER SEEING KARIN AGAIN. UPSET AND ANGRY, KARIN SOUGHT OUT KENTA TO APOLOGIZE AND BEG HIM TO IGNORE HER FAMILY'S DEMAND, BUT IN THE PROCESS, SHE REVEALED WHY HER BLEEDING IS WORSE WHEN HE'S AROUND. ANGRY AND IN DISBELIEF, KENTA REACTED HARSHLY AND RAN AWAY.

THE MAAKA FAMILY

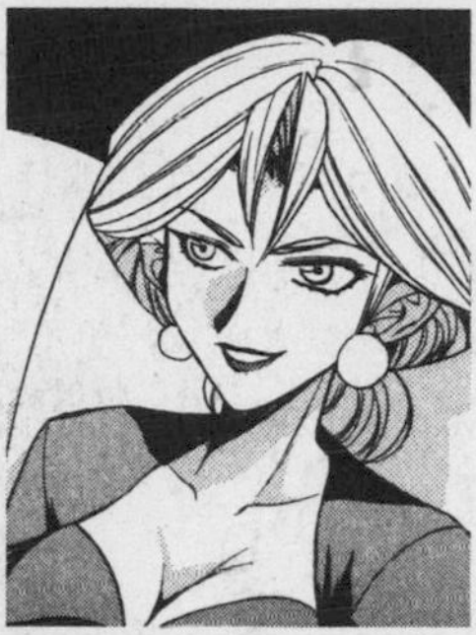

CALERA MARKER

Karin's overbearing mother. While Calera resents that Karin wasn't born a normal vampire, she does love her daughter in her own obnoxious way. Calera has chosen to keep her European last name.

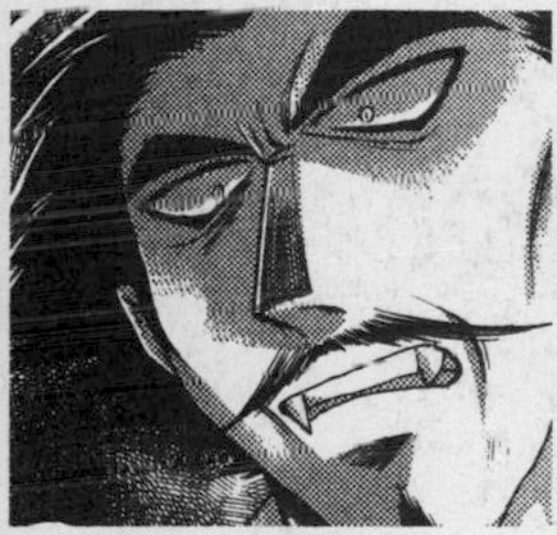

HENRY MARKER

Karin's father. In general, Henry treats Karin a lot better than her mother does, but the pants in this particular family are worn by Calera. Henry has also chosen to keep his European last name.

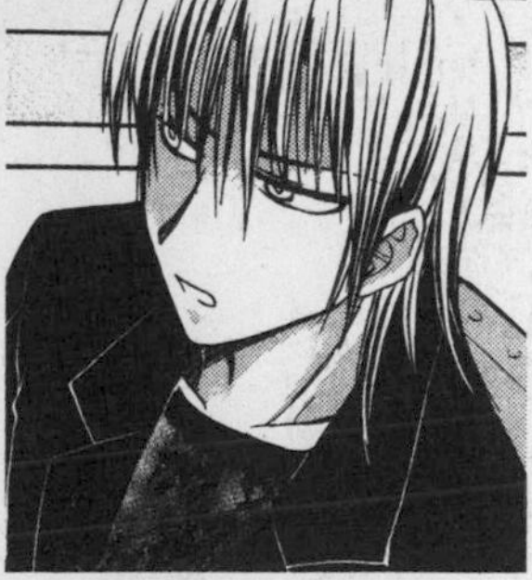

REN MAAKA

Karin's older brother. Ren milks the "sexy creature of the night" thing for all it's worth and spends his nights in the arms (and beds) of attractive young women.

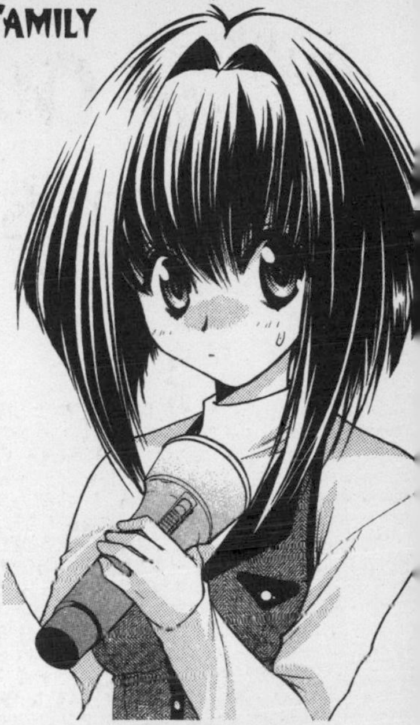

KARIN MAAKA

Our little heroine. Karin is a vampire living in Japan, but instead of sucking blood from her victims, she actually GIVES them some of her blood. She's a vampire in reverse.

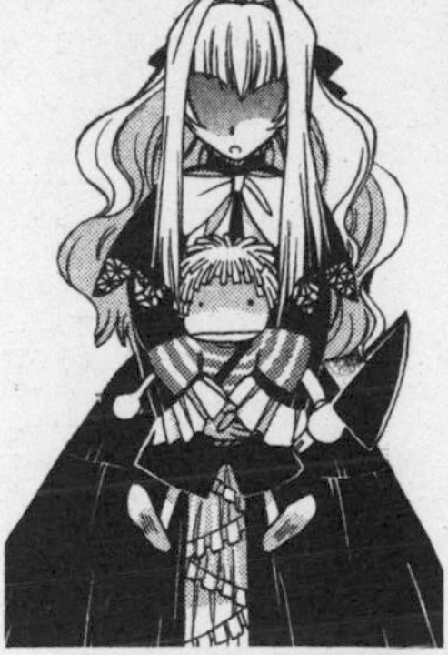

ANJU MAAKA

Karin's little sister. Anju has not yet awoken as a full vampire, but she can control bats and is usually the one who cleans up after Karin's messes. Rarely seen without her "talking" doll, Boogie.

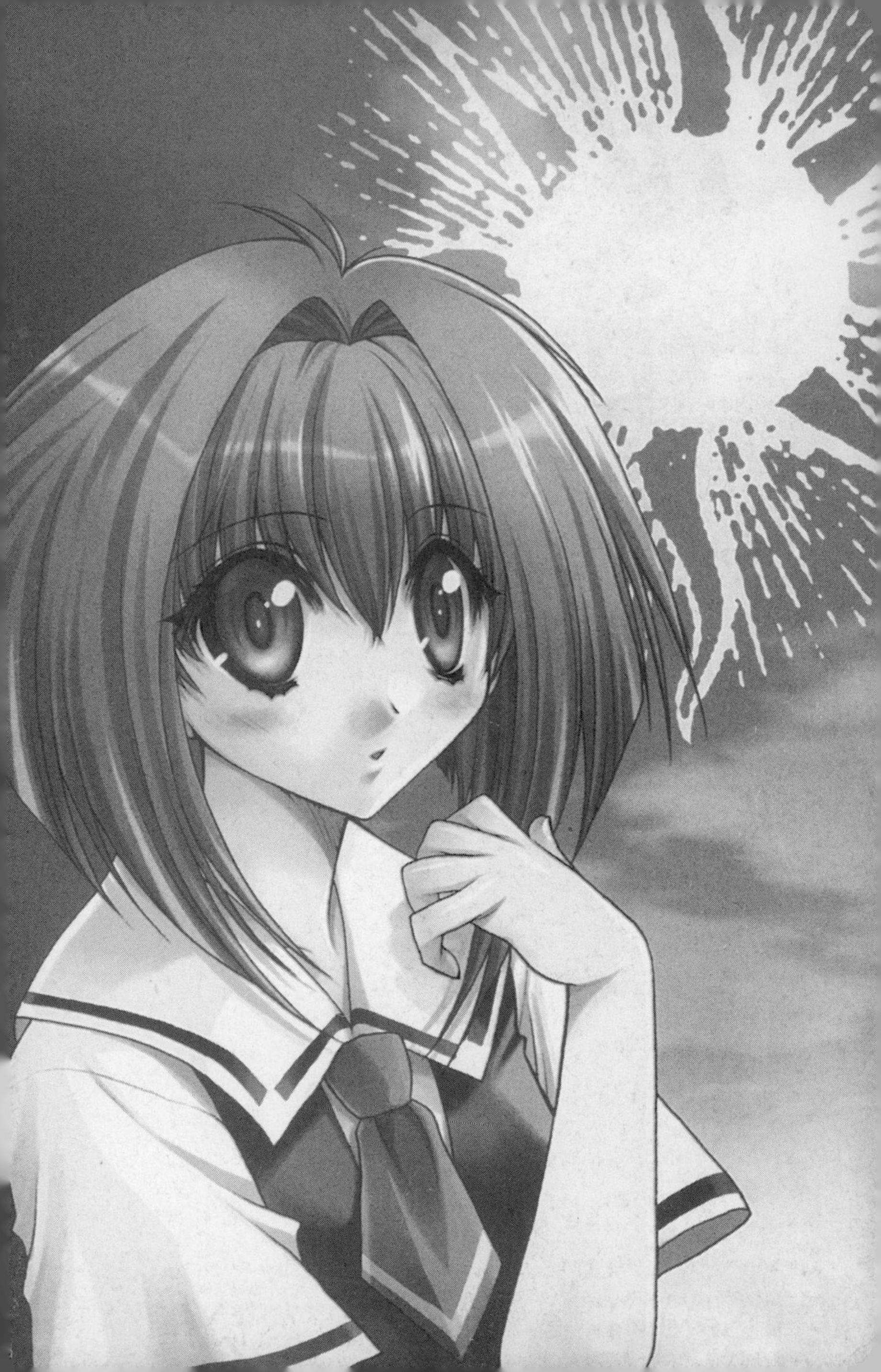

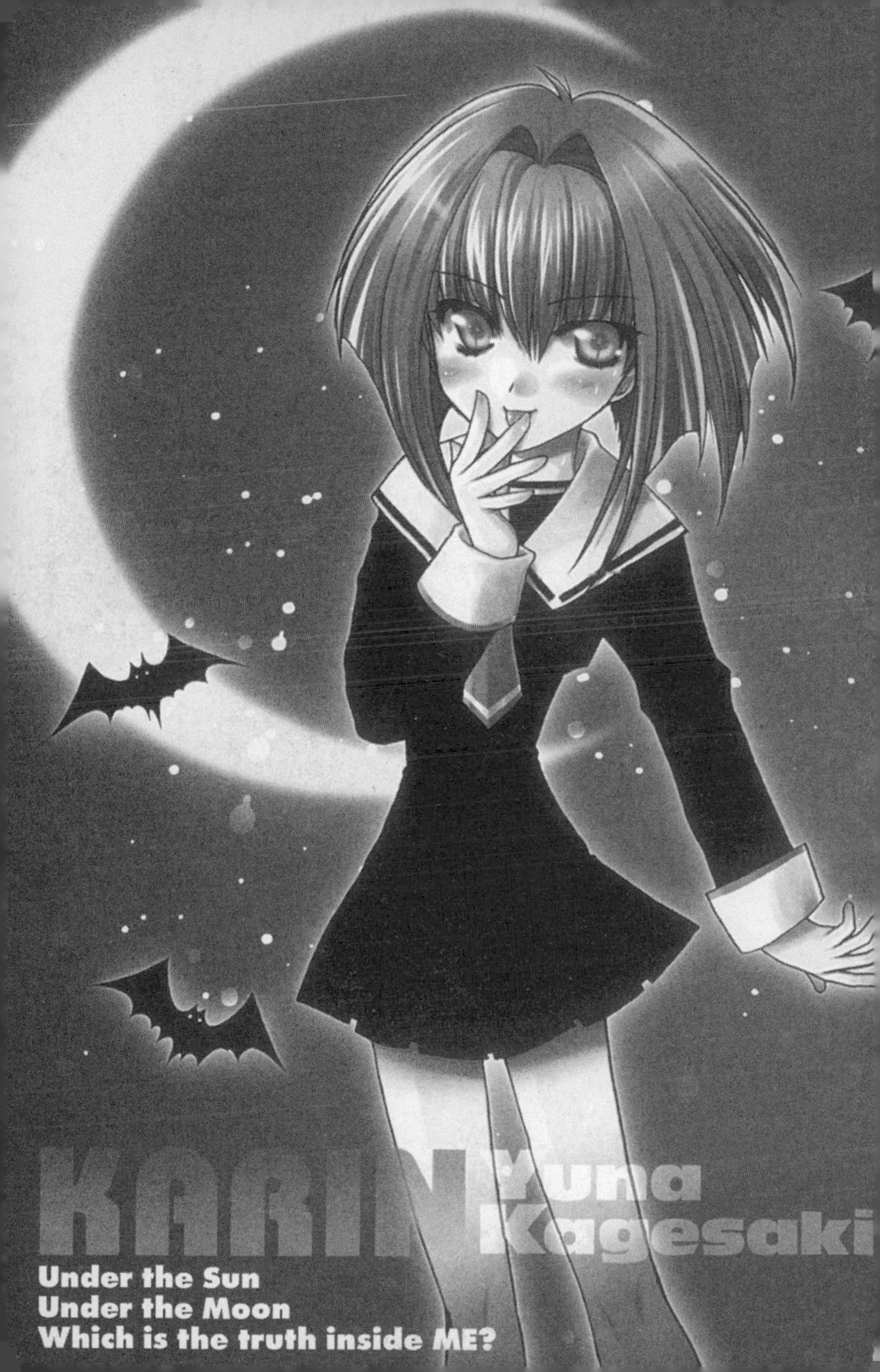
KARIN
Yuna Kagesaki
Under the Sun
Under the Moon
Which is the truth inside ME?

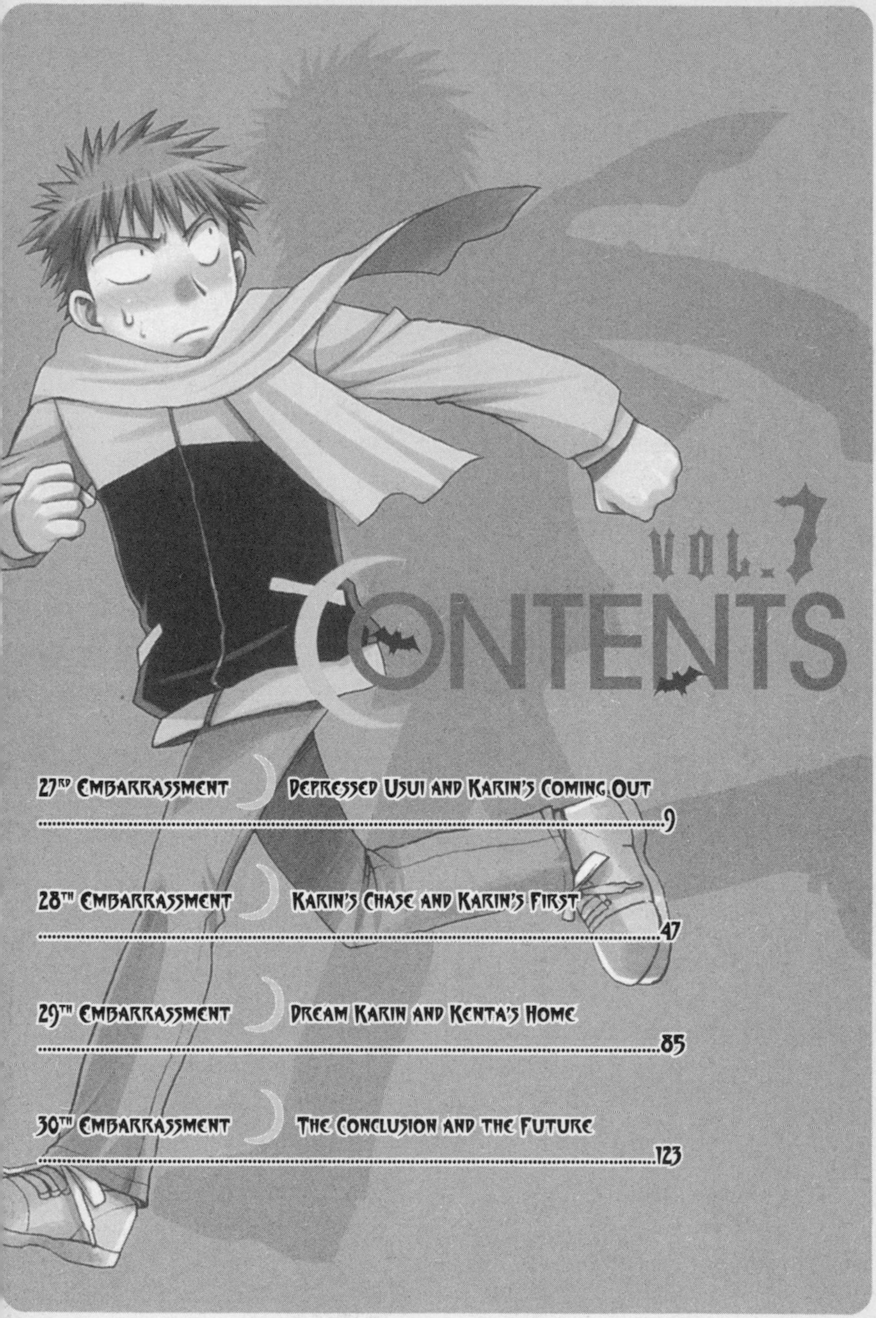

Vol. 7 Contents

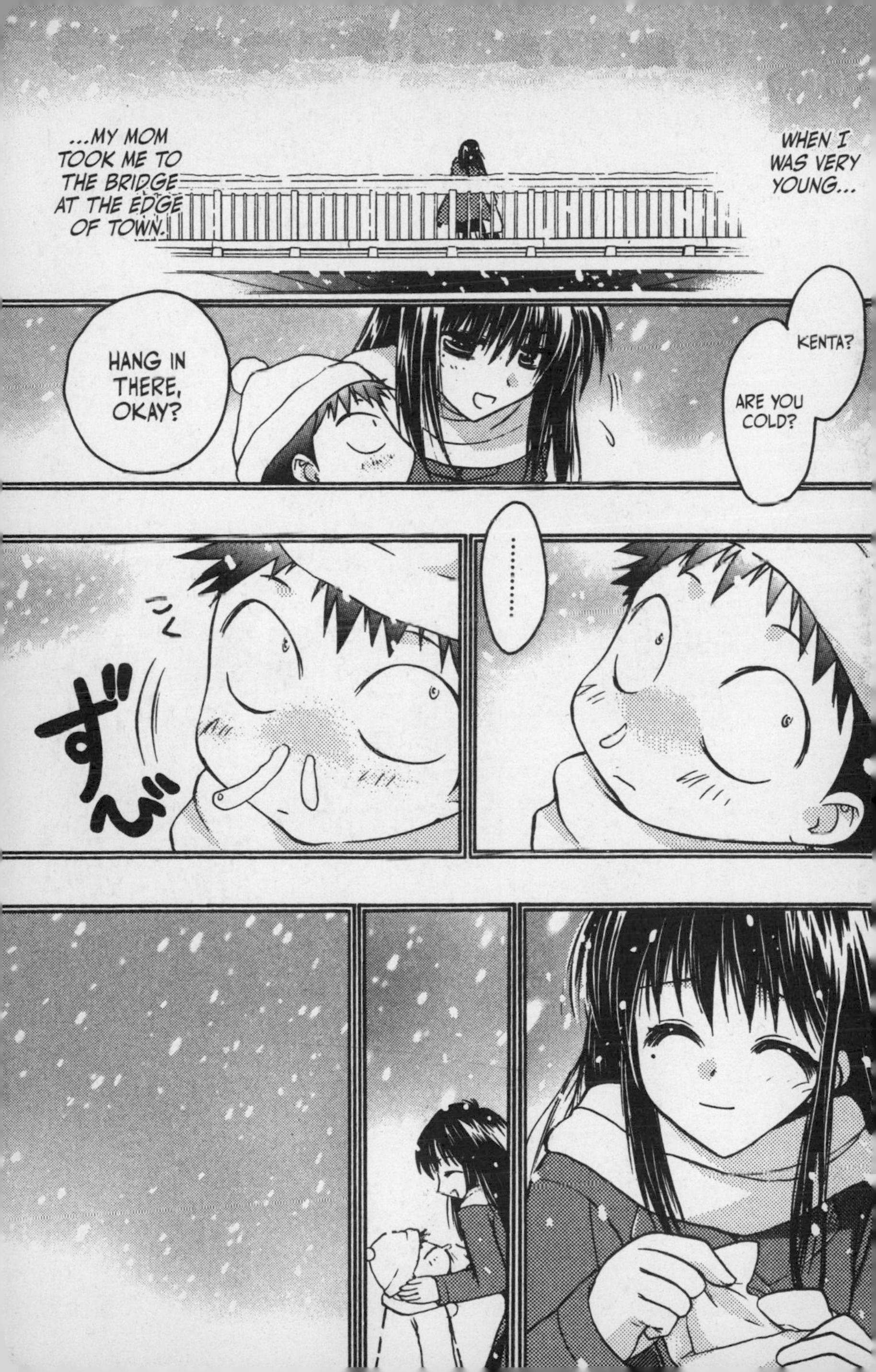
WHEN I WAS VERY YOUNG...
...MY MOM TOOK ME TO THE BRIDGE AT THE EDGE OF TOWN.
KENTA?
ARE YOU COLD?
HANG IN THERE, OKAY?
......
ずび

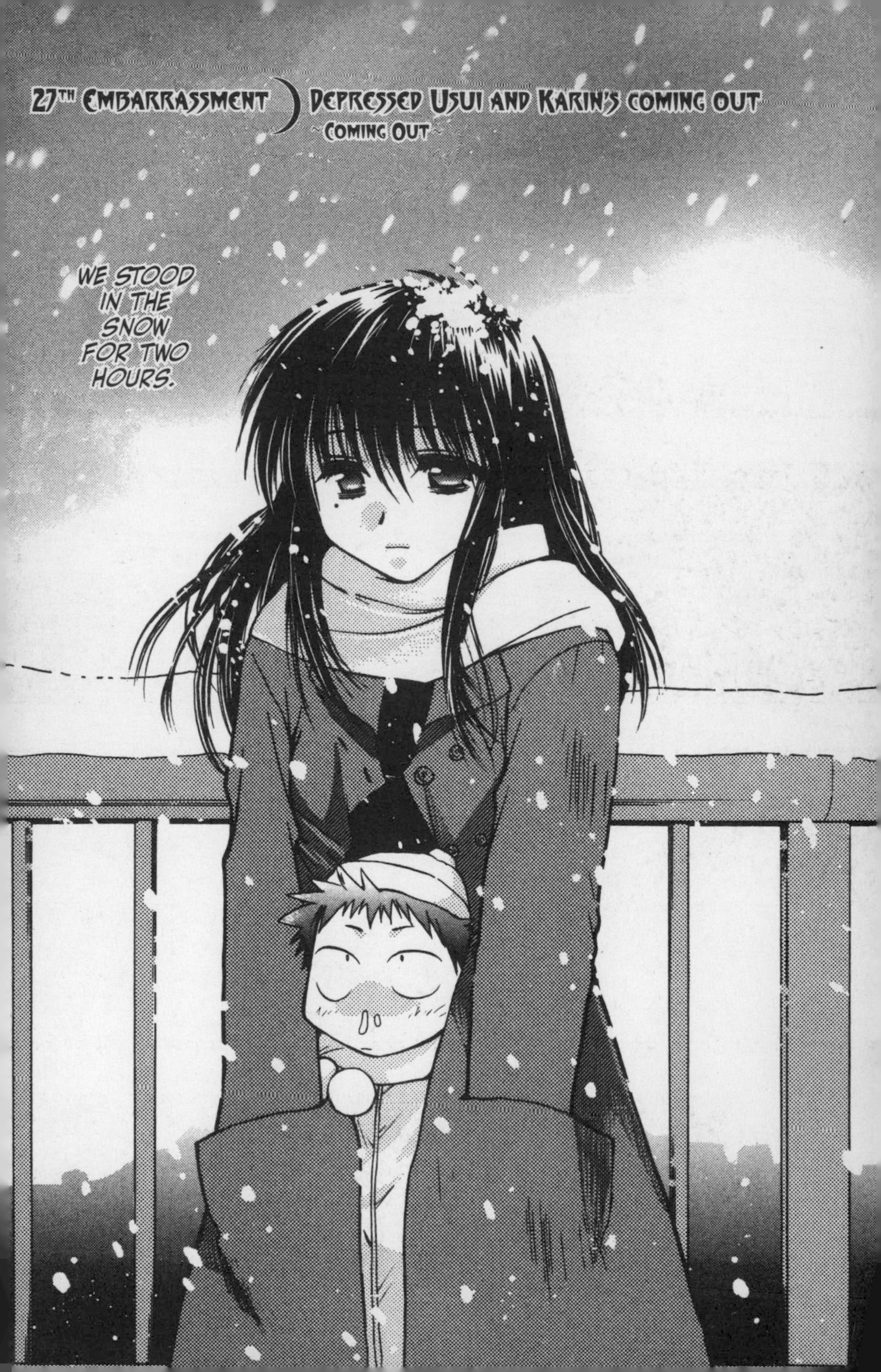
27TH EMBARRASSMENT
DEPRESSED USUI AND KARIN'S COMING OUT
~COMING OUT~
WE STOOD IN THE SNOW FOR TWO HOURS.

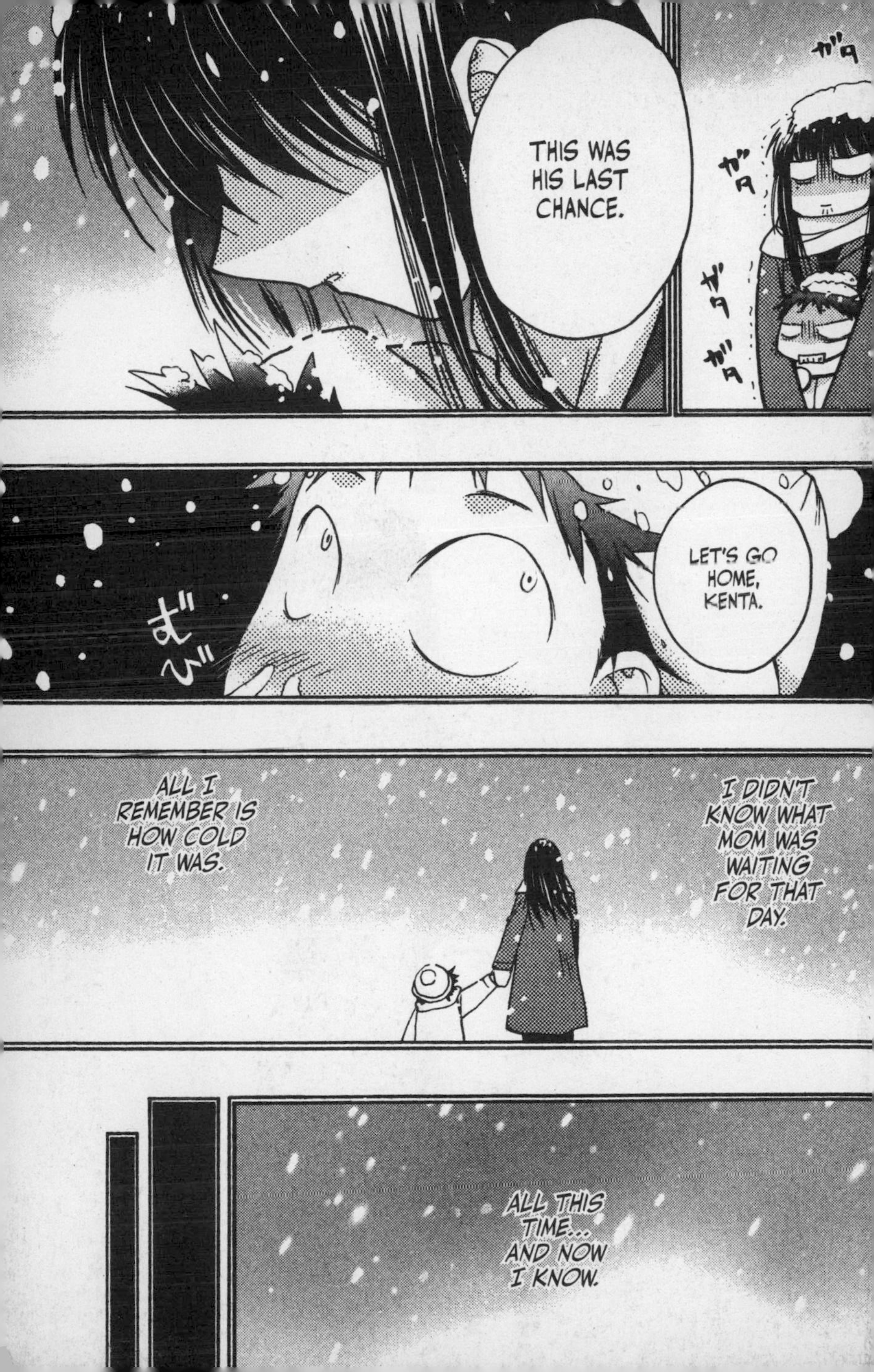
ガタ
ガタ
ガタ
ガタ
THIS WAS HIS LAST CHANCE.
LET'S GO HOME, KENTA.
ずび
I DIDN'T KNOW WHAT MOM WAS WAITING FOR THAT DAY.
ALL I REMEMBER IS HOW COLD IT WAS.
ALL THIS TIME... AND NOW I KNOW.

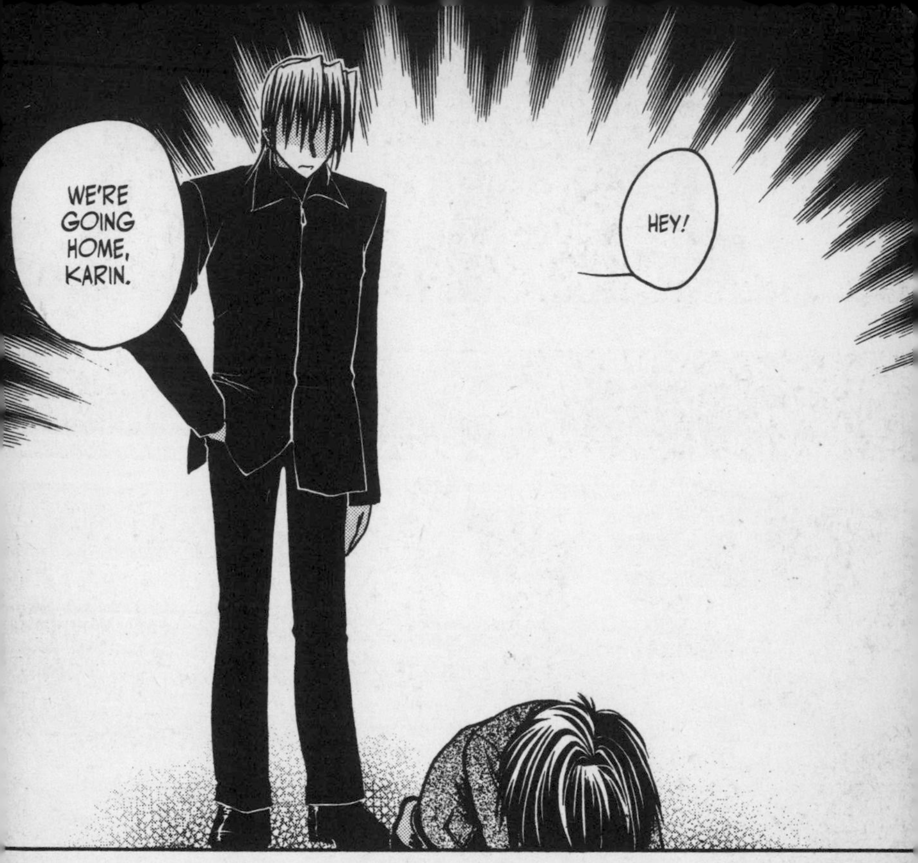
HEY!
WE'RE GOING HOME, KARIN.

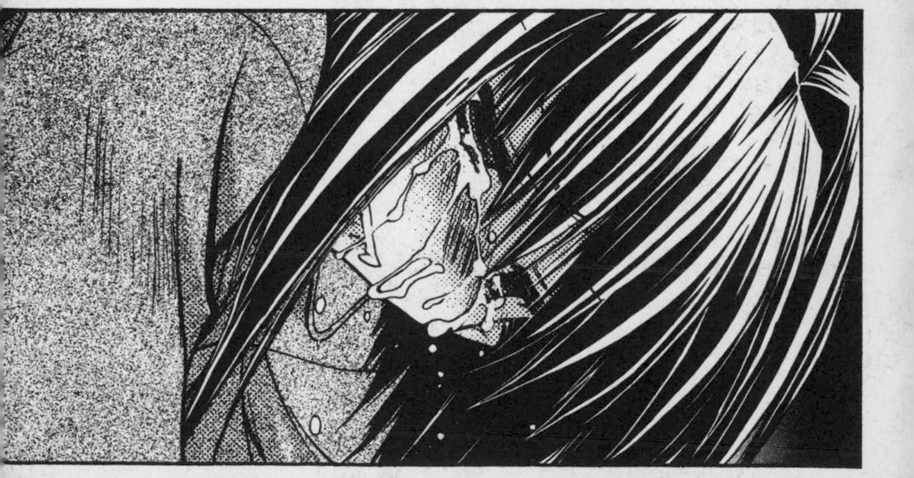

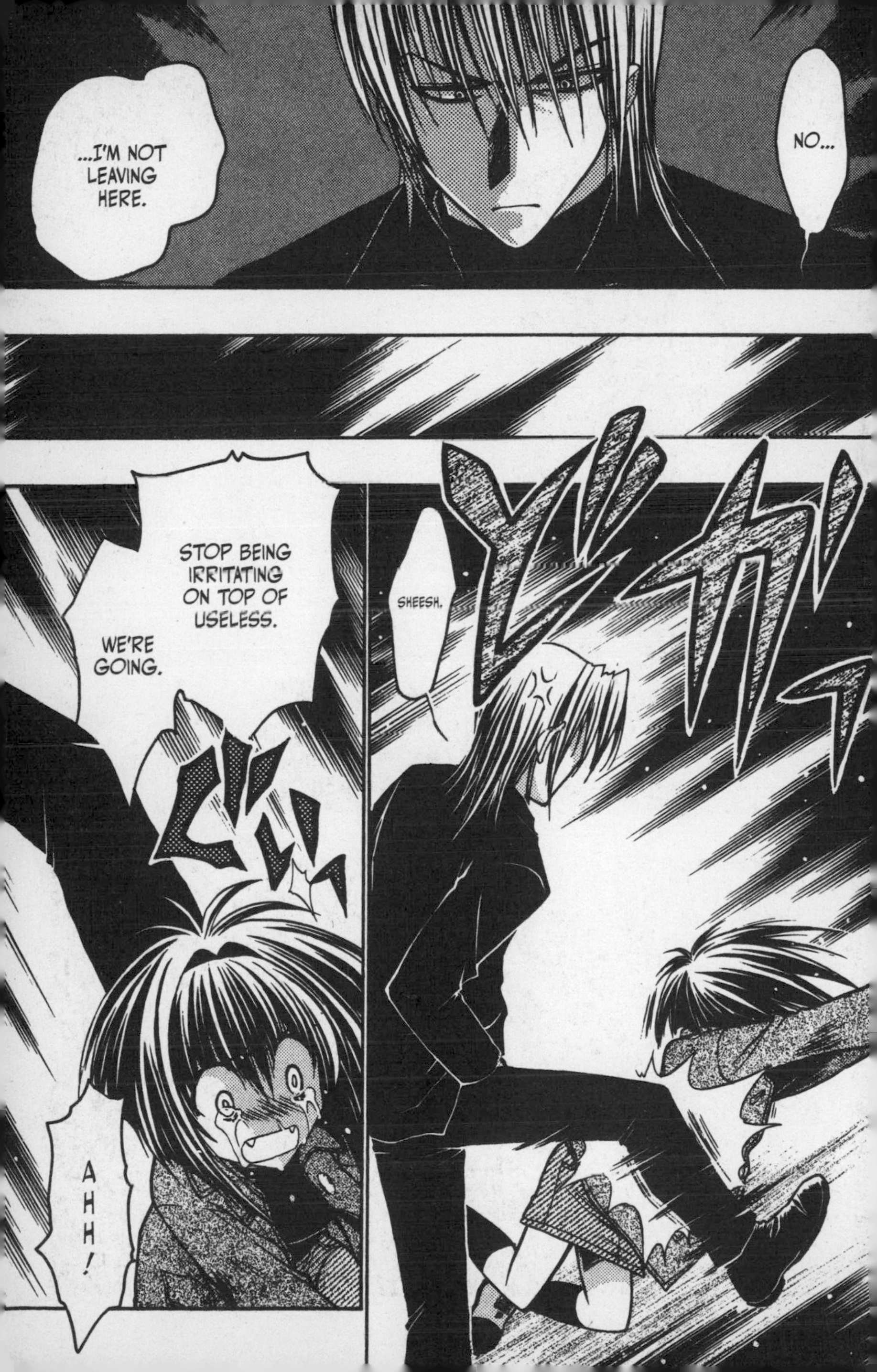
NO...
...I'M NOT LEAVING HERE.
SHEESH.
STOP BEING IRRITATING ON TOP OF USELESS.
WE'RE GOING.
AHH!

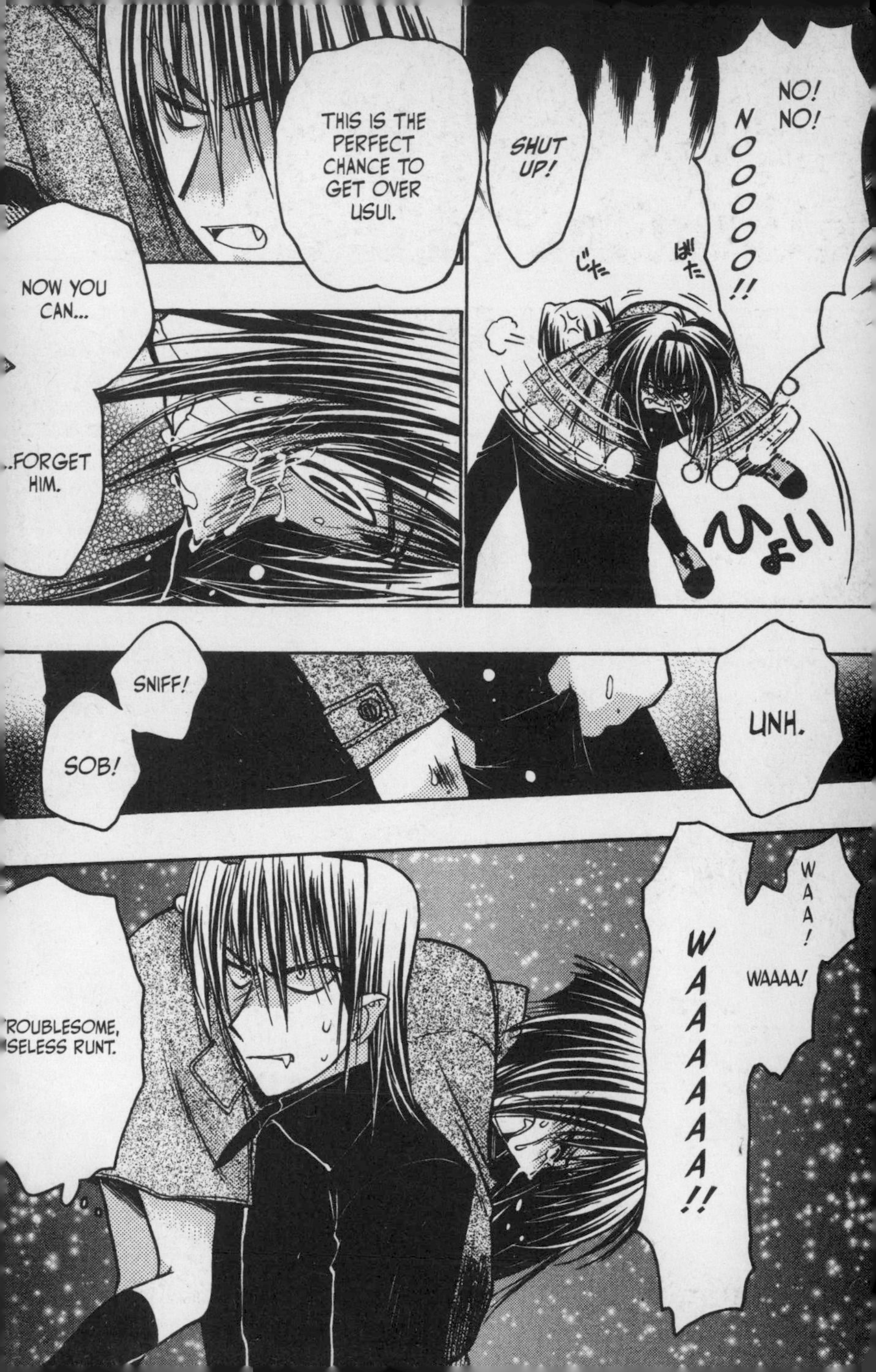

NO! NO!
NOOOOOO!!
SHUT UP!
ばた
じた
ひょい
THIS IS THE PERFECT CHANCE TO GET OVER USUI.
NOW YOU CAN...
..FORGET HIM.
UNH.
SNIFF!
SOB!
WAA!
WAAAA!
WAAAAAAA!!
ROUBLESOME, SELESS RUNT.

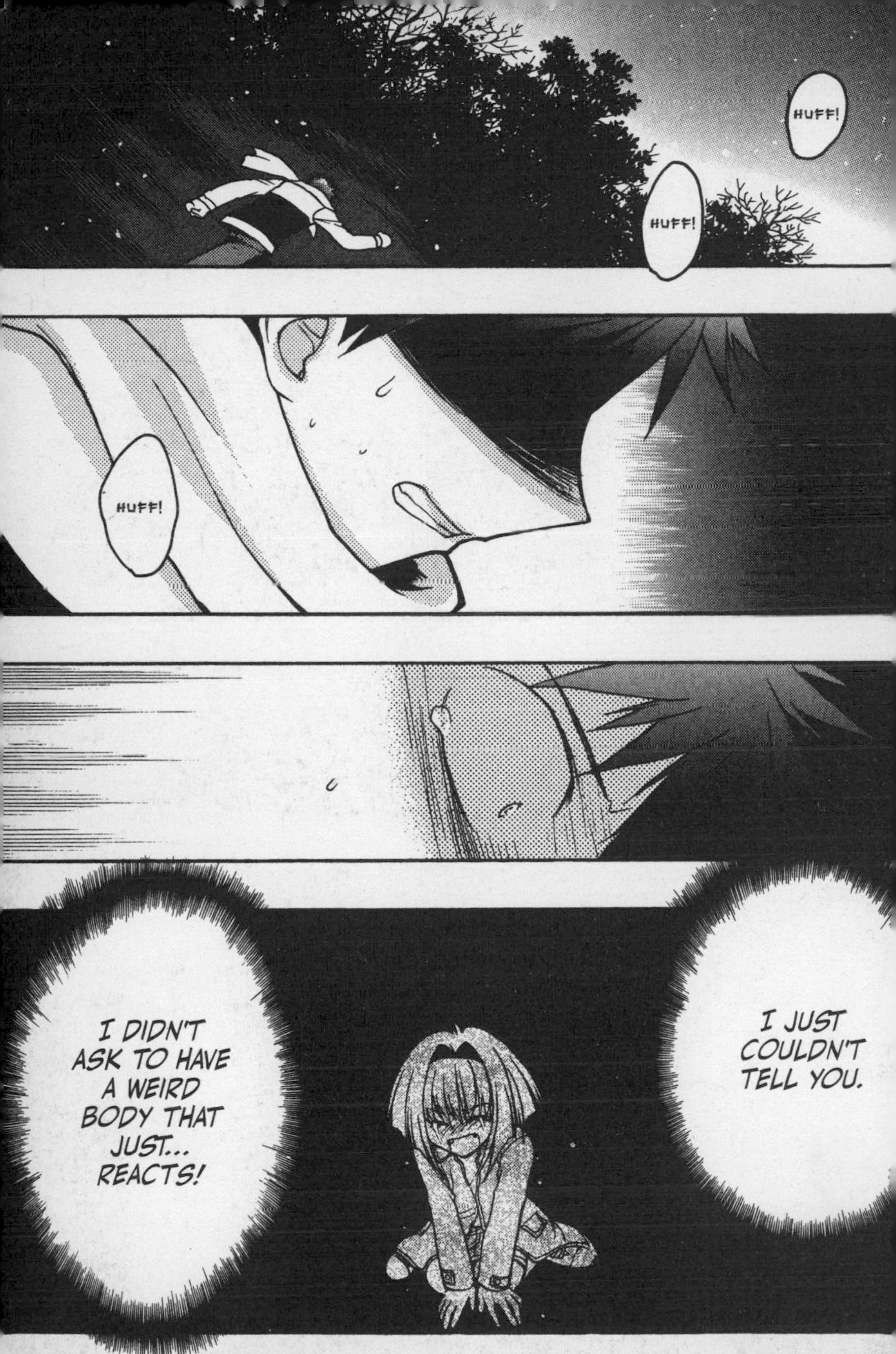
HUFF!
HUFF!
HUFF!
I JUST COULDN'T TELL YOU.
I DIDN'T ASK TO HAVE A WEIRD BODY THAT JUST... REACTS!

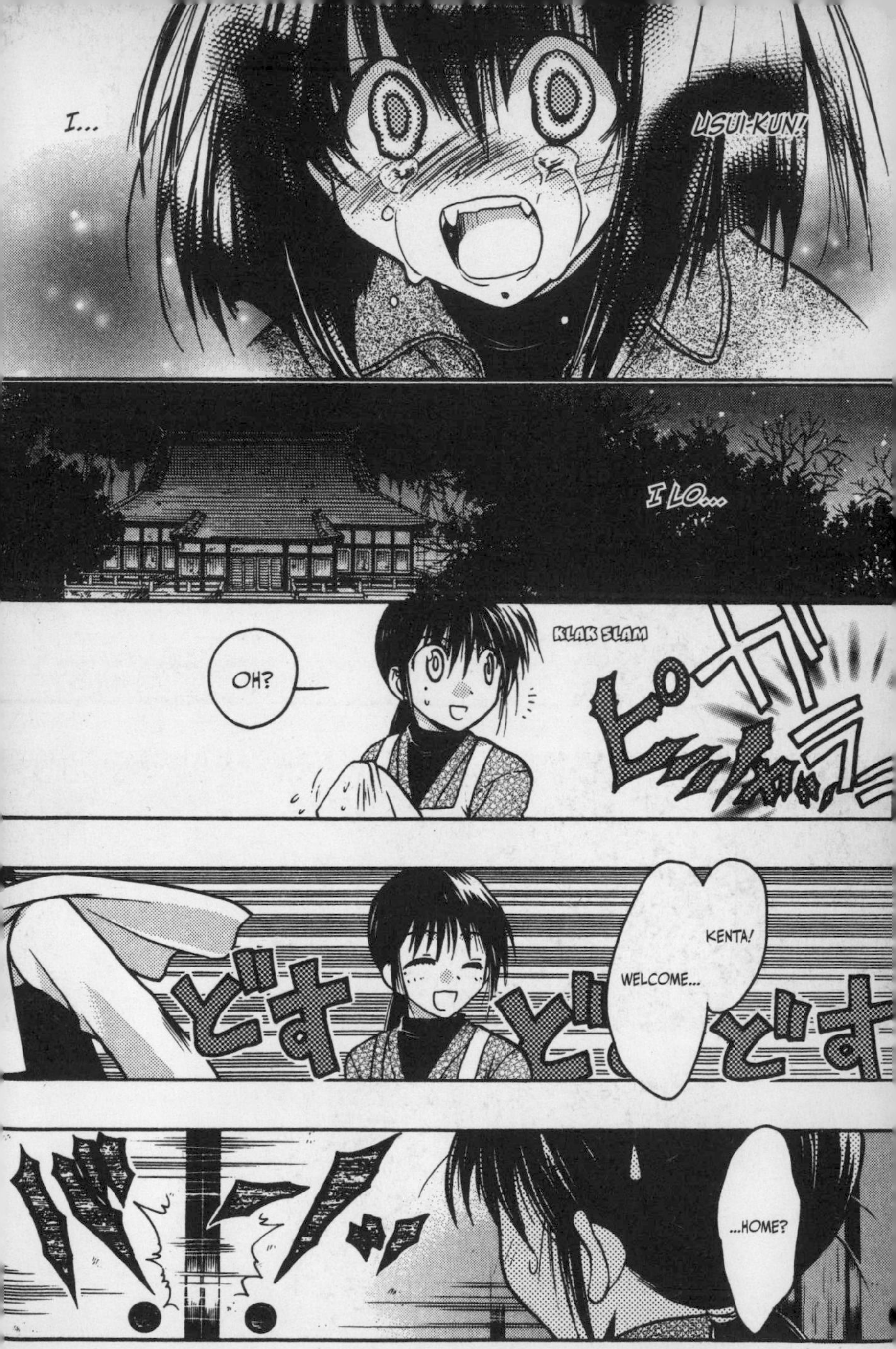
USUI-KUN!
I...
I LO...
KLAK SLAM
OH?
KENTA!
WELCOME...
...HOME?

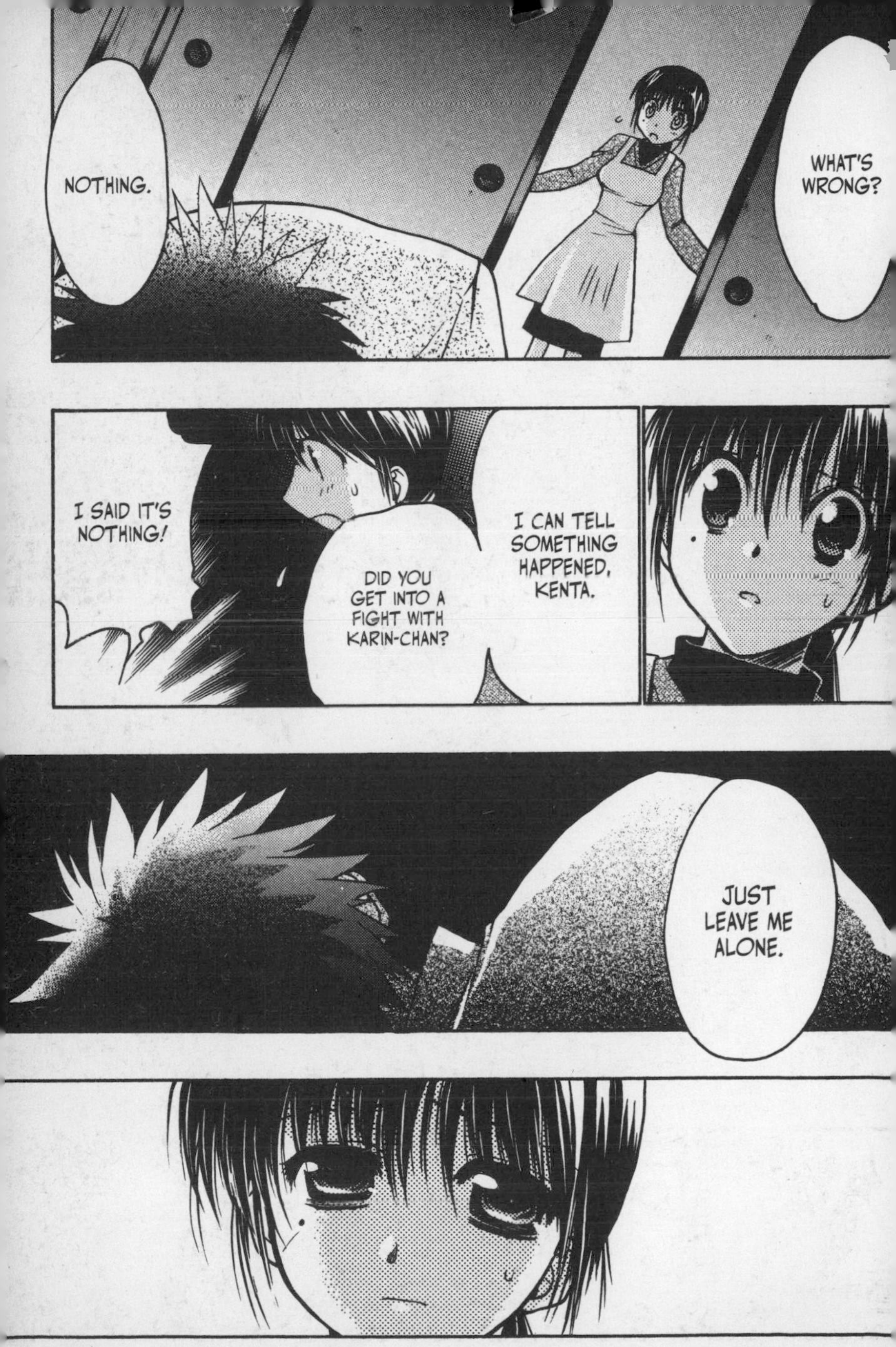
WHAT'S WRONG?
NOTHING.
I CAN TELL SOMETHING HAPPENED, KENTA.
DID YOU GET INTO A FIGHT WITH KARIN-CHAN?
I SAID IT'S NOTHING!
JUST LEAVE ME ALONE.

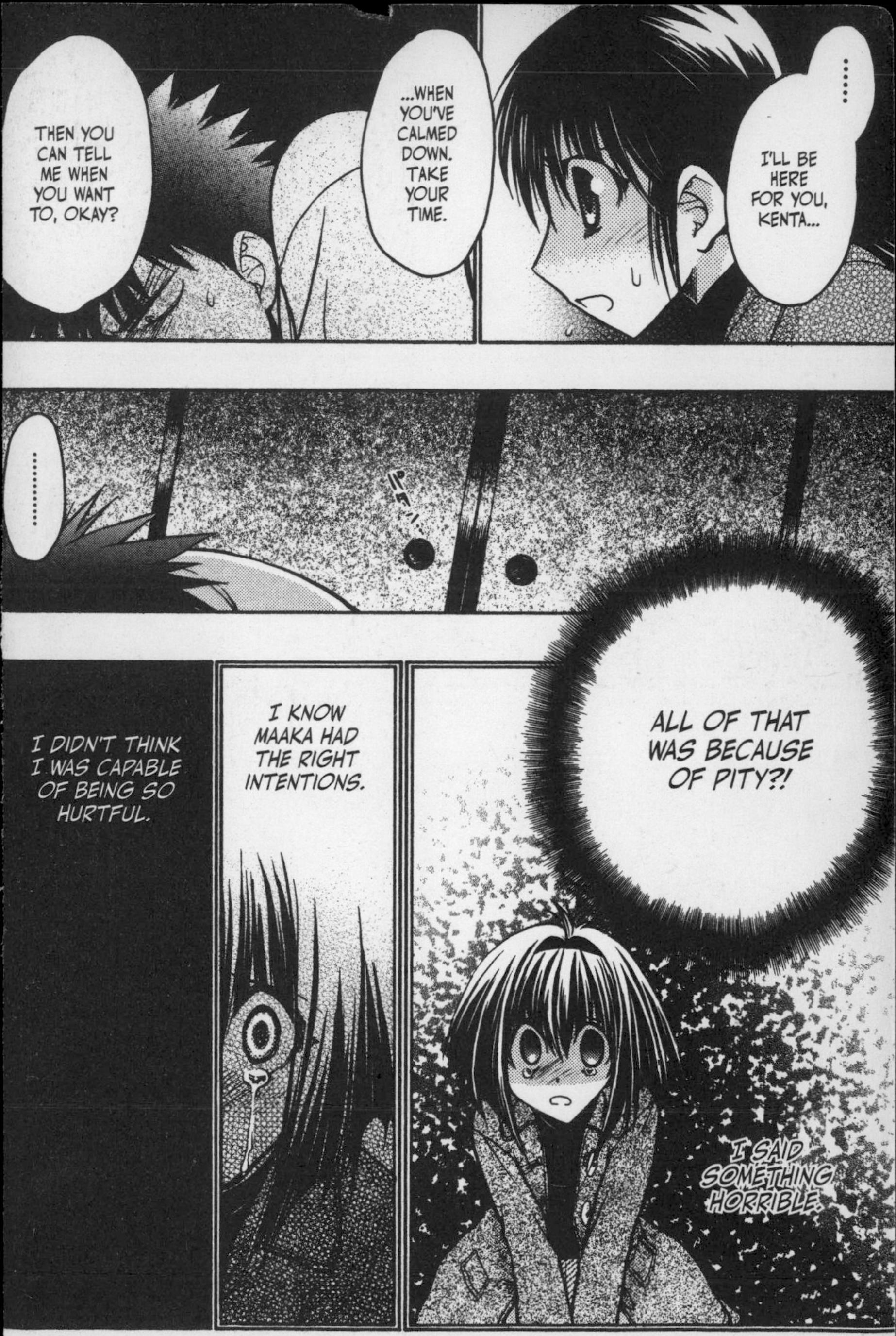
......
I'LL BE HERE FOR YOU, KENTA...
...WHEN YOU'VE CALMED DOWN. TAKE YOUR TIME.
THEN YOU CAN TELL ME WHEN YOU WANT TO, OKAY?
......
ALL OF THAT WAS BECAUSE OF PITY?!
I SAID SOMETHING HORRIBLE.
I KNOW MAAKA HAD THE RIGHT INTENTIONS.
I DIDN'T THINK I WAS CAPABLE OF BEING SO HURTFUL.

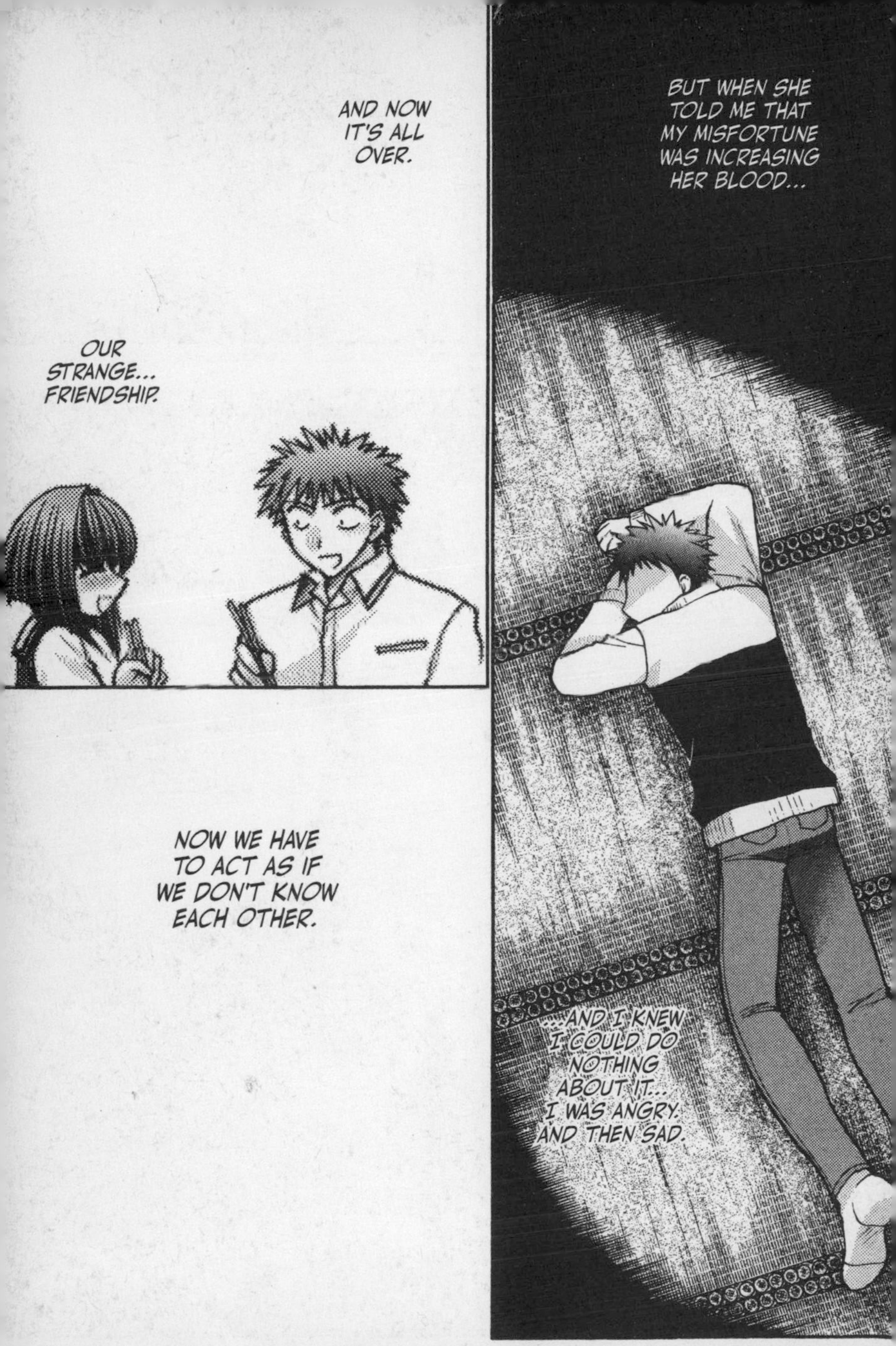
BUT WHEN SHE TOLD ME THAT MY MISFORTUNE WAS INCREASING HER BLOOD...
...AND I KNEW I COULD DO NOTHING ABOUT IT... I WAS ANGRY. AND THEN SAD.
AND NOW IT'S ALL OVER.
OUR STRANGE... FRIENDSHIP.
NOW WE HAVE TO ACT AS IF WE DON'T KNOW EACH OTHER.

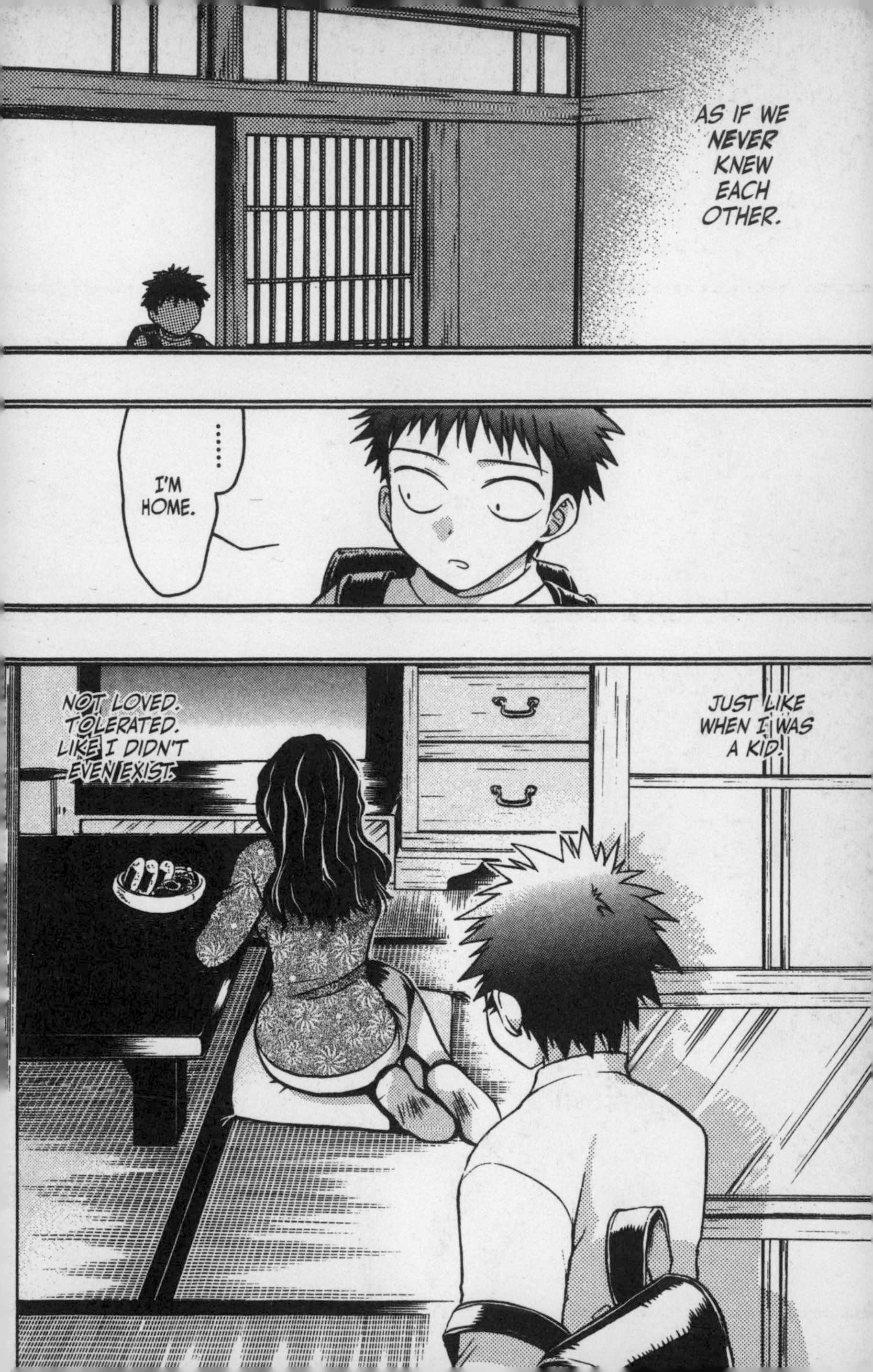
AS IF WE NEVER KNEW EACH OTHER.
......
I'M HOME.
JUST LIKE WHEN I WAS A KID.
NOT LOVED. TOLERATED. LIKE I DIDN'T EVEN EXIST.

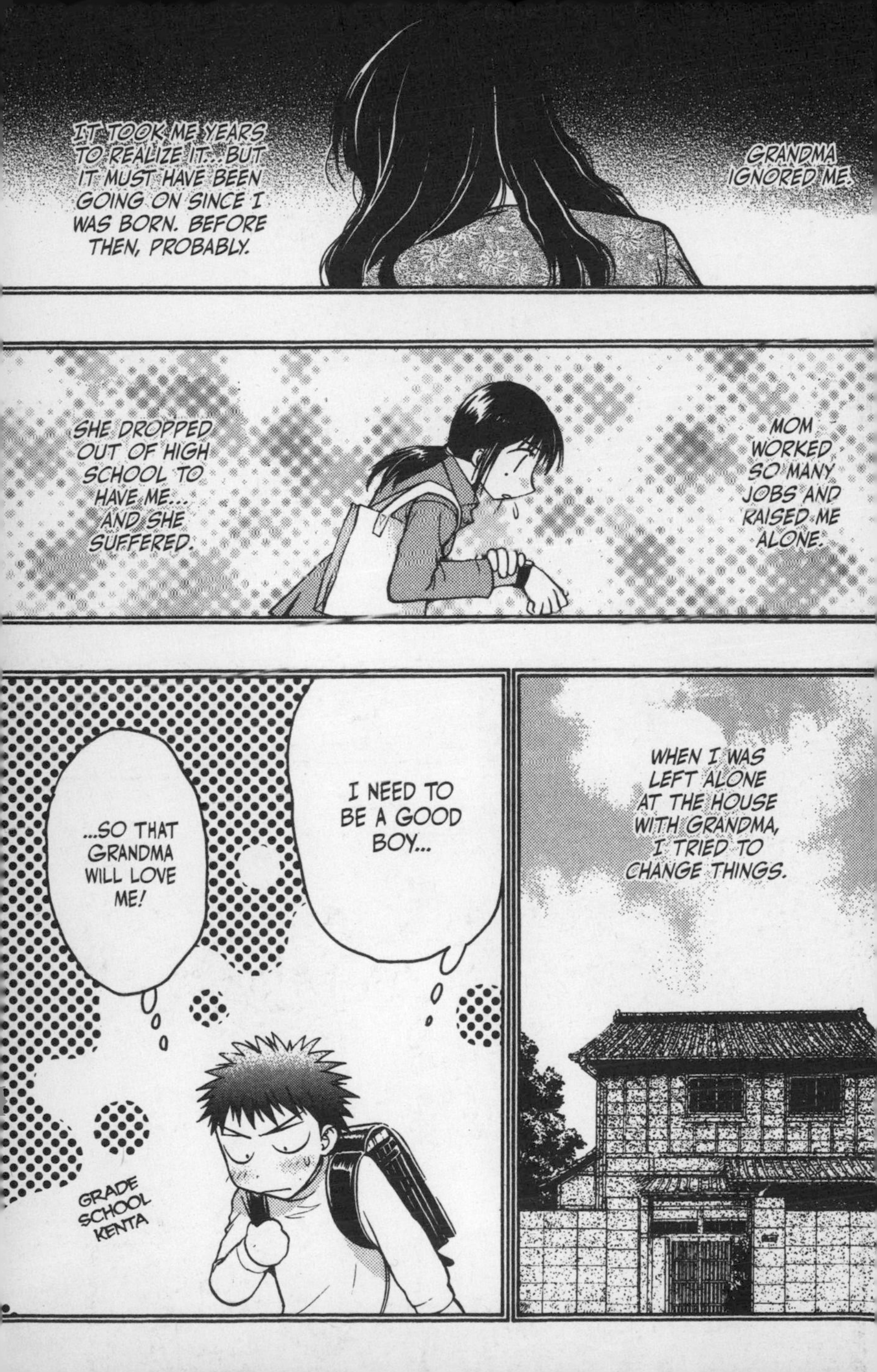
GRANDMA IGNORED ME.
IT TOOK ME YEARS TO REALIZE IT...BUT IT MUST HAVE BEEN GOING ON SINCE I WAS BORN. BEFORE THEN, PROBABLY.
MOM WORKED SO MANY JOBS AND RAISED ME ALONE.
SHE DROPPED OUT OF HIGH SCHOOL TO HAVE ME... AND SHE SUFFERED.
WHEN I WAS LEFT ALONE AT THE HOUSE WITH GRANDMA, I TRIED TO CHANGE THINGS.
I NEED TO BE A GOOD BOY...
...SO THAT GRANDMA WILL LOVE ME!
GRADE SCHOOL KENTA

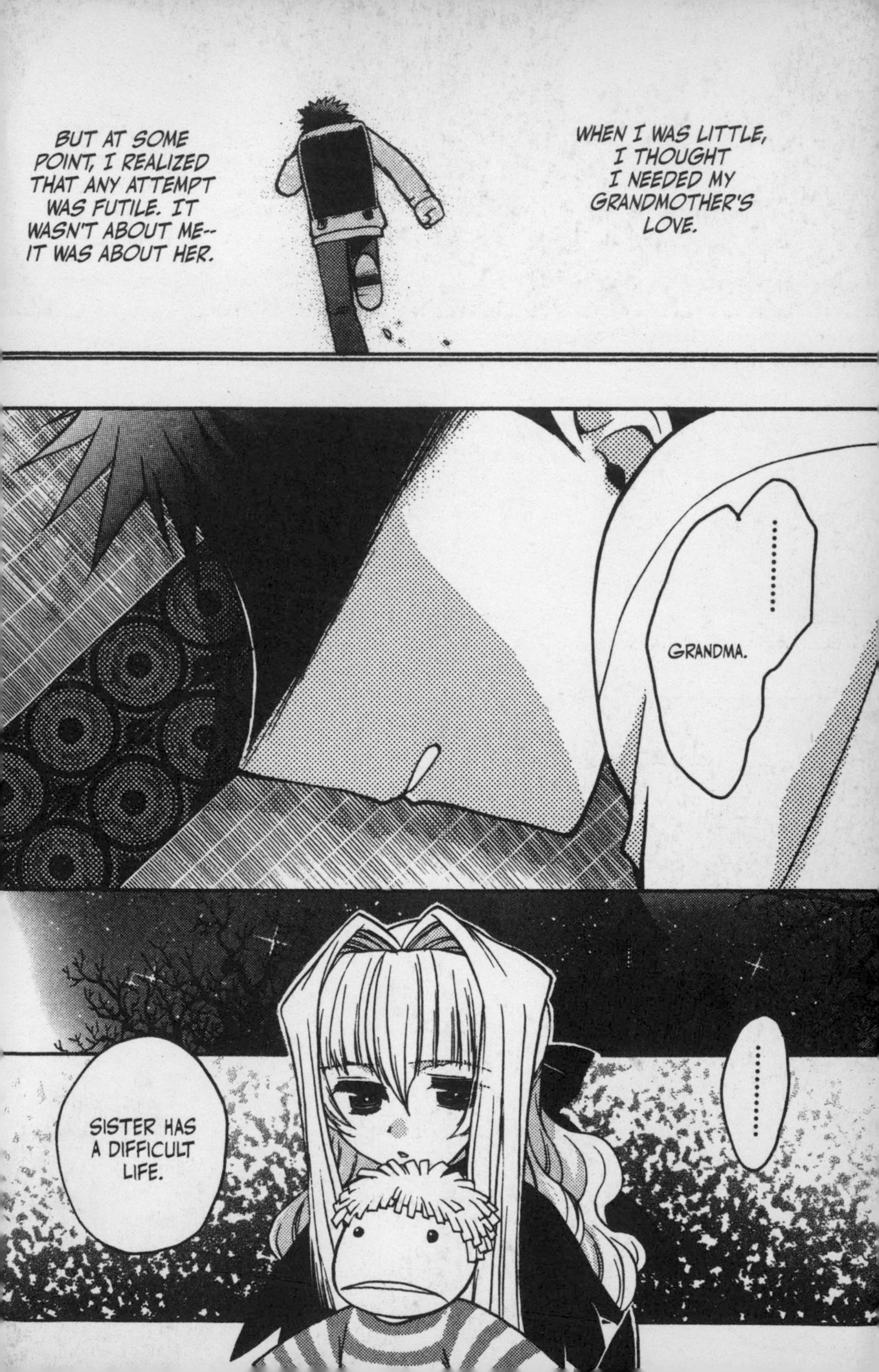
WHEN I WAS LITTLE, I THOUGHT I NEEDED MY GRANDMOTHER'S LOVE.
BUT AT SOME POINT, I REALIZED THAT ANY ATTEMPT WAS FUTILE. IT WASN'T ABOUT ME-- IT WAS ABOUT HER.
......
GRANDMA.
......
SISTER HAS A DIFFICULT LIFE.

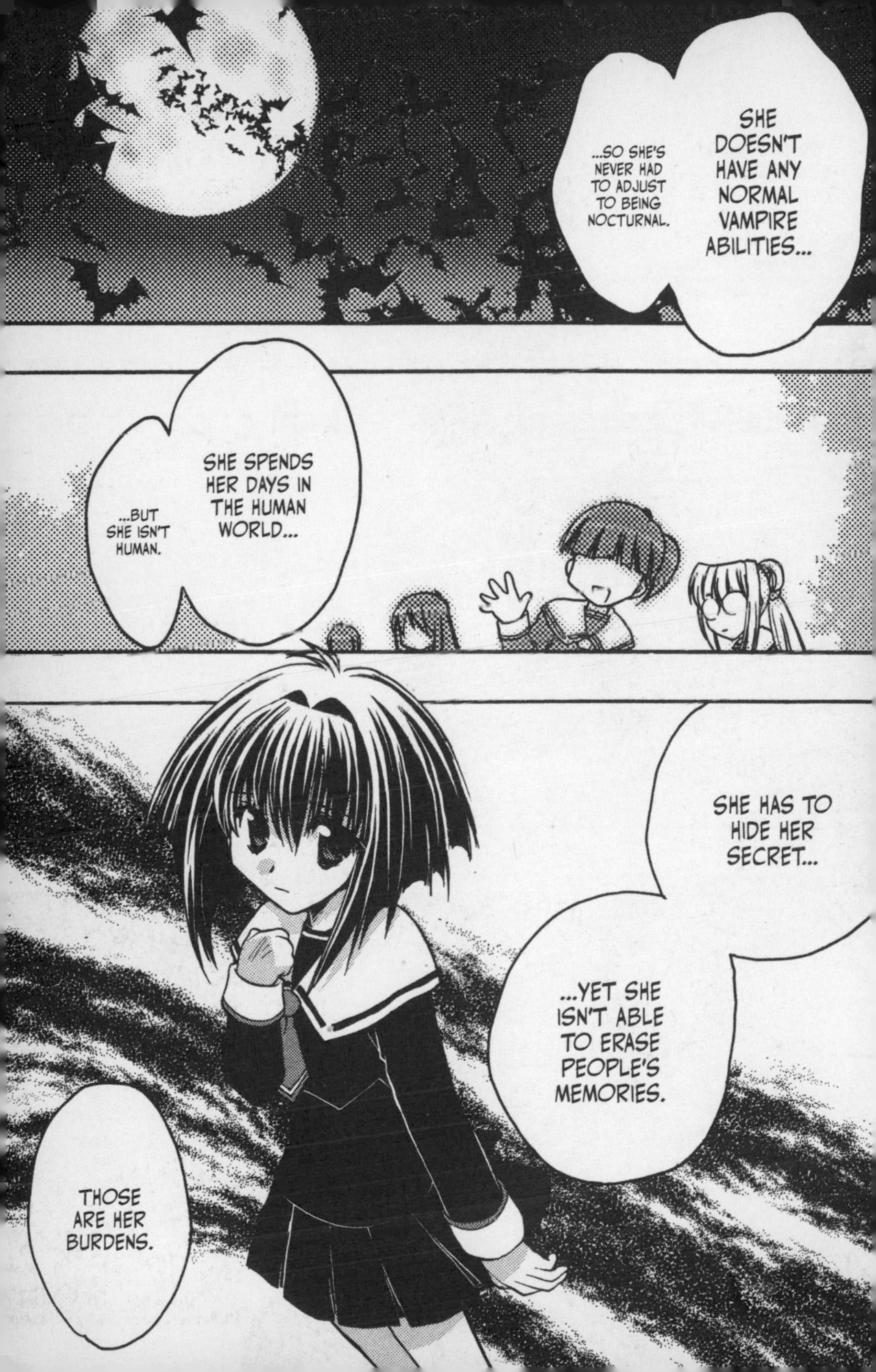
SHE DOESN'T HAVE ANY NORMAL VAMPIRE ABILITIES...
...SO SHE'S NEVER HAD TO ADJUST TO BEING NOCTURNAL.
SHE SPENDS HER DAYS IN THE HUMAN WORLD...
...BUT SHE ISN'T HUMAN.
SHE HAS TO HIDE HER SECRET...
...YET SHE ISN'T ABLE TO ERASE PEOPLE'S MEMORIES.
THOSE ARE HER BURDENS.

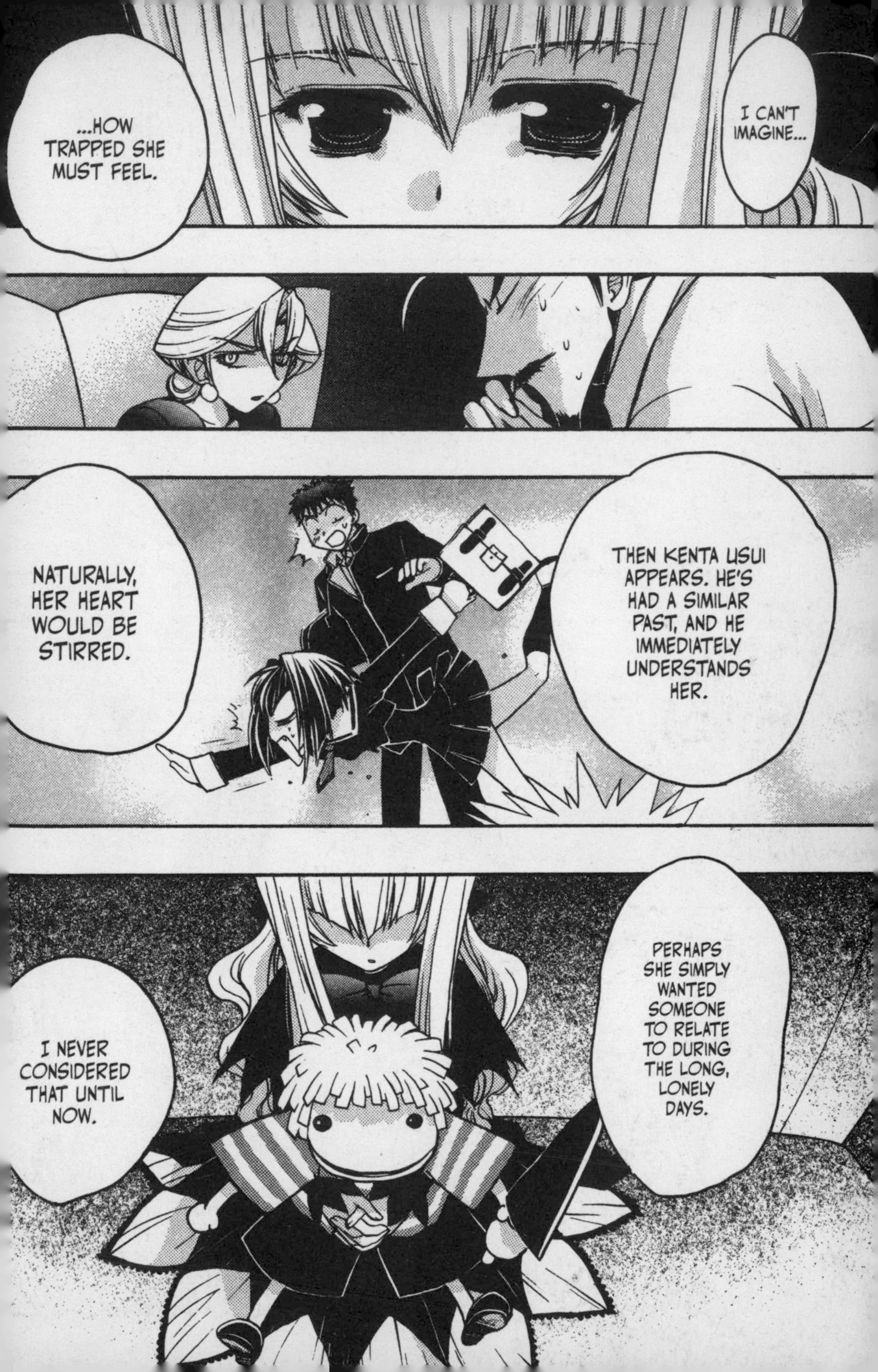
I CAN'T IMAGINE...
...HOW TRAPPED SHE MUST FEEL.
THEN KENTA USUI APPEARS. HE'S HAD A SIMILAR PAST, AND HE IMMEDIATELY UNDERSTANDS HER.
NATURALLY, HER HEART WOULD BE STIRRED.
PERHAPS SHE SIMPLY WANTED SOMEONE TO RELATE TO DURING THE LONG, LONELY DAYS.
I NEVER CONSIDERED THAT UNTIL NOW.

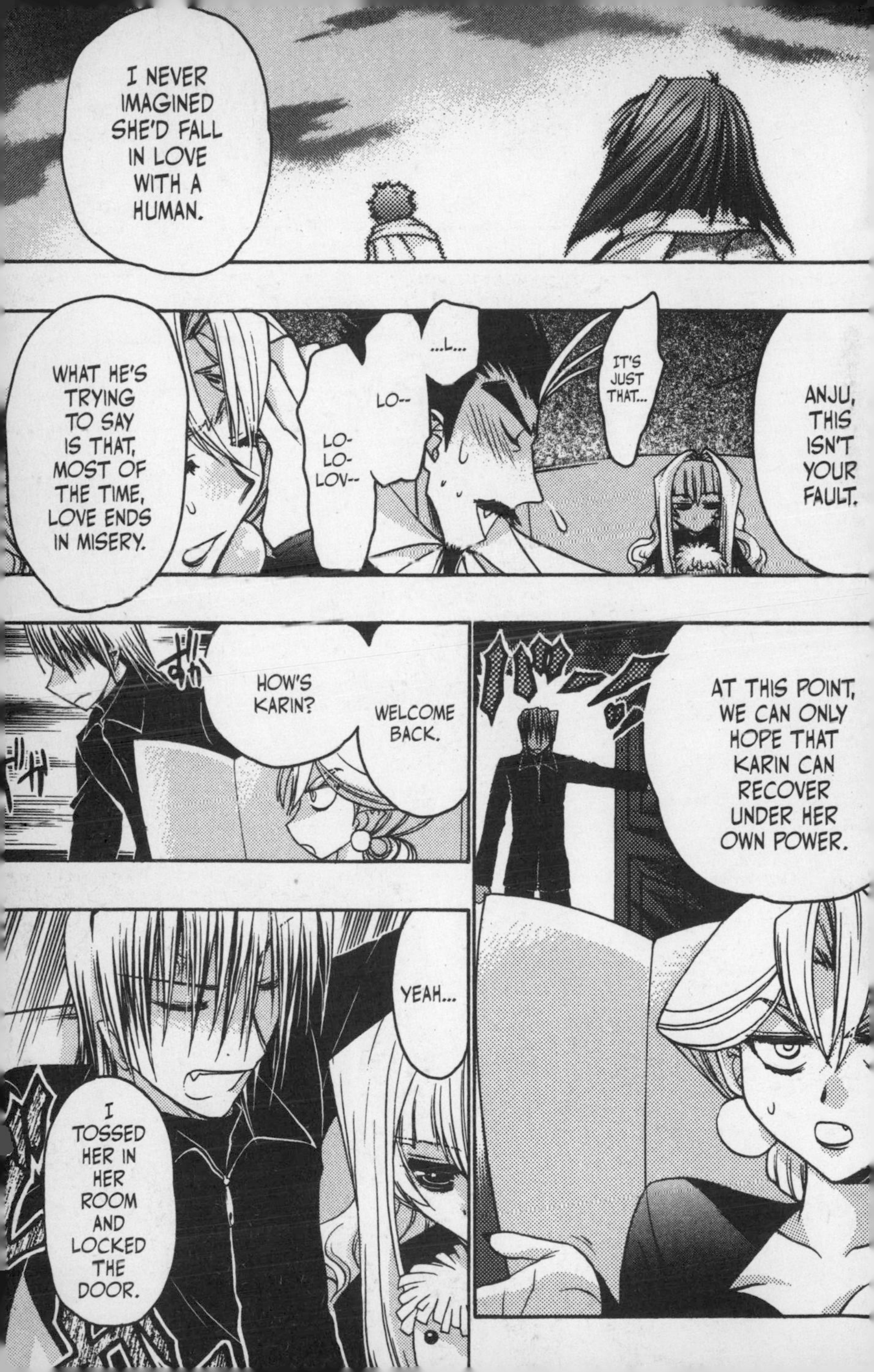
I NEVER IMAGINED SHE'D FALL IN LOVE WITH A HUMAN.
ANJU, THIS ISN'T YOUR FAULT.
IT'S JUST THAT...
...L...
LO--
LO-LO-LOV--
WHAT HE'S TRYING TO SAY IS THAT, MOST OF THE TIME, LOVE ENDS IN MISERY.
AT THIS POINT, WE CAN ONLY HOPE THAT KARIN CAN RECOVER UNDER HER OWN POWER.
WELCOME BACK.
HOW'S KARIN?
YEAH...
I TOSSED HER IN HER ROOM AND LOCKED THE DOOR.

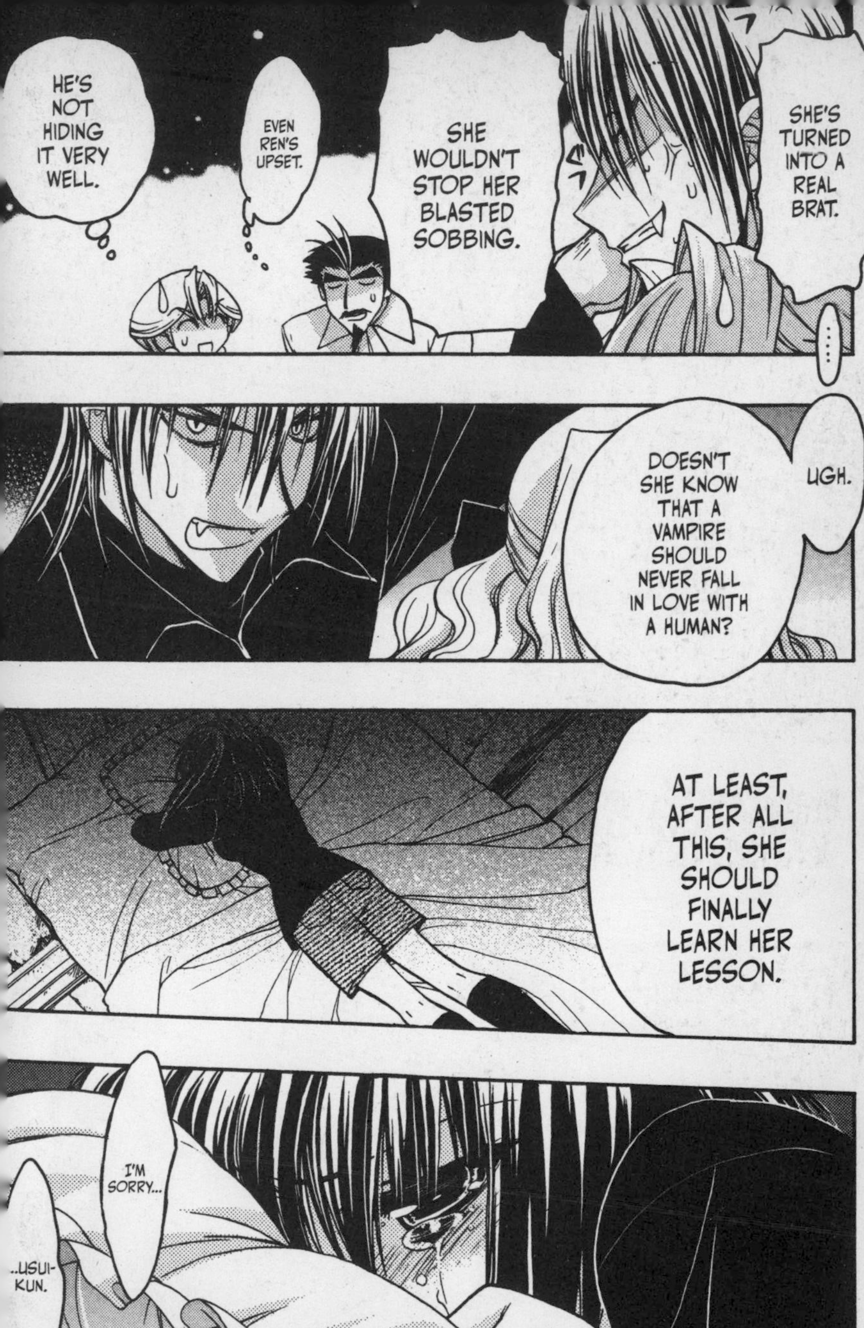
SHE'S TURNED INTO A REAL BRAT.
.....
SHE WOULDN'T STOP HER BLASTED SOBBING.
EVEN REN'S UPSET.
HE'S NOT HIDING IT VERY WELL.
UGH.
DOESN'T SHE KNOW THAT A VAMPIRE SHOULD NEVER FALL IN LOVE WITH A HUMAN?
AT LEAST, AFTER ALL THIS, SHE SHOULD FINALLY LEARN HER LESSON.
I'M SORRY...
..USUI-KUN.

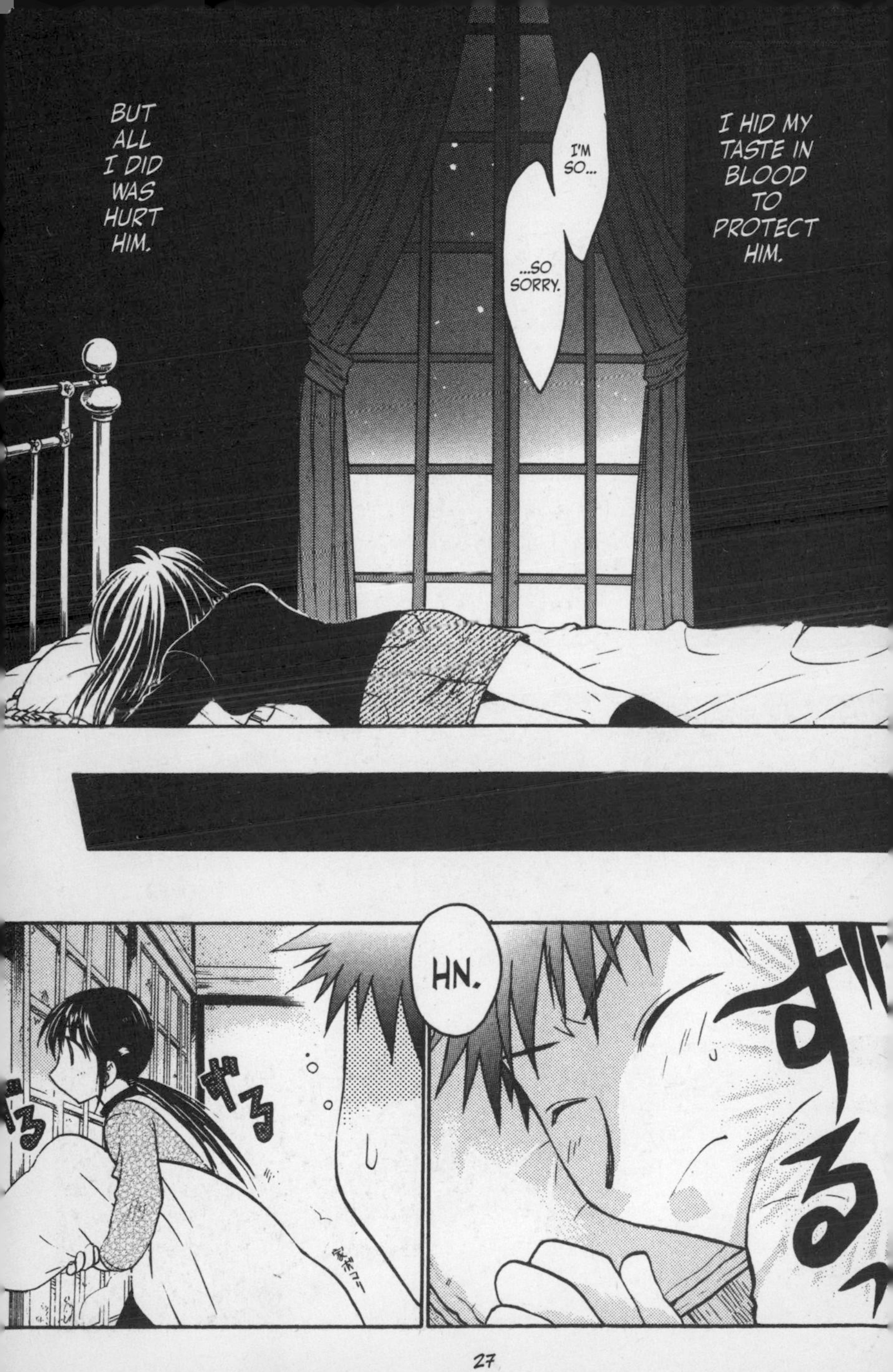
I HID MY TASTE IN BLOOD TO PROTECT HIM.
I'M SO...
...SO SORRY.
BUT ALL I DID WAS HURT HIM.
HN.
ずる
ずる

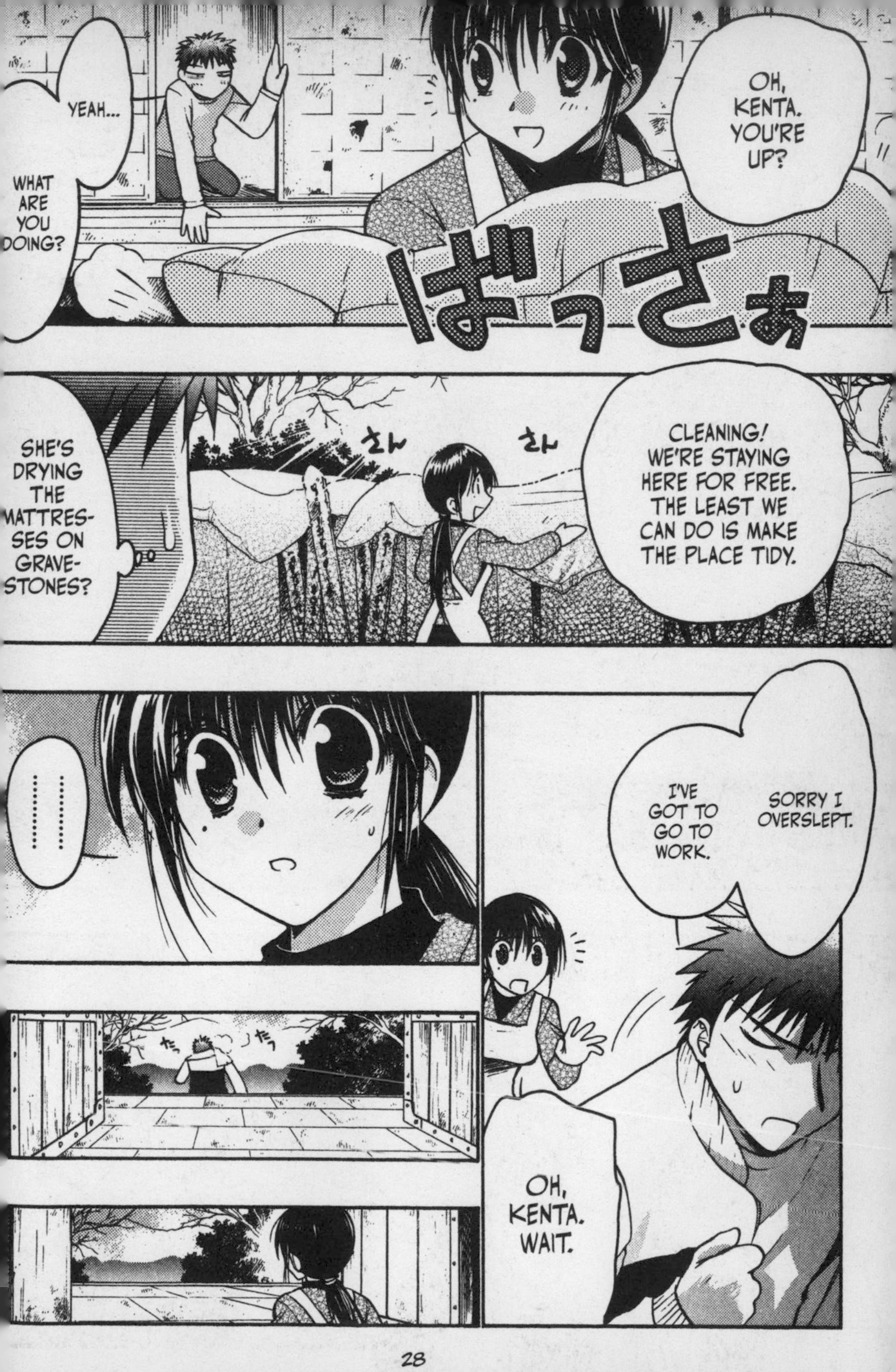
OH, KENTA. YOU'RE UP?
ぱっさぁ
YEAH...
WHAT ARE YOU DOING?
CLEANING! WE'RE STAYING HERE FOR FREE. THE LEAST WE CAN DO IS MAKE THE PLACE TIDY.
さん
さん
SHE'S DRYING THE MATTRES-SES ON GRAVE-STONES?
SORRY I OVERSLEPT.
I'VE GOT TO GO TO WORK.
OH, KENTA. WAIT.
......
たっ
たっ

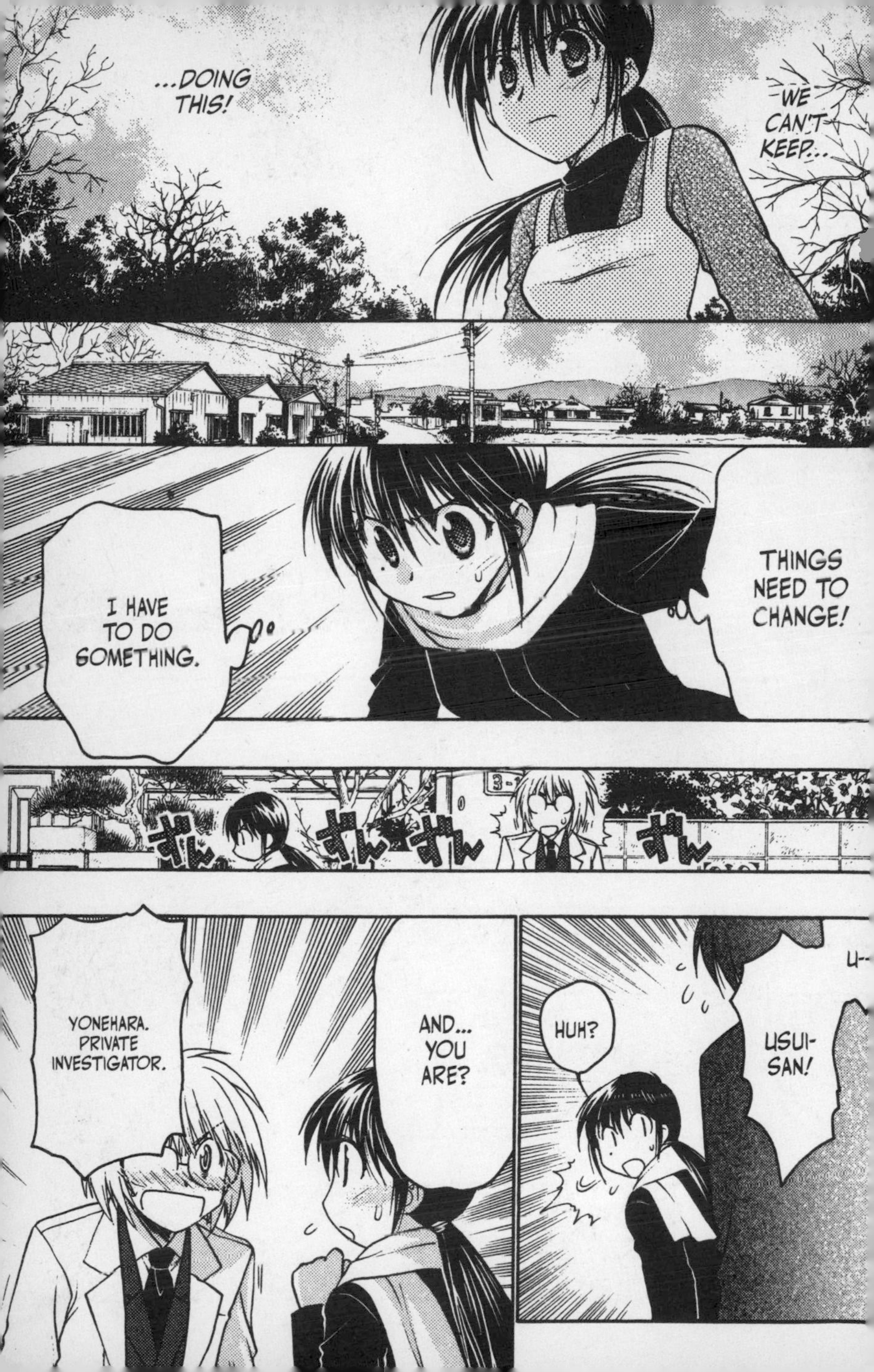
WE CAN'T KEEP...
...DOING THIS!
THINGS NEED TO CHANGE!
I HAVE TO DO SOMETHING.
U--
USUI-SAN!
HUH?
AND... YOU ARE?
YONEHARA. PRIVATE INVESTIGATOR.

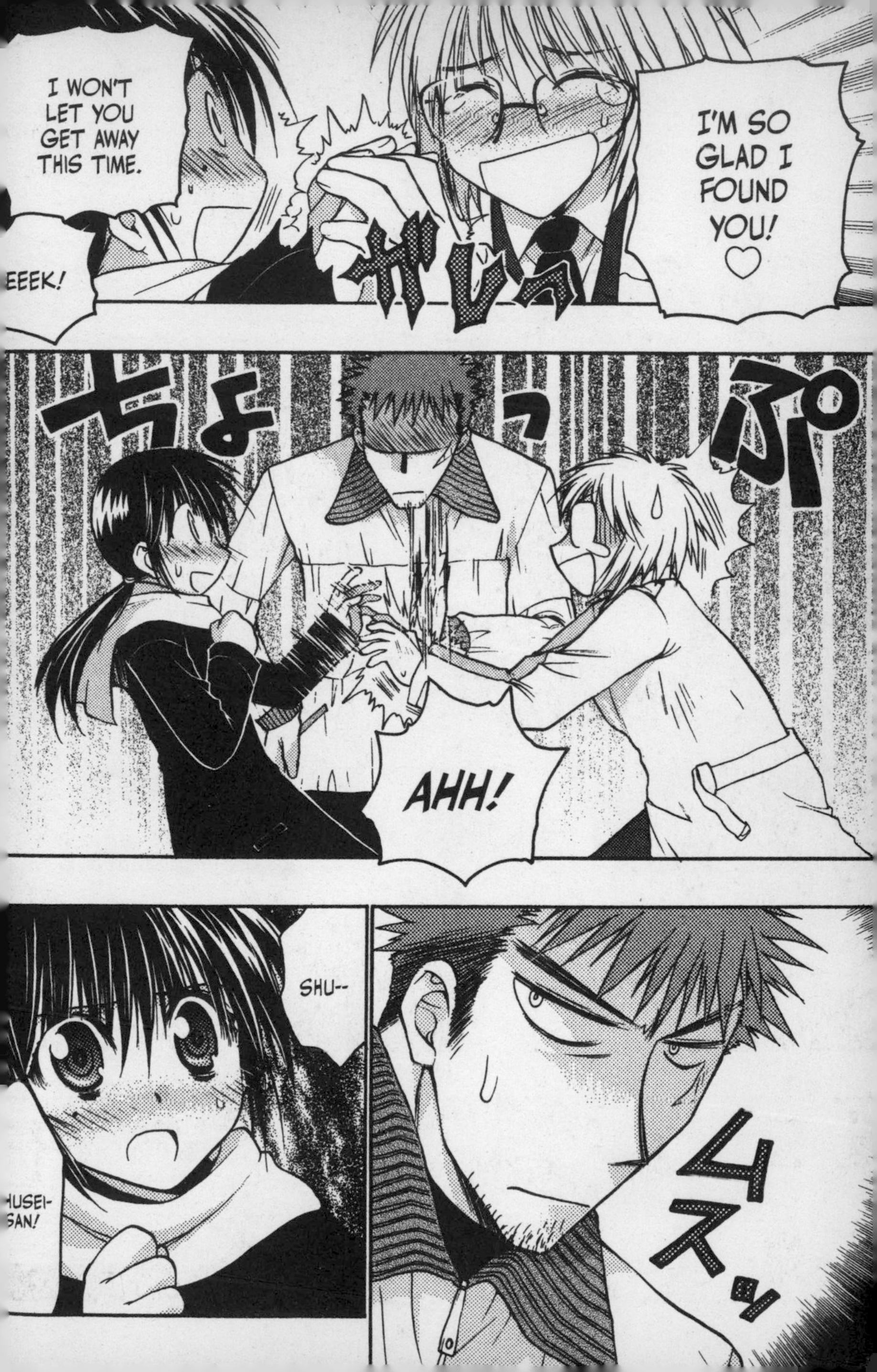
I'M SO GLAD I FOUND YOU! ♡
ガしっ
I WON'T LET YOU GET AWAY THIS TIME.
EEEK!
ちょっぷ
AHH!
ムスッ
SHU--
HUSEI-SAN!

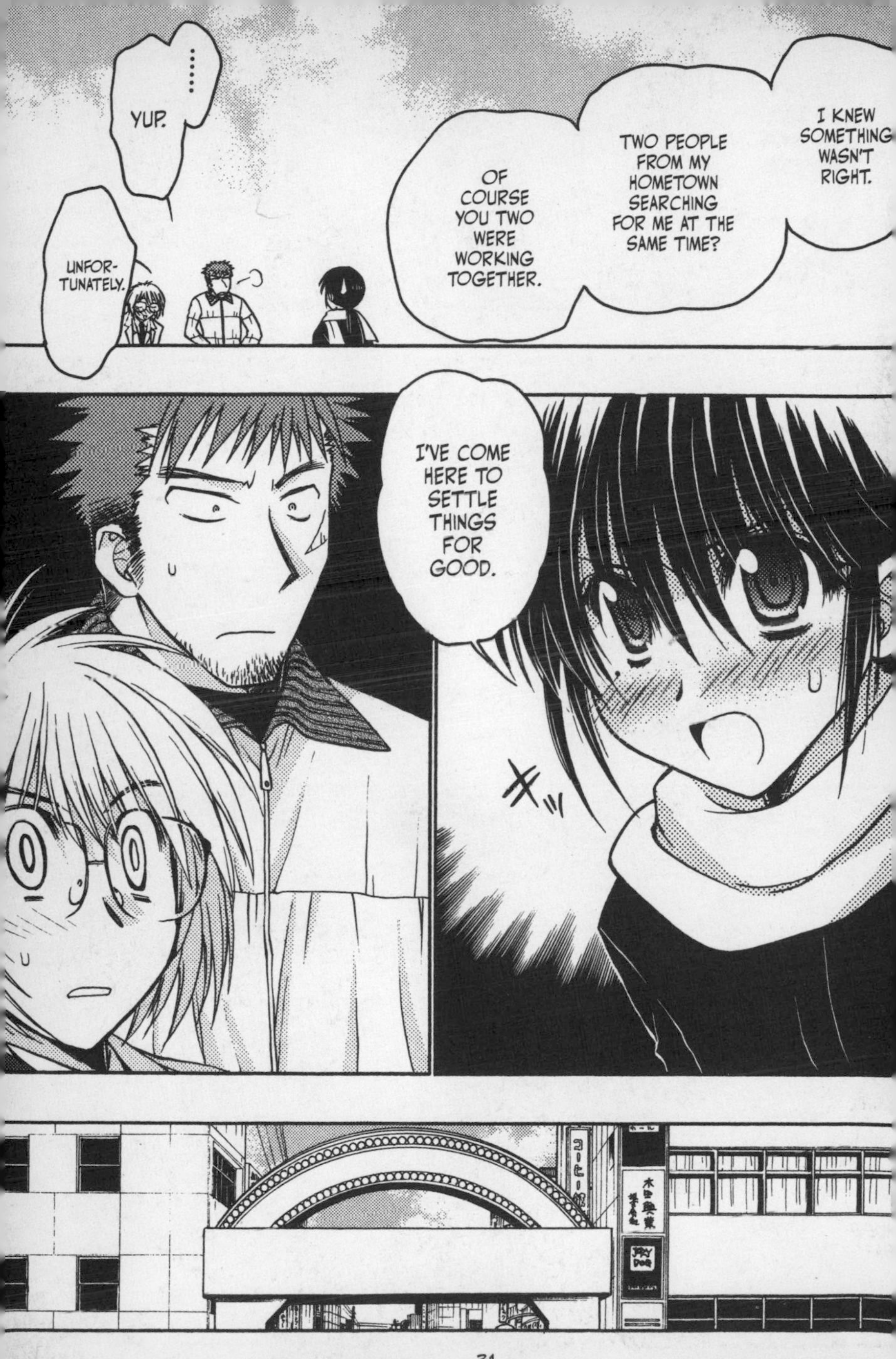
I KNEW SOMETHING WASN'T RIGHT.
TWO PEOPLE FROM MY HOMETOWN SEARCHING FOR ME AT THE SAME TIME?
OF COURSE YOU TWO WERE WORKING TOGETHER.
......
YUP.
UNFOR-TUNATELY.
I'VE COME HERE TO SETTLE THINGS FOR GOOD.

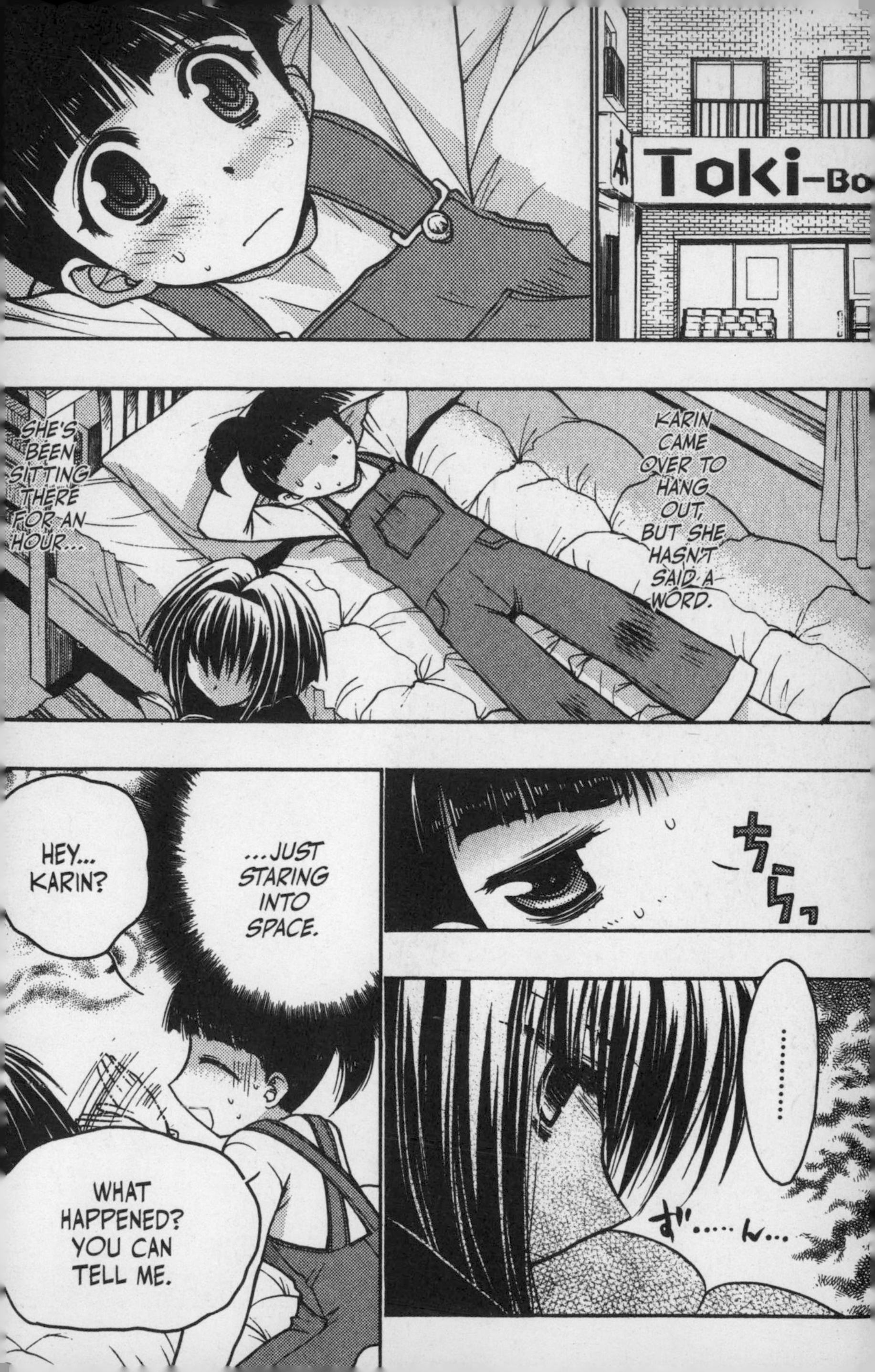
本
Toki-Bo
KARIN CAME OVER TO HANG OUT, BUT SHE HASN'T SAID A WORD.
SHE'S BEEN SITTING THERE FOR AN HOUR...
ちらっ
......
ず……ん……
...JUST STARING INTO SPACE.
HEY... KARIN?
WHAT HAPPENED? YOU CAN TELL ME.

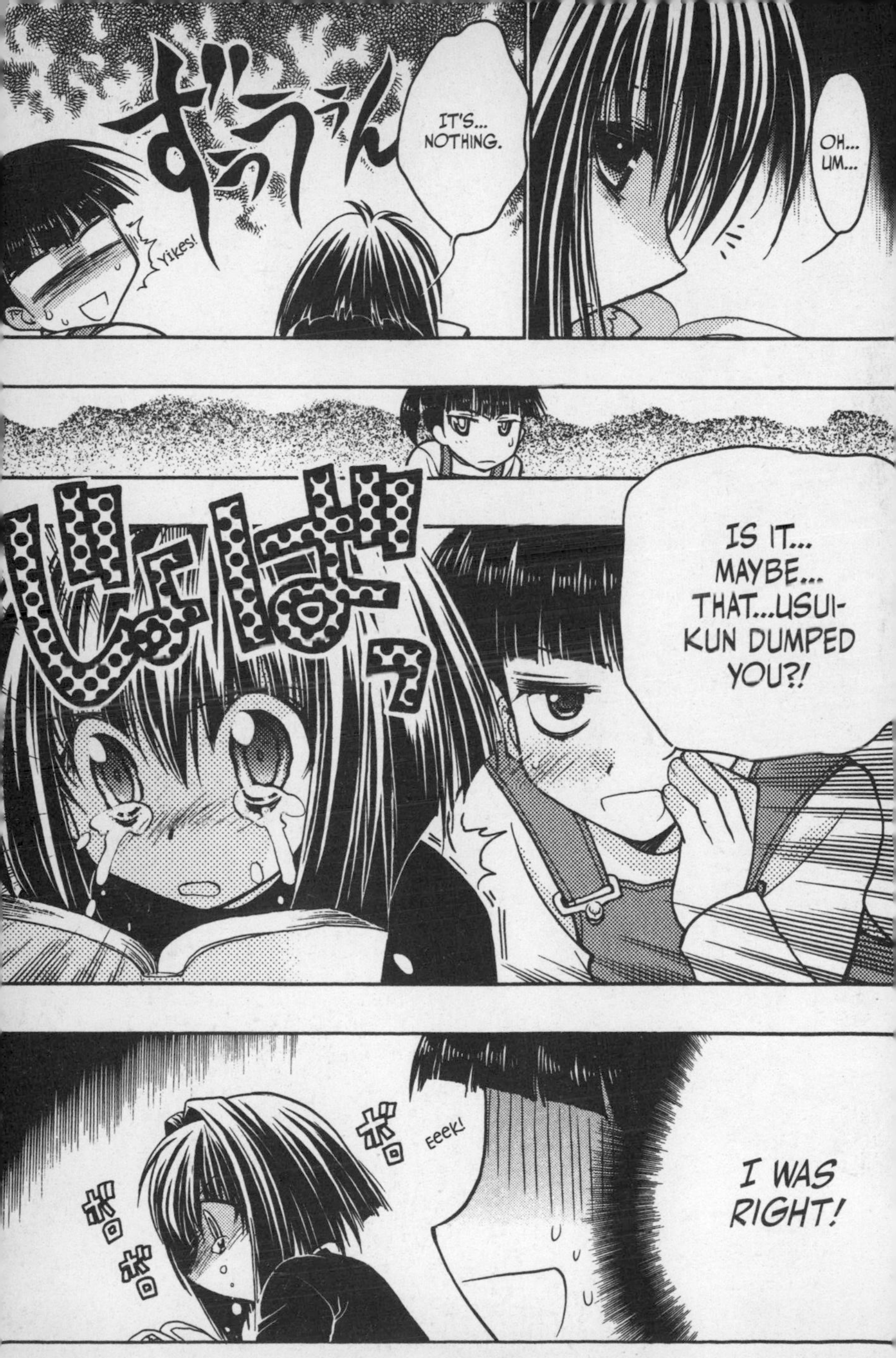
OH... UM...
IT'S... NOTHING.
YIKES!
IS IT... MAYBE... THAT...USUI-KUN DUMPED YOU?!
I WAS RIGHT!
EEEK!
ボロ
ボロ
ボロ

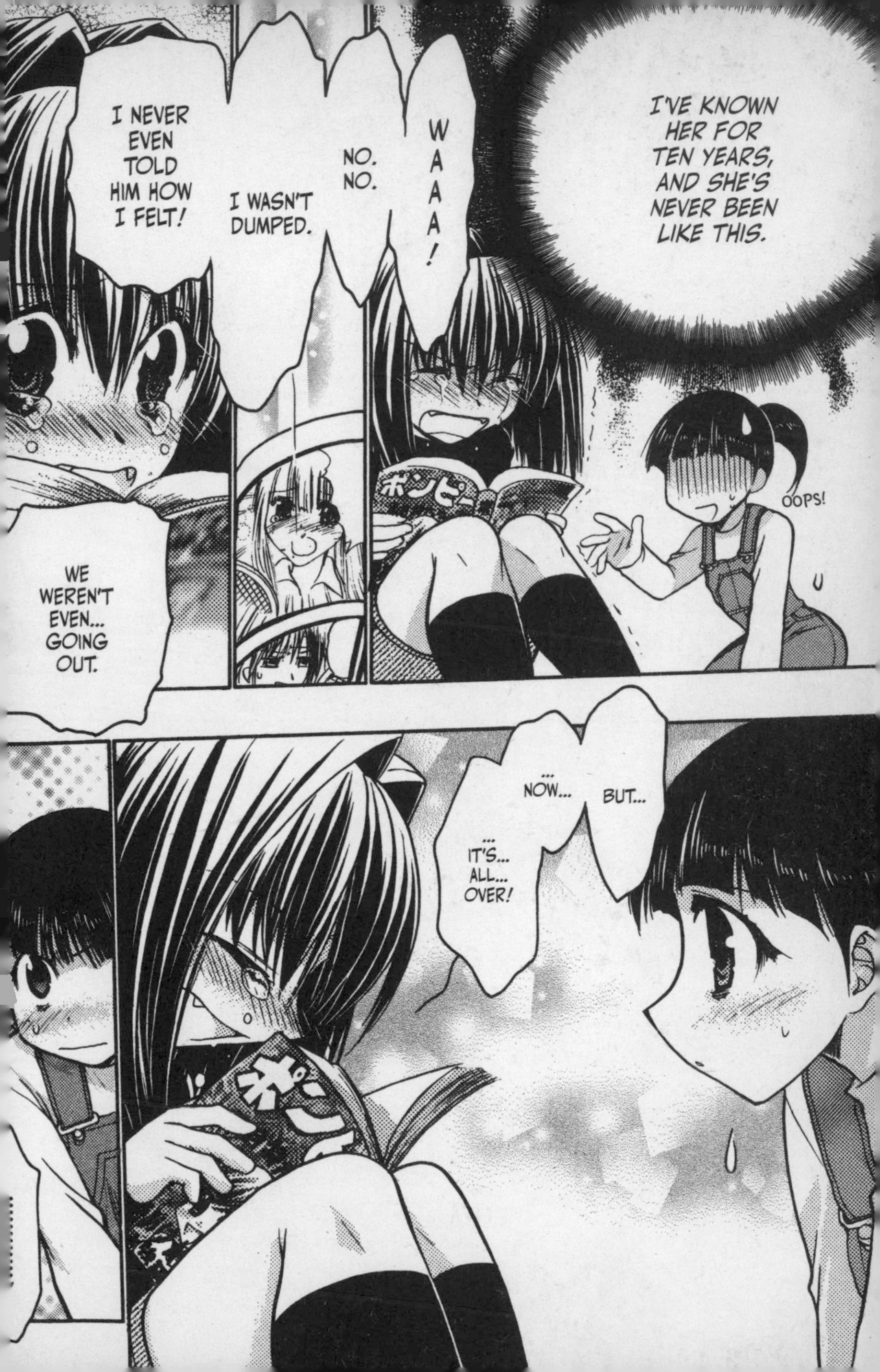
I'VE KNOWN HER FOR TEN YEARS, AND SHE'S NEVER BEEN LIKE THIS.
OOPS!
WAAAA!
NO. NO.
I WASN'T DUMPED.
I NEVER EVEN TOLD HIM HOW I FELT!
WE WEREN'T EVEN... GOING OUT.
BUT...
...NOW...
...IT'S... ALL... OVER!

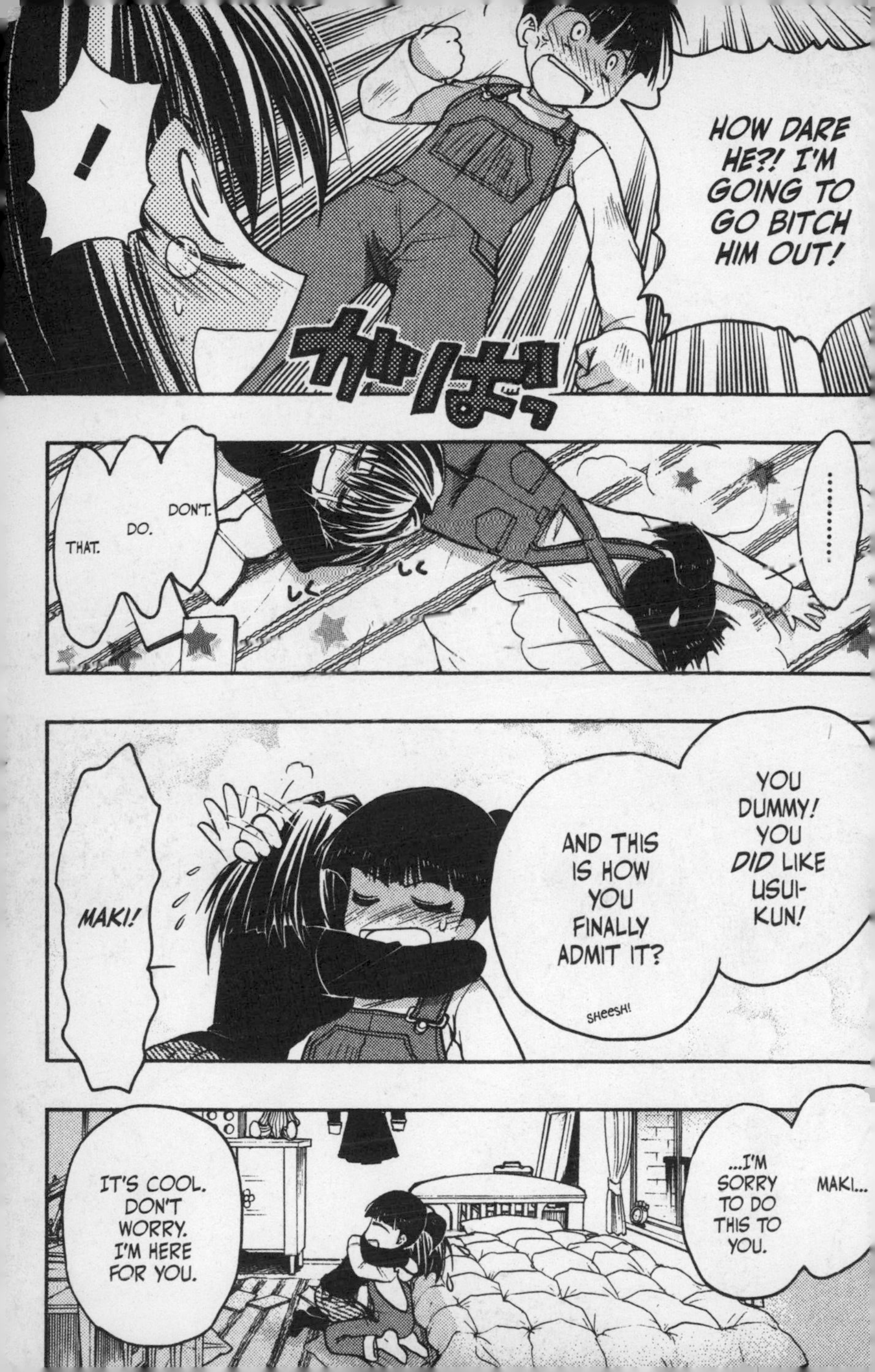
HOW DARE HE?! I'M GOING TO GO BITCH HIM OUT!
!
がばっ
......
DON'T. DO. THAT.
しく しく
YOU DUMMY! YOU *DID* LIKE USUI-KUN!
AND THIS IS HOW YOU FINALLY ADMIT IT?
SHEESH!
MAKI!
MAKI...
...I'M SORRY TO DO THIS TO YOU.
IT'S COOL. DON'T WORRY. I'M HERE FOR YOU.

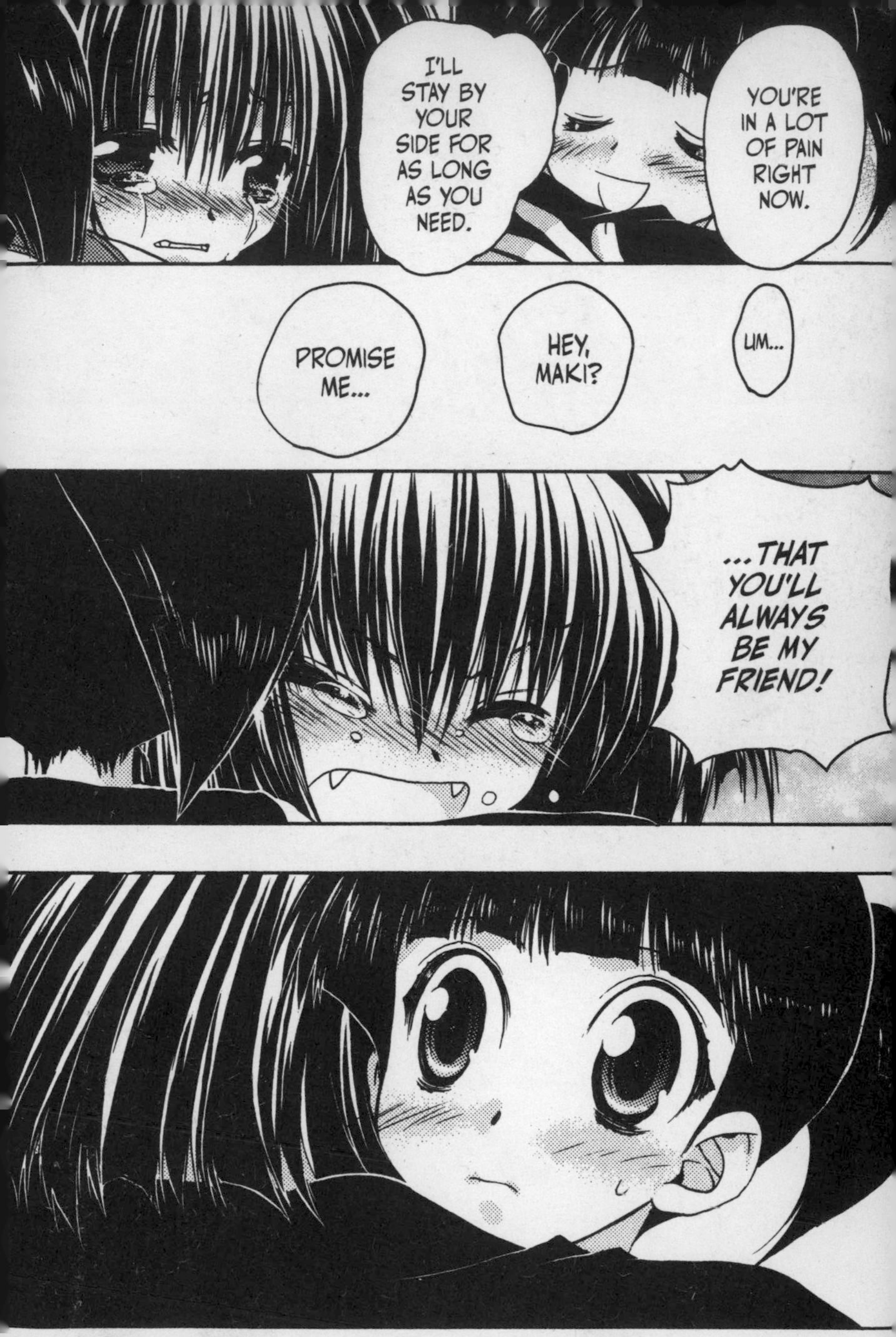
YOU'RE IN A LOT OF PAIN RIGHT NOW.
I'LL STAY BY YOUR SIDE FOR AS LONG AS YOU NEED.
UM...
HEY, MAKI?
PROMISE ME...
...THAT YOU'LL ALWAYS BE MY FRIEND!

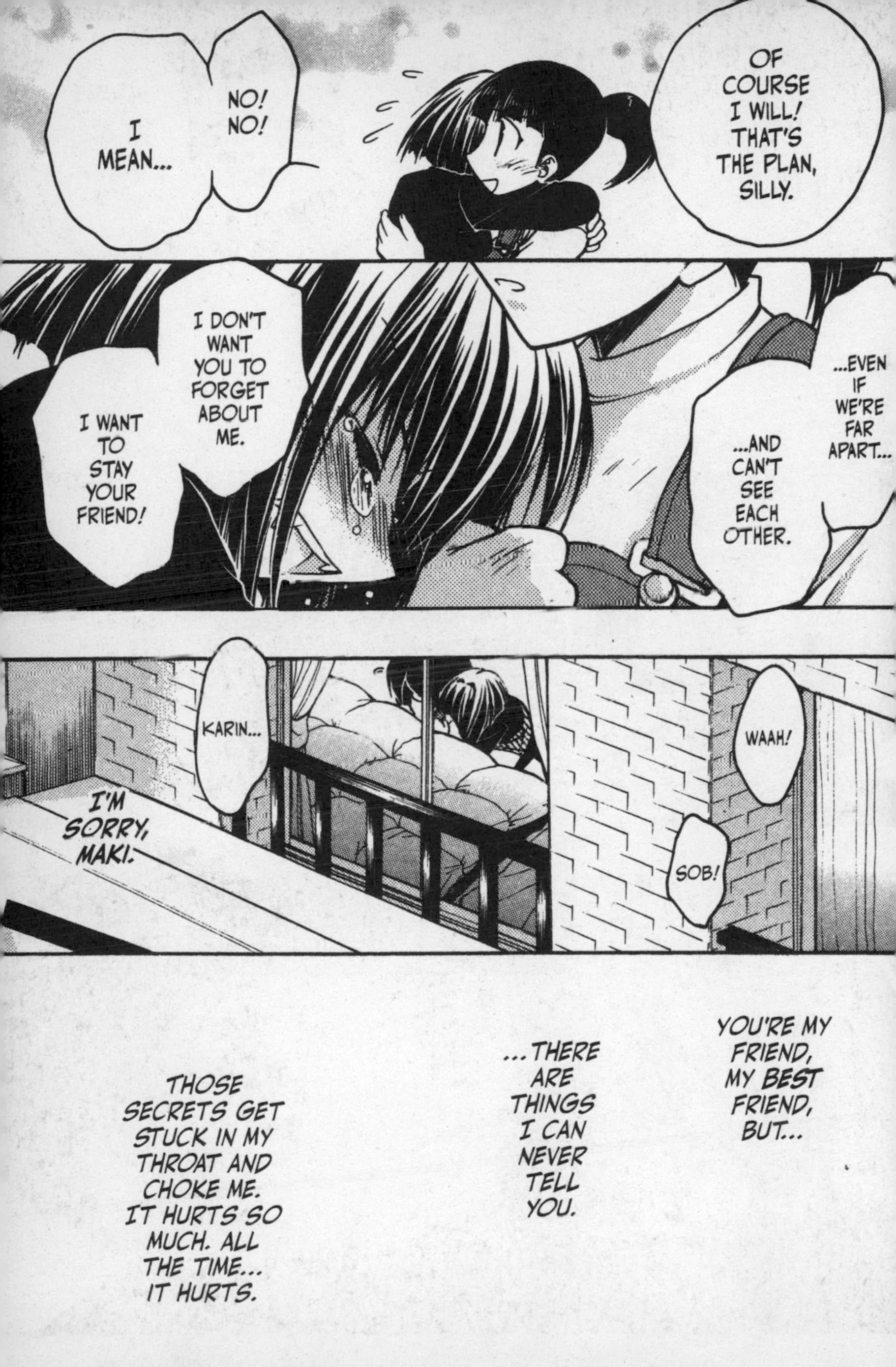
OF COURSE I WILL! THAT'S THE PLAN, SILLY.
NO! NO!
I MEAN...
...EVEN IF WE'RE FAR APART...
...AND CAN'T SEE EACH OTHER.
I DON'T WANT YOU TO FORGET ABOUT ME.
I WANT TO STAY YOUR FRIEND!
WAAH!
SOB!
KARIN...
I'M SORRY, MAKI.
YOU'RE MY FRIEND, MY *BEST* FRIEND, BUT...
...THERE ARE THINGS I CAN NEVER TELL YOU.
THOSE SECRETS GET STUCK IN MY THROAT AND CHOKE ME. IT HURTS SO MUCH. ALL THE TIME... IT HURTS.

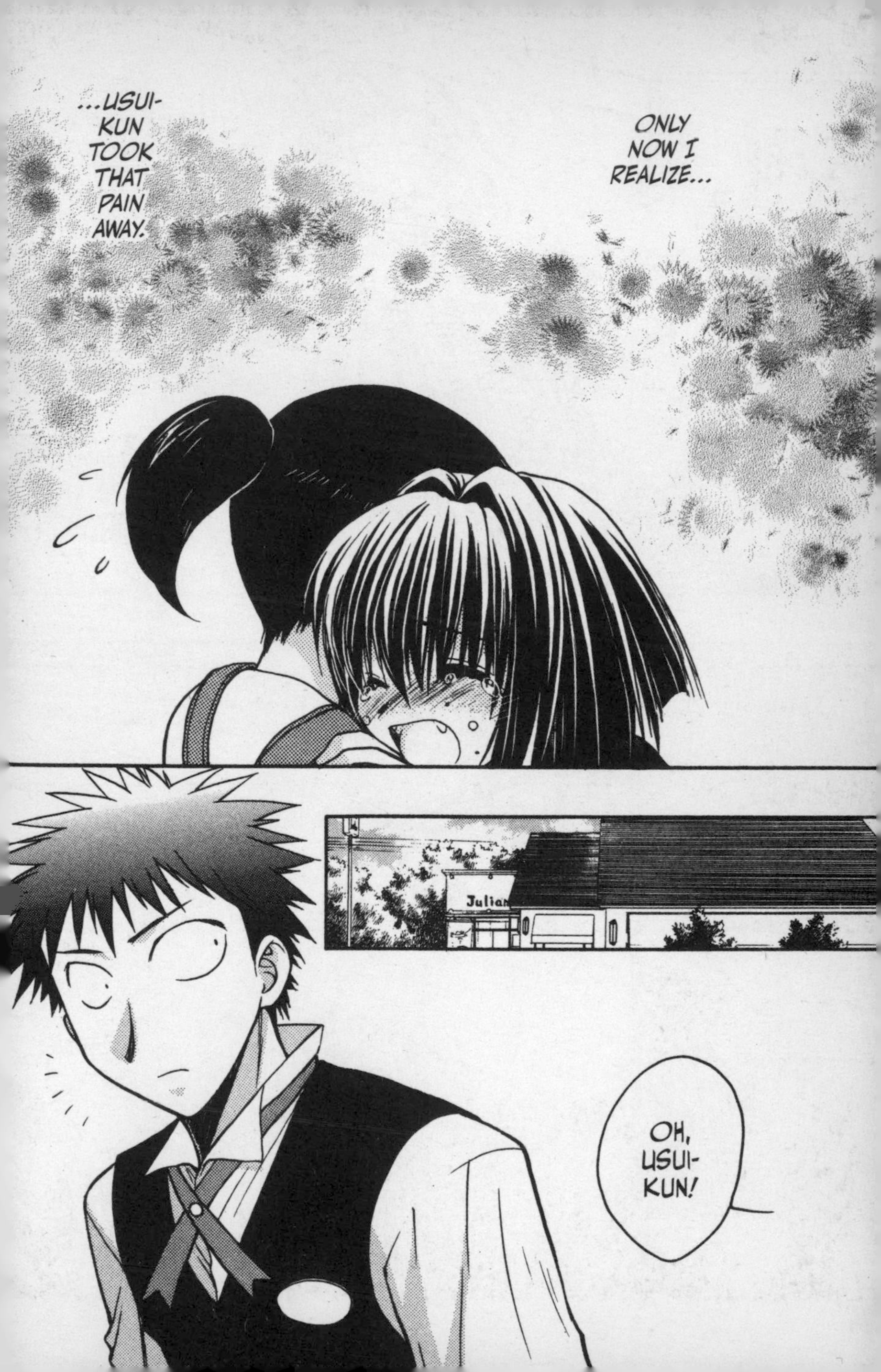
ONLY NOW I REALIZE...
...USUI-KUN TOOK THAT PAIN AWAY.
OH, USUI-KUN!

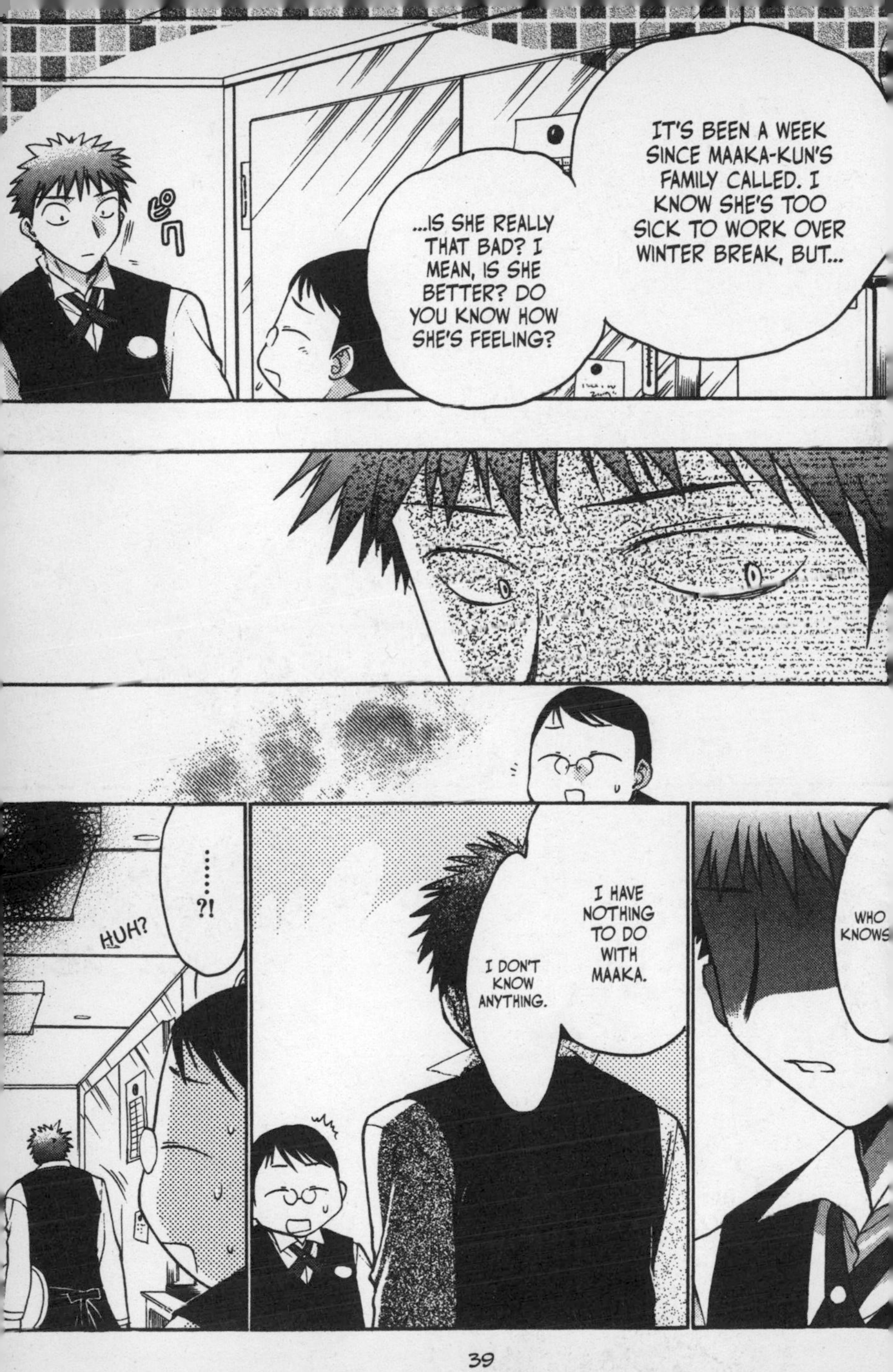
IT'S BEEN A WEEK SINCE MAAKA-KUN'S FAMILY CALLED. I KNOW SHE'S TOO SICK TO WORK OVER WINTER BREAK, BUT...
...IS SHE REALLY THAT BAD? I MEAN, IS SHE BETTER? DO YOU KNOW HOW SHE'S FEELING?
WHO KNOWS
I HAVE NOTHING TO DO WITH MAAKA.
I DON'T KNOW ANYTHING.
......
?!
HUH?

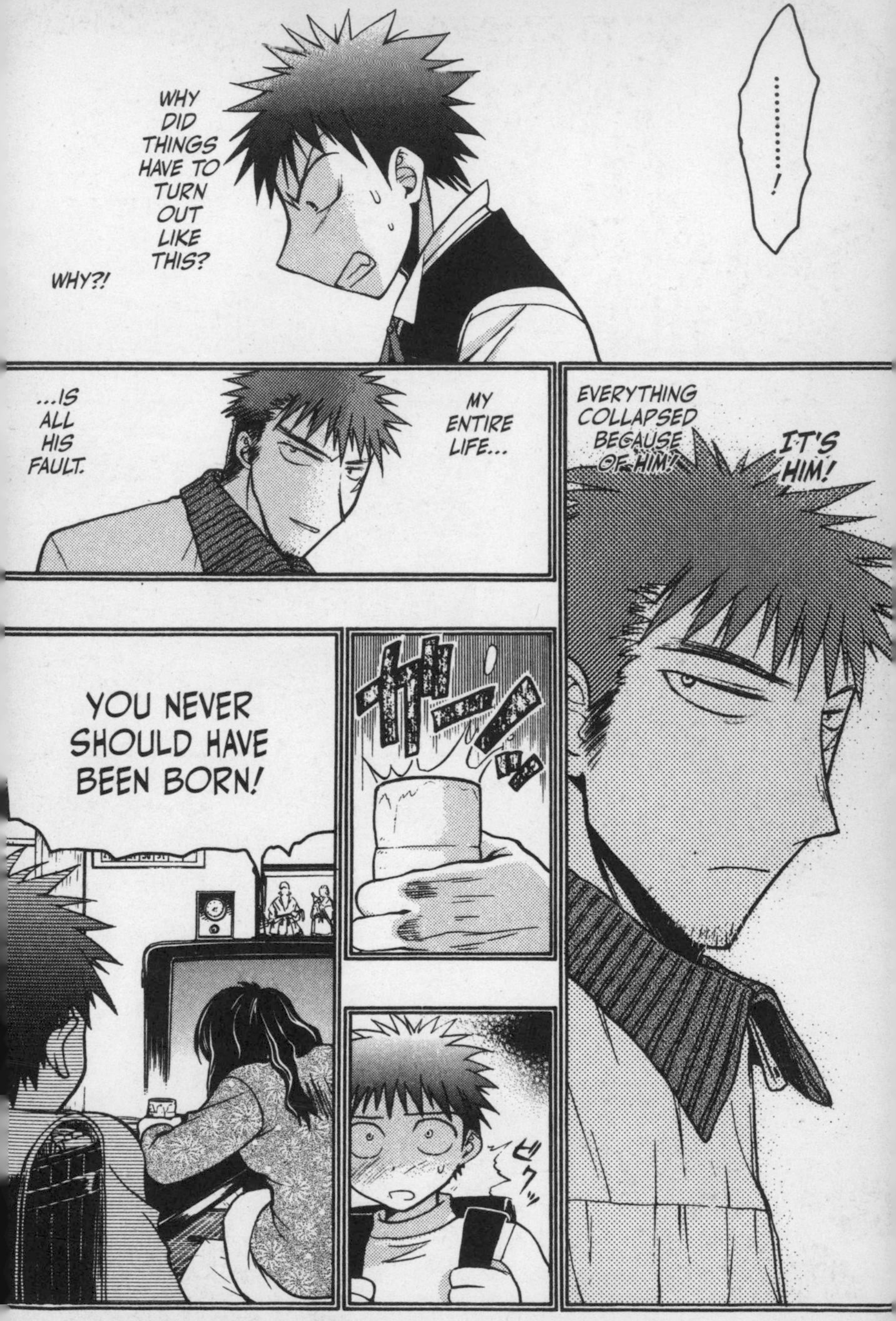
......!
WHY DID THINGS HAVE TO TURN OUT LIKE THIS?
WHY?!
IT'S HIM!
EVERYTHING COLLAPSED BECAUSE OF HIM!
MY ENTIRE LIFE...
...IS ALL HIS FAULT.
YOU NEVER SHOULD HAVE BEEN BORN!

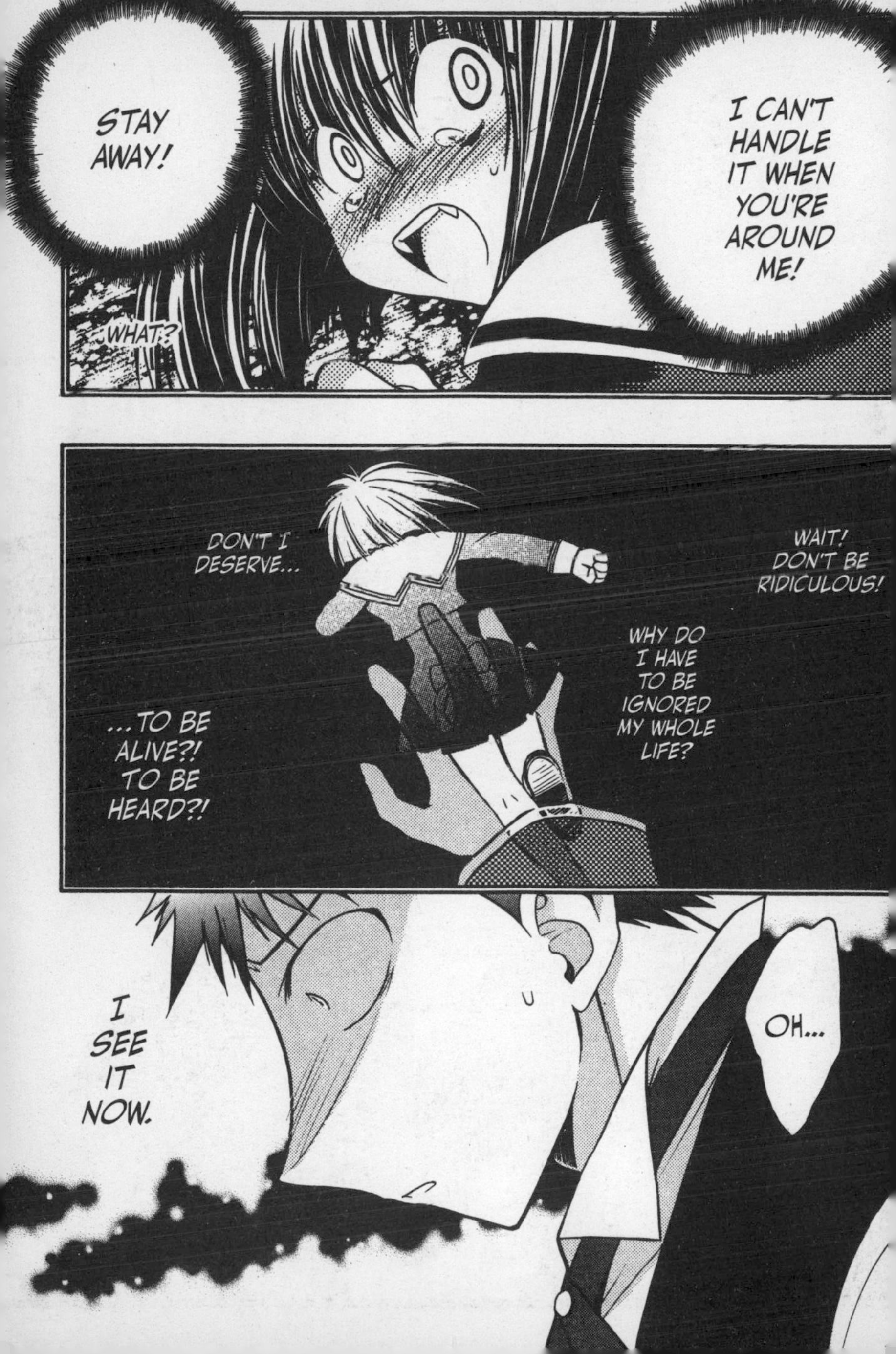
I CAN'T HANDLE IT WHEN YOU'RE AROUND ME!
STAY AWAY!
WHAT?
WAIT! DON'T BE RIDICULOUS!
WHY DO I HAVE TO BE IGNORED MY WHOLE LIFE?
DON'T I DESERVE...
...TO BE ALIVE?! TO BE HEARD?!
OH...
I SEE IT NOW.

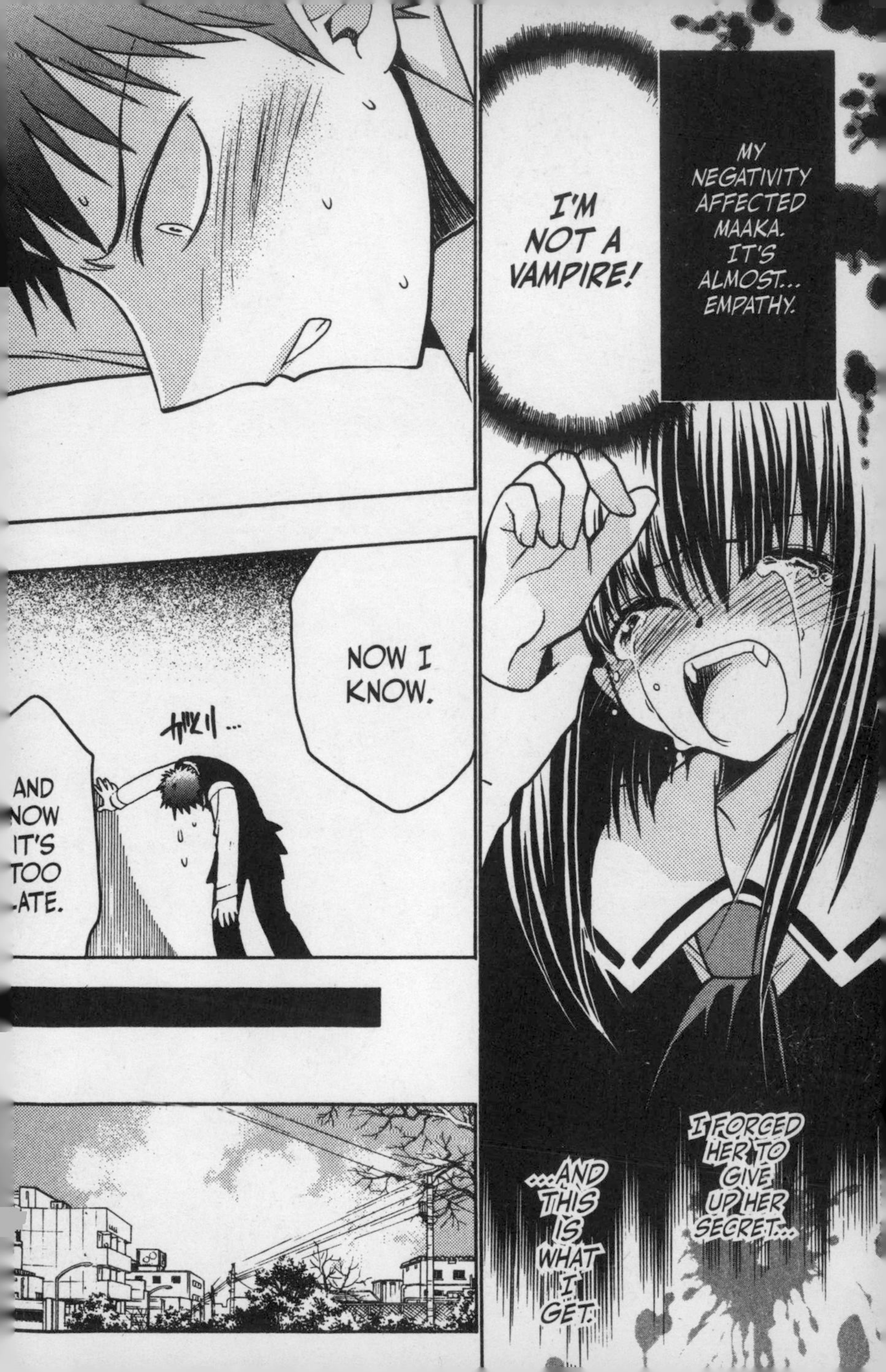

MY NEGATIVITY AFFECTED MAAKA. IT'S ALMOST... EMPATHY.
I'M NOT A VAMPIRE!
I FORCED HER TO GIVE UP HER SECRET...
...AND THIS IS WHAT I GET.
NOW I KNOW.
AND NOW IT'S TOO LATE.

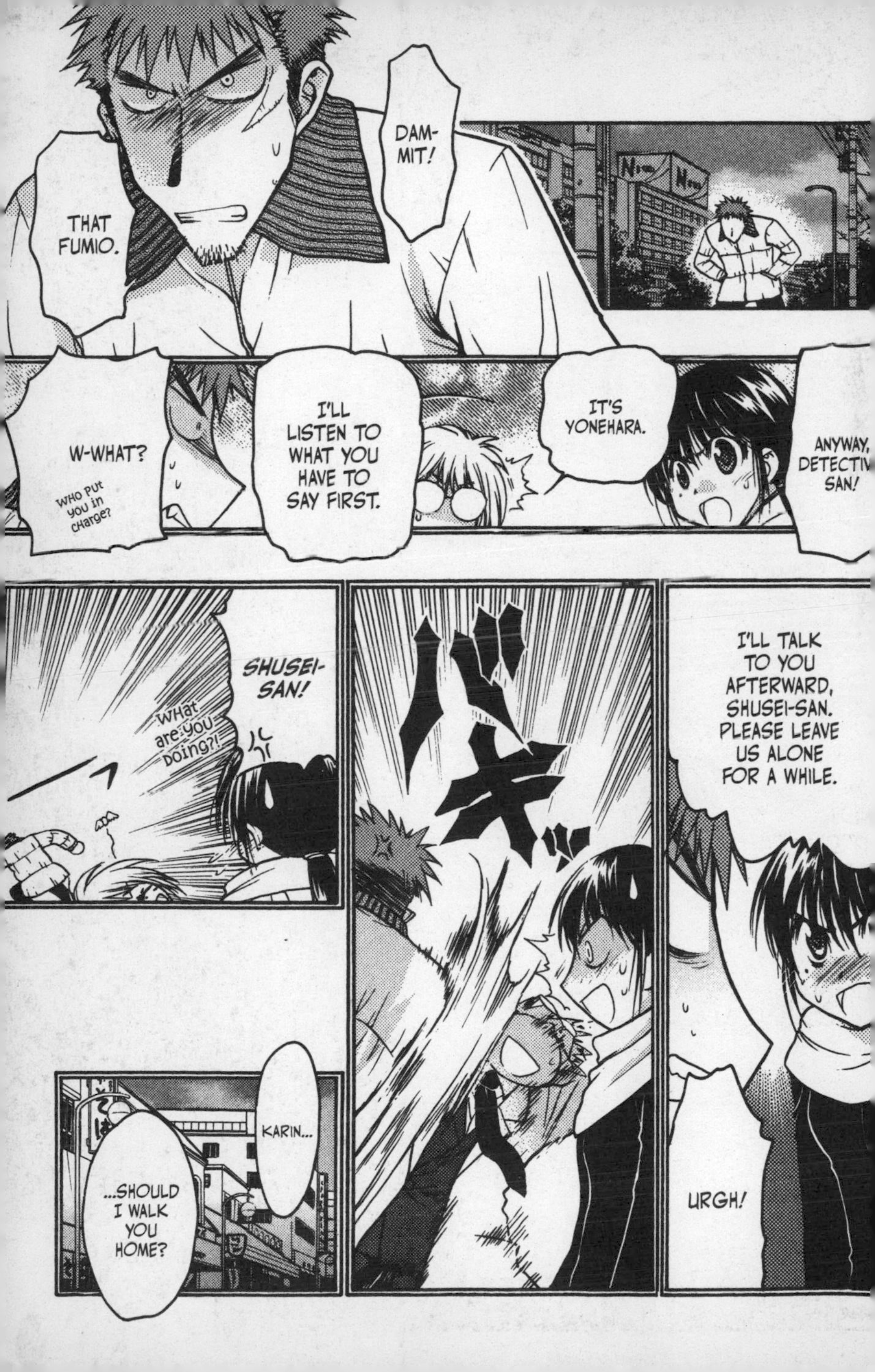
DAM-MIT!
THAT FUMIO.
ANYWAY, DETECTIV SAN!
IT'S YONEHARA.
I'LL LISTEN TO WHAT YOU HAVE TO SAY FIRST.
W-WHAT?
Who put you in charge?
I'LL TALK TO YOU AFTERWARD, SHUSEI-SAN. PLEASE LEAVE US ALONE FOR A WHILE.
URGH!
バキッ
SHUSEI-SAN!
What are you doing?!
KARIN...
...SHOULD I WALK YOU HOME?

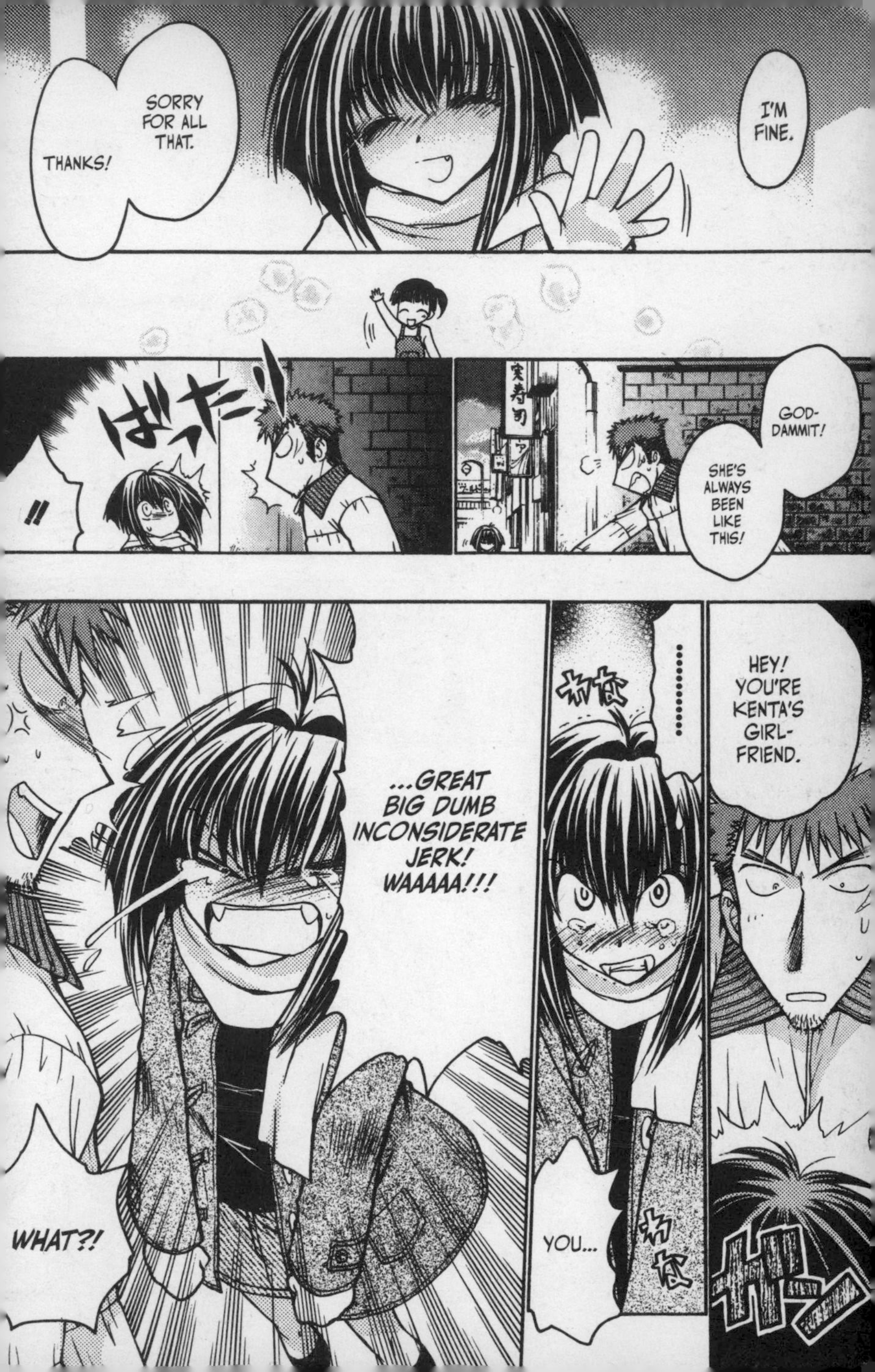
I'M FINE.
SORRY FOR ALL THAT.
THANKS!
GOD-DAMMIT!
SHE'S ALWAYS BEEN LIKE THIS!
!!
HEY! YOU'RE KENTA'S GIRL-FRIEND.
....
わな
YOU...
わな
...GREAT BIG DUMB INCONSIDERATE JERK! WAAAAA!!!
WHAT?!

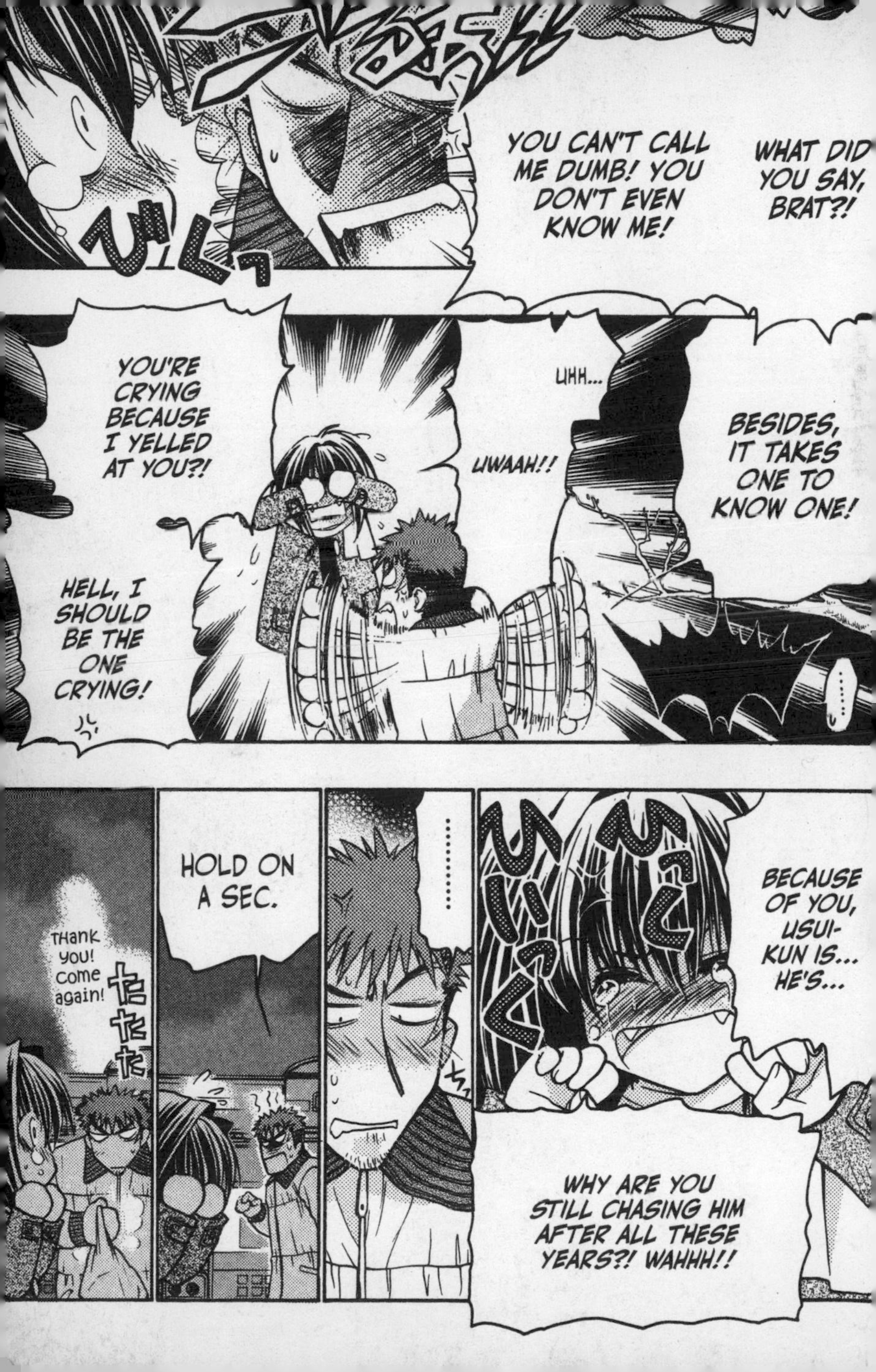
WHAT DID YOU SAY, BRAT?!
YOU CAN'T CALL ME DUMB! YOU DON'T EVEN KNOW ME!
BESIDES, IT TAKES ONE TO KNOW ONE!
.....
UHH...
UWAAH!!
YOU'RE CRYING BECAUSE I YELLED AT YOU?!
HELL, I SHOULD BE THE ONE CRYING!
BECAUSE OF YOU, USUI-KUN IS... HE'S...
WHY ARE YOU STILL CHASING HIM AFTER ALL THESE YEARS?! WAHHH!!
....
HOLD ON A SEC.
Thank you! Come again!

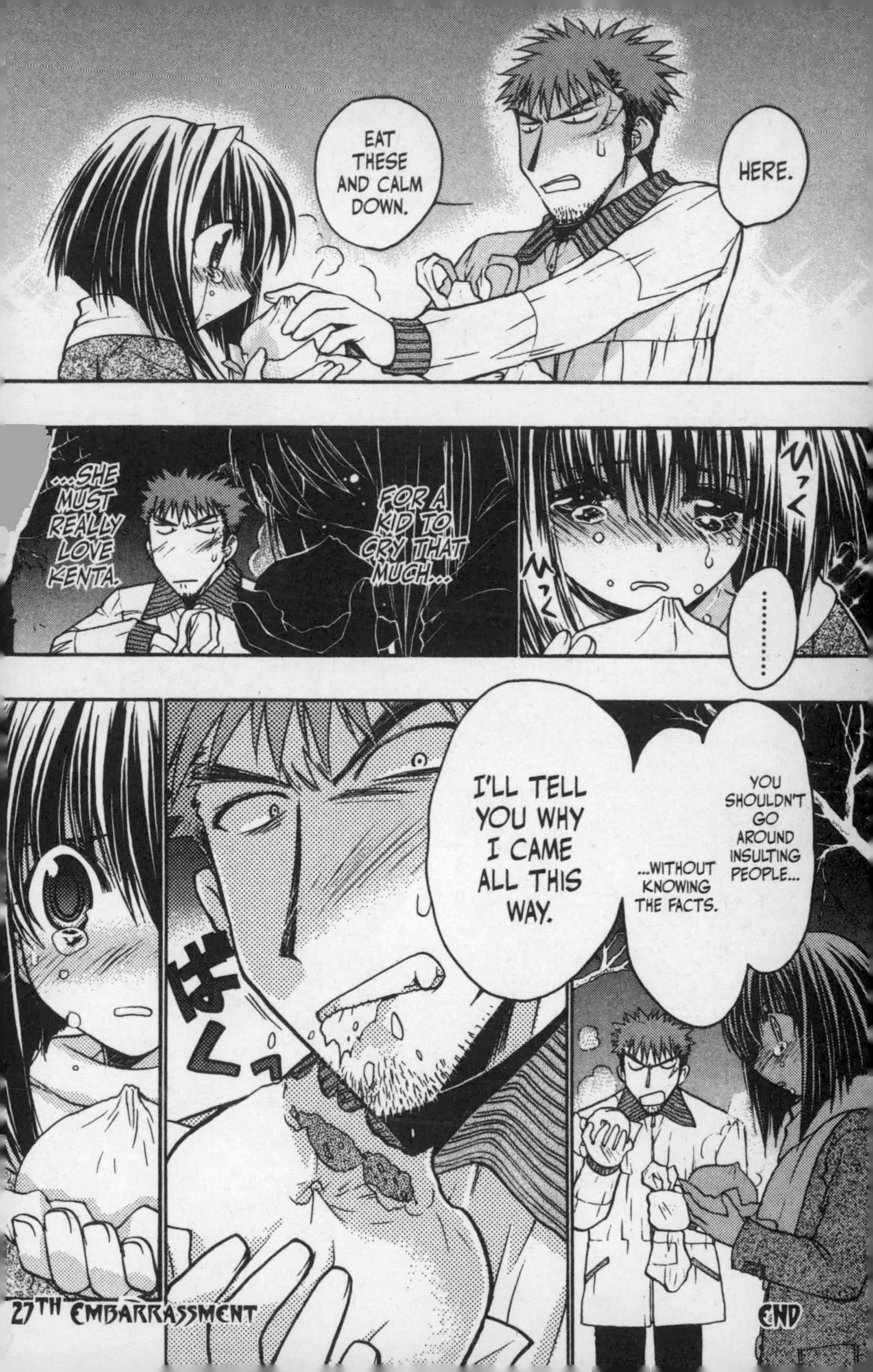
HERE.
EAT THESE AND CALM DOWN.
ひっく
......
FOR A KID TO CRY THAT MUCH...
...SHE MUST REALLY LOVE KENTA.
YOU SHOULDN'T GO AROUND INSULTING PEOPLE...
...WITHOUT KNOWING THE FACTS.
I'LL TELL YOU WHY I CAME ALL THIS WAY.
END
27TH EMBARRASSMENT

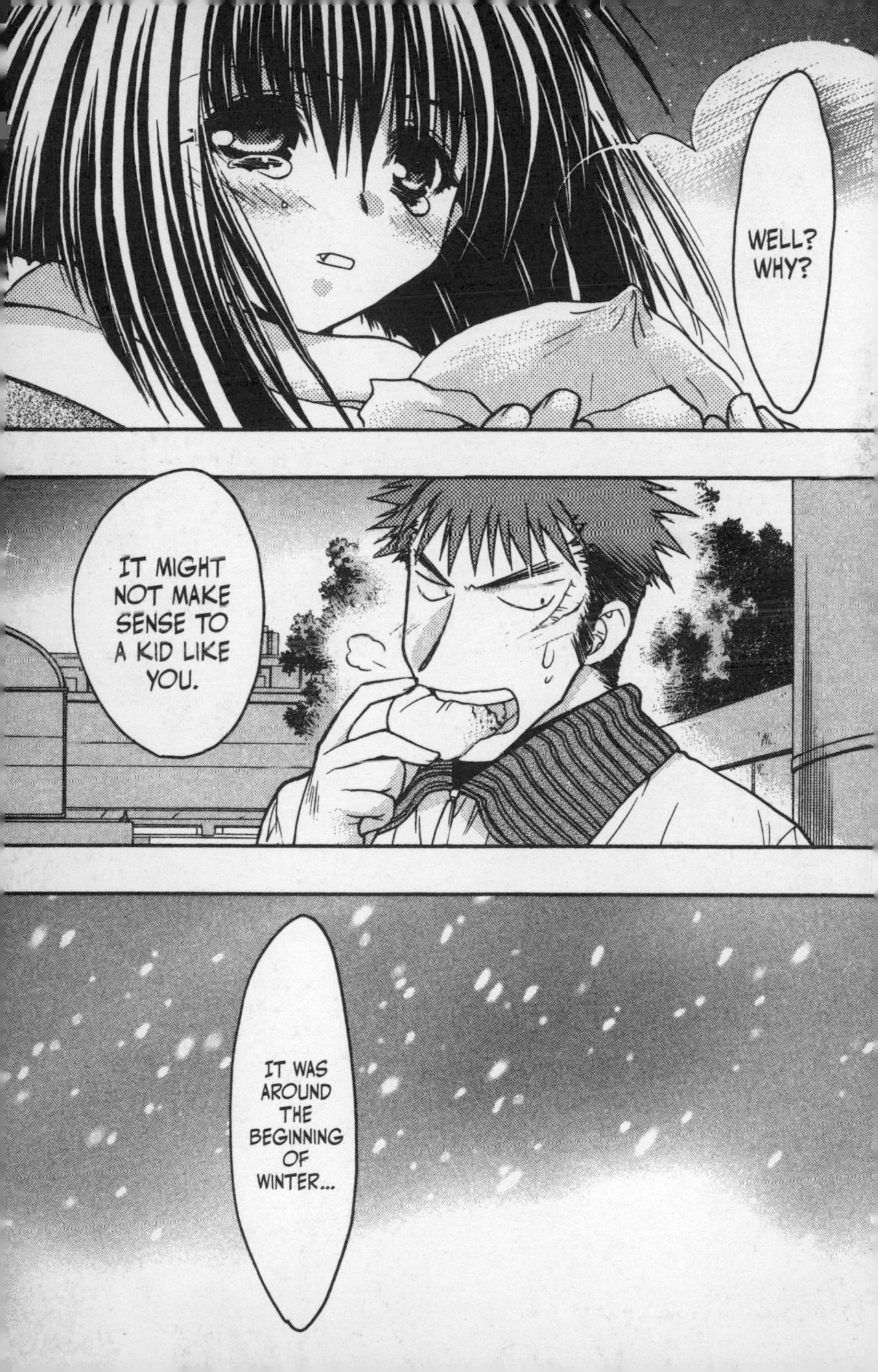
WELL? WHY?
IT MIGHT NOT MAKE SENSE TO A KID LIKE YOU.
IT WAS AROUND THE BEGINNING OF WINTER...

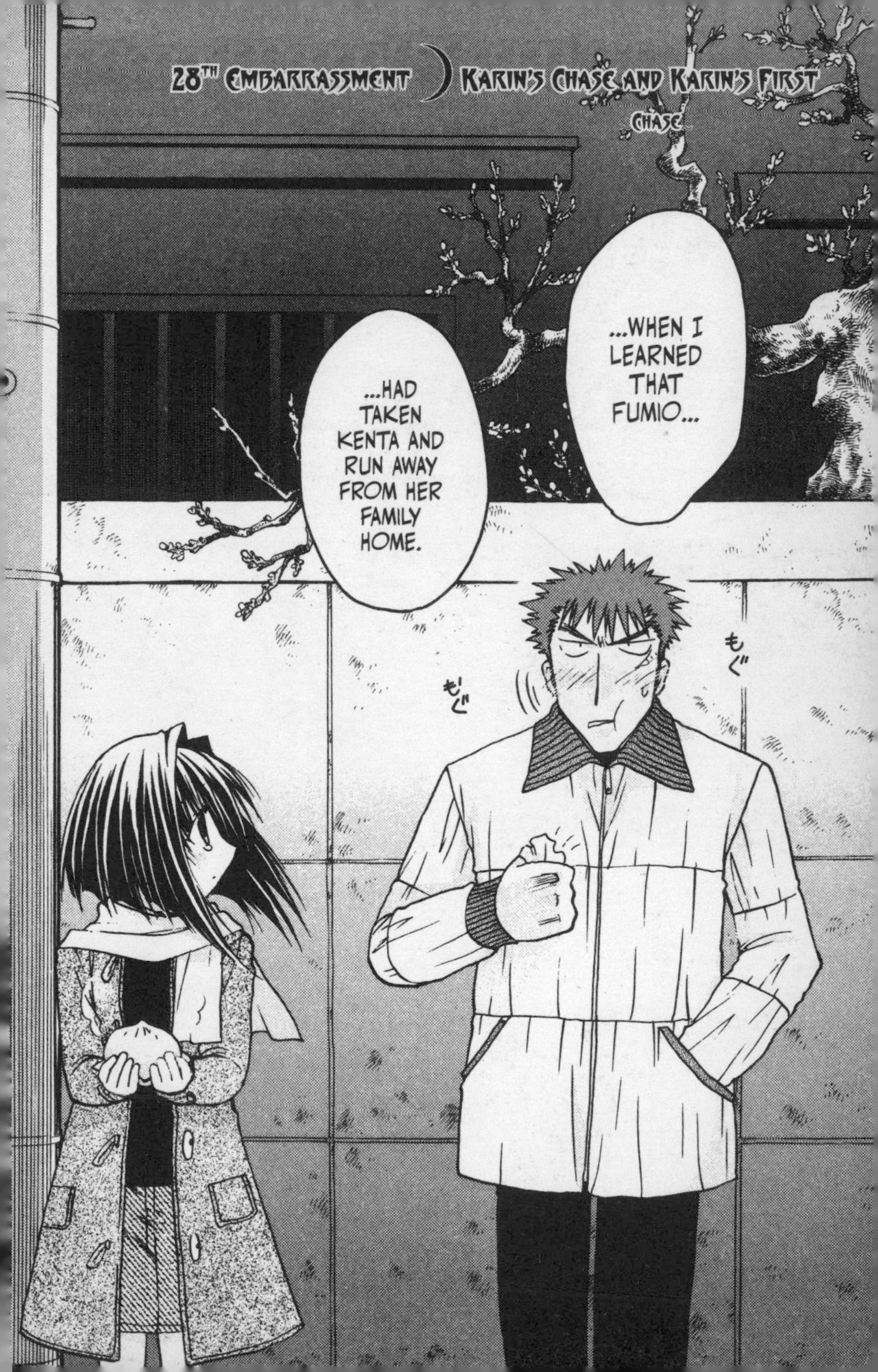
28TH EMBARRASSMENT
KARIN'S CHASE AND KARIN'S FIRST CHASE
...WHEN I LEARNED THAT FUMIO...
...HAD TAKEN KENTA AND RUN AWAY FROM HER FAMILY HOME.
もぐ
もぐ

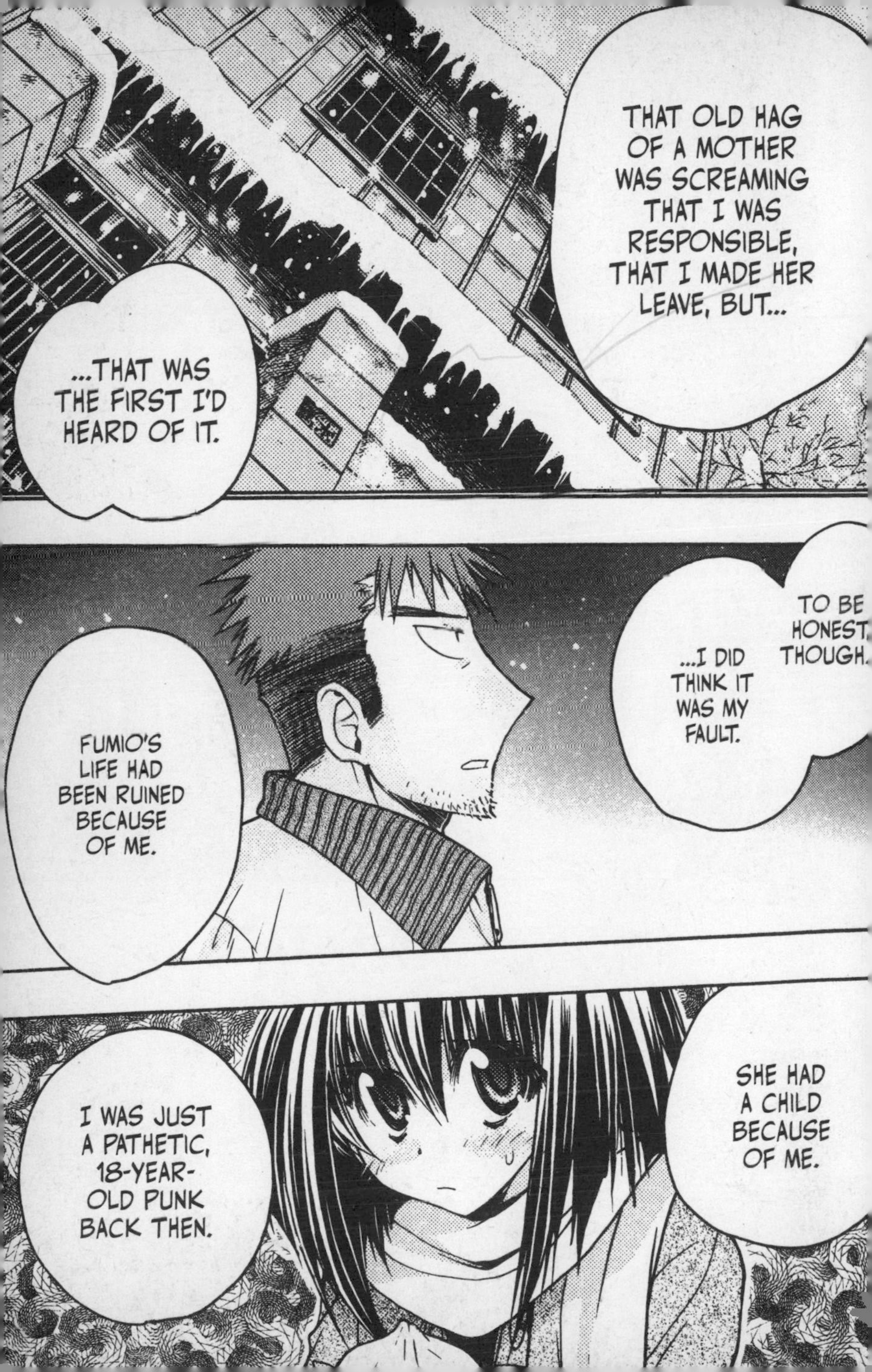
THAT OLD HAG OF A MOTHER WAS SCREAMING THAT I WAS RESPONSIBLE, THAT I MADE HER LEAVE, BUT...
...THAT WAS THE FIRST I'D HEARD OF IT.
TO BE HONEST, THOUGH.
...I DID THINK IT WAS MY FAULT.
FUMIO'S LIFE HAD BEEN RUINED BECAUSE OF ME.
SHE HAD A CHILD BECAUSE OF ME.
I WAS JUST A PATHETIC, 18-YEAR-OLD PUNK BACK THEN.

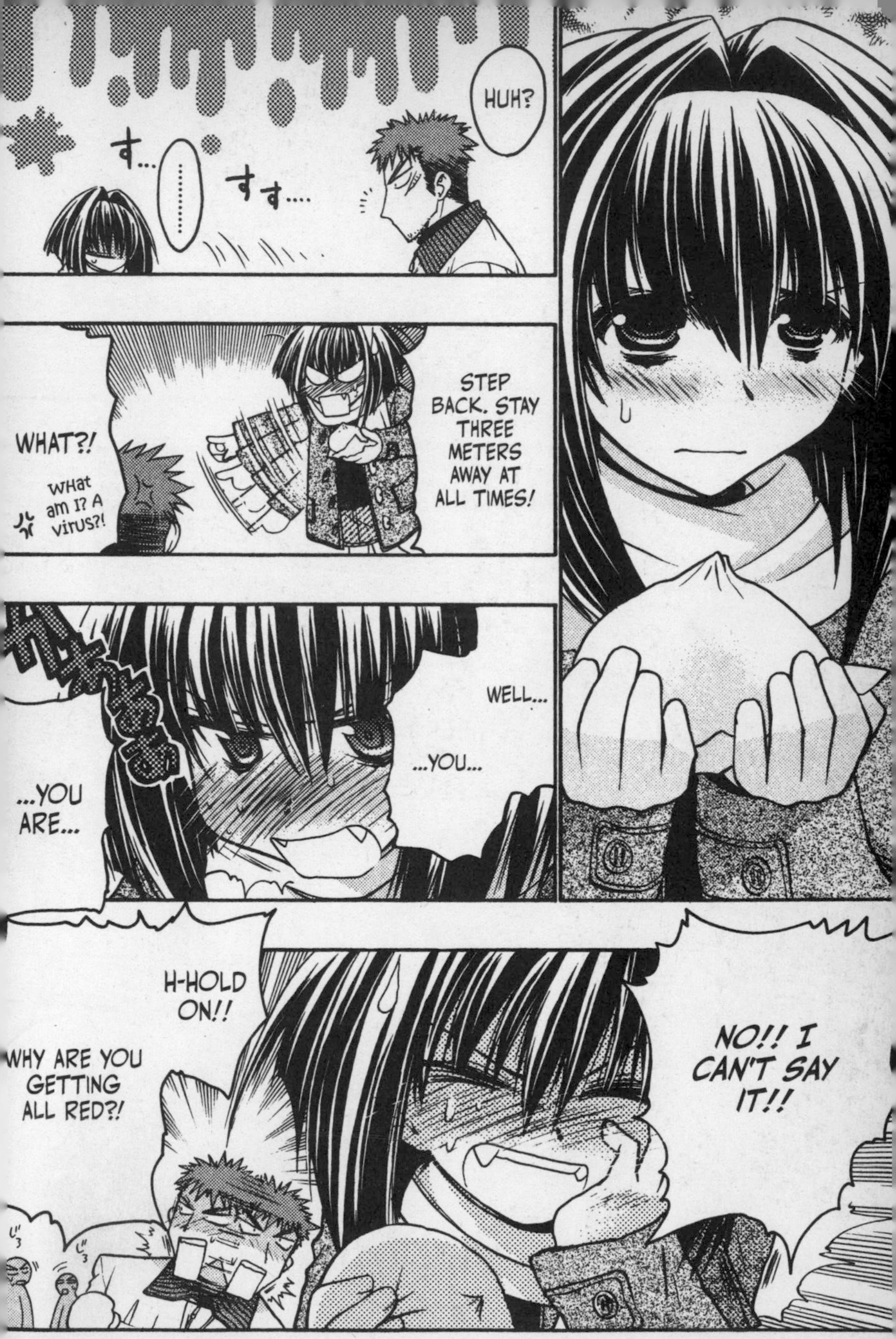
HUH?
すす....
......
す...
STEP BACK. STAY THREE METERS AWAY AT ALL TIMES!
WHAT?!
What am I? A virus?!
WELL...
...YOU...
...YOU ARE...
NO!! I CAN'T SAY IT!!
H-HOLD ON!!
WHY ARE YOU GETTING ALL RED?!

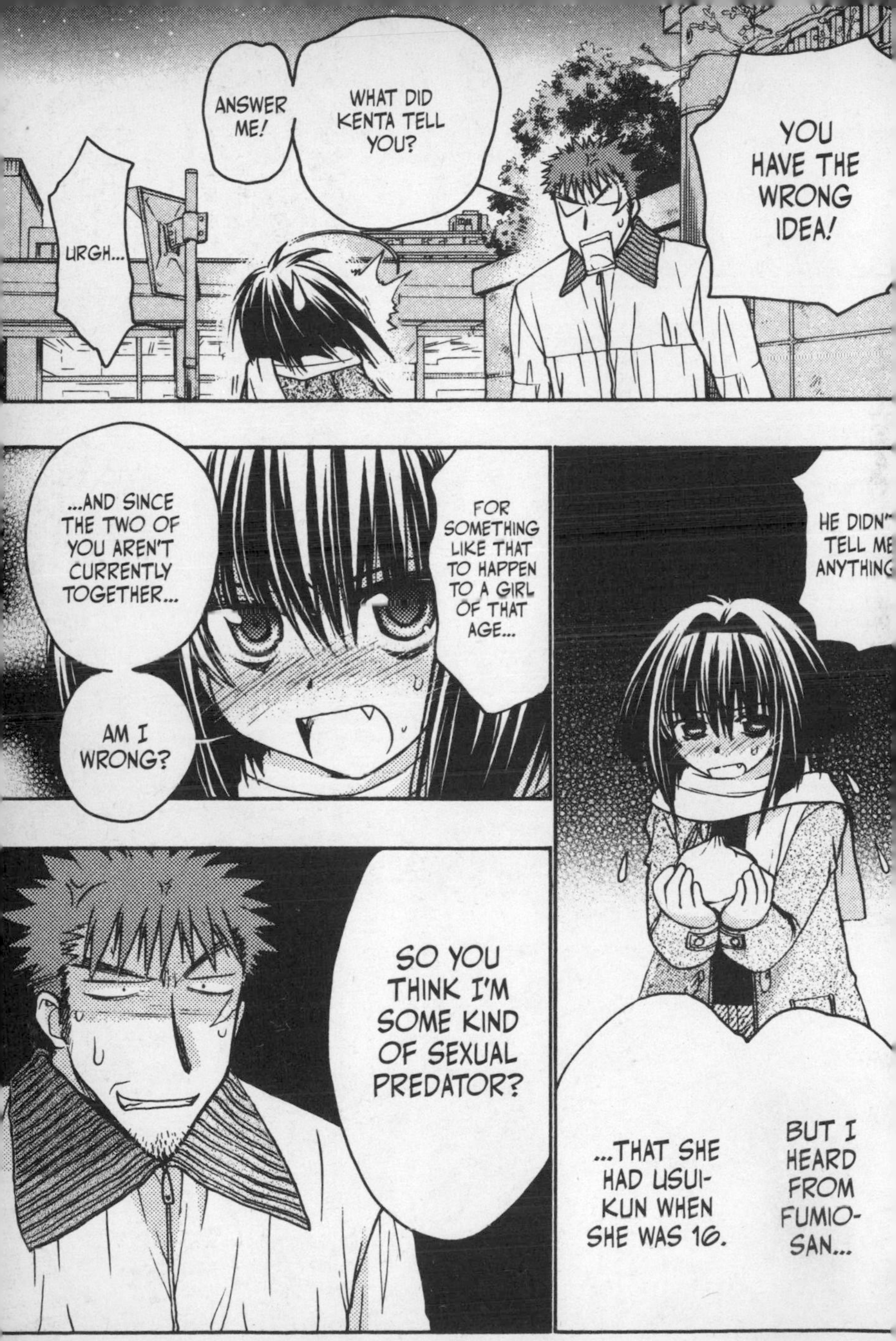
YOU HAVE THE WRONG IDEA!
WHAT DID KENTA TELL YOU?
ANSWER ME!
URGH...
HE DIDN'T TELL ME ANYTHING
BUT I HEARD FROM FUMIO-SAN...
...THAT SHE HAD USUI-KUN WHEN SHE WAS 16.
FOR SOMETHING LIKE THAT TO HAPPEN TO A GIRL OF THAT AGE...
...AND SINCE THE TWO OF YOU AREN'T CURRENTLY TOGETHER...
AM I WRONG?
SO YOU THINK I'M SOME KIND OF SEXUAL PREDATOR?

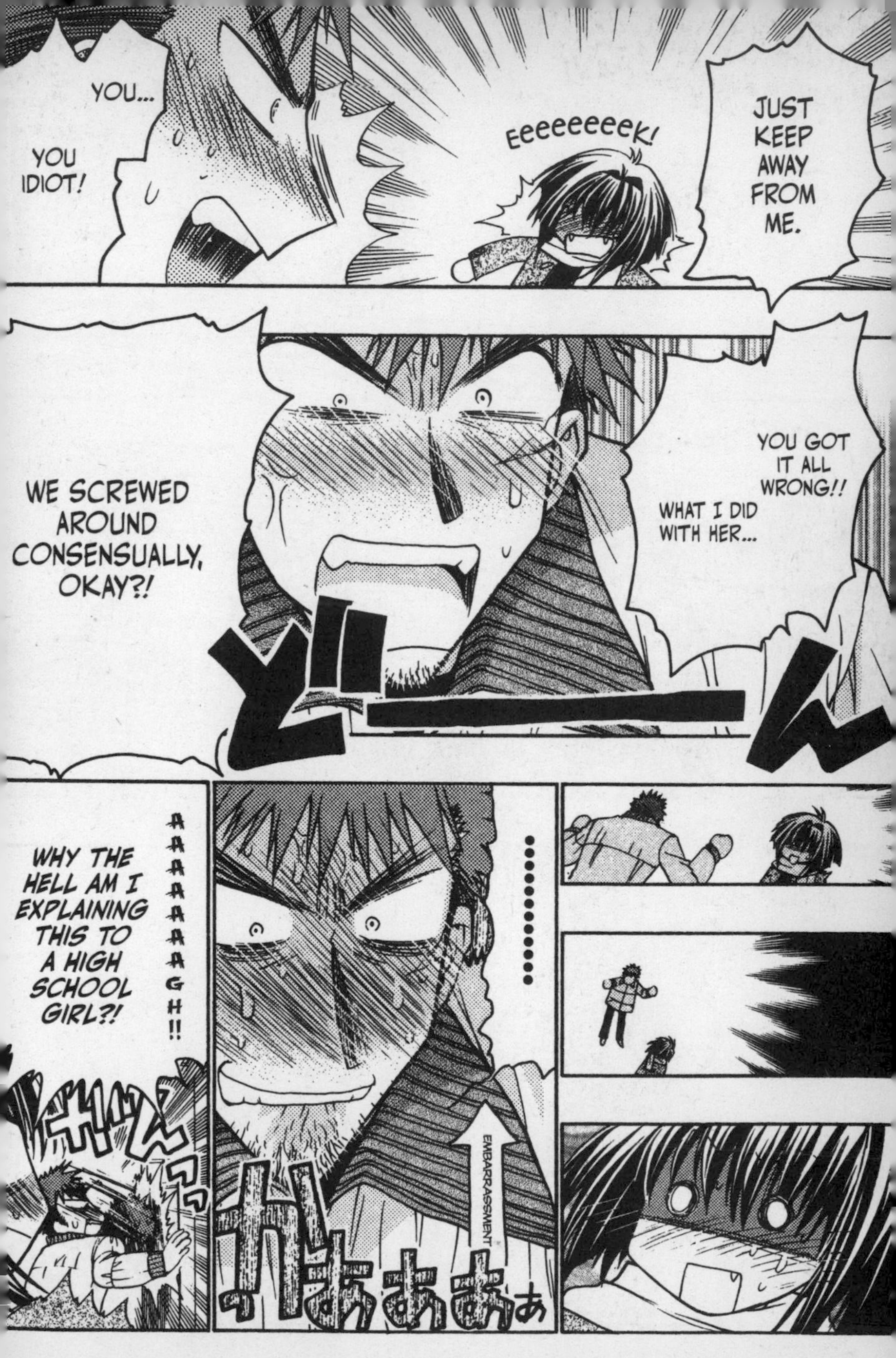
JUST KEEP AWAY FROM ME.
Eeeeeeeeek!
YOU...
YOU IDIOT!
YOU GOT IT ALL WRONG!!
WHAT I DID WITH HER...
WE SCREWED AROUND CONSENSUALLY, OKAY?!
....
EMBARRASSMENT
AAAAAAAAAGH!!
WHY THE HELL AM I EXPLAINING THIS TO A HIGH SCHOOL GIRL?!

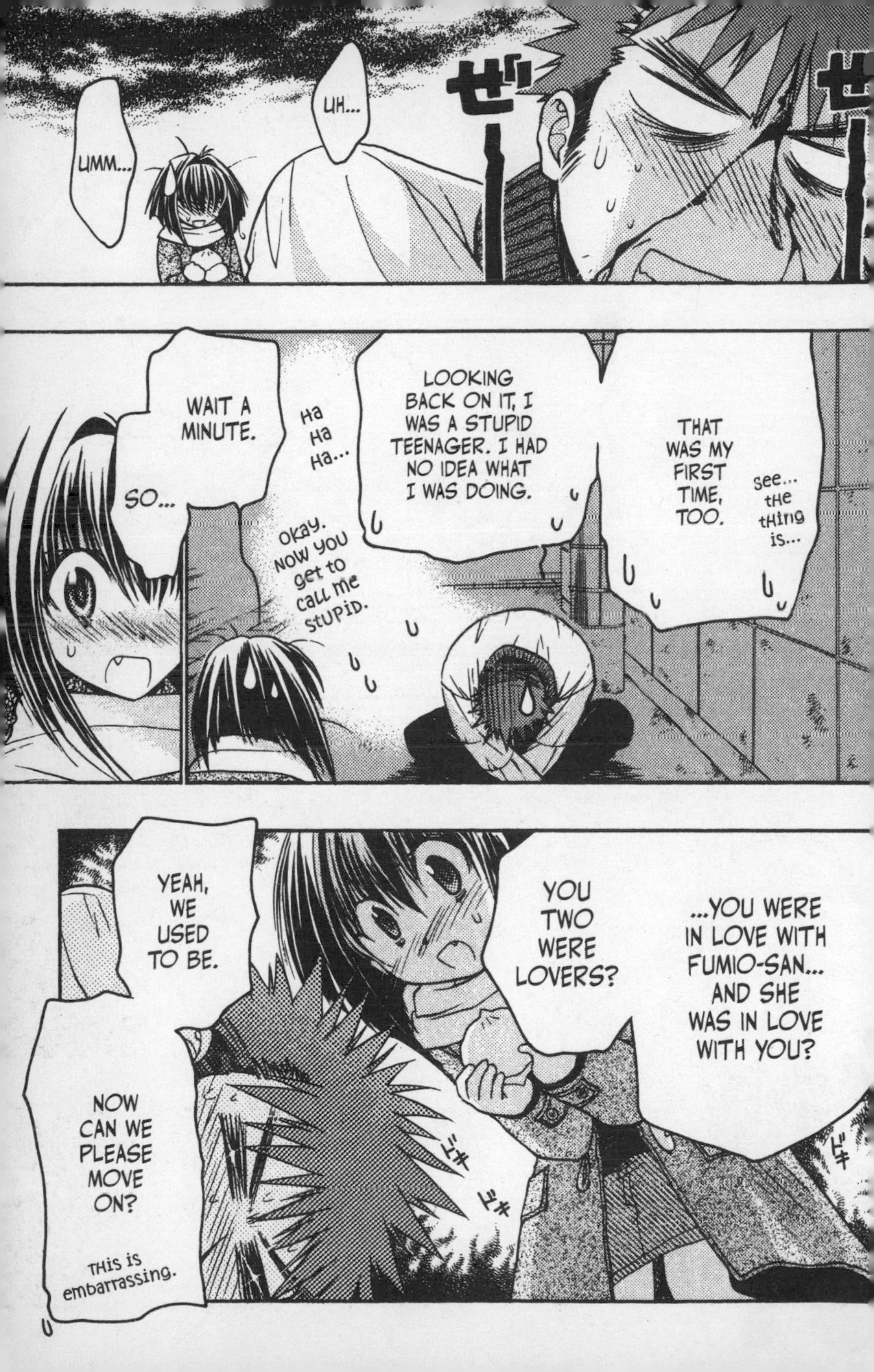
UH...
UMM...
THAT WAS MY FIRST TIME, TOO.
see... the thing is...
LOOKING BACK ON IT, I WAS A STUPID TEENAGER. I HAD NO IDEA WHAT I WAS DOING.
Ha Ha Ha...
Okay. Now you get to call me stupid.
WAIT A MINUTE.
SO...
...YOU WERE IN LOVE WITH FUMIO-SAN... AND SHE WAS IN LOVE WITH YOU?
YOU TWO WERE LOVERS?
ドキ
ドキ
ドキ
YEAH, WE USED TO BE.
NOW CAN WE PLEASE MOVE ON?
This is embarrassing.

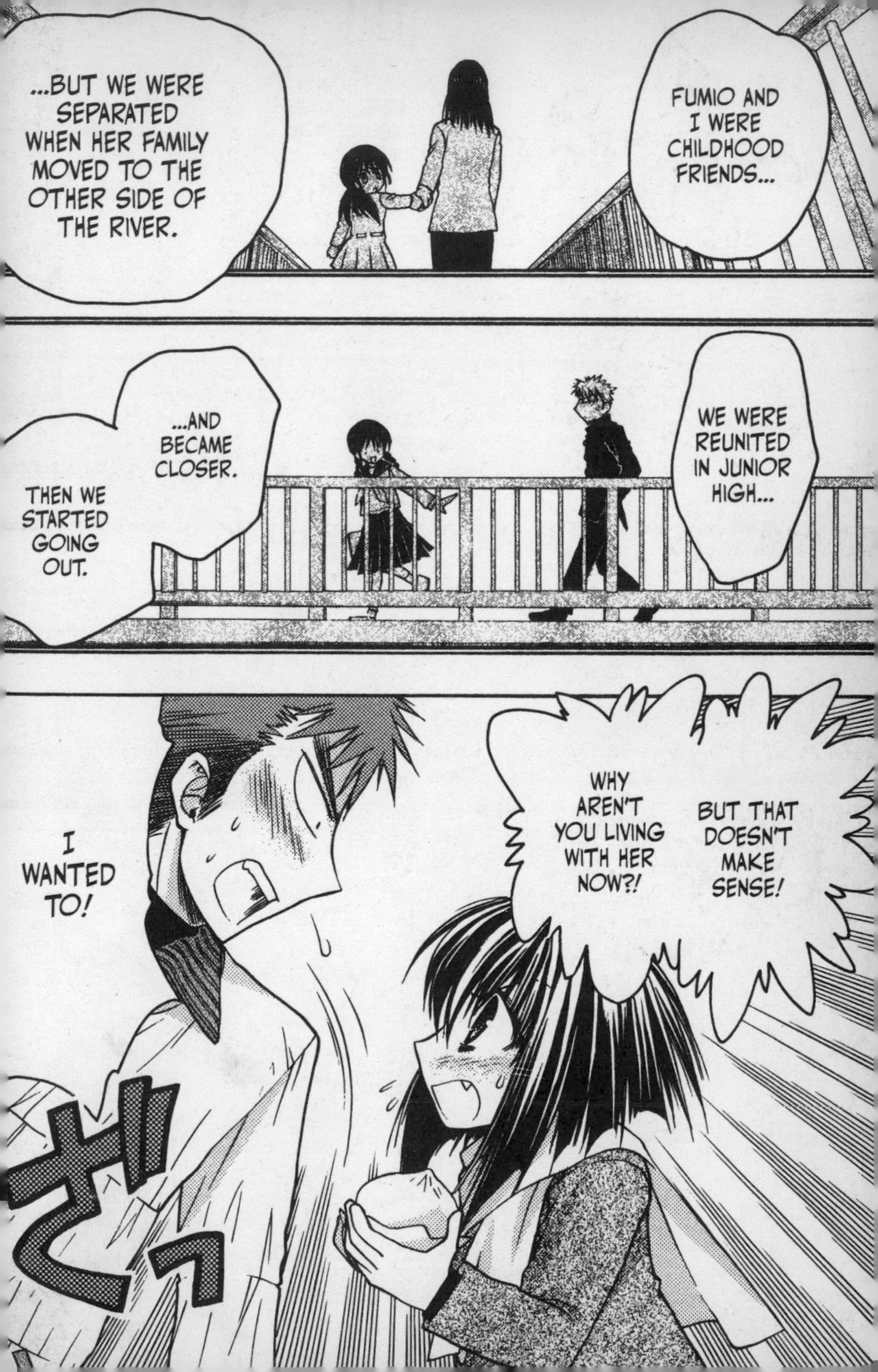
FUMIO AND I WERE CHILDHOOD FRIENDS...
...BUT WE WERE SEPARATED WHEN HER FAMILY MOVED TO THE OTHER SIDE OF THE RIVER.
WE WERE REUNITED IN JUNIOR HIGH...
...AND BECAME CLOSER.
THEN WE STARTED GOING OUT.
BUT THAT DOESN'T MAKE SENSE!
WHY AREN'T YOU LIVING WITH HER NOW?!
I WANTED TO!

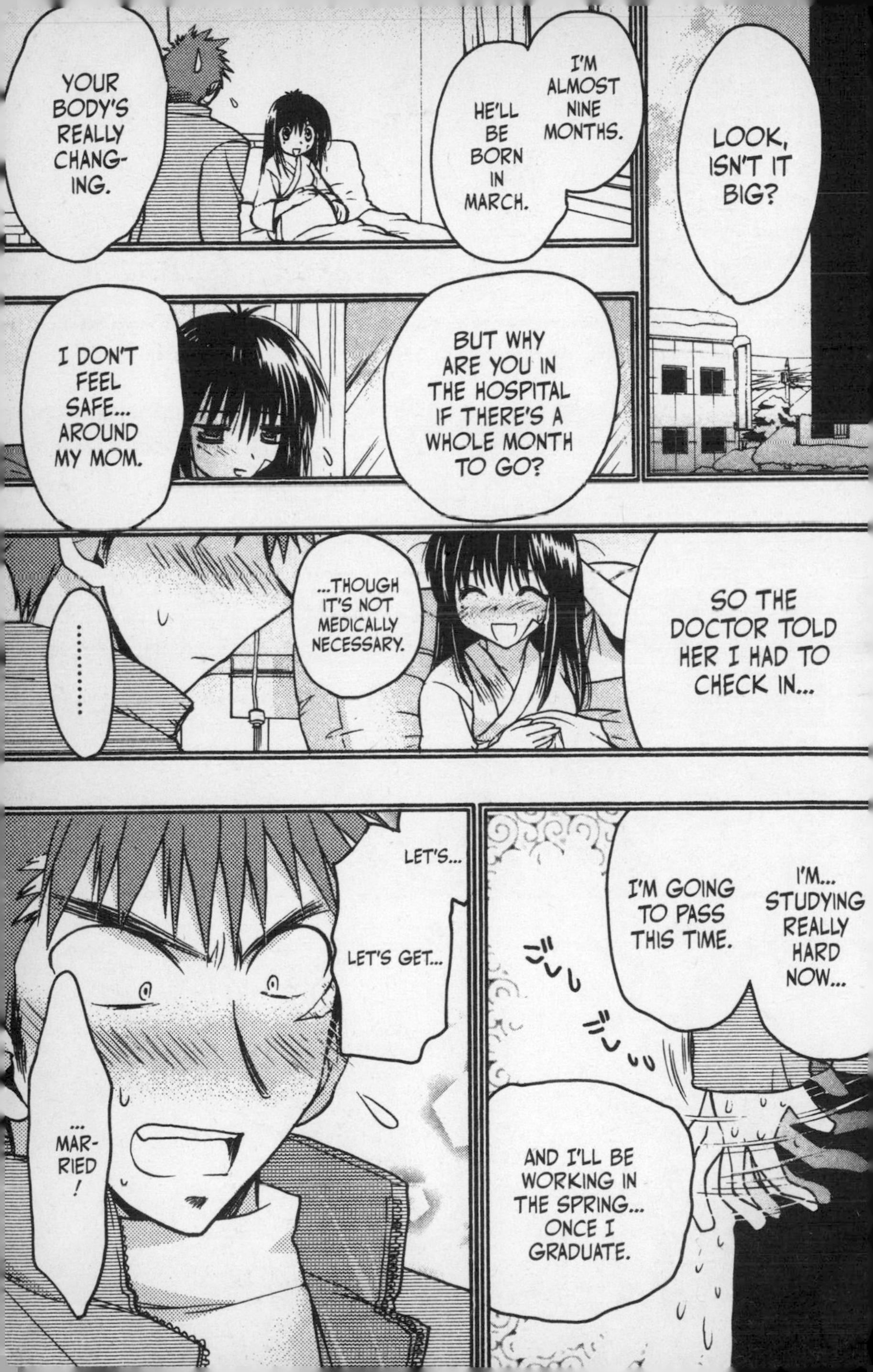
LOOK, ISN'T IT BIG?
I'M ALMOST NINE MONTHS.
HE'LL BE BORN IN MARCH.
YOUR BODY'S REALLY CHANG-ING.
BUT WHY ARE YOU IN THE HOSPITAL IF THERE'S A WHOLE MONTH TO GO?
I DON'T FEEL SAFE... AROUND MY MOM.
SO THE DOCTOR TOLD HER I HAD TO CHECK IN...
...THOUGH IT'S NOT MEDICALLY NECESSARY.
....
I'M... STUDYING REALLY HARD NOW...
I'M GOING TO PASS THIS TIME.
AND I'LL BE WORKING IN THE SPRING... ONCE I GRADUATE.
LET'S...
LET'S GET...
...MAR-RIED!

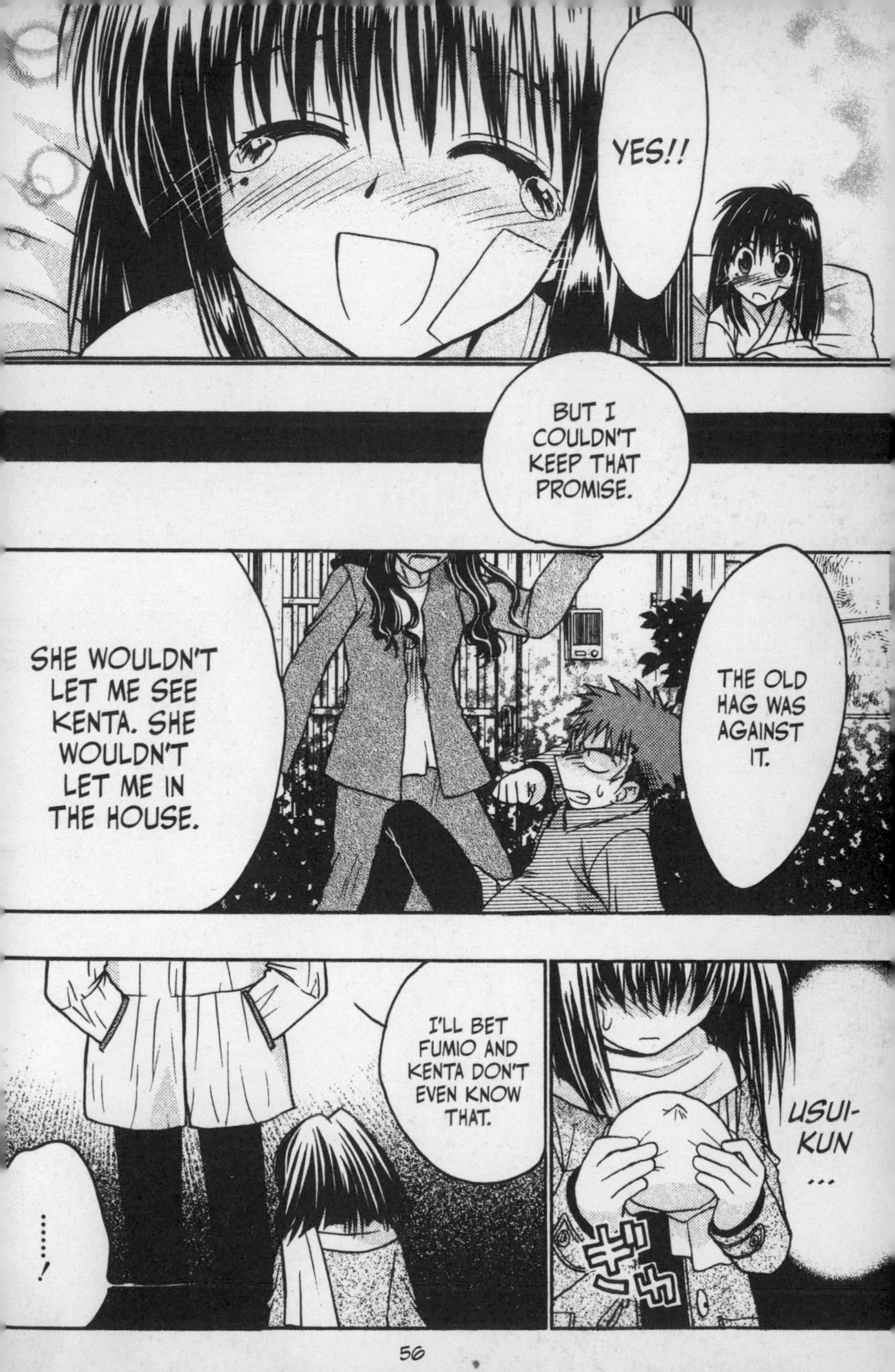
YES!!
BUT I COULDN'T KEEP THAT PROMISE.
THE OLD HAG WAS AGAINST IT.
SHE WOULDN'T LET ME SEE KENTA. SHE WOULDN'T LET ME IN THE HOUSE.
USUI-KUN ...
I'LL BET FUMIO AND KENTA DON'T EVEN KNOW THAT.
......!

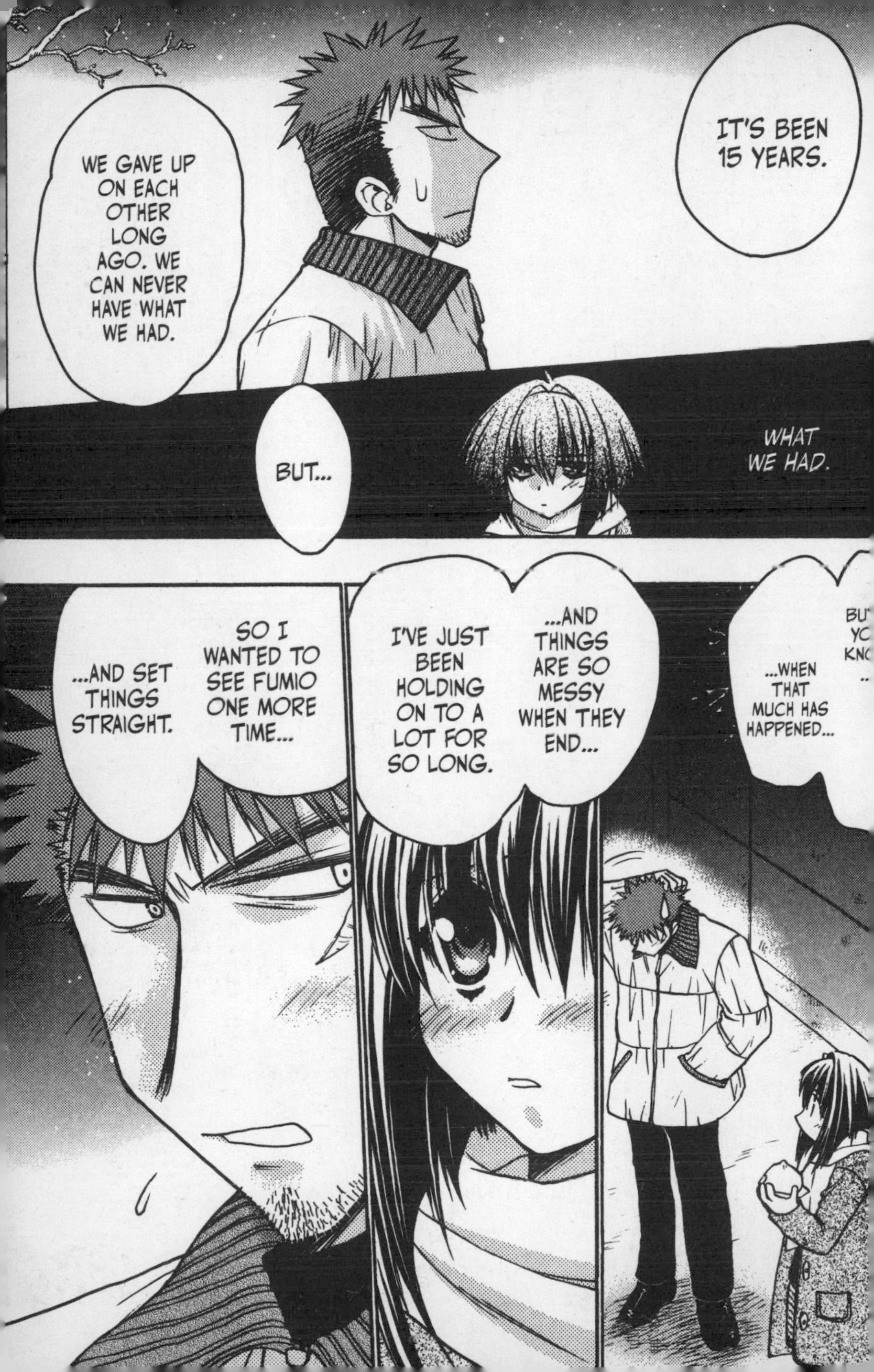
IT'S BEEN 15 YEARS.
WE GAVE UP ON EACH OTHER LONG AGO. WE CAN NEVER HAVE WHAT WE HAD.
WHAT WE HAD.
BUT...
...WHEN THAT MUCH HAS HAPPENED...
...AND THINGS ARE SO MESSY WHEN THEY END...
I'VE JUST BEEN HOLDING ON TO A LOT FOR SO LONG.
SO I WANTED TO SEE FUMIO ONE MORE TIME...
...AND SET THINGS STRAIGHT.

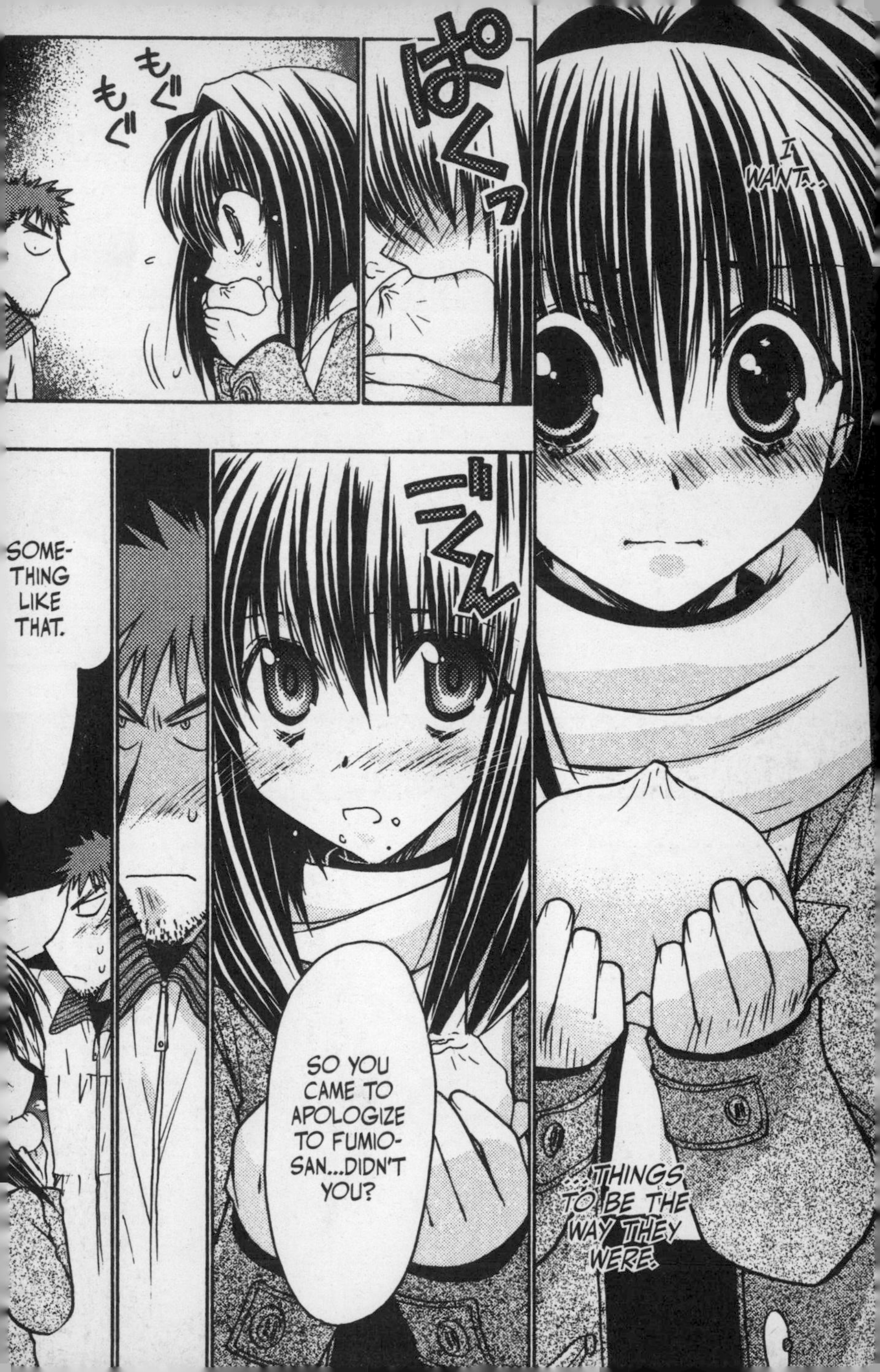
I WANT...
...THINGS TO BE THE WAY THEY WERE.
ぱくっ
もぐもぐ
ごくん
SO YOU CAME TO APOLOGIZE TO FUMIO-SAN...DIDN'T YOU?
SOME-THING LIKE THAT.

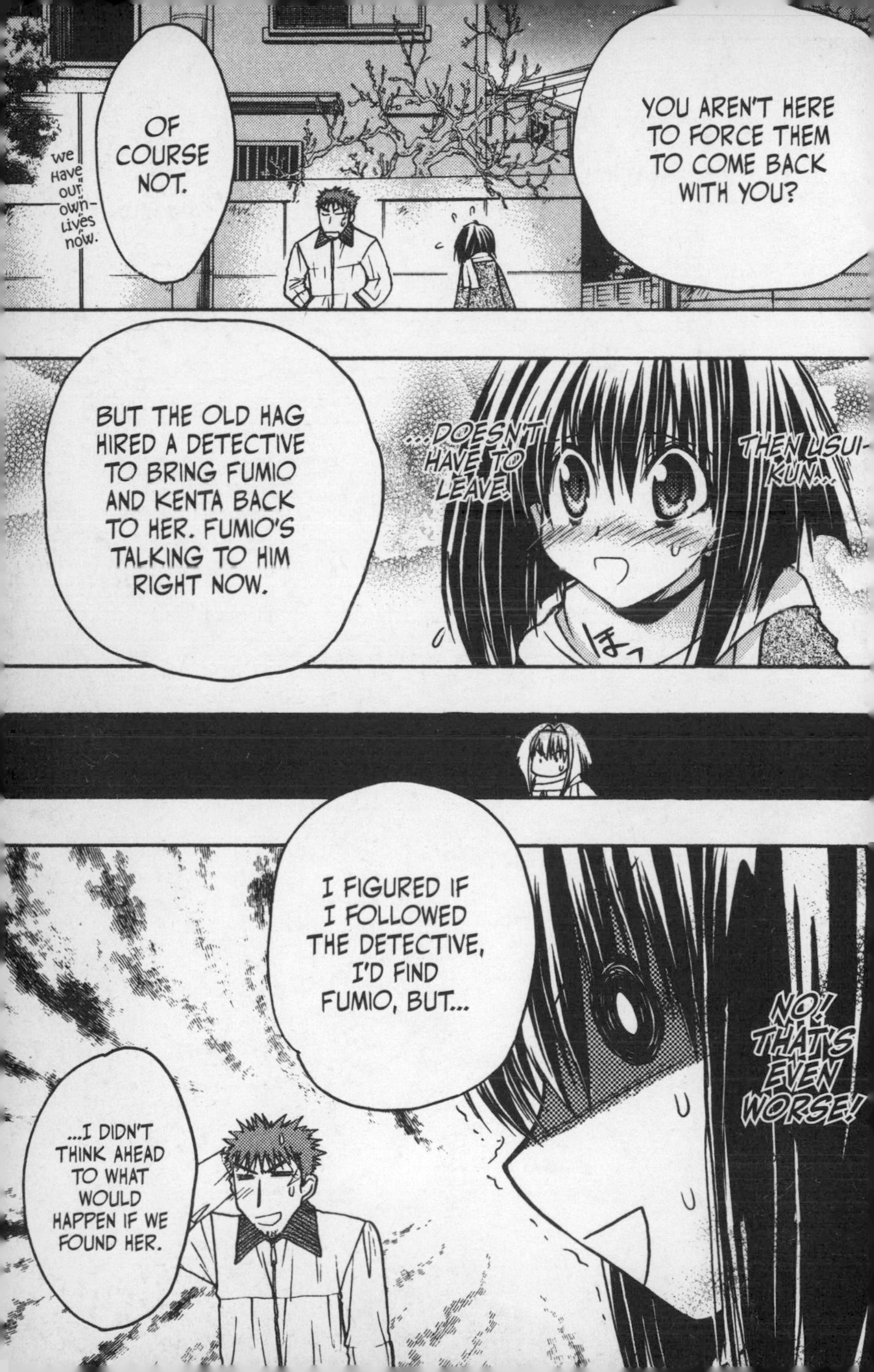
YOU AREN'T HERE TO FORCE THEM TO COME BACK WITH YOU?
OF COURSE NOT.
We have our own lives now.
THEN USUI-KUN...
...DOESN'T HAVE TO LEAVE.
ほっ
BUT THE OLD HAG HIRED A DETECTIVE TO BRING FUMIO AND KENTA BACK TO HER. FUMIO'S TALKING TO HIM RIGHT NOW.
I FIGURED IF I FOLLOWED THE DETECTIVE, I'D FIND FUMIO, BUT...
...I DIDN'T THINK AHEAD TO WHAT WOULD HAPPEN IF WE FOUND HER.
NO! THAT'S EVEN WORSE!

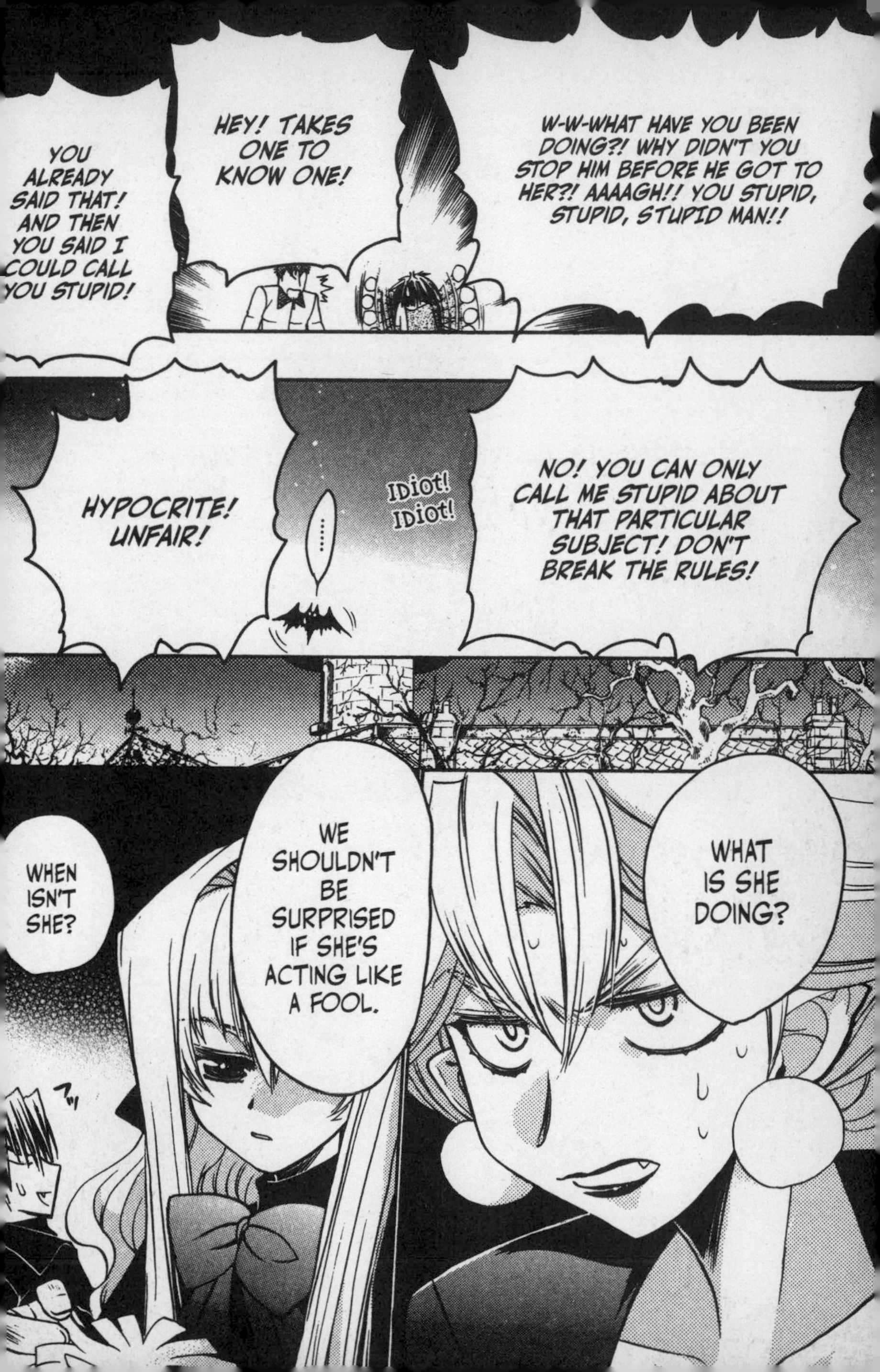
W-W-WHAT HAVE YOU BEEN DOING?! WHY DIDN'T YOU STOP HIM BEFORE HE GOT TO HER?! AAAAGH!! YOU STUPID, STUPID, STUPID MAN!!
HEY! TAKES ONE TO KNOW ONE!
YOU ALREADY SAID THAT! AND THEN YOU SAID I COULD CALL YOU STUPID!
NO! YOU CAN ONLY CALL ME STUPID ABOUT THAT PARTICULAR SUBJECT! DON'T BREAK THE RULES!
IDIOT! IDIOT!
......
HYPOCRITE! UNFAIR!
WHAT IS SHE DOING?
WE SHOULDN'T BE SURPRISED IF SHE'S ACTING LIKE A FOOL.
WHEN ISN'T SHE?

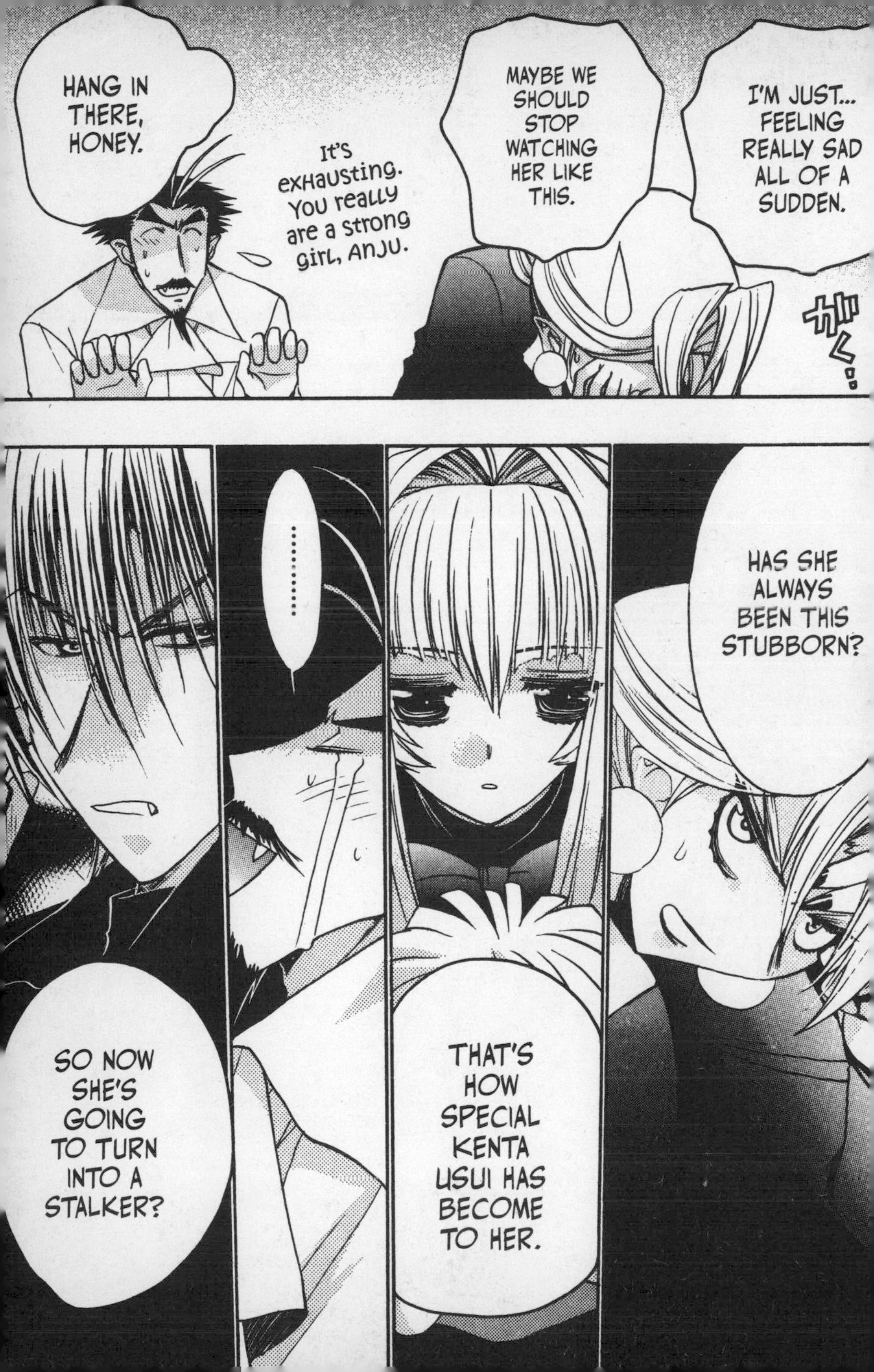
I'M JUST... FEELING REALLY SAD ALL OF A SUDDEN.
MAYBE WE SHOULD STOP WATCHING HER LIKE THIS.
HANG IN THERE, HONEY.
It's exhausting. You really are a strong girl, Anju.
HAS SHE ALWAYS BEEN THIS STUBBORN?
THAT'S HOW SPECIAL KENTA USUI HAS BECOME TO HER.
......
SO NOW SHE'S GOING TO TURN INTO A STALKER?

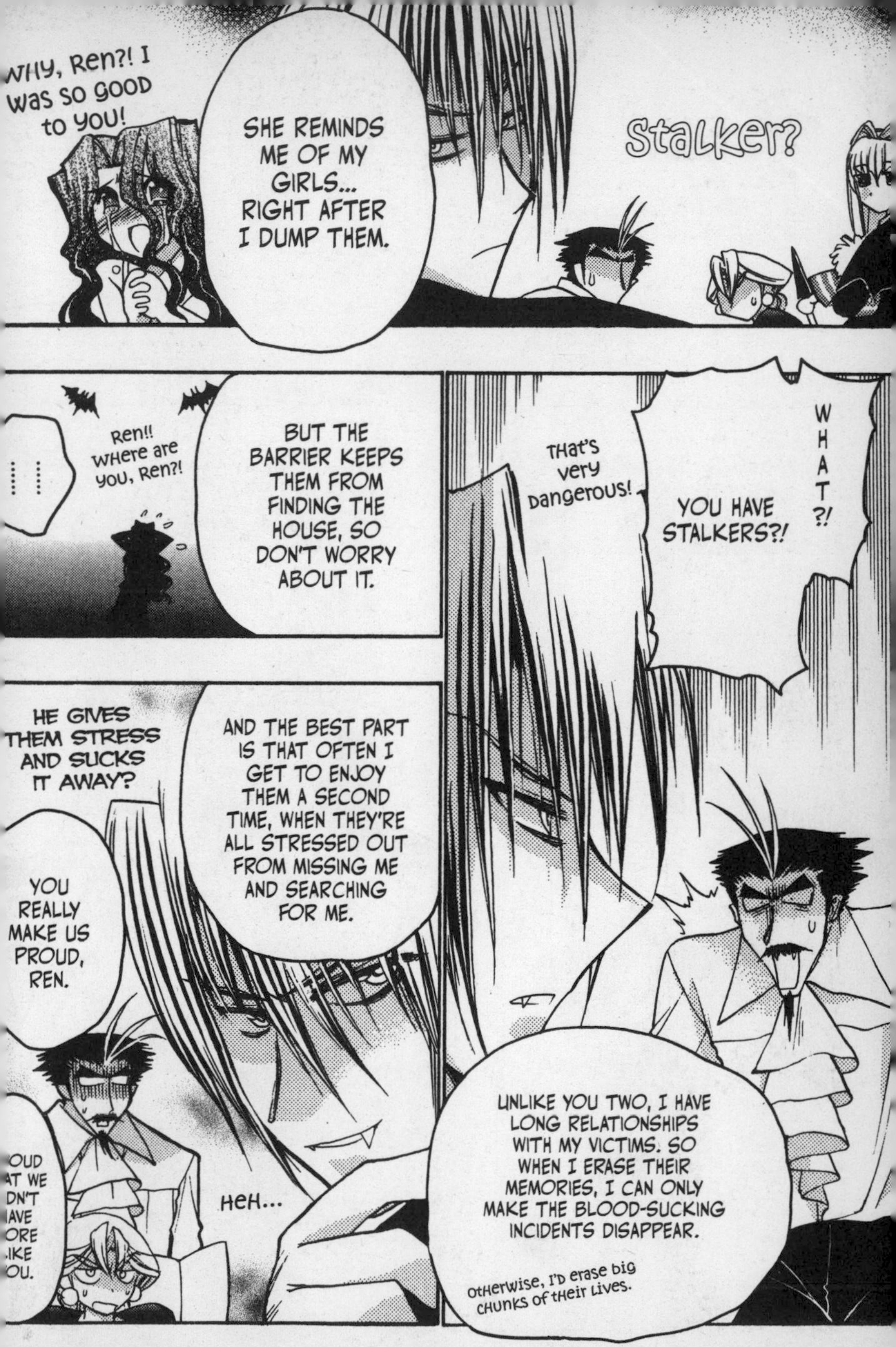
Stalker?
SHE REMINDS ME OF MY GIRLS... RIGHT AFTER I DUMP THEM.
WHY, Ren?! I was so good to you!
WHAT?!
YOU HAVE STALKERS?!
That's very Dangerous!
UNLIKE YOU TWO, I HAVE LONG RELATIONSHIPS WITH MY VICTIMS. SO WHEN I ERASE THEIR MEMORIES, I CAN ONLY MAKE THE BLOOD-SUCKING INCIDENTS DISAPPEAR.
Otherwise, I'D erase big chunks of their lives.
BUT THE BARRIER KEEPS THEM FROM FINDING THE HOUSE, SO DON'T WORRY ABOUT IT.
Ren!! Where are you, Ren?!
......
AND THE BEST PART IS THAT OFTEN I GET TO ENJOY THEM A SECOND TIME, WHEN THEY'RE ALL STRESSED OUT FROM MISSING ME AND SEARCHING FOR ME.
HE GIVES THEM STRESS AND SUCKS IT AWAY?
YOU REALLY MAKE US PROUD, REN.
HeH...
ROUD AT WE DN'T AVE ORE IKE OU.

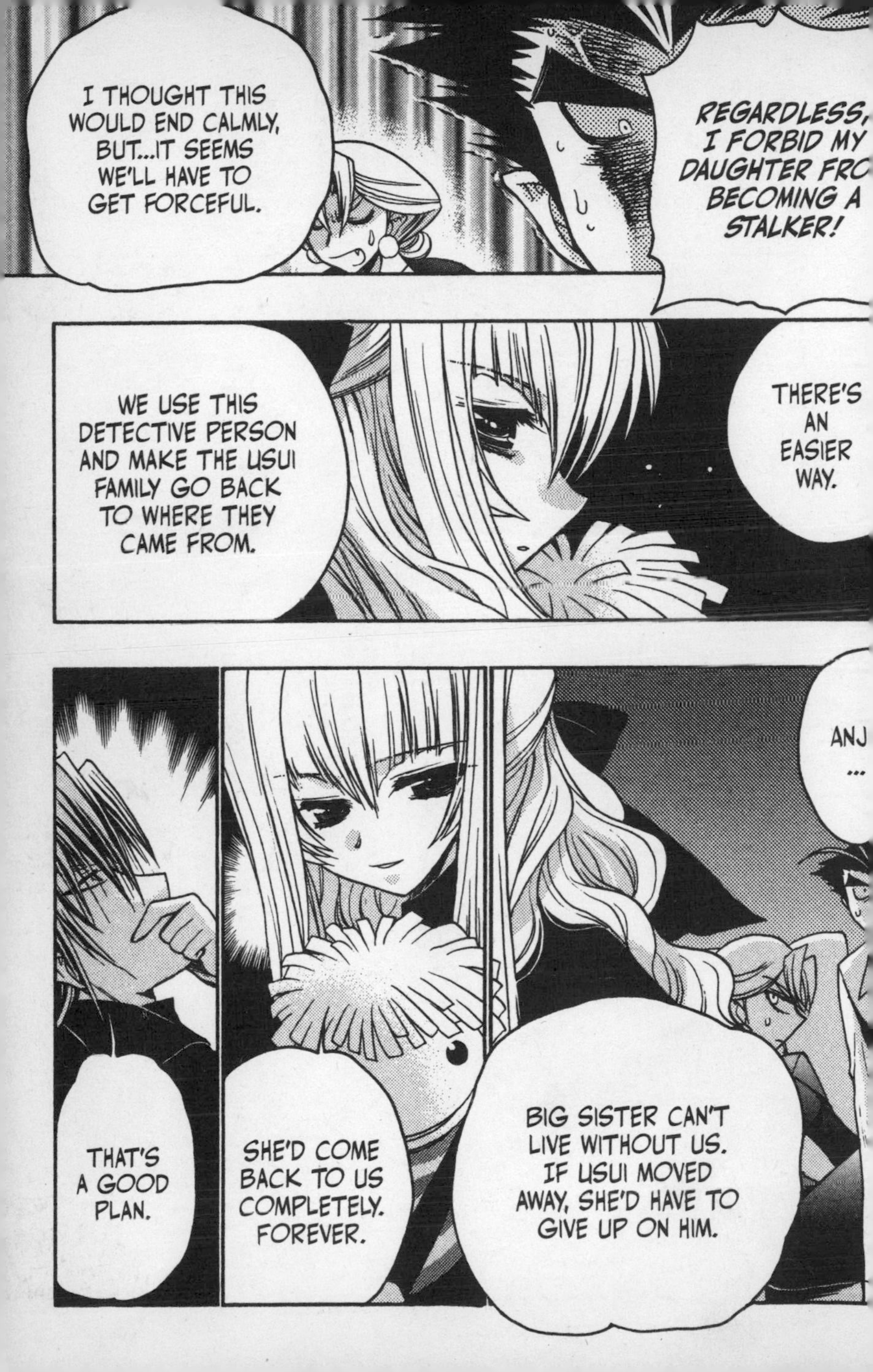
REGARDLESS, I FORBID MY DAUGHTER FRO BECOMING A STALKER!
I THOUGHT THIS WOULD END CALMLY, BUT...IT SEEMS WE'LL HAVE TO GET FORCEFUL.
THERE'S AN EASIER WAY.
WE USE THIS DETECTIVE PERSON AND MAKE THE USUI FAMILY GO BACK TO WHERE THEY CAME FROM.
ANJ ...
BIG SISTER CAN'T LIVE WITHOUT US. IF USUI MOVED AWAY, SHE'D HAVE TO GIVE UP ON HIM.
SHE'D COME BACK TO US COMPLETELY. FOREVER.
THAT'S A GOOD PLAN.

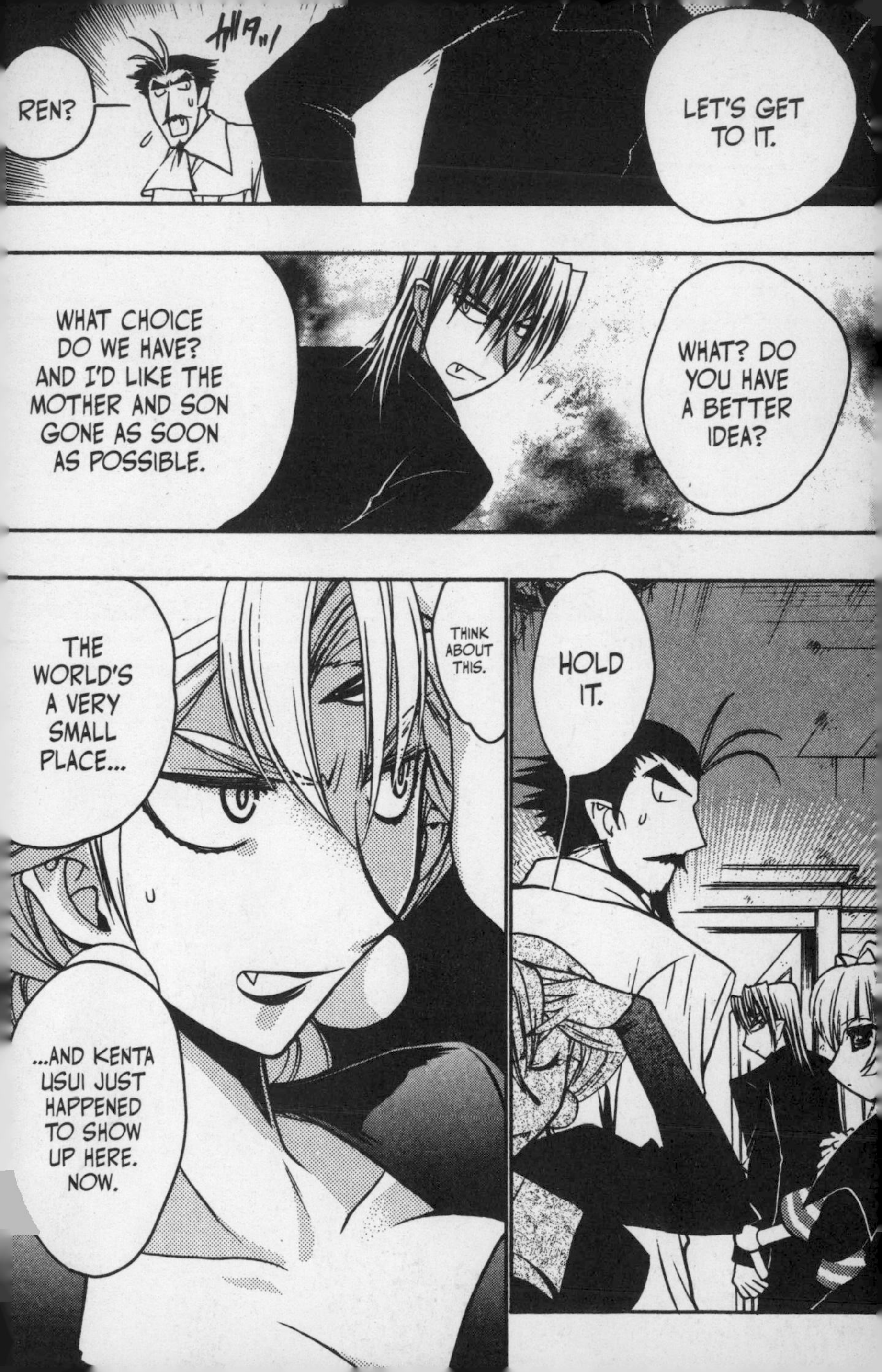
LET'S GET TO IT.
REN?
WHAT? DO YOU HAVE A BETTER IDEA?
WHAT CHOICE DO WE HAVE? AND I'D LIKE THE MOTHER AND SON GONE AS SOON AS POSSIBLE.
HOLD IT.
THINK ABOUT THIS.
THE WORLD'S A VERY SMALL PLACE...
...AND KENTA USUI JUST HAPPENED TO SHOW UP HERE. NOW.

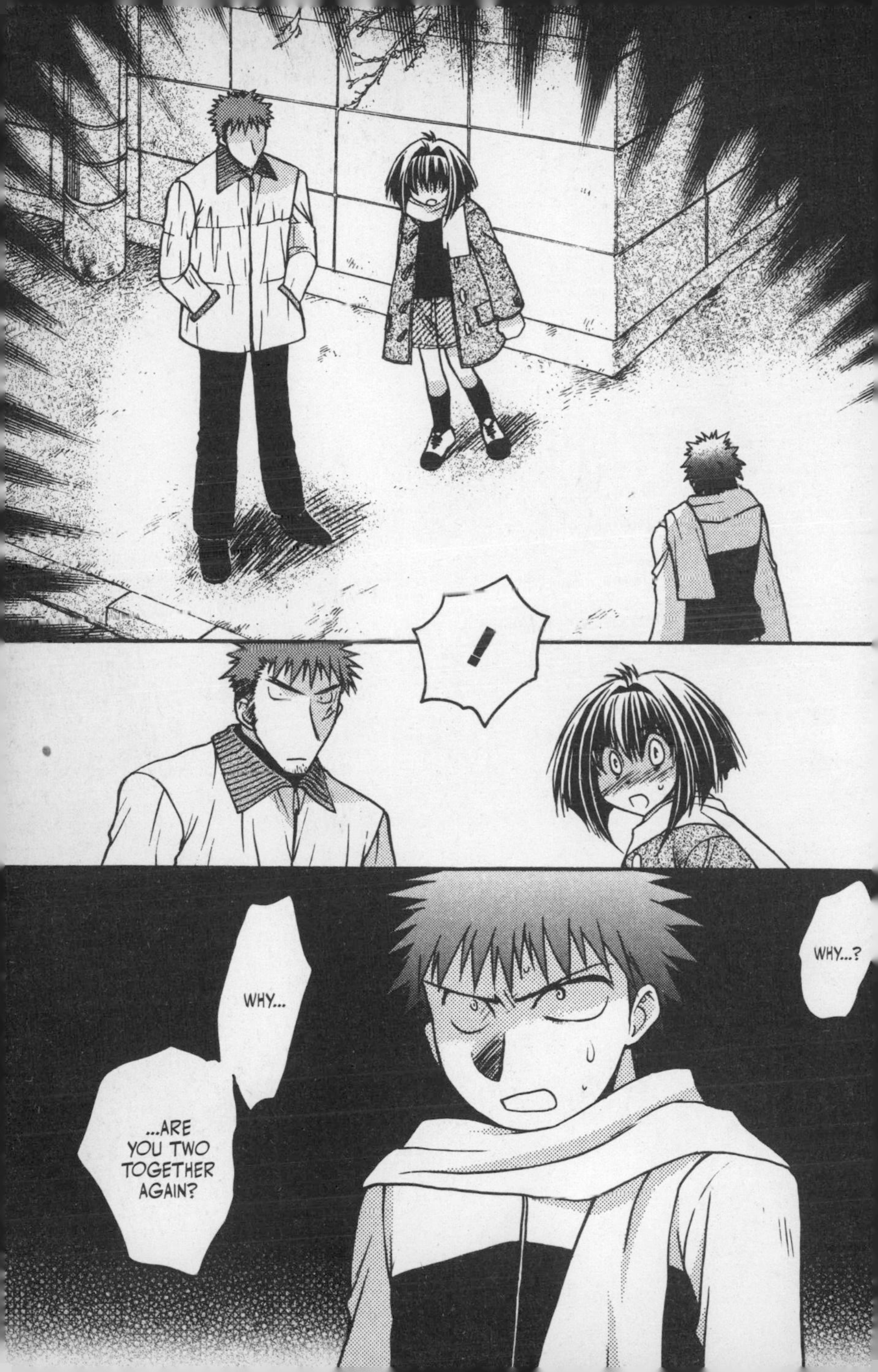
!
WHY...?
WHY...
...ARE YOU TWO TOGETHER AGAIN?

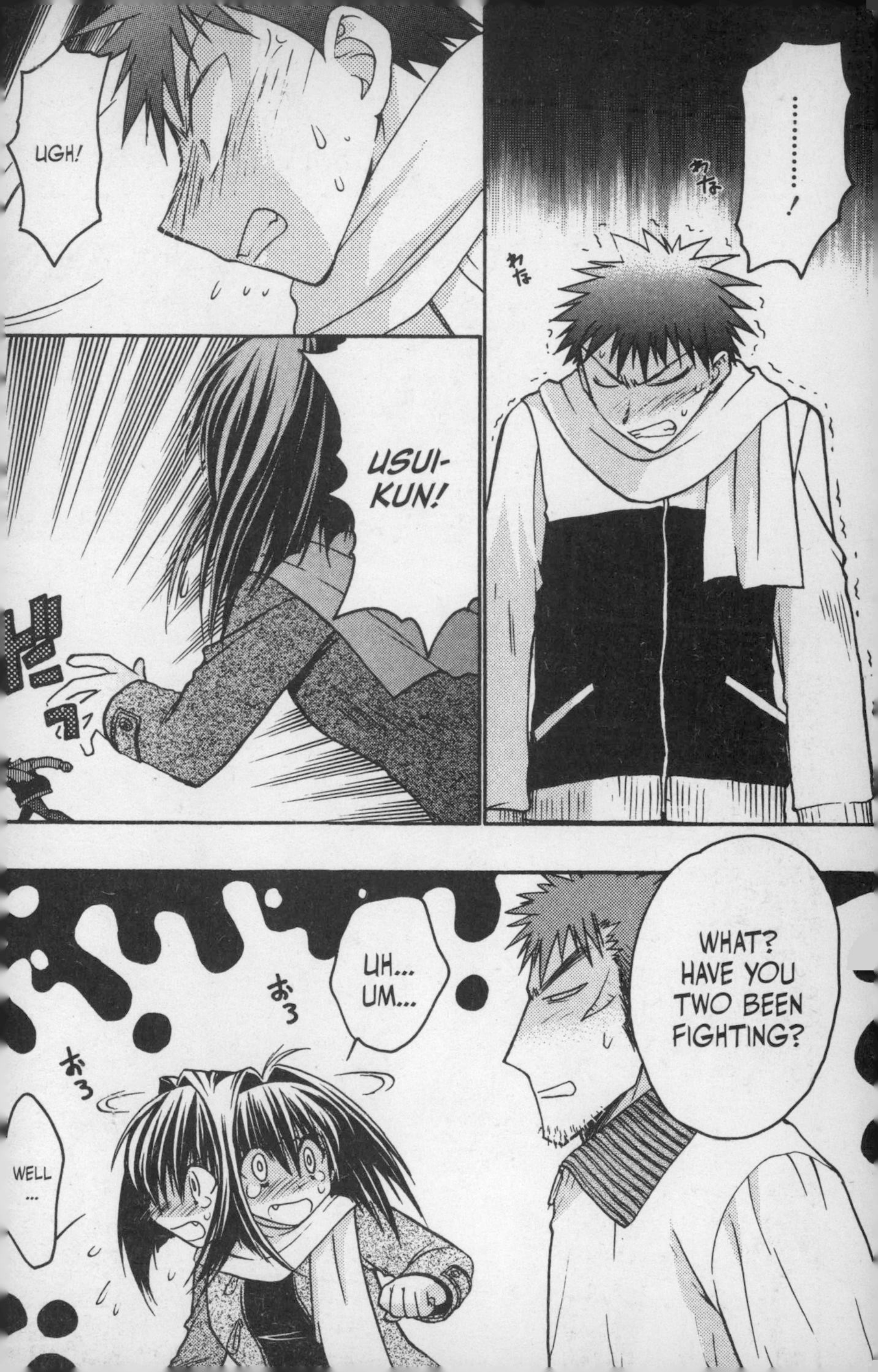
......!
わな
わな
UGH!
USUI-KUN!
ダッ
WHAT? HAVE YOU TWO BEEN FIGHTING?
UH... UM...
おろ
おろ
WELL ...

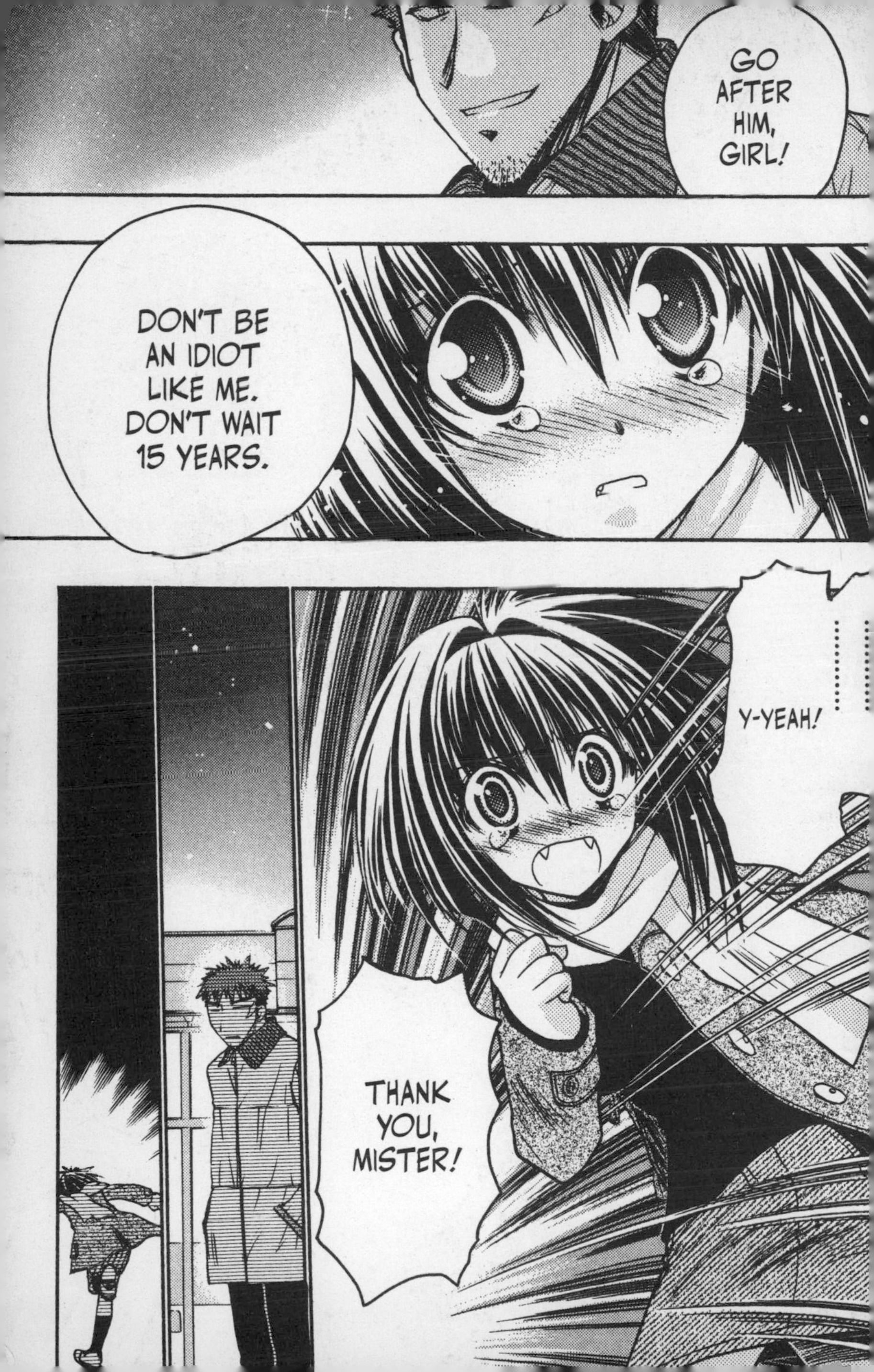
GO AFTER HIM, GIRL!
DON'T BE AN IDIOT LIKE ME. DON'T WAIT 15 YEARS.
......
Y-YEAH!
THANK YOU, MISTER!

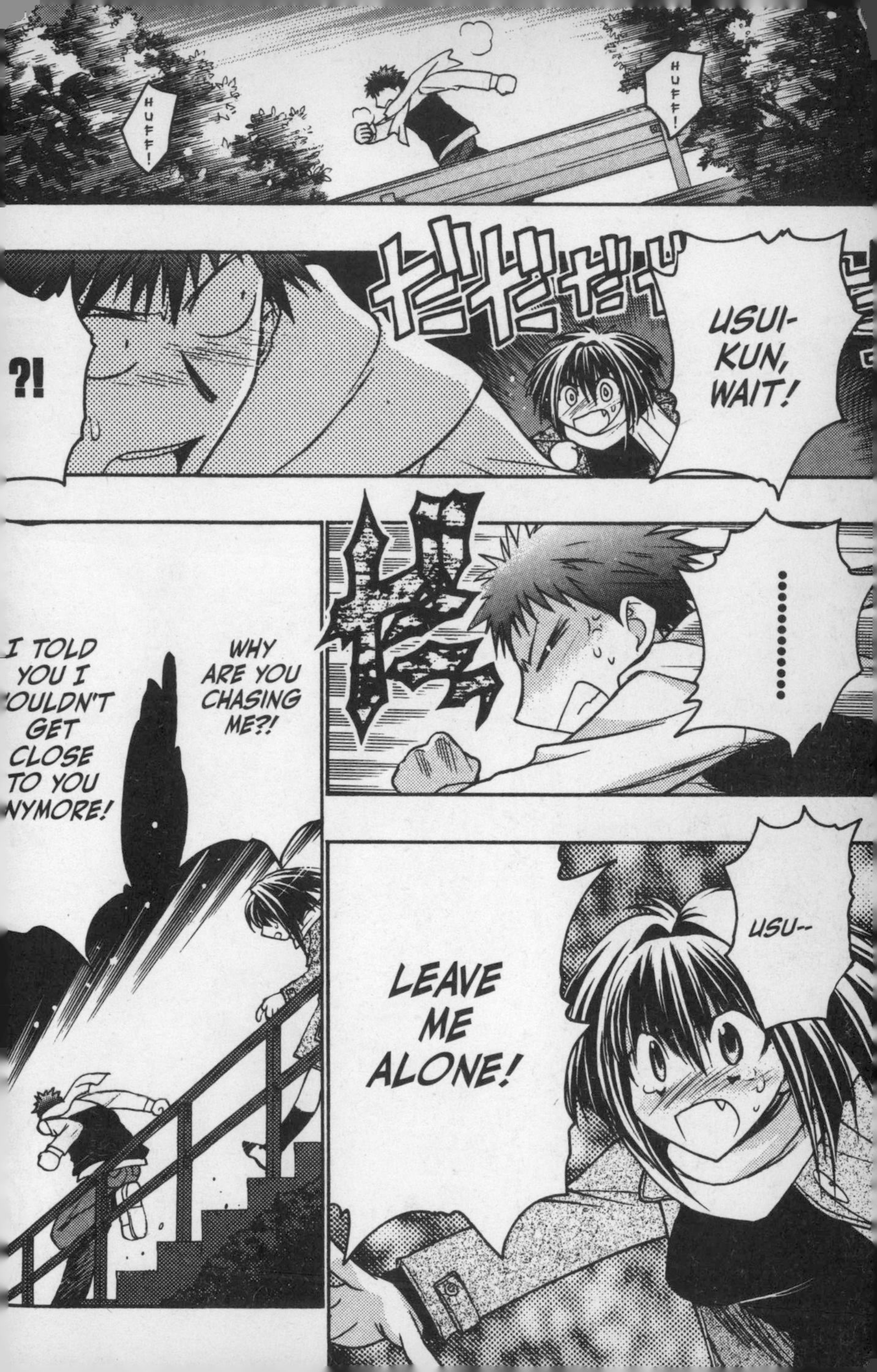
HUFF!
HUFF!
USUI-KUN, WAIT!
?!
....
USU--
LEAVE ME ALONE!
WHY ARE YOU CHASING ME?!
I TOLD YOU I 'OULDN'T GET CLOSE TO YOU NYMORE!

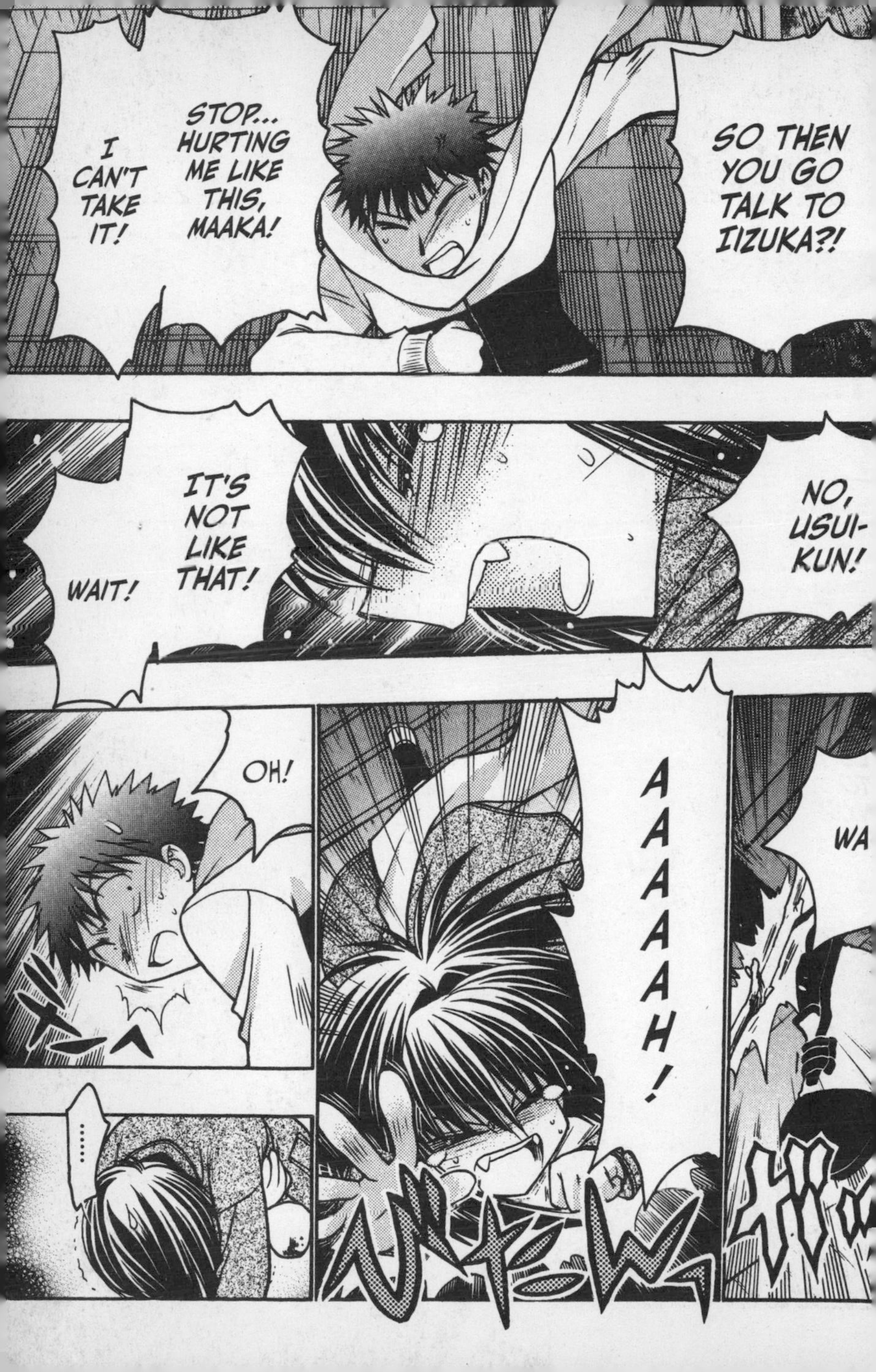
SO THEN YOU GO TALK TO IIZUKA?!
STOP... HURTING ME LIKE THIS, MAAKA!
I CAN'T TAKE IT!
NO, USUI-KUN!
IT'S NOT LIKE THAT!
WAIT!
WA
AAAAAAH!
OH!
......

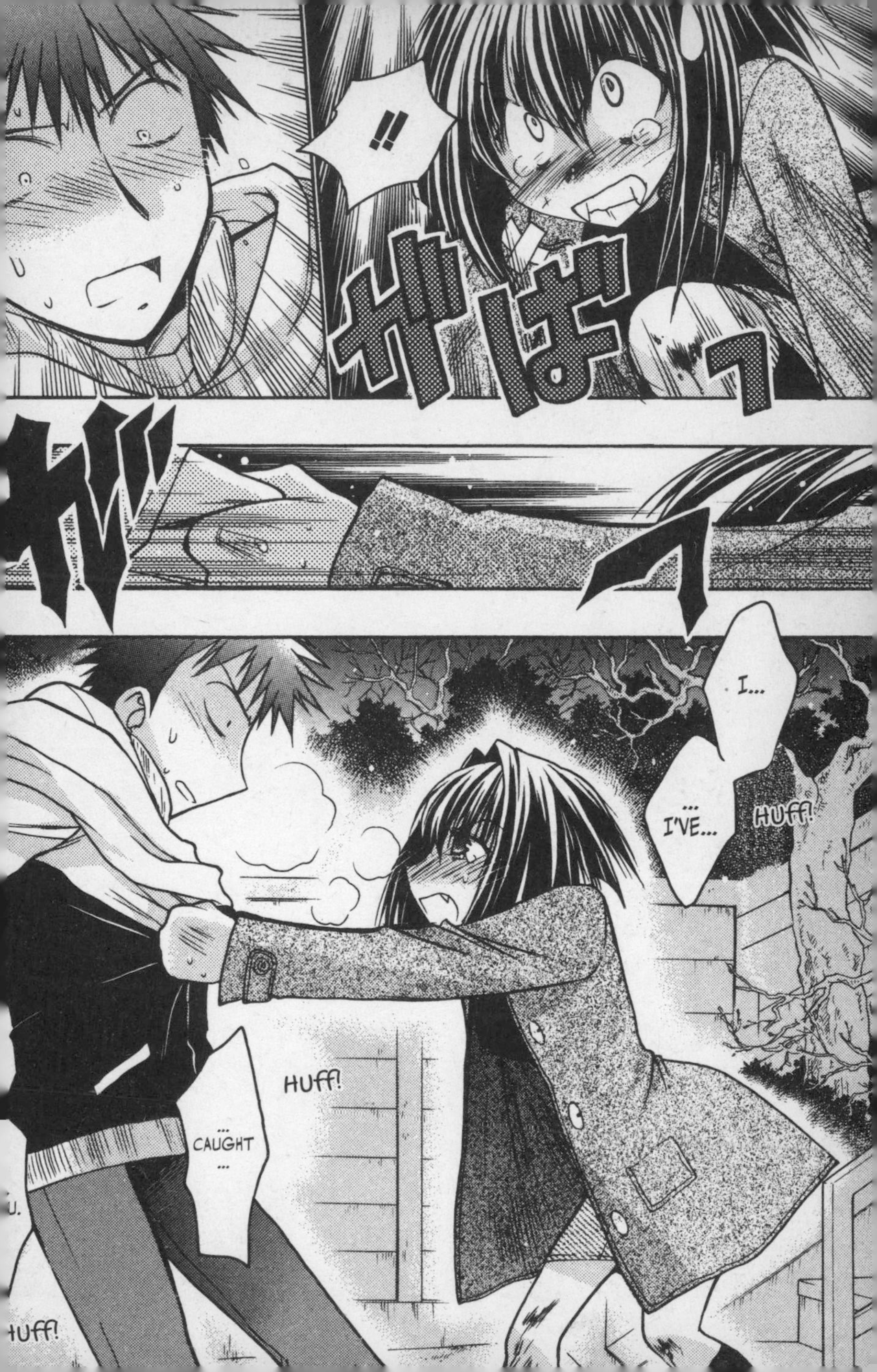
!!
I...
...I'VE...
HUFF!
HUFF!
...CAUGHT...
HUFF!

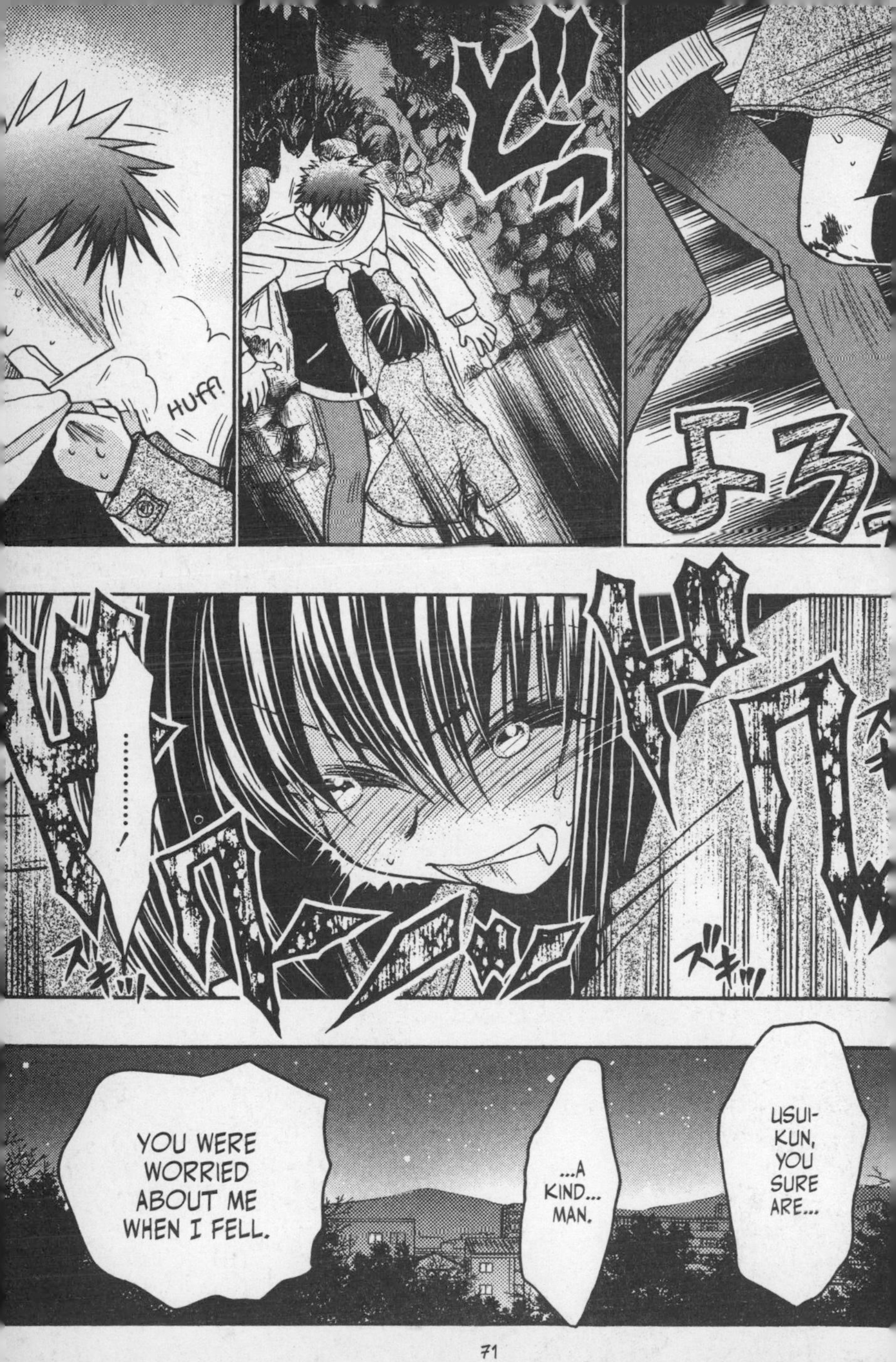
よろっ
どっ
HUFF!
......!
ズキッ
ズキッ
USUI-KUN, YOU SURE ARE...
...A KIND... MAN.
YOU WERE WORRIED ABOUT ME WHEN I FELL.

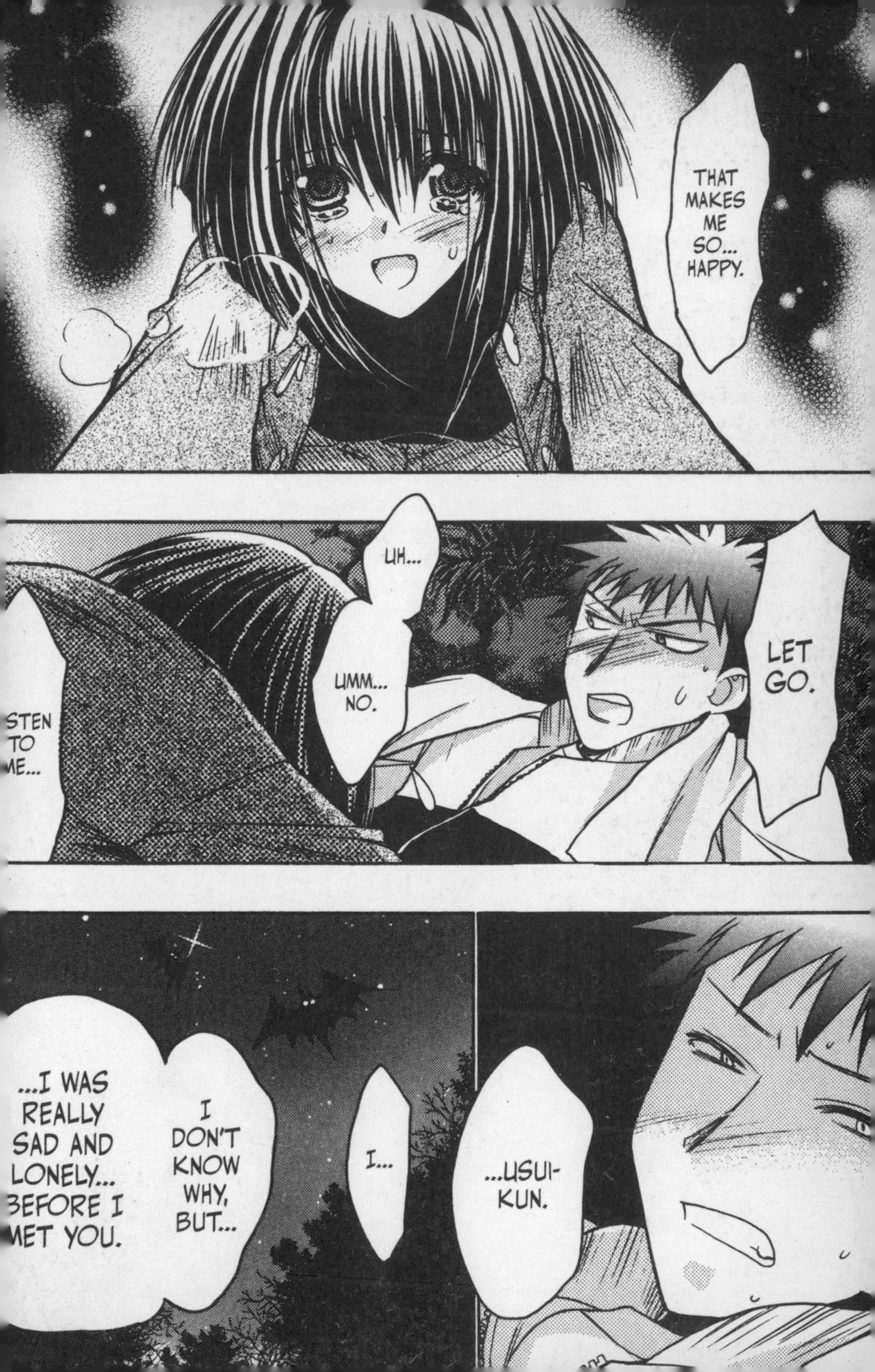
THAT MAKES ME SO... HAPPY.
LET GO.
UH...
UMM... NO.
STEN TO ME...
...USUI-KUN.
I...
I DON'T KNOW WHY, BUT...
...I WAS REALLY SAD AND LONELY... BEFORE I MET YOU.

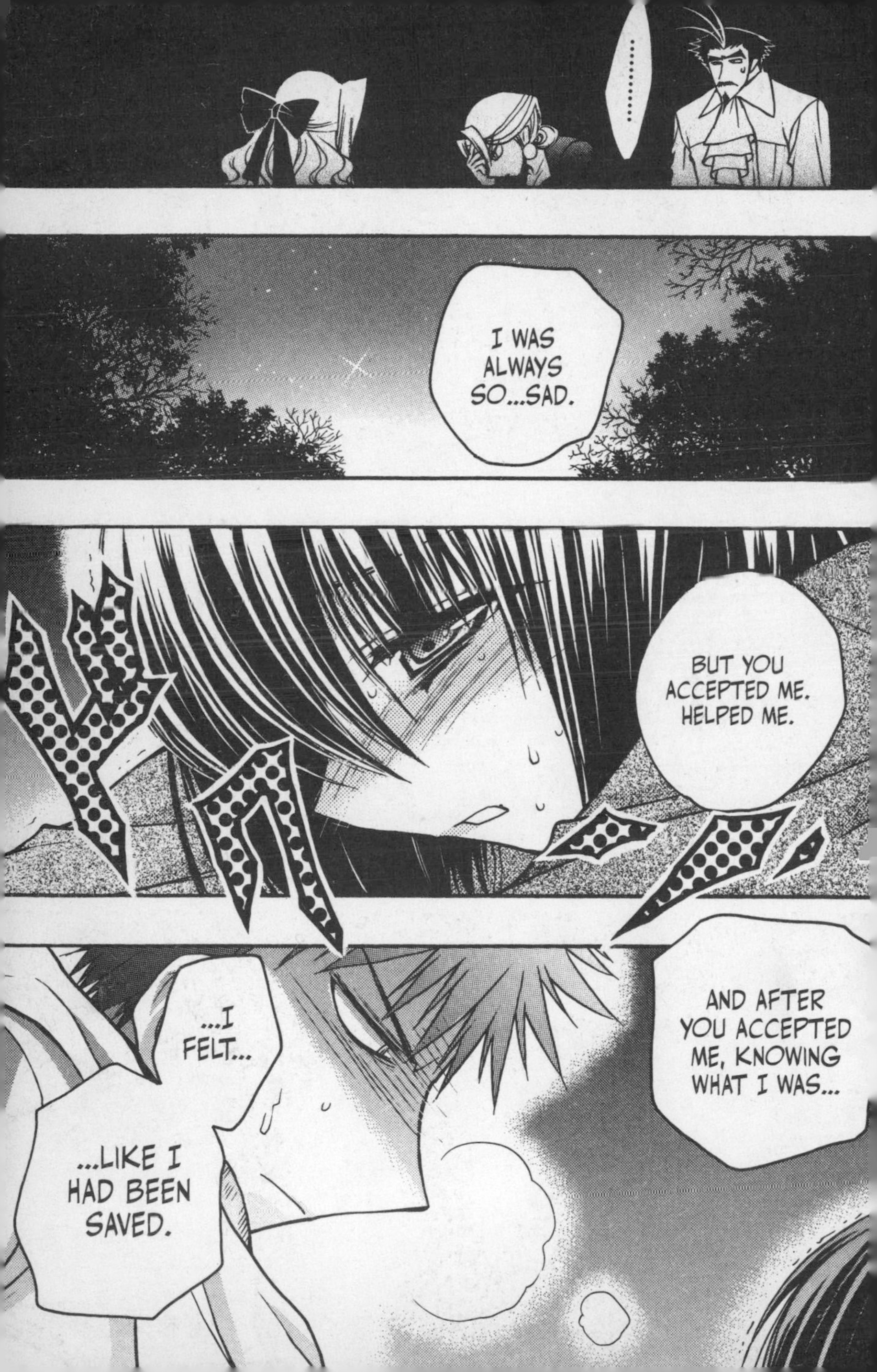
......
I WAS ALWAYS SO...SAD.
BUT YOU ACCEPTED ME. HELPED ME.
AND AFTER YOU ACCEPTED ME, KNOWING WHAT I WAS...
...I FELT...
...LIKE I HAD BEEN SAVED.

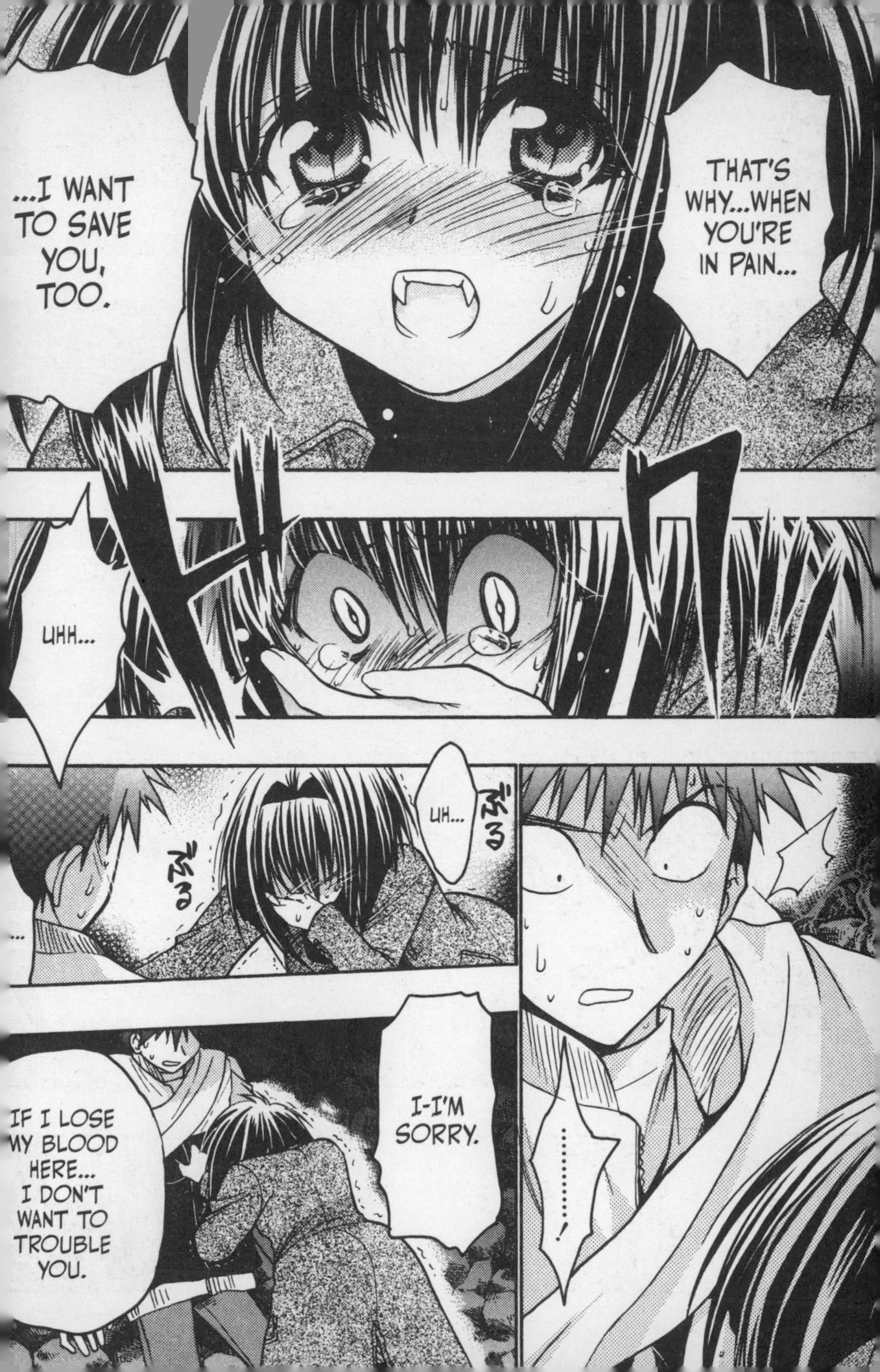
THAT'S WHY...WHEN YOU'RE IN PAIN...
...I WANT TO SAVE YOU, TOO.
UHH...
......!
ずる
UH...
ずる
I-I'M SORRY.
IF I LOSE MY BLOOD HERE... I DON'T WANT TO TROUBLE YOU.

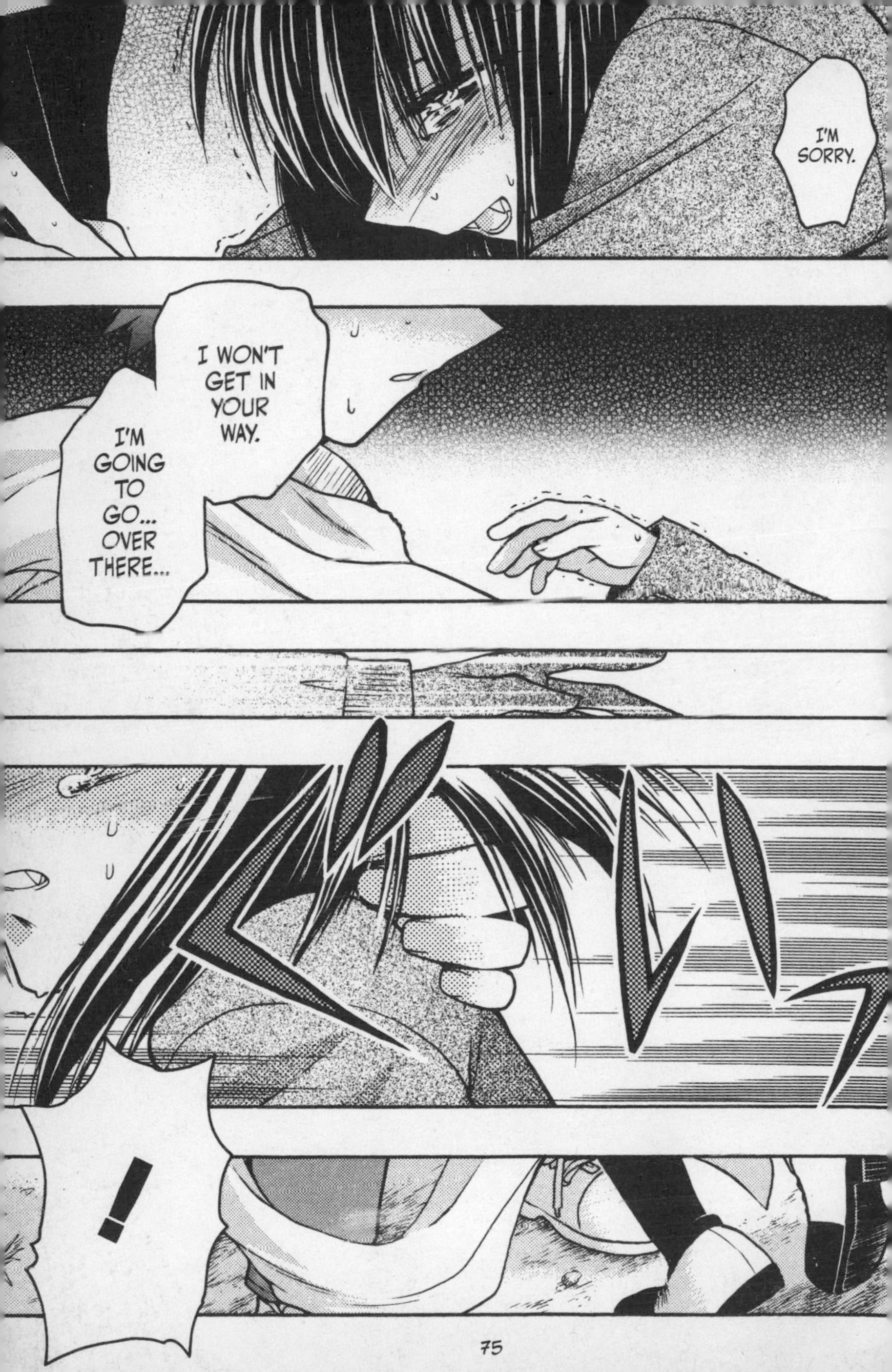
I'M SORRY.
I WON'T GET IN YOUR WAY.
I'M GOING TO GO... OVER THERE...
!

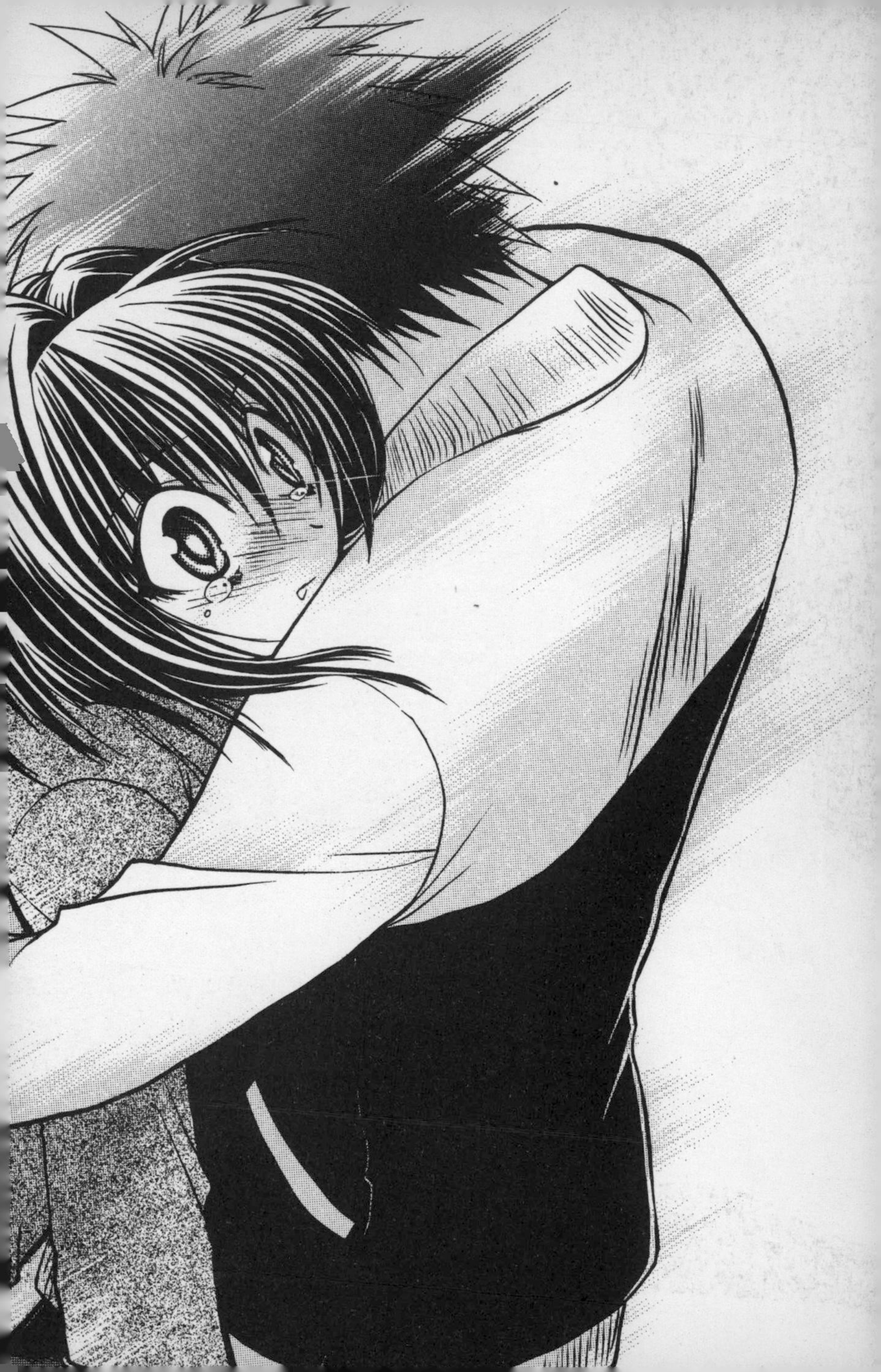

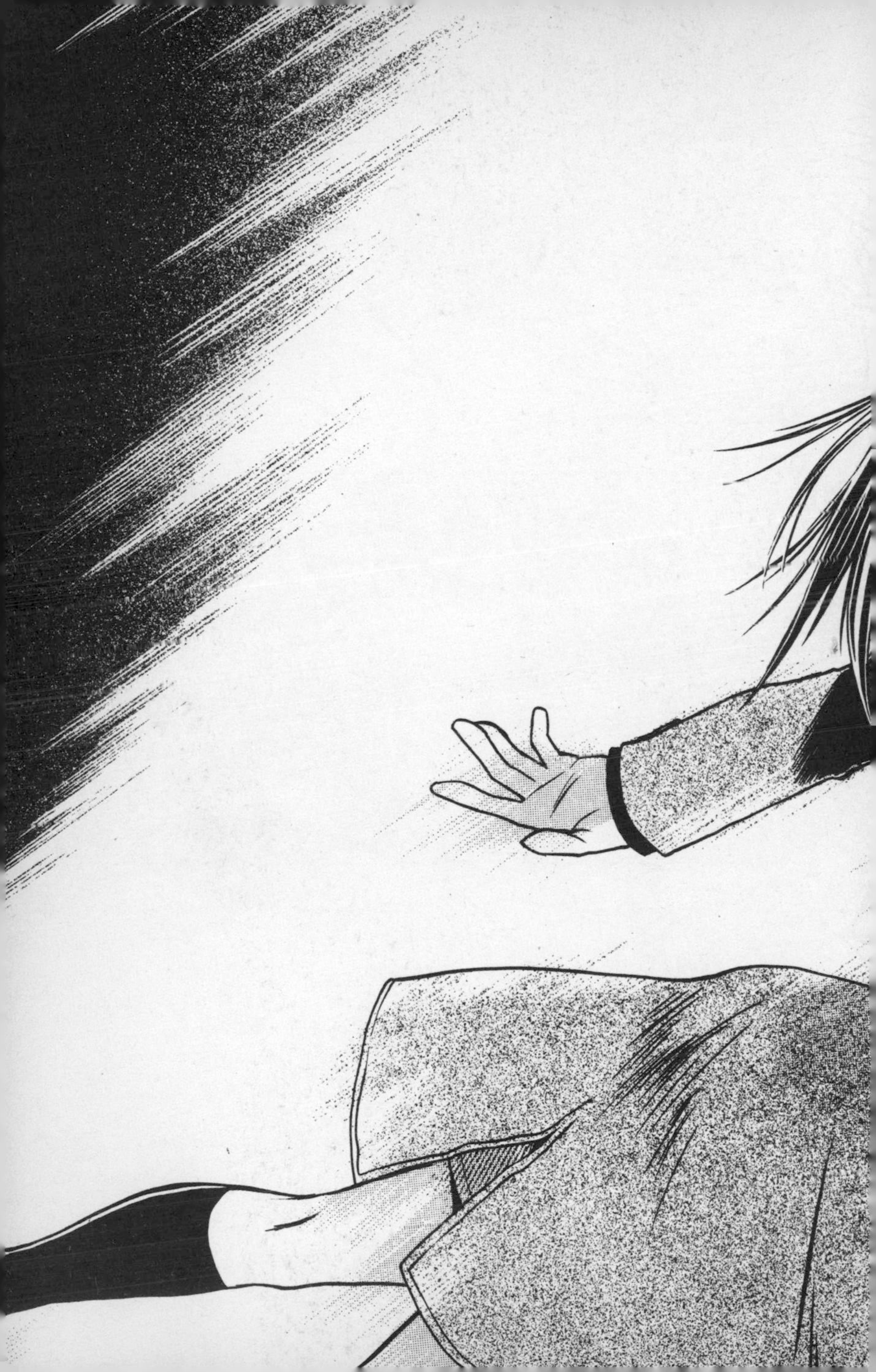

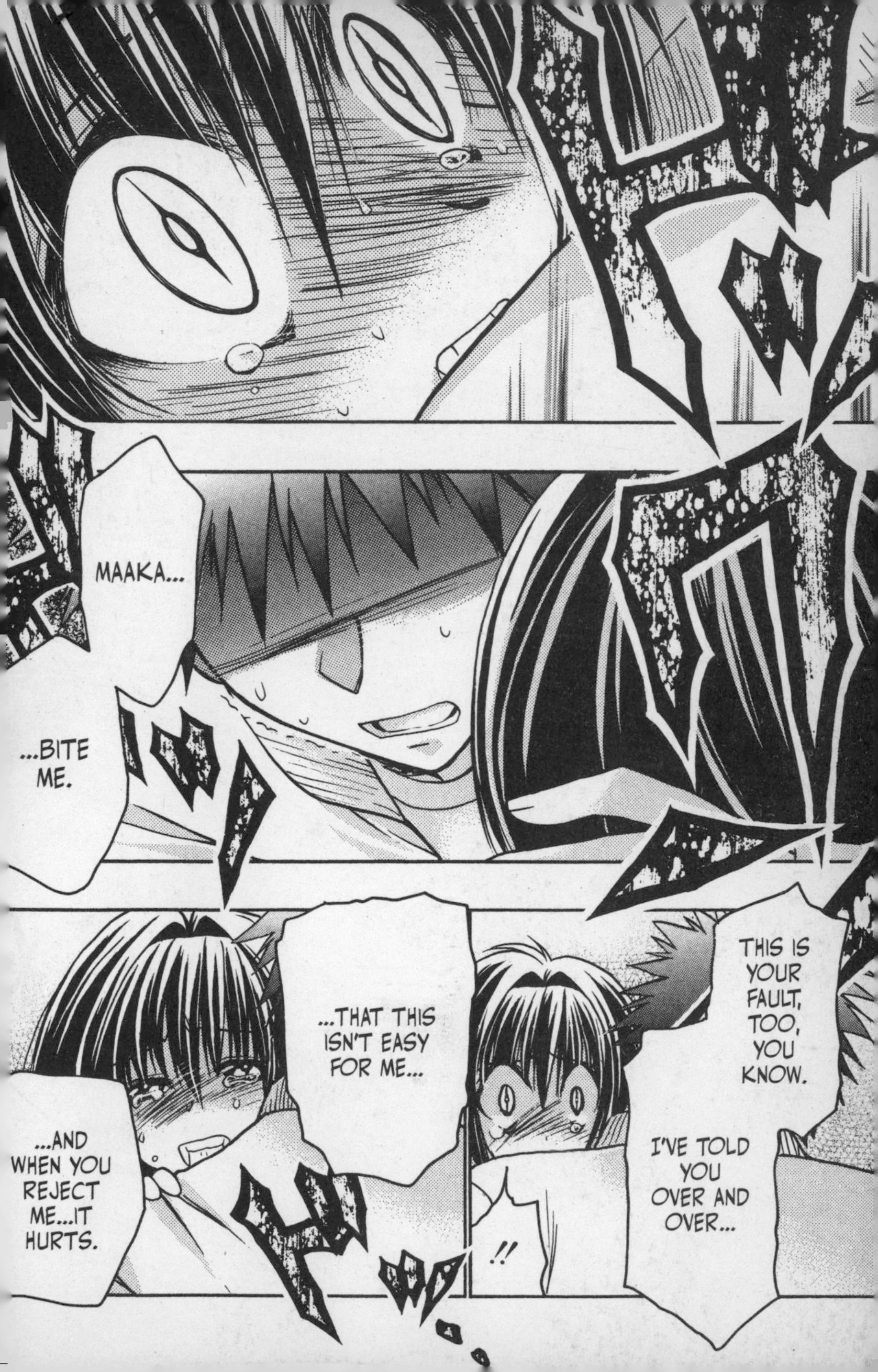
MAAKA...
...BITE ME.
THIS IS YOUR FAULT, TOO, YOU KNOW.
I'VE TOLD YOU OVER AND OVER...
!!
...THAT THIS ISN'T EASY FOR ME...
...AND WHEN YOU REJECT ME...IT HURTS.

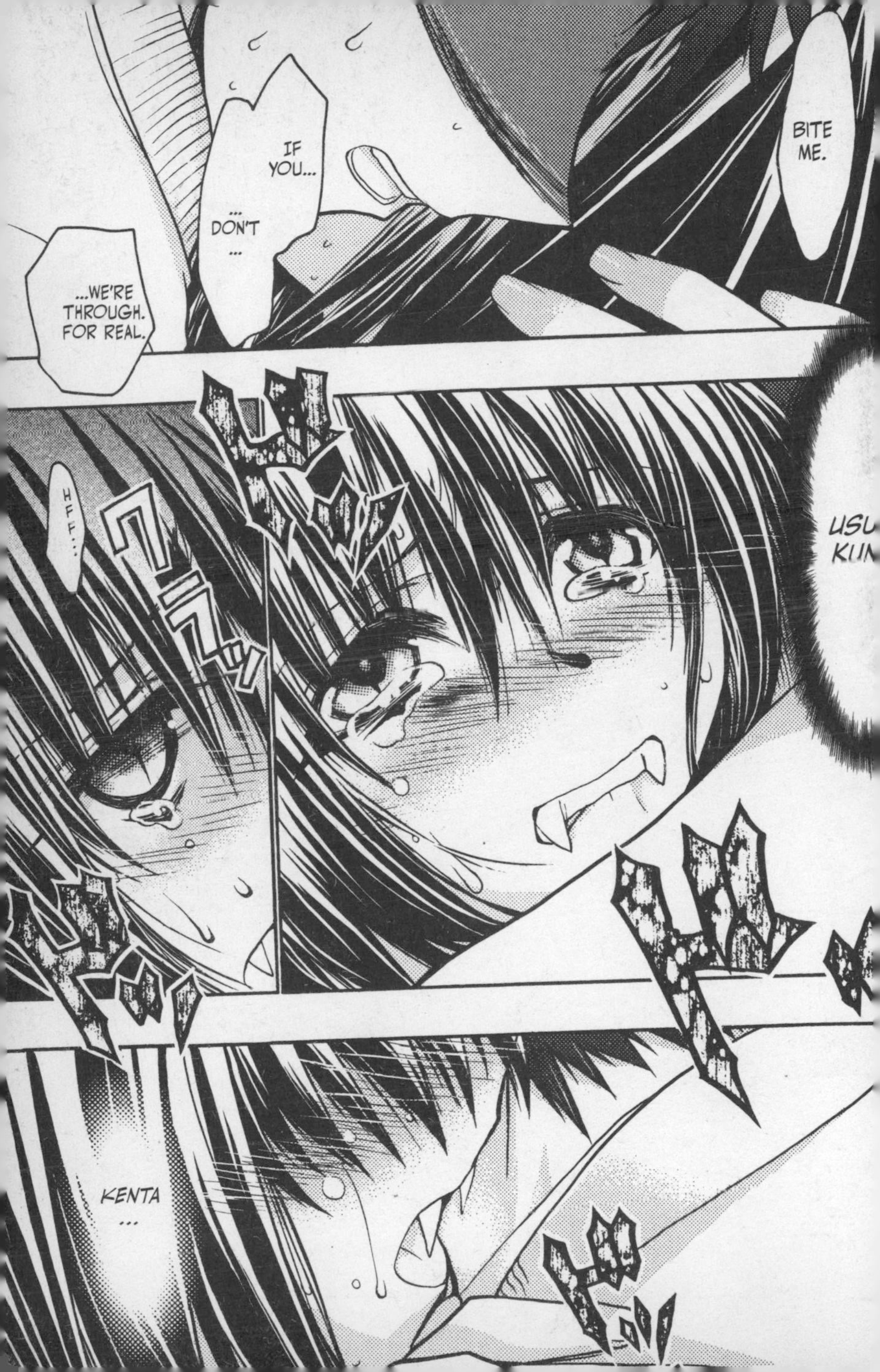
BITE ME.
IF YOU...
...DON'T...
...WE'RE THROUGH. FOR REAL.
USU KUN
HFF...
KENTA ...

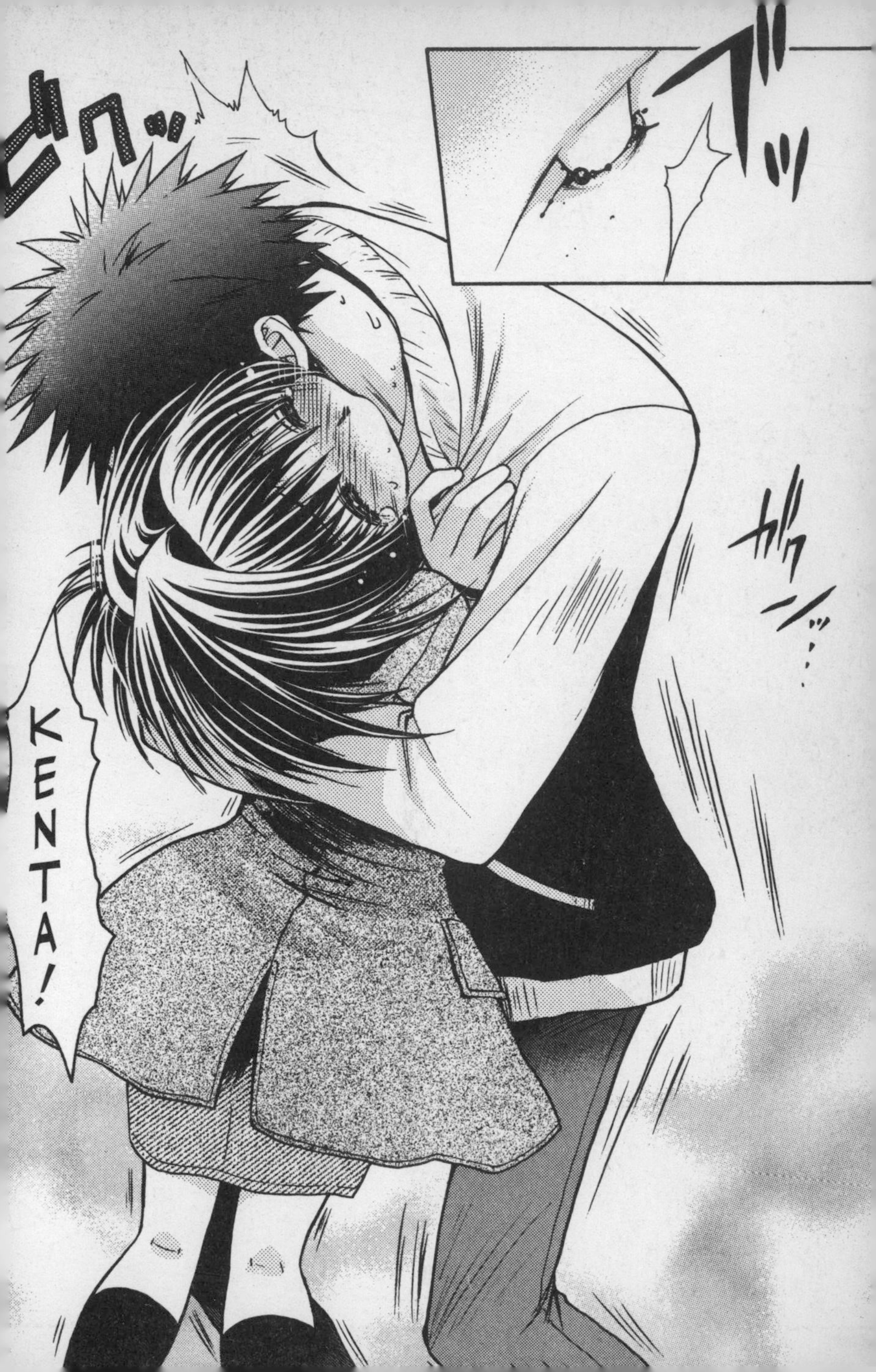
KENTA!

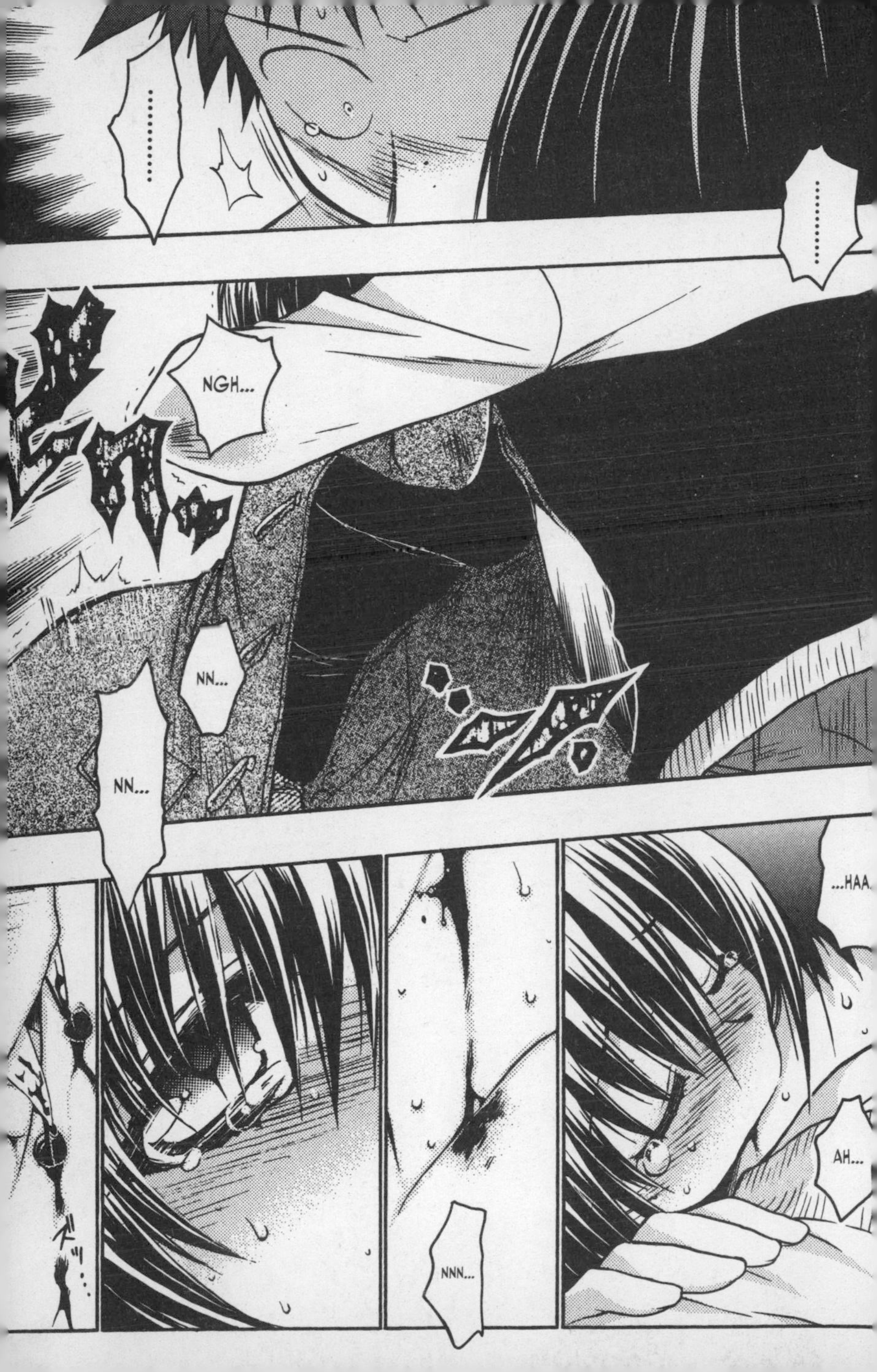
......
......
NGH...
NN...
NN...
...HAA.
AH...
NNN...

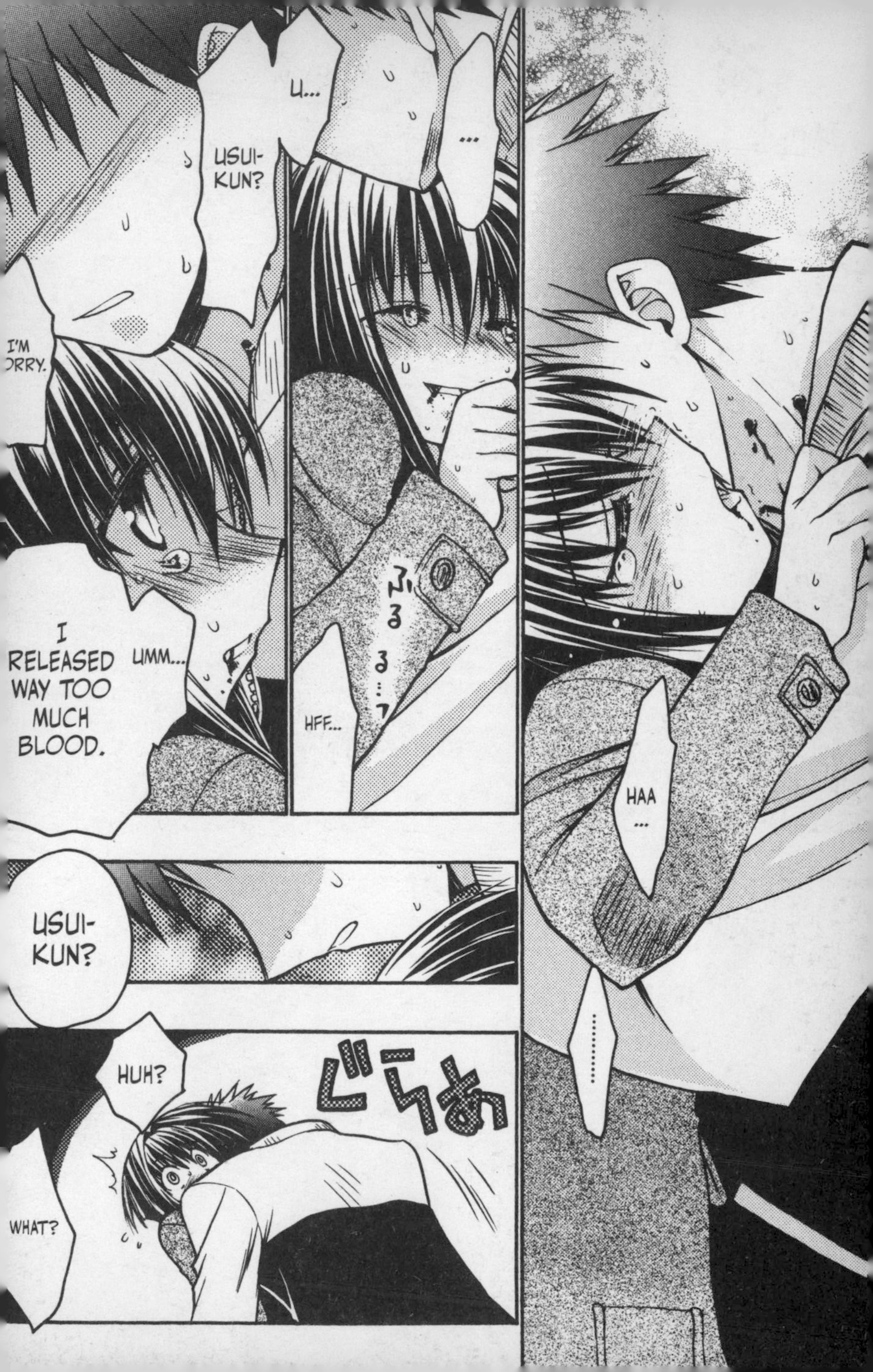
HAA ...
......
U...
...
ぷるる…っ
HFF...
USUI-KUN?
I'M ORRY.
UMM...
I RELEASED WAY TOO MUCH BLOOD.
USUI-KUN?
HUH?
ぐらあ
WHAT?

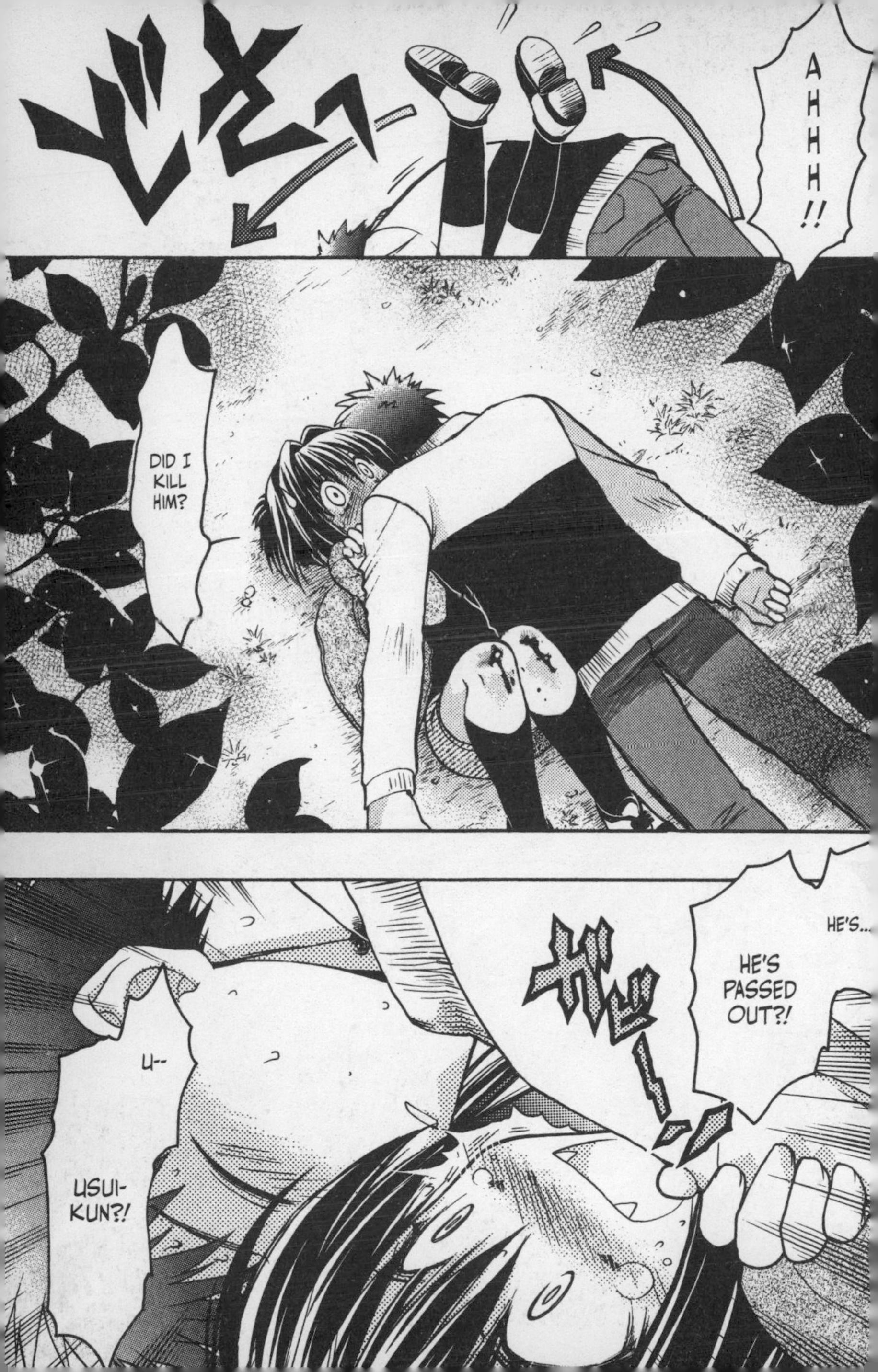
AHHHH!!
DID I KILL HIM?
HE'S...
HE'S PASSED OUT?!
U--
USUI-KUN?!

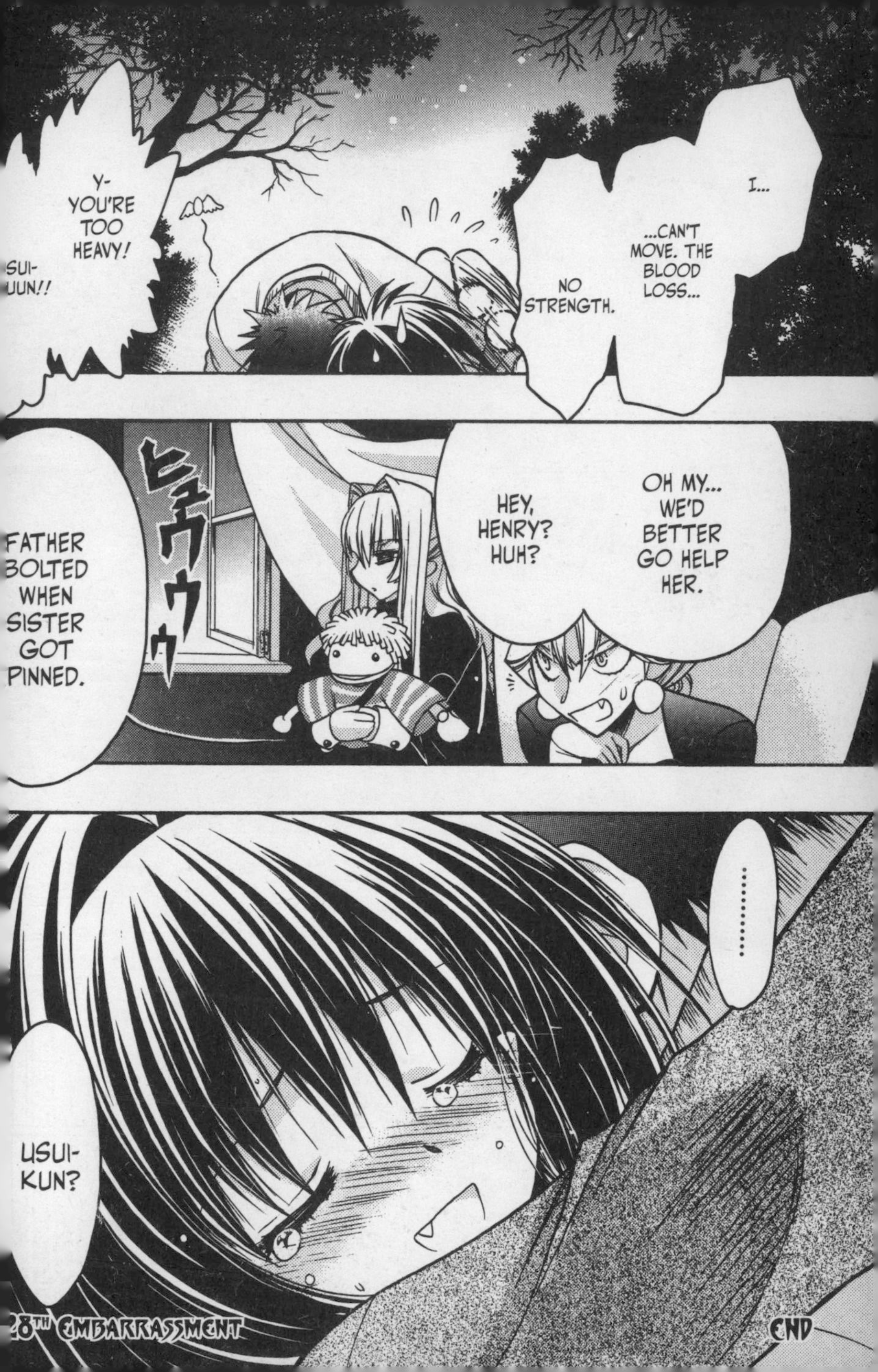
I...
...CAN'T MOVE. THE BLOOD LOSS...
NO STRENGTH.
Y-YOU'RE TOO HEAVY!
SUI-UUN!!
OH MY... WE'D BETTER GO HELP HER.
HEY, HENRY? HUH?
ヒュウウウ
FATHER BOLTED WHEN SISTER GOT PINNED.
....
USUI-KUN?
28TH EMBARRASSMENT
END

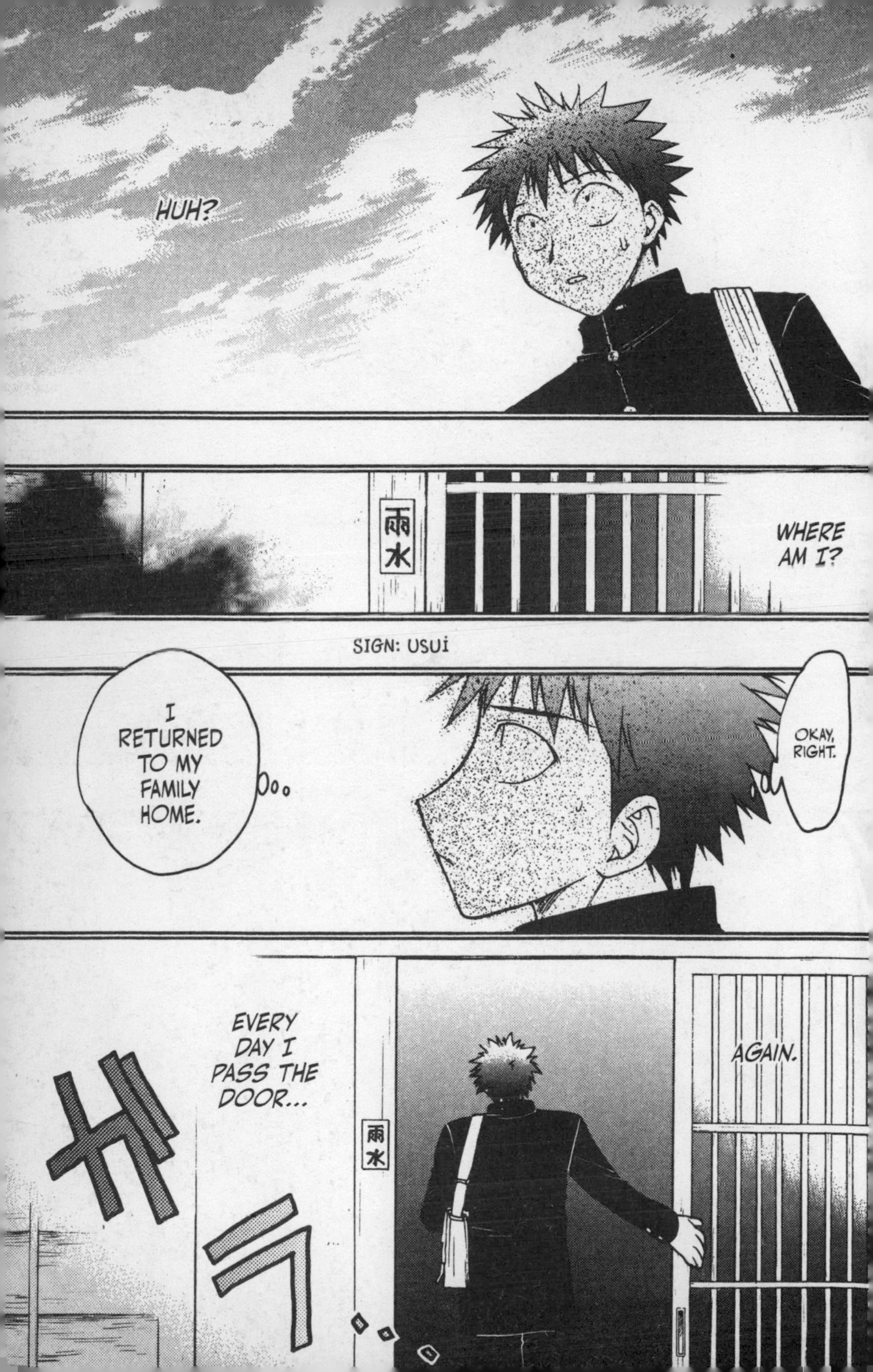
HUH?
WHERE AM I?
雨水
SIGN: USUI
OKAY, RIGHT.
I RETURNED TO MY FAMILY HOME.
Ooo
AGAIN.
EVERY DAY I PASS THE DOOR...
雨水
ガラ

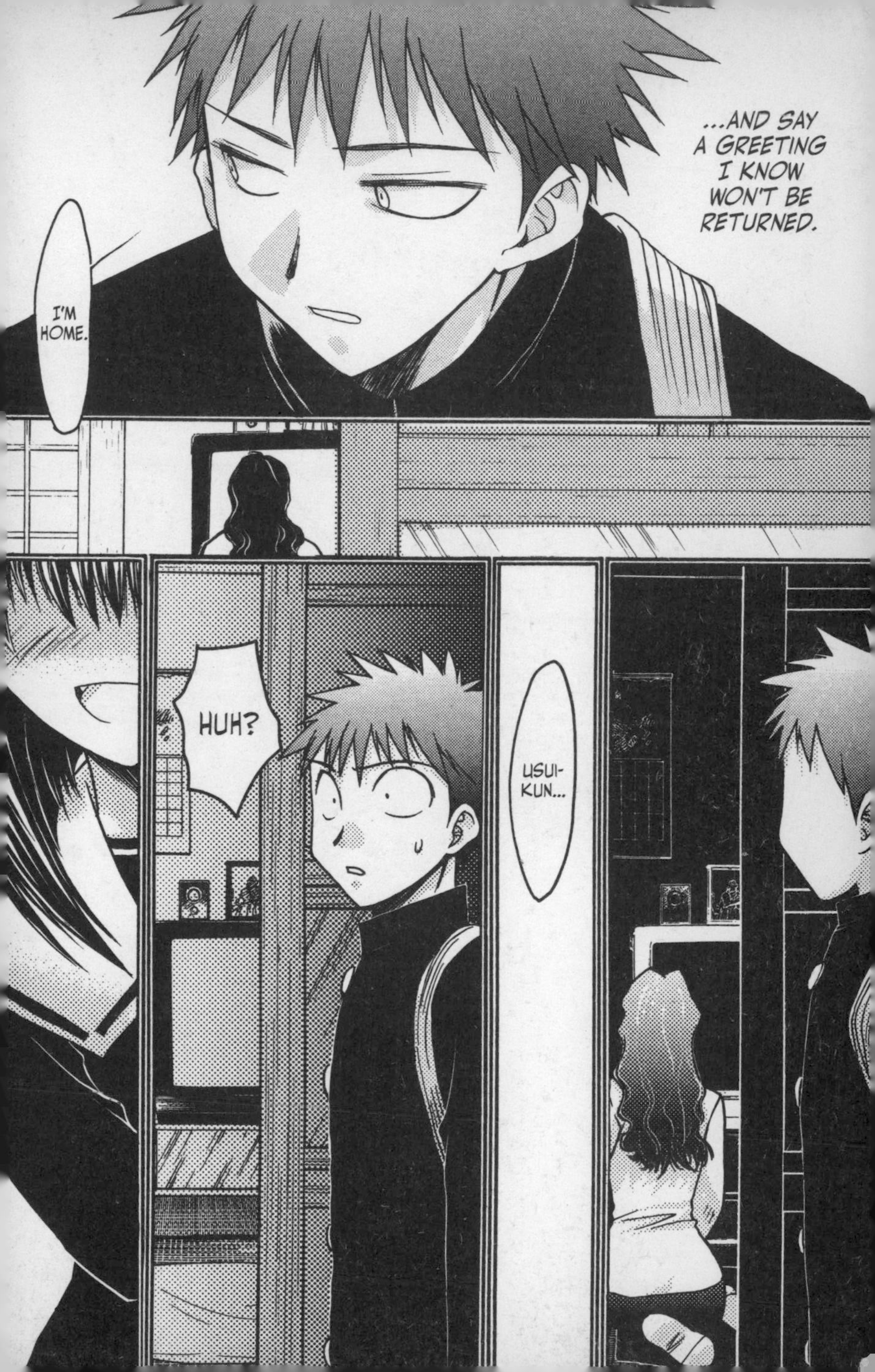
...AND SAY A GREETING I KNOW WON'T BE RETURNED.
I'M HOME.
USUI-KUN...
HUH?

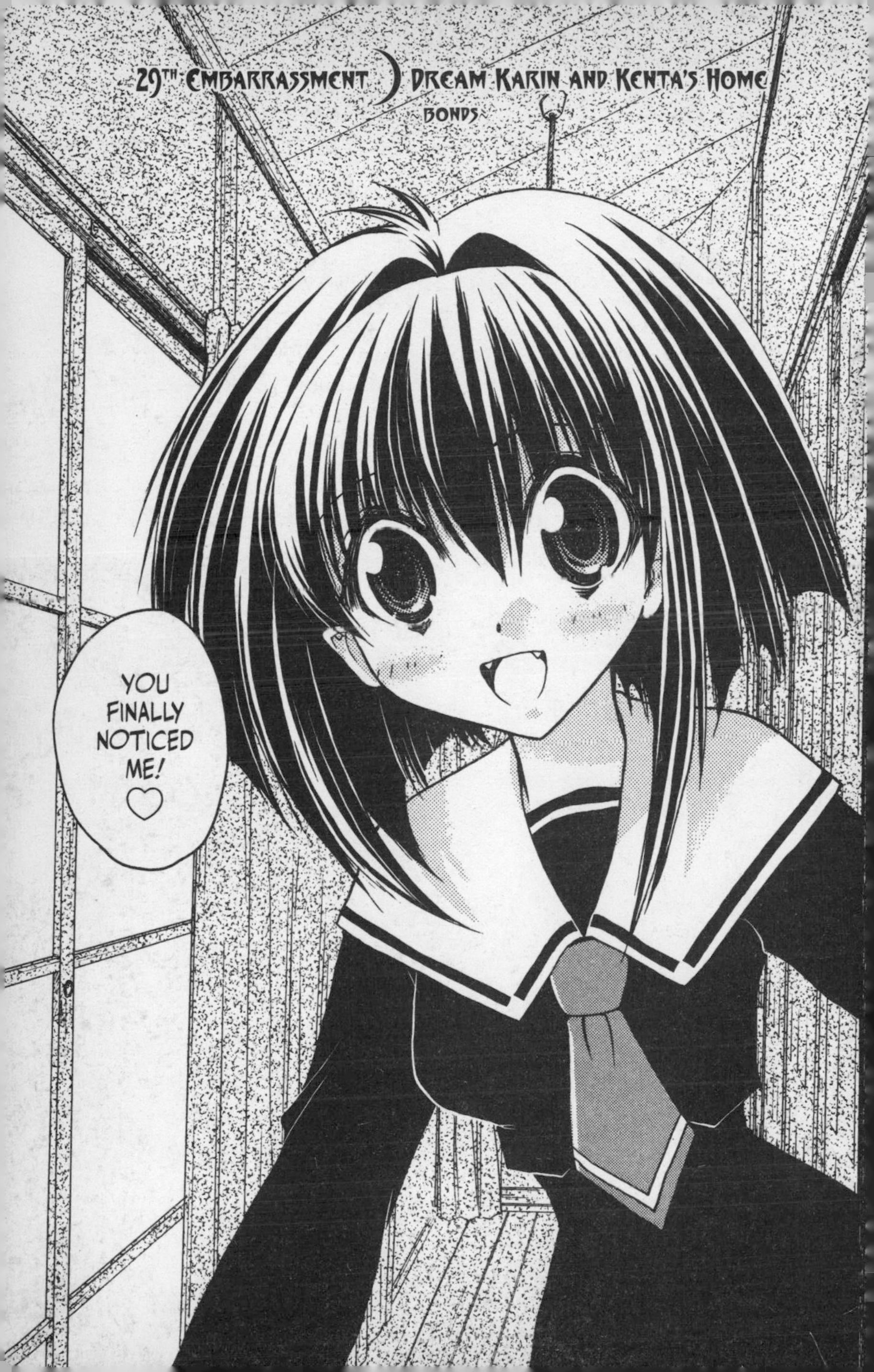
29TH EMBARRASSMENT) DREAM KARIN AND KENTA'S HOME
~BONDS~
YOU FINALLY NOTICED ME! ♡

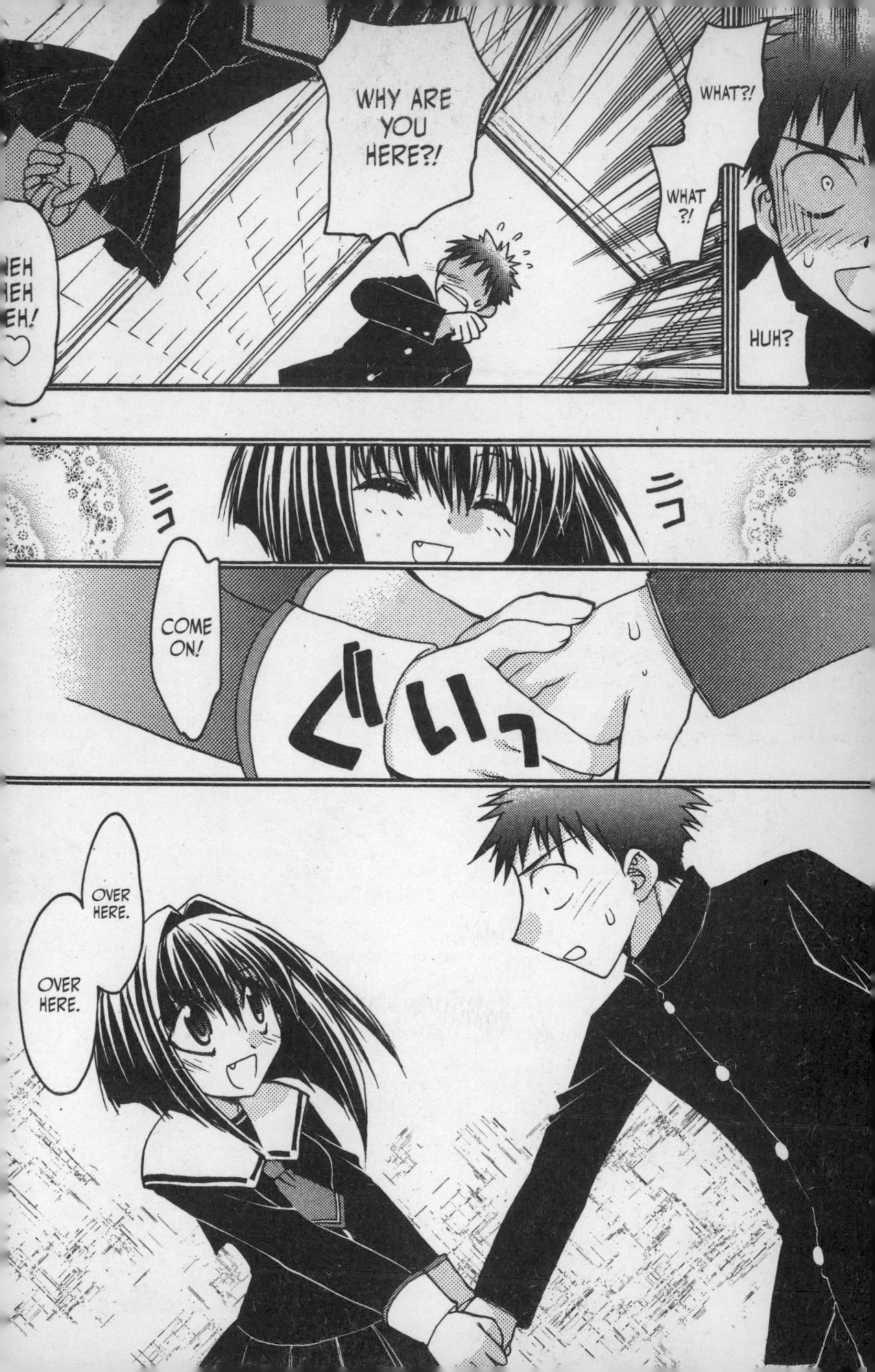
WHAT?!
WHAT ?!
HUH?
WHY ARE YOU HERE?!
HEH HEH EH! ♡
ニコ
ニコ
COME ON!
ぐいっ
OVER HERE.
OVER HERE.

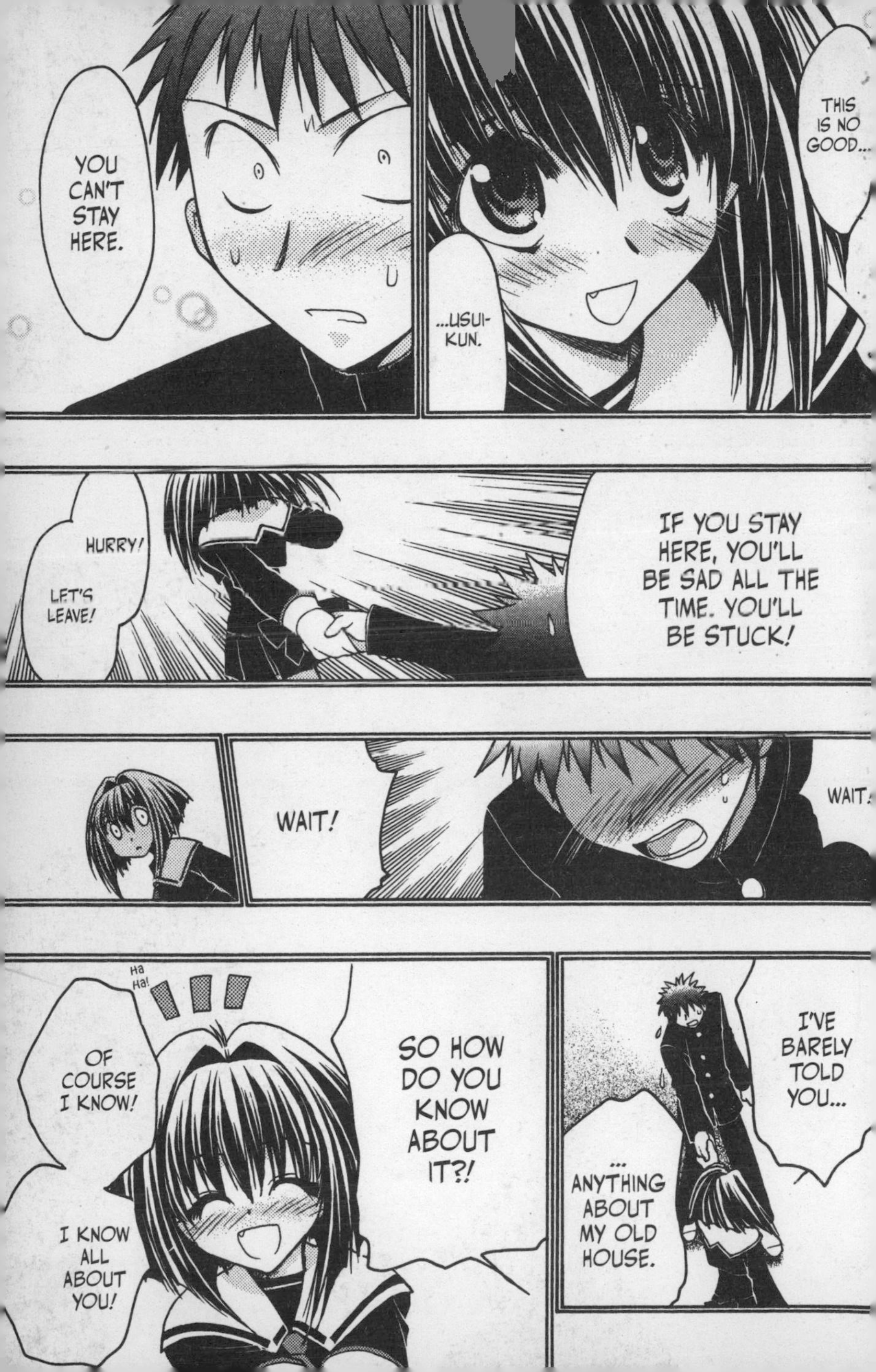
THIS IS NO GOOD...
...USUI-KUN.
YOU CAN'T STAY HERE.
IF YOU STAY HERE, YOU'LL BE SAD ALL THE TIME. YOU'LL BE STUCK!
HURRY!
LET'S LEAVE!
WAIT.
WAIT!
I'VE BARELY TOLD YOU...
...ANYTHING ABOUT MY OLD HOUSE.
SO HOW DO YOU KNOW ABOUT IT?!
Ha Ha!
OF COURSE I KNOW!
I KNOW ALL ABOUT YOU!

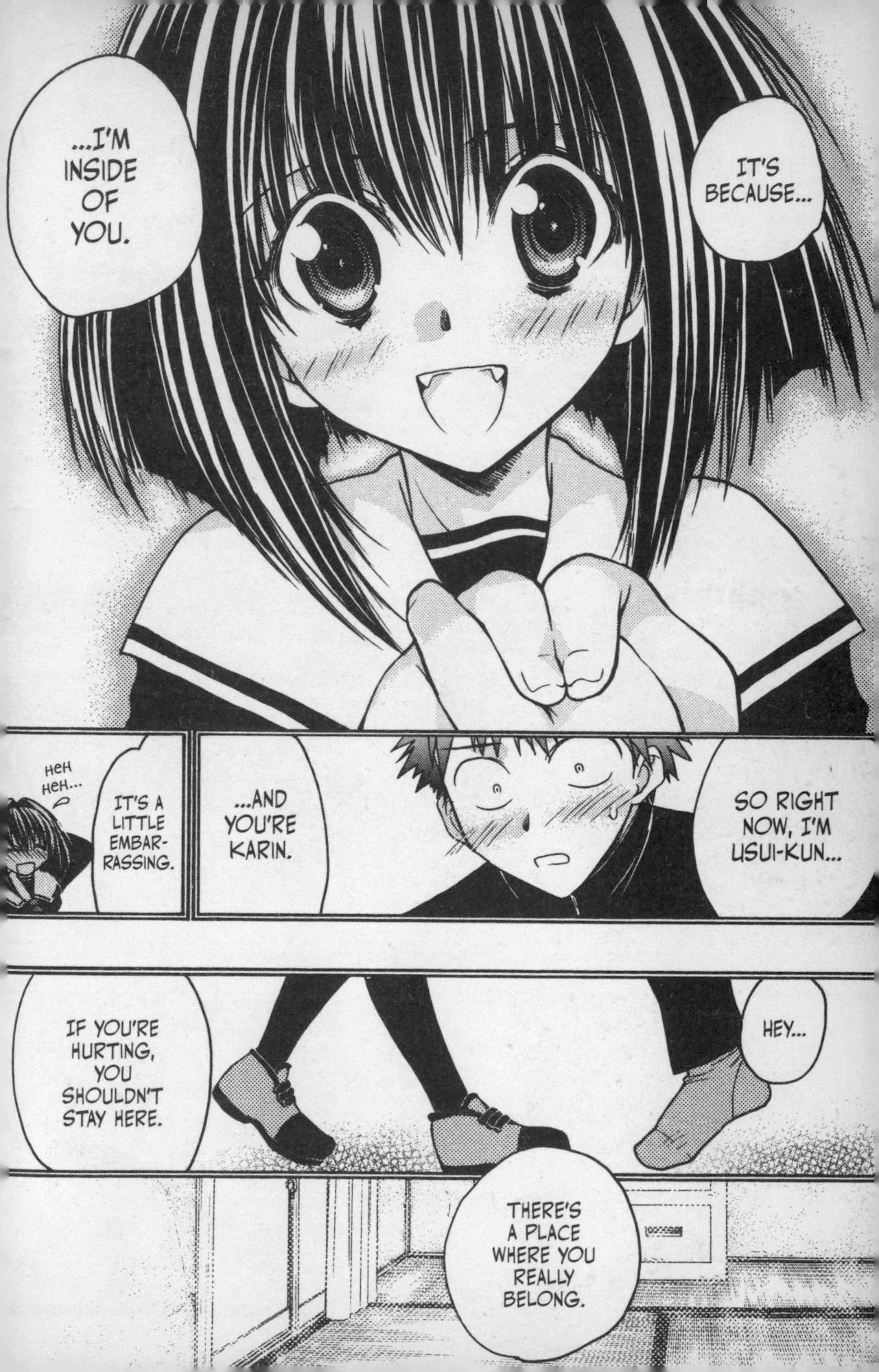
IT'S BECAUSE...
...I'M INSIDE OF YOU.
SO RIGHT NOW, I'M USUI-KUN...
...AND YOU'RE KARIN.
IT'S A LITTLE EMBAR-RASSING.
HEH HEH...
HEY...
IF YOU'RE HURTING, YOU SHOULDN'T STAY HERE.
THERE'S A PLACE WHERE YOU REALLY BELONG.

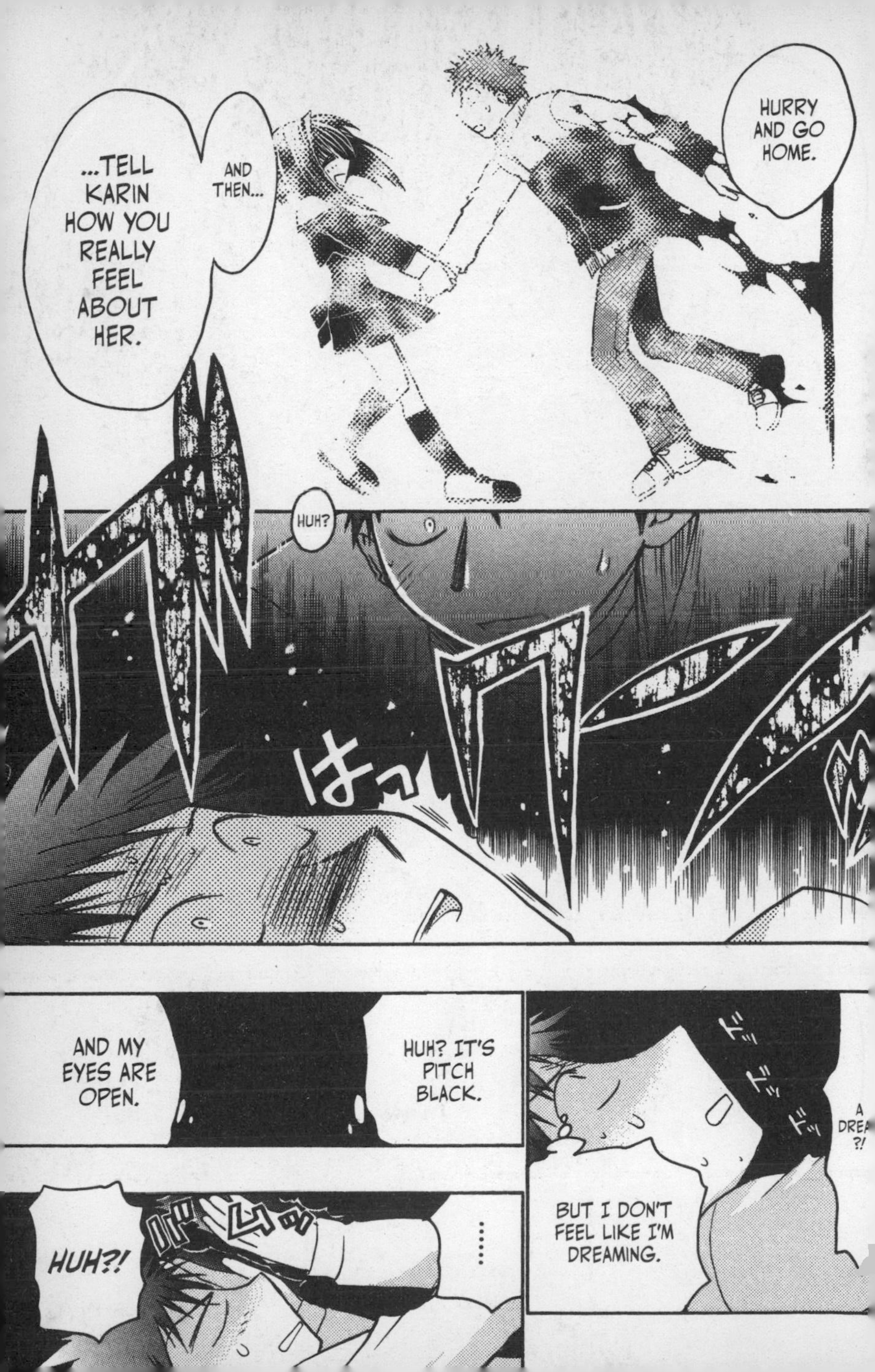
HURRY AND GO HOME.
AND THEN...
...TELL KARIN HOW YOU REALLY FEEL ABOUT HER.
HUH?
はっ
ドッ ドッ ドッ
A DREA ?!
BUT I DON'T FEEL LIKE I'M DREAMING.
HUH? IT'S PITCH BLACK.
AND MY EYES ARE OPEN.
......
HUH?!

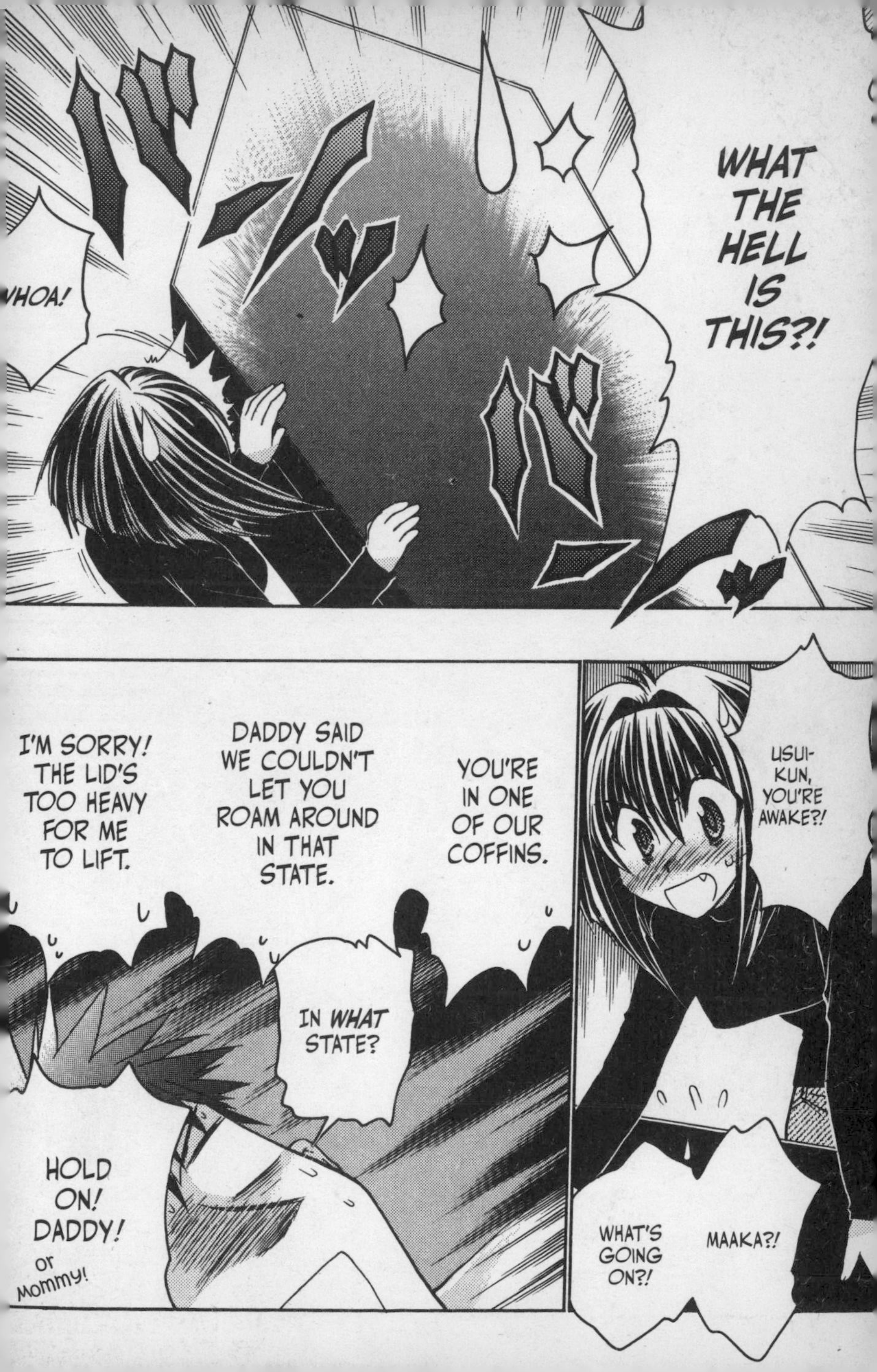
WHAT THE HELL IS THIS?!
WHOA!
USUI-KUN, YOU'RE AWAKE?!
MAAKA?!
WHAT'S GOING ON?!
YOU'RE IN ONE OF OUR COFFINS.
DADDY SAID WE COULDN'T LET YOU ROAM AROUND IN THAT STATE.
I'M SORRY! THE LID'S TOO HEAVY FOR ME TO LIFT.
IN *WHAT* STATE?
HOLD ON! DADDY!
or Mommy!

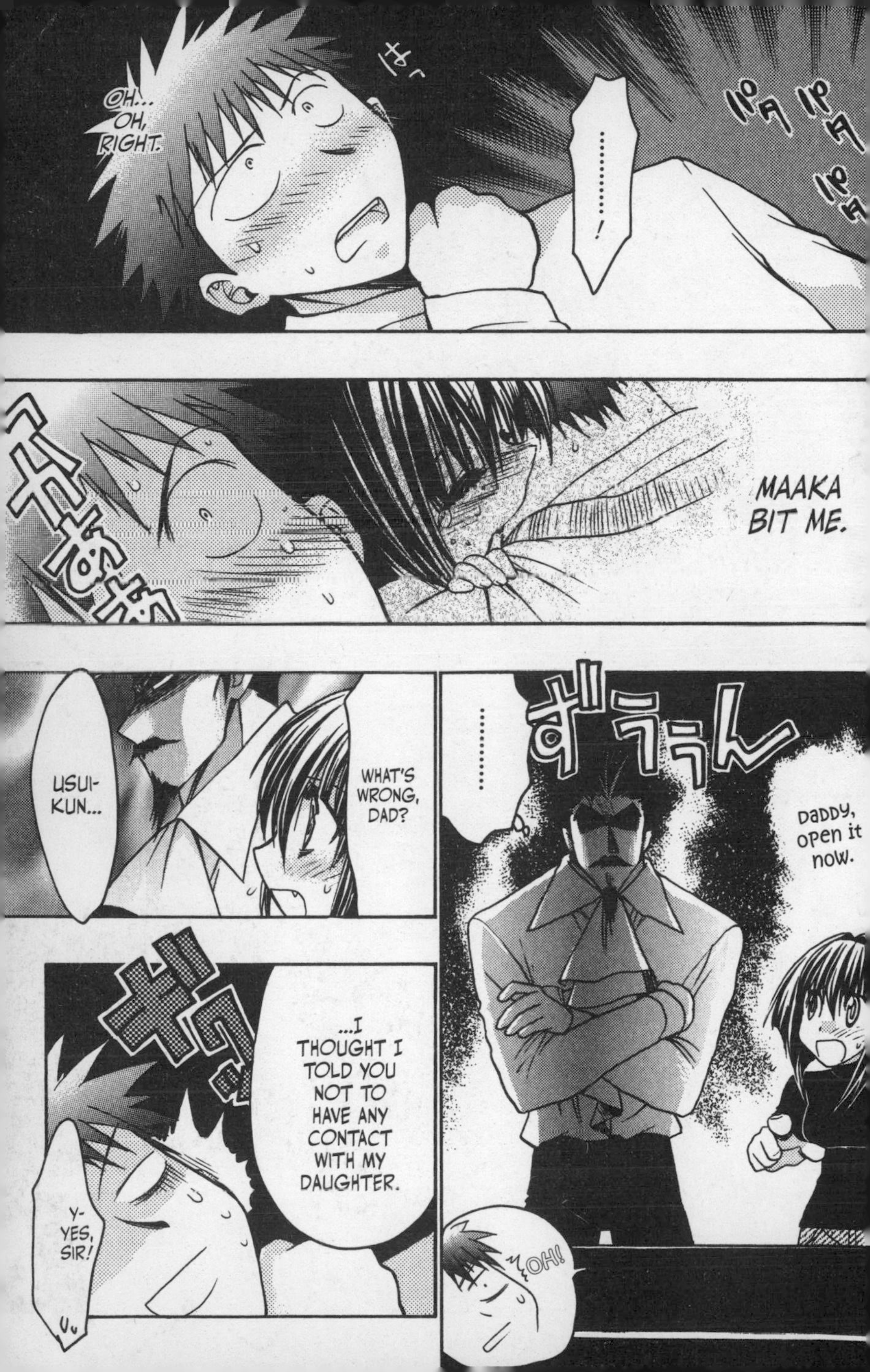

パタパタパタ
......!
はっ
Oh... oh, right.
Maaka bit me.
ずううん
......
Daddy, open it now.
Oh!
What's wrong, dad?
Usui-kun...
...I thought I told you not to have any contact with my daughter.
Y-yes, sir!

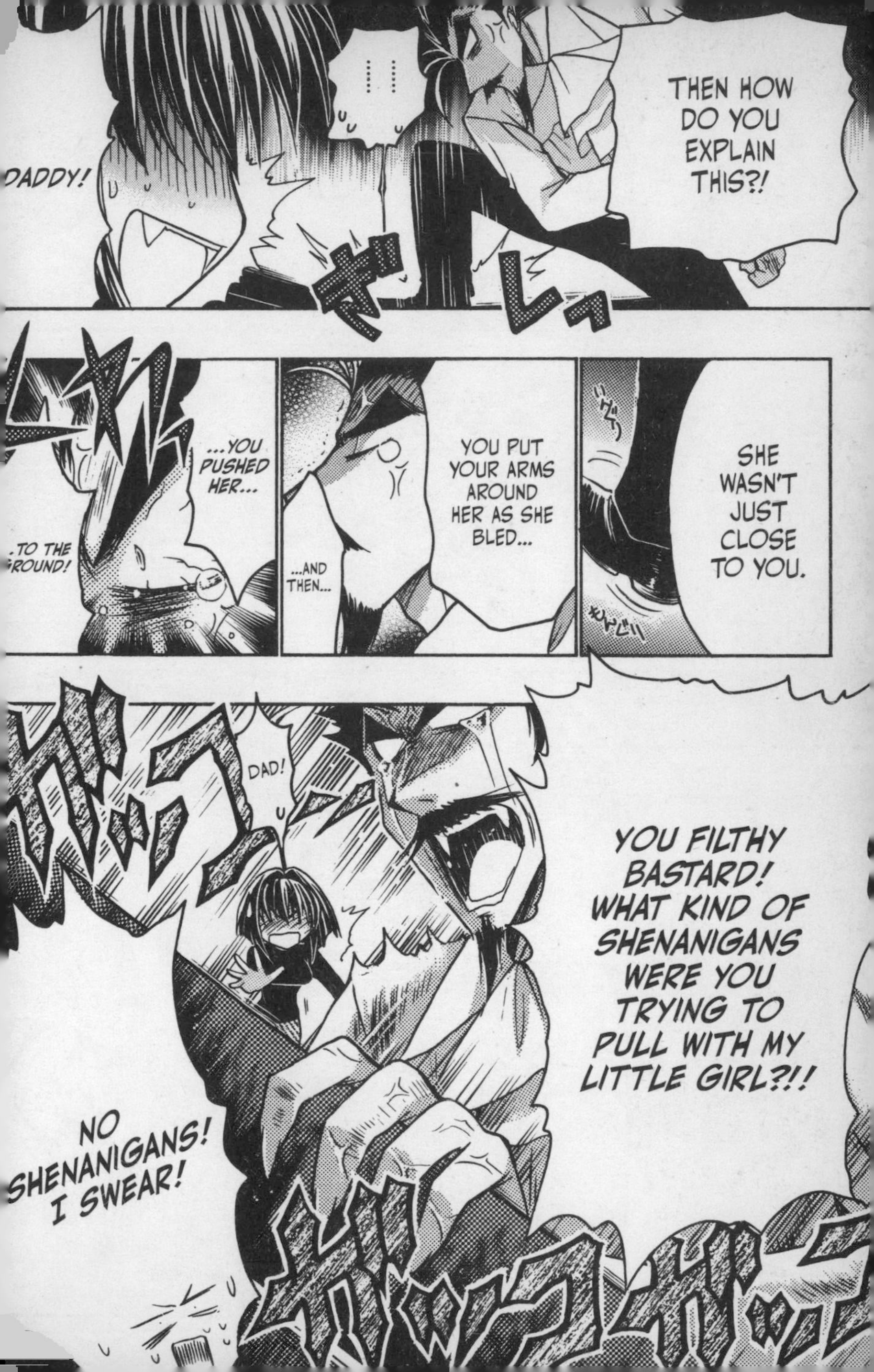
THEN HOW DO YOU EXPLAIN THIS?!
...
DADDY!
SHE WASN'T JUST CLOSE TO YOU.
YOU PUT YOUR ARMS AROUND HER AS SHE BLED...
...AND THEN...
...YOU PUSHED HER...
...TO THE GROUND!
YOU FILTHY BASTARD! WHAT KIND OF SHENANIGANS WERE YOU TRYING TO PULL WITH MY LITTLE GIRL?!!
DAD!
NO SHENANIGANS! I SWEAR!

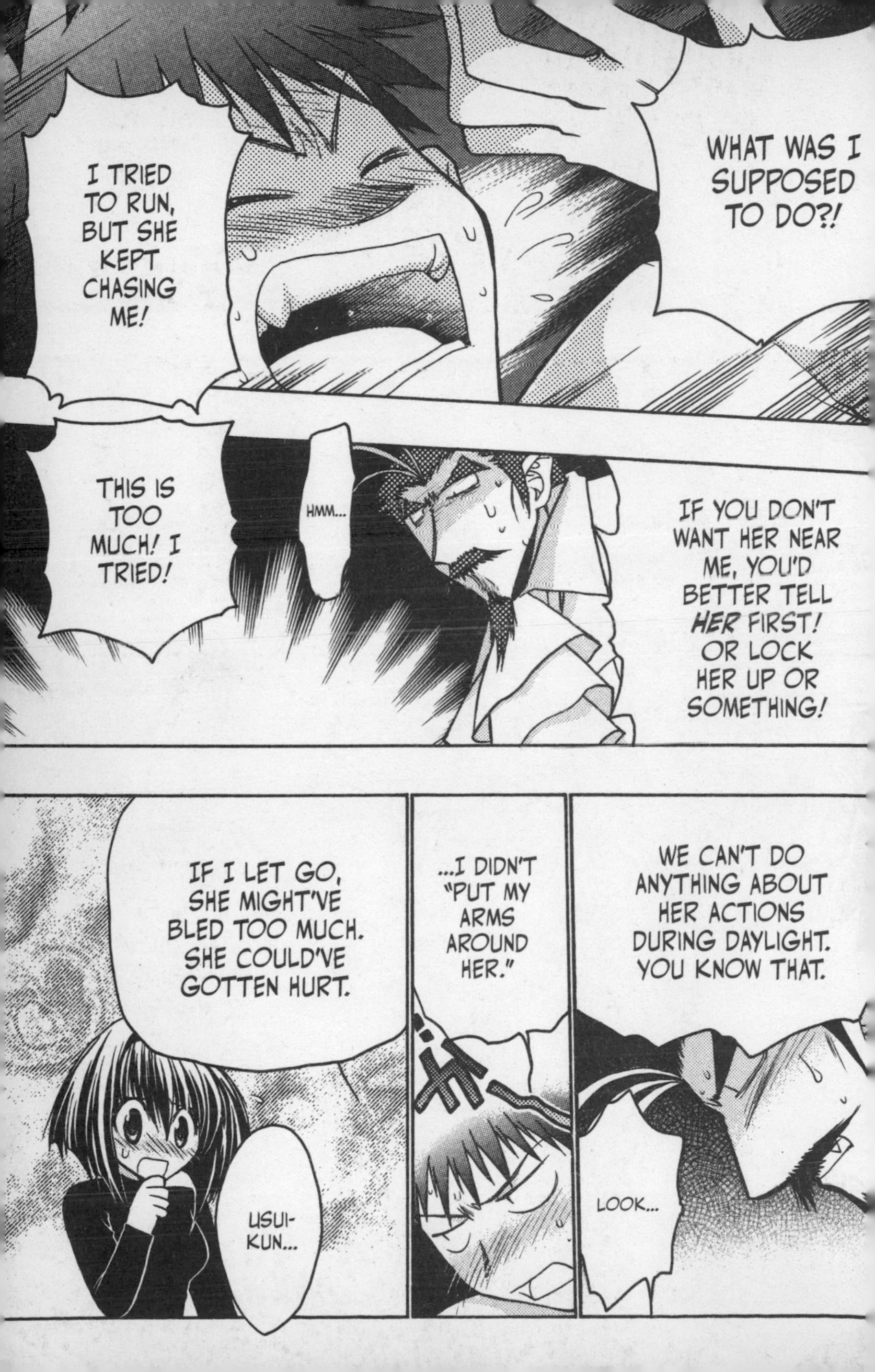
WHAT WAS I SUPPOSED TO DO?!
I TRIED TO RUN, BUT SHE KEPT CHASING ME!
IF YOU DON'T WANT HER NEAR ME, YOU'D BETTER TELL *HER* FIRST! OR LOCK HER UP OR SOMETHING!
HMM...
THIS IS TOO MUCH! I TRIED!
WE CAN'T DO ANYTHING ABOUT HER ACTIONS DURING DAYLIGHT. YOU KNOW THAT.
LOOK...
...I DIDN'T "PUT MY ARMS AROUND HER."
IF I LET GO, SHE MIGHT'VE BLED TOO MUCH. SHE COULD'VE GOTTEN HURT.
USUI-KUN...

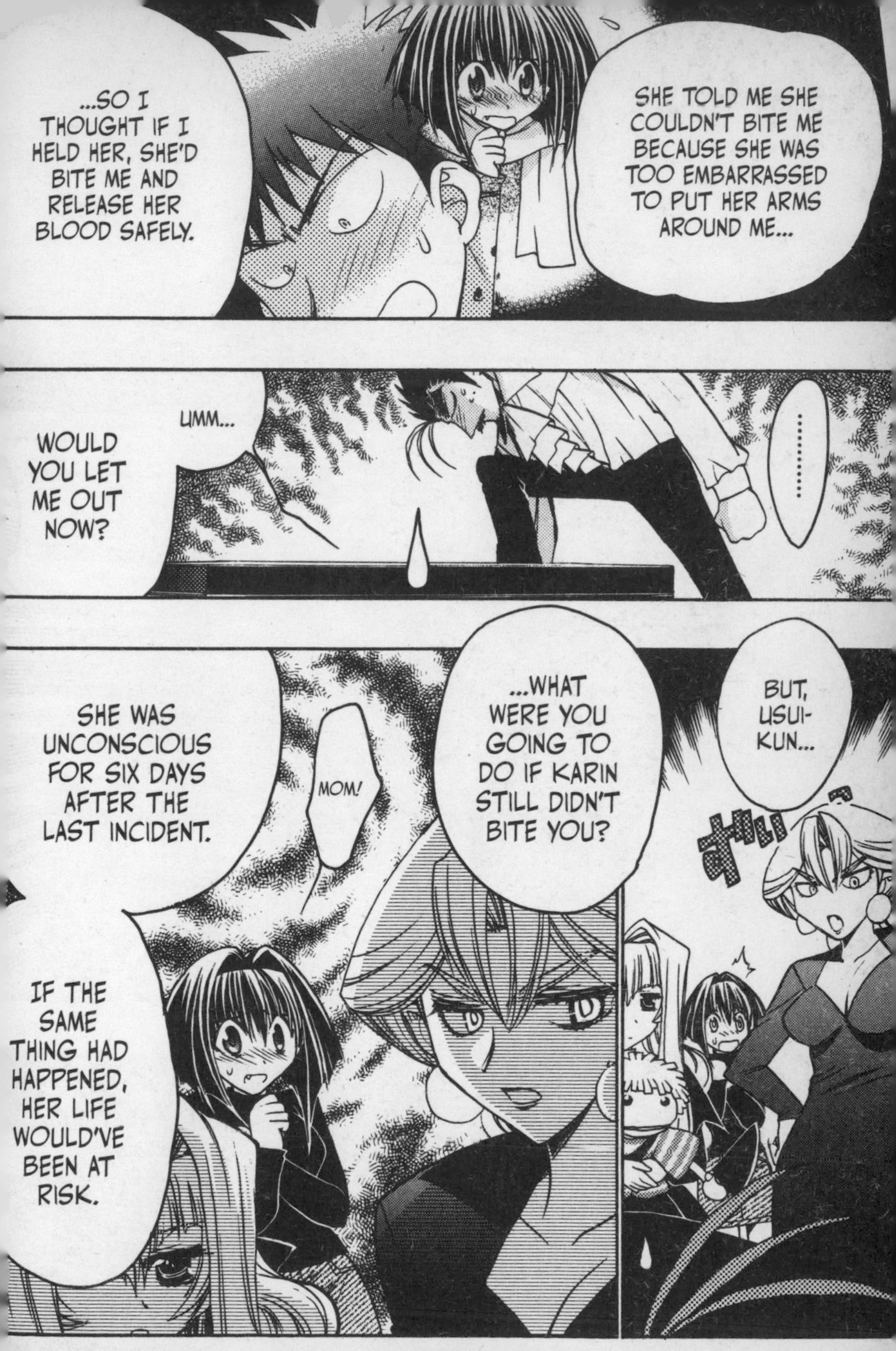
SHE TOLD ME SHE COULDN'T BITE ME BECAUSE SHE WAS TOO EMBARRASSED TO PUT HER ARMS AROUND ME...
...SO I THOUGHT IF I HELD HER, SHE'D BITE ME AND RELEASE HER BLOOD SAFELY.
....
UMM...
WOULD YOU LET ME OUT NOW?
BUT, USUI-KUN...
...WHAT WERE YOU GOING TO DO IF KARIN STILL DIDN'T BITE YOU?
MOM!
SHE WAS UNCONSCIOUS FOR SIX DAYS AFTER THE LAST INCIDENT.
IF THE SAME THING HAD HAPPENED, HER LIFE WOULD'VE BEEN AT RISK.

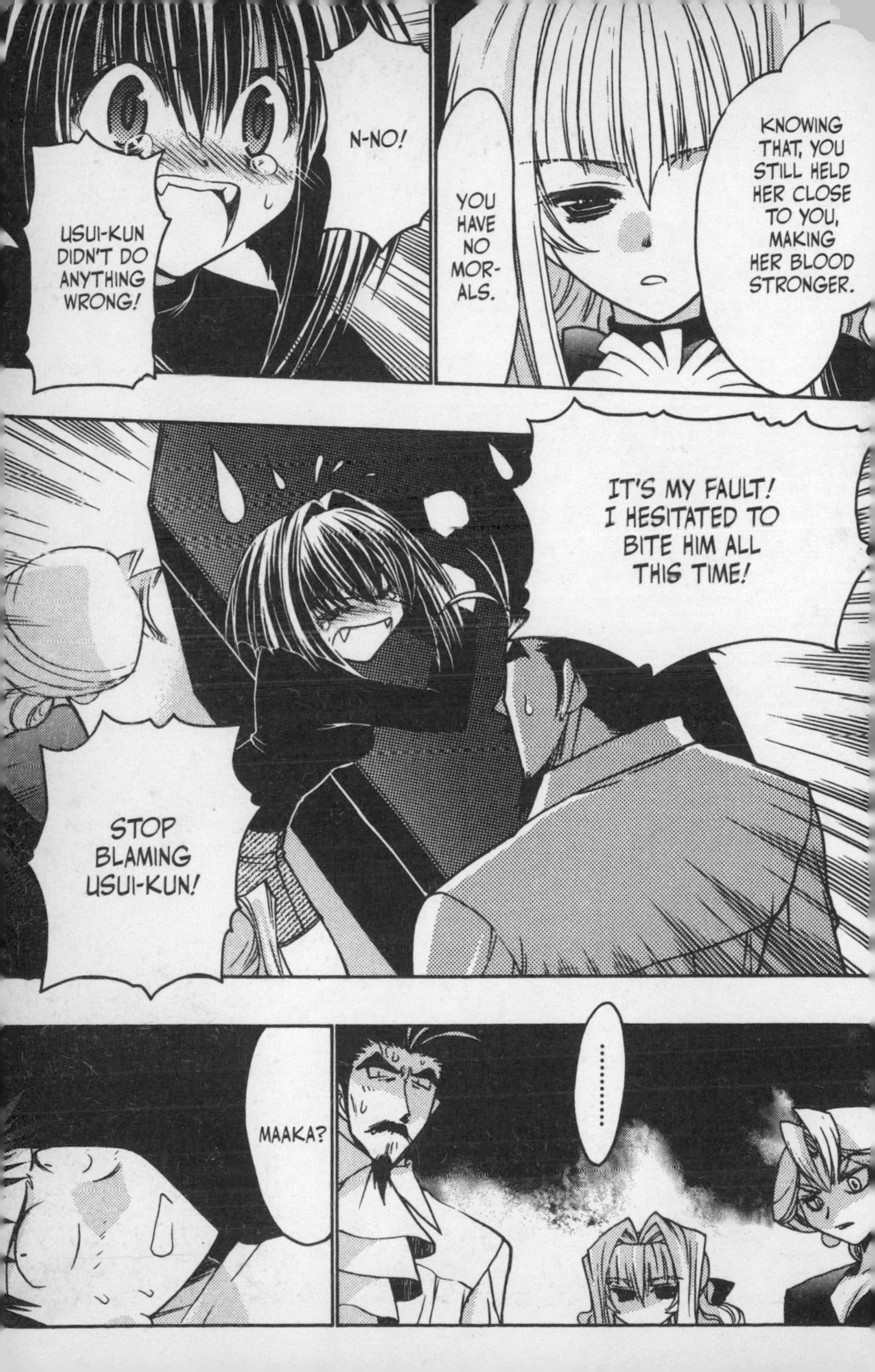
KNOWING THAT, YOU STILL HELD HER CLOSE TO YOU, MAKING HER BLOOD STRONGER.
YOU HAVE NO MOR-ALS.
N-NO!
USUI-KUN DIDN'T DO ANYTHING WRONG!
IT'S MY FAULT! I HESITATED TO BITE HIM ALL THIS TIME!
STOP BLAMING USUI-KUN!
....
MAAKA?

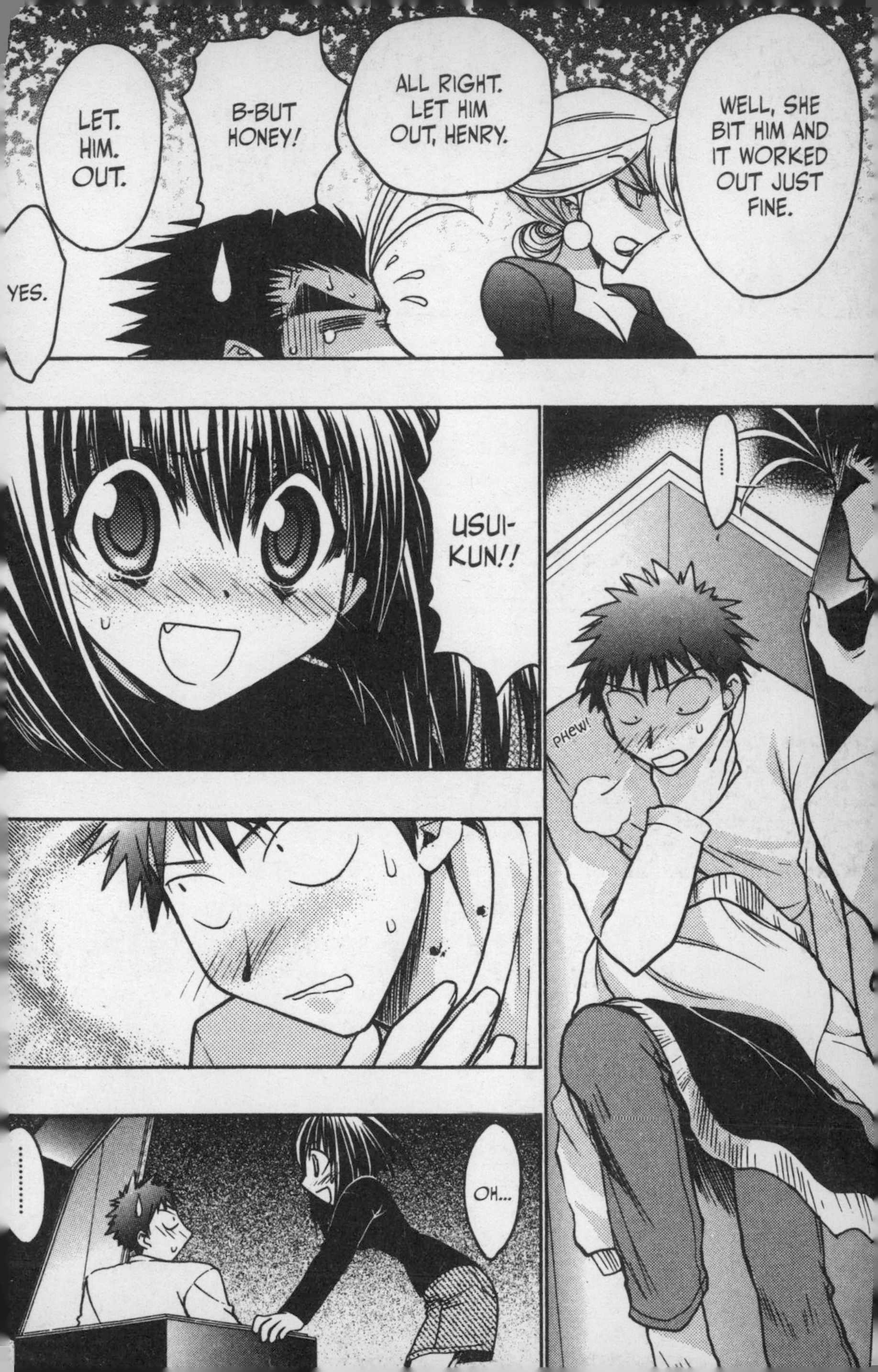
WELL, SHE BIT HIM AND IT WORKED OUT JUST FINE.
ALL RIGHT. LET HIM OUT, HENRY.
B-BUT HONEY!
LET. HIM. OUT.
YES.
......
PHEW!
USUI-KUN!!
OH...
......

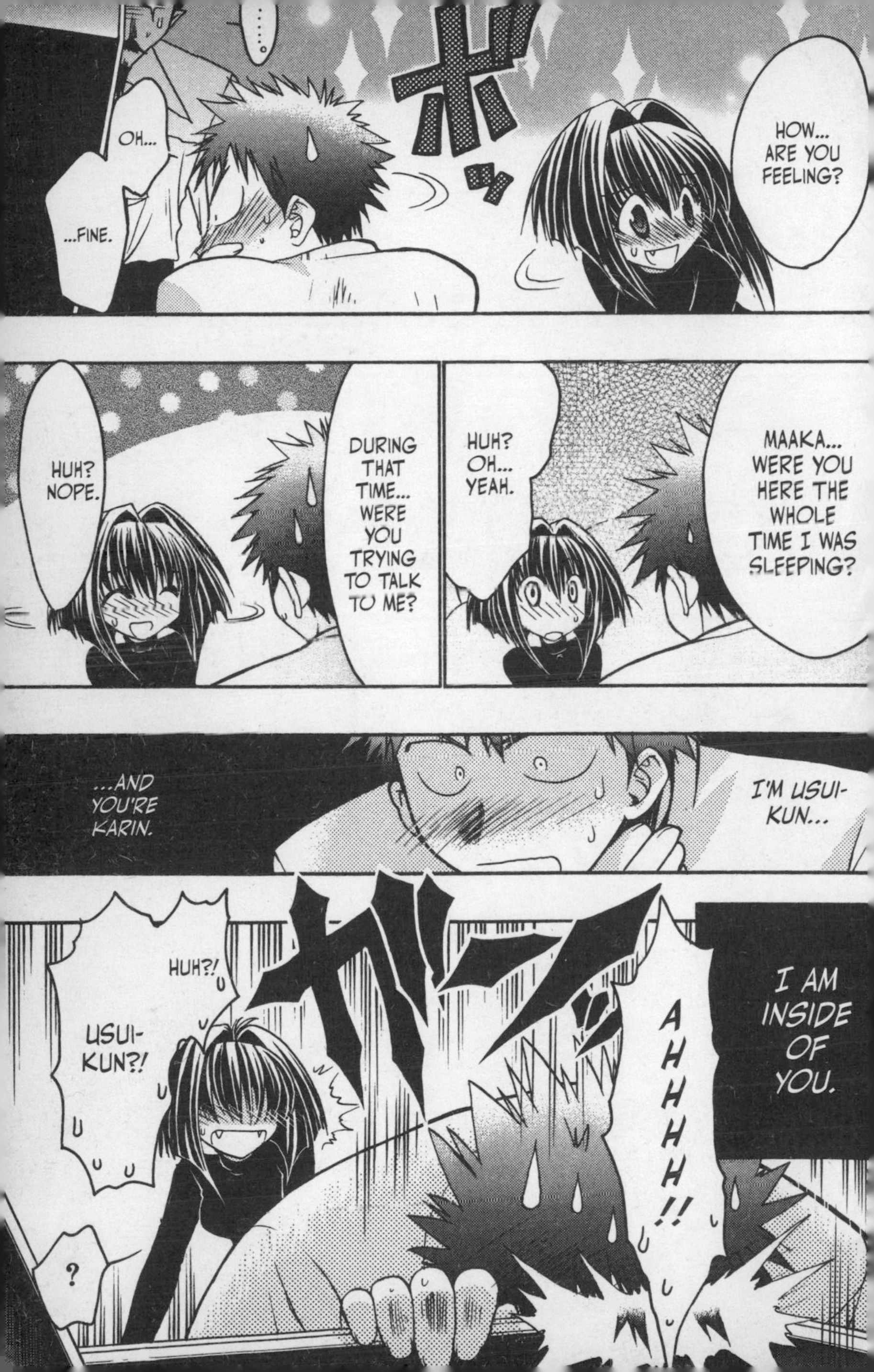
HOW... ARE YOU FEELING?
OH...
...FINE.
MAAKA... WERE YOU HERE THE WHOLE TIME I WAS SLEEPING?
HUH? OH... YEAH.
DURING THAT TIME... WERE YOU TRYING TO TALK TO ME?
HUH? NOPE.
I'M USUI-KUN...
...AND YOU'RE KARIN.
I AM INSIDE OF YOU.
AHHHHH!!
HUH?!
USUI-KUN?!
?

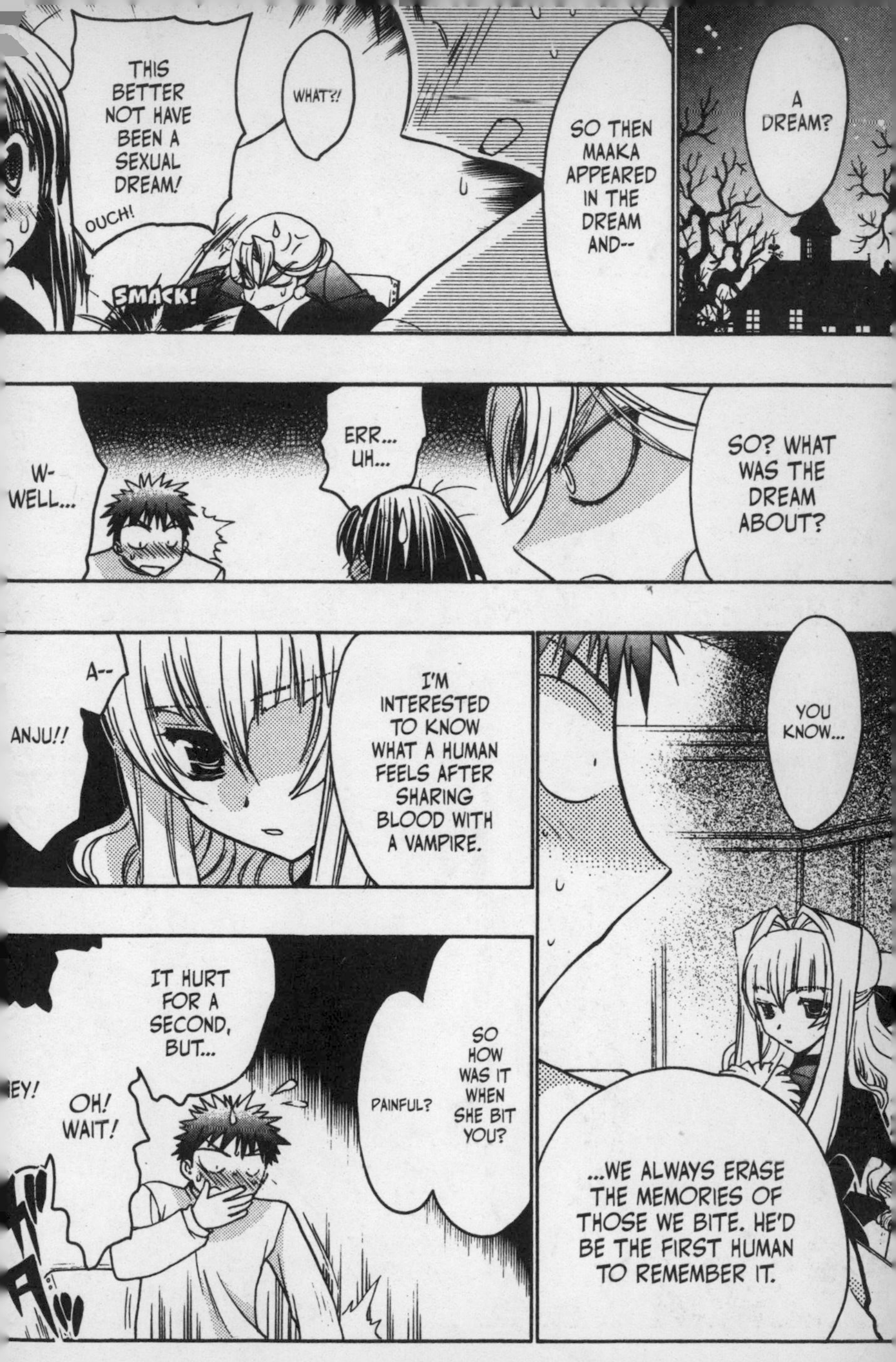
A DREAM?
SO THEN MAAKA APPEARED IN THE DREAM AND--
WHAT?!
THIS BETTER NOT HAVE BEEN A SEXUAL DREAM!
OUCH!
SMACK!
SO? WHAT WAS THE DREAM ABOUT?
ERR... UH...
W- WELL...
YOU KNOW...
...WE ALWAYS ERASE THE MEMORIES OF THOSE WE BITE. HE'D BE THE FIRST HUMAN TO REMEMBER IT.
I'M INTERESTED TO KNOW WHAT A HUMAN FEELS AFTER SHARING BLOOD WITH A VAMPIRE.
A--
ANJU!!
SO HOW WAS IT WHEN SHE BIT YOU?
PAINFUL?
IT HURT FOR A SECOND, BUT...
OH! WAIT!
EY!

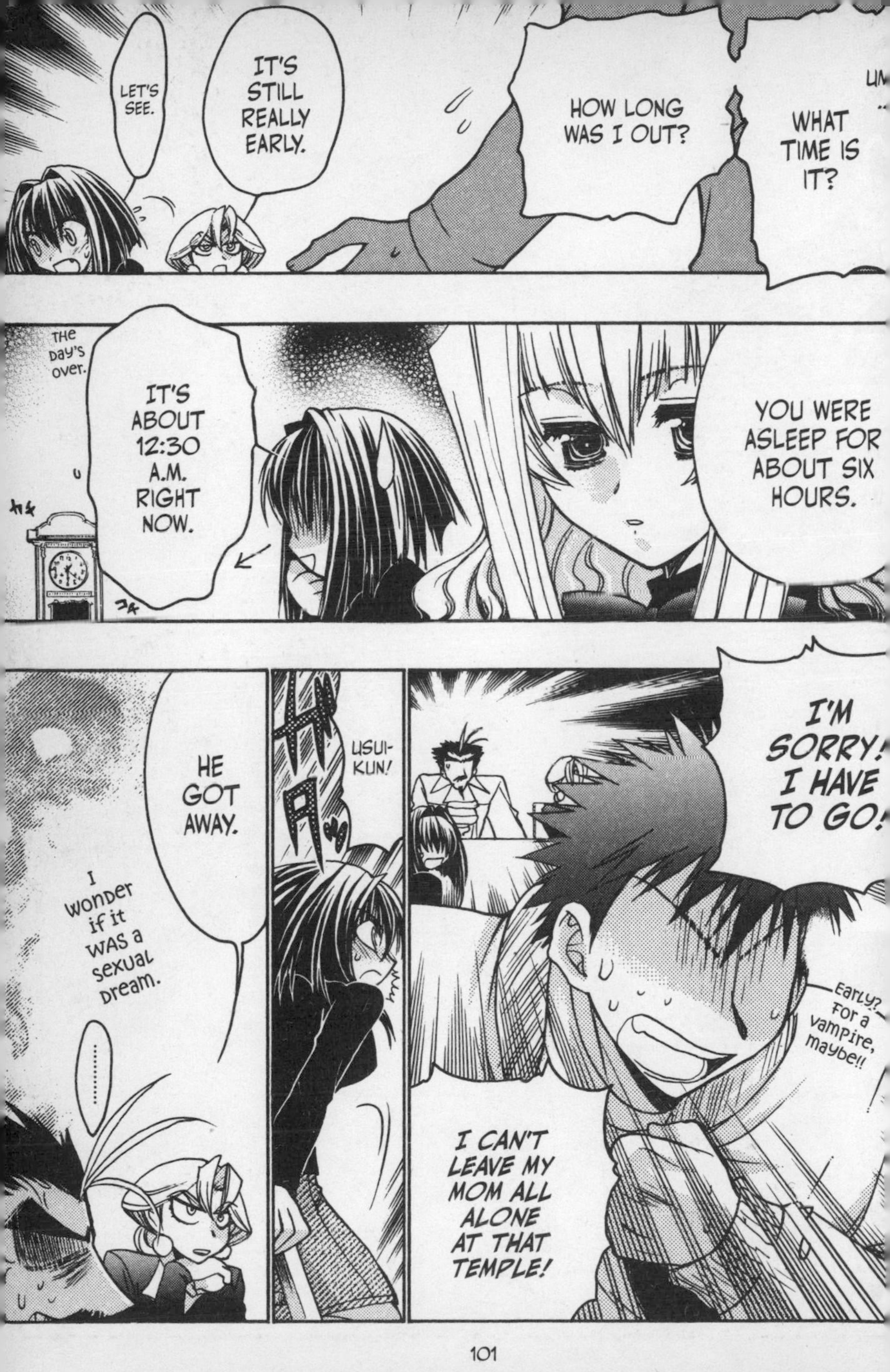
UM
WHAT TIME IS IT?
HOW LONG WAS I OUT?
IT'S STILL REALLY EARLY.
LET'S SEE.
YOU WERE ASLEEP FOR ABOUT SIX HOURS.
IT'S ABOUT 12:30 A.M. RIGHT NOW.
THE DAY'S OVER.
I'M SORRY! I HAVE TO GO!
Early? For a vampire, maybe!!
I CAN'T LEAVE MY MOM ALL ALONE AT THAT TEMPLE!
USUI-KUN!
HE GOT AWAY.
I wonder if it was a sexual dream.
....

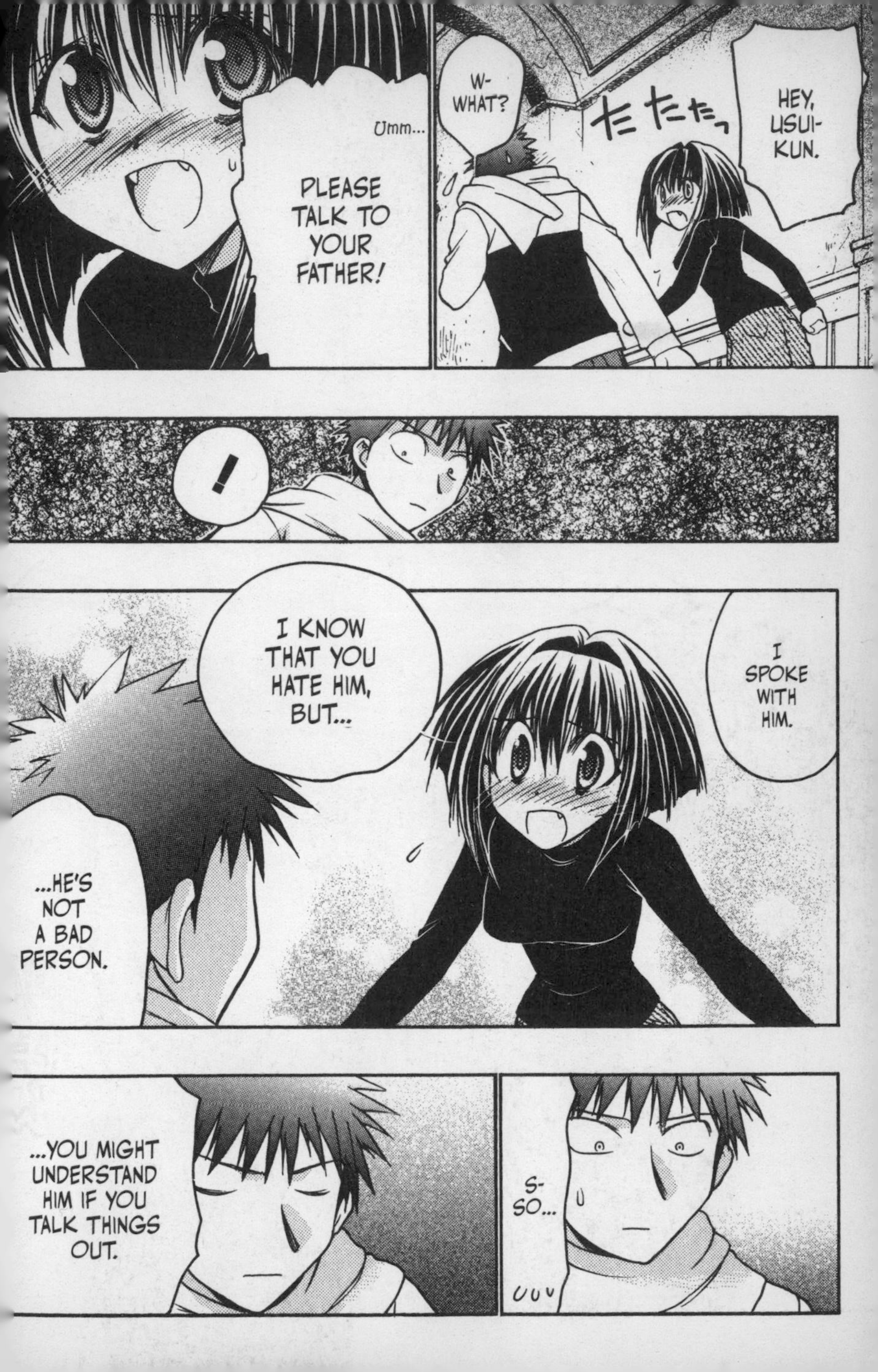
HEY, USUI-KUN.
たたたっ
W-WHAT?
Umm...
PLEASE TALK TO YOUR FATHER!
!
I SPOKE WITH HIM.
I KNOW THAT YOU HATE HIM, BUT...
...HE'S NOT A BAD PERSON.
S-SO...
...YOU MIGHT UNDERSTAND HIM IF YOU TALK THINGS OUT.

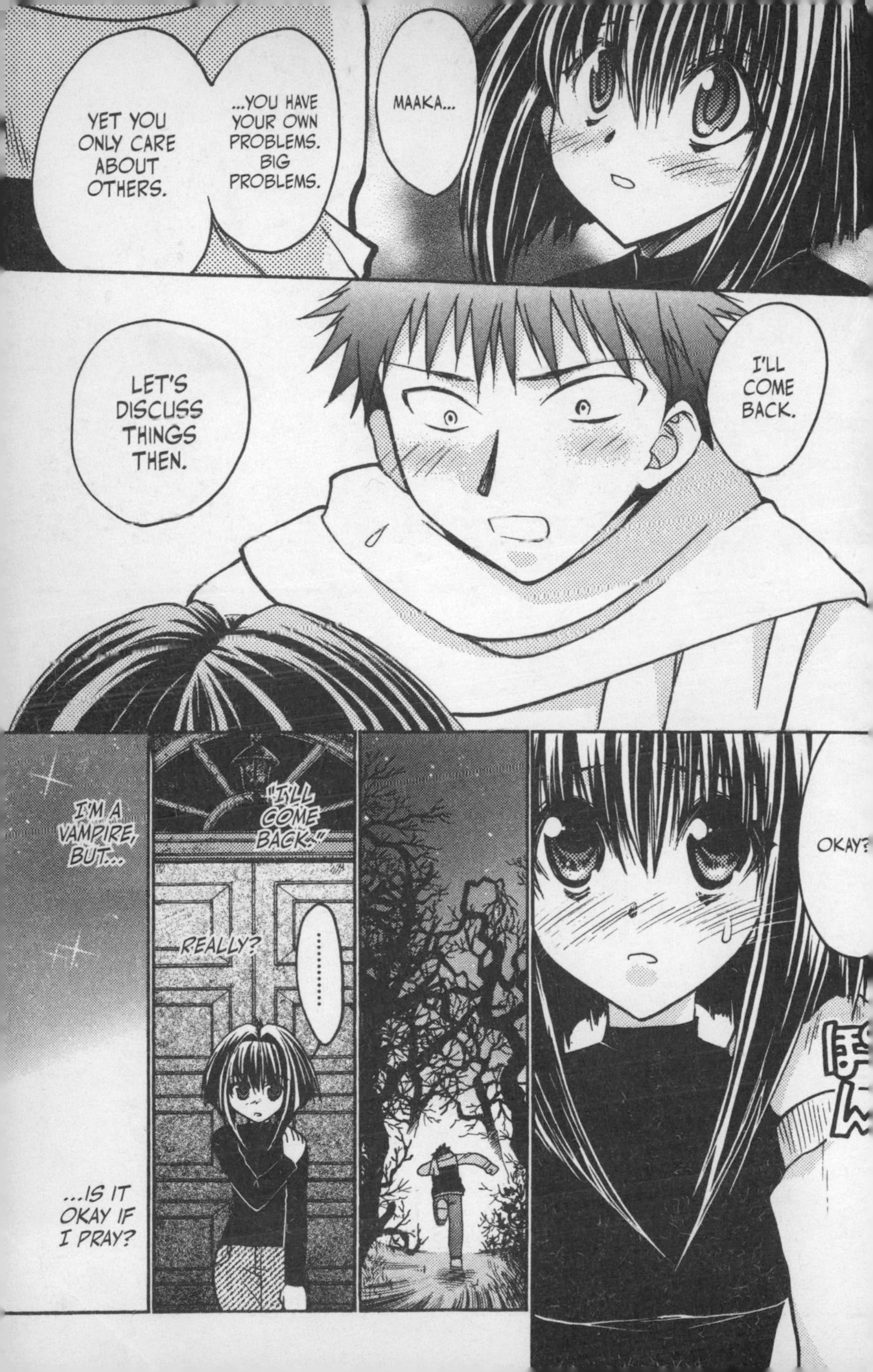
MAAKA...
...YOU HAVE YOUR OWN PROBLEMS. BIG PROBLEMS.
YET YOU ONLY CARE ABOUT OTHERS.
I'LL COME BACK.
LET'S DISCUSS THINGS THEN.
OKAY?
ぽん
"I'LL COME BACK."
......
REALLY?
I'M A VAMPIRE, BUT...
...IS IT OKAY IF I PRAY?

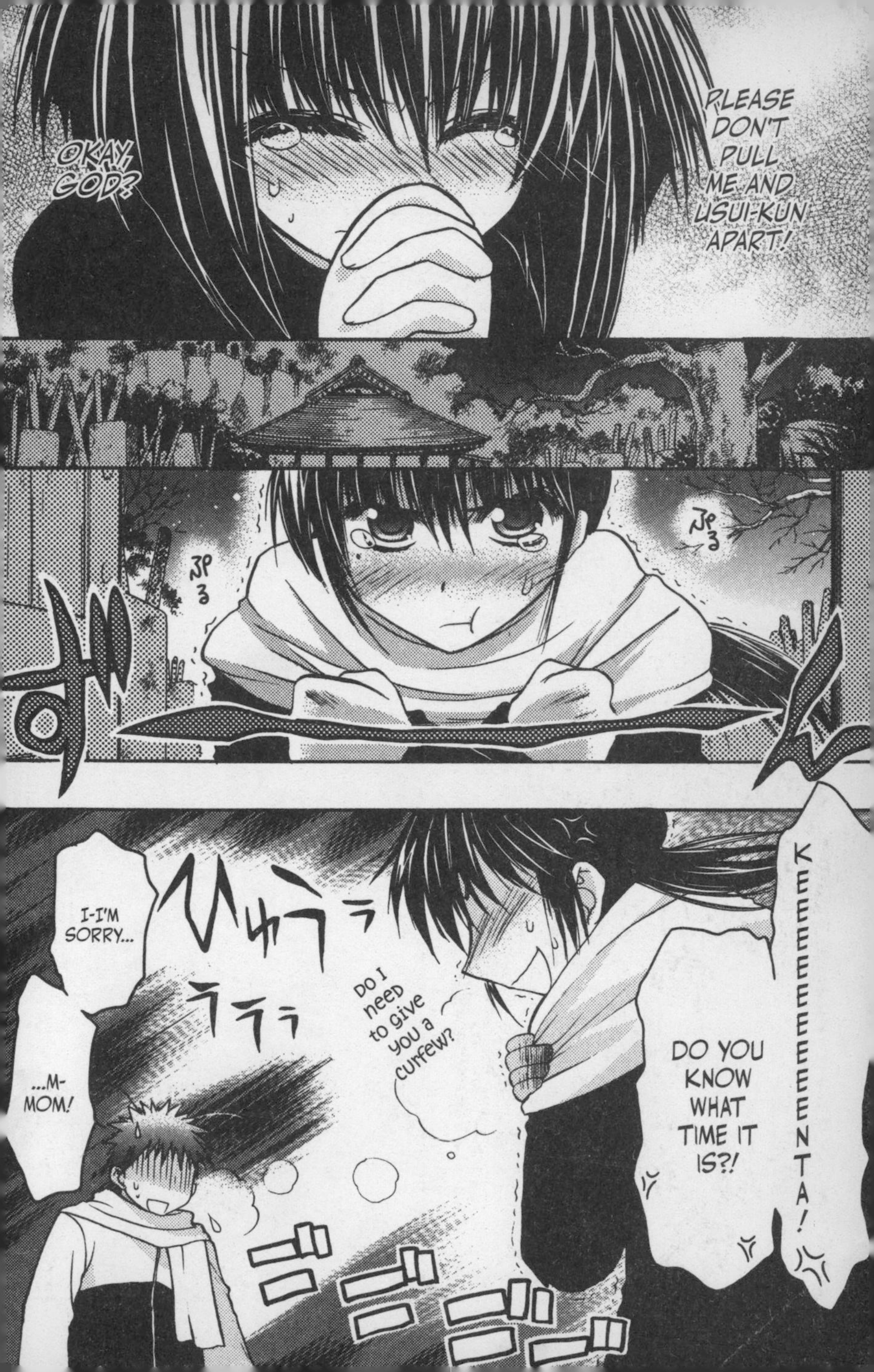
PLEASE DON'T PULL ME AND USUI-KUN APART!
OKAY, GOD?
KEEEEEEEEEEEEENTA!
DO YOU KNOW WHAT TIME IT IS?!
DO I NEED TO GIVE YOU A CURFEW?
I-I'M SORRY...
...M-MOM!

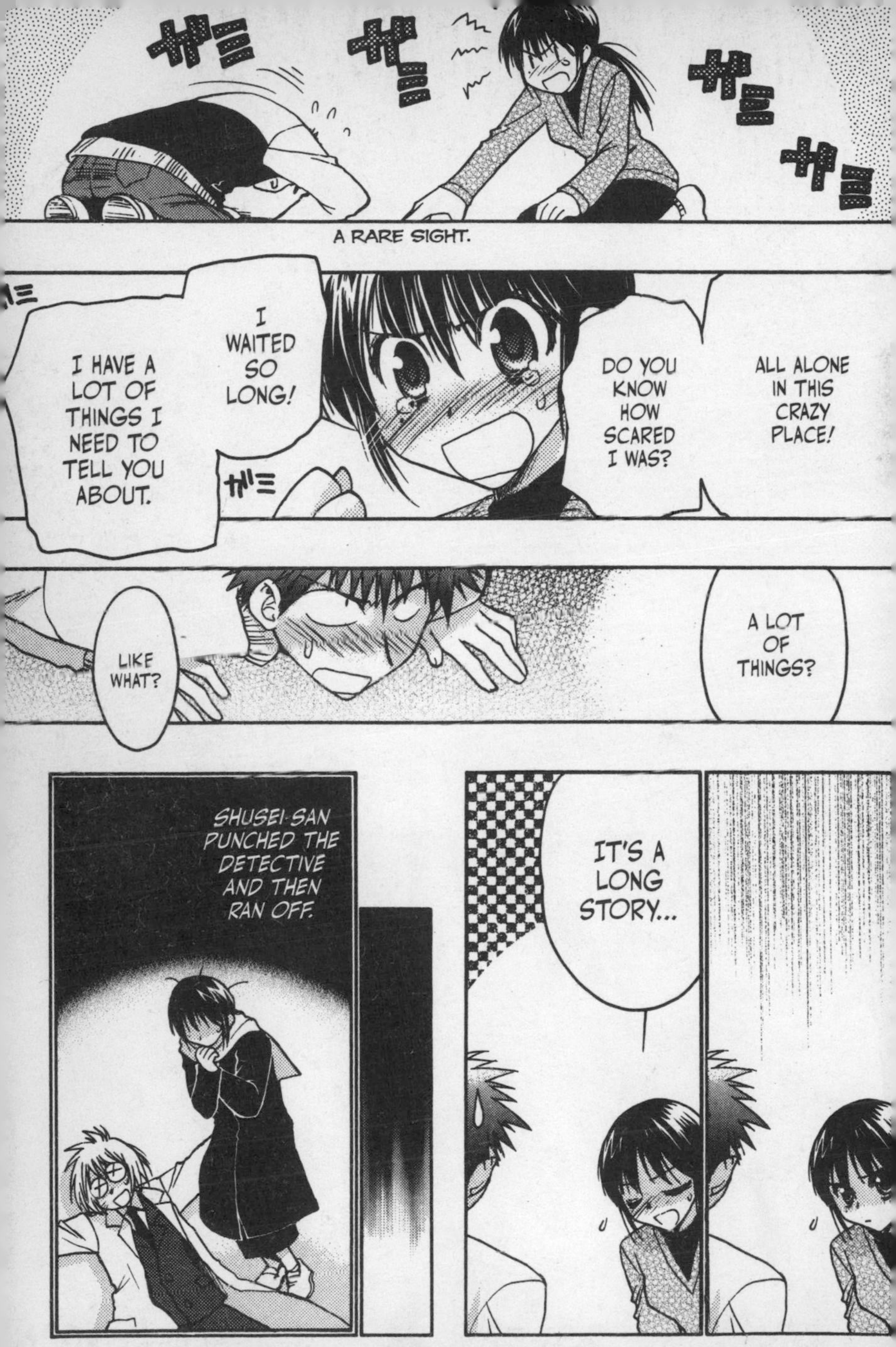
ガミ
ガミ
ガミ
ガミ
A RARE SIGHT.
ALL ALONE IN THIS CRAZY PLACE!
DO YOU KNOW HOW SCARED I WAS?
I WAITED SO LONG!
ガミ
I HAVE A LOT OF THINGS I NEED TO TELL YOU ABOUT.
A LOT OF THINGS?
LIKE WHAT?
IT'S A LONG STORY...
SHUSEI-SAN PUNCHED THE DETECTIVE AND THEN RAN OFF.

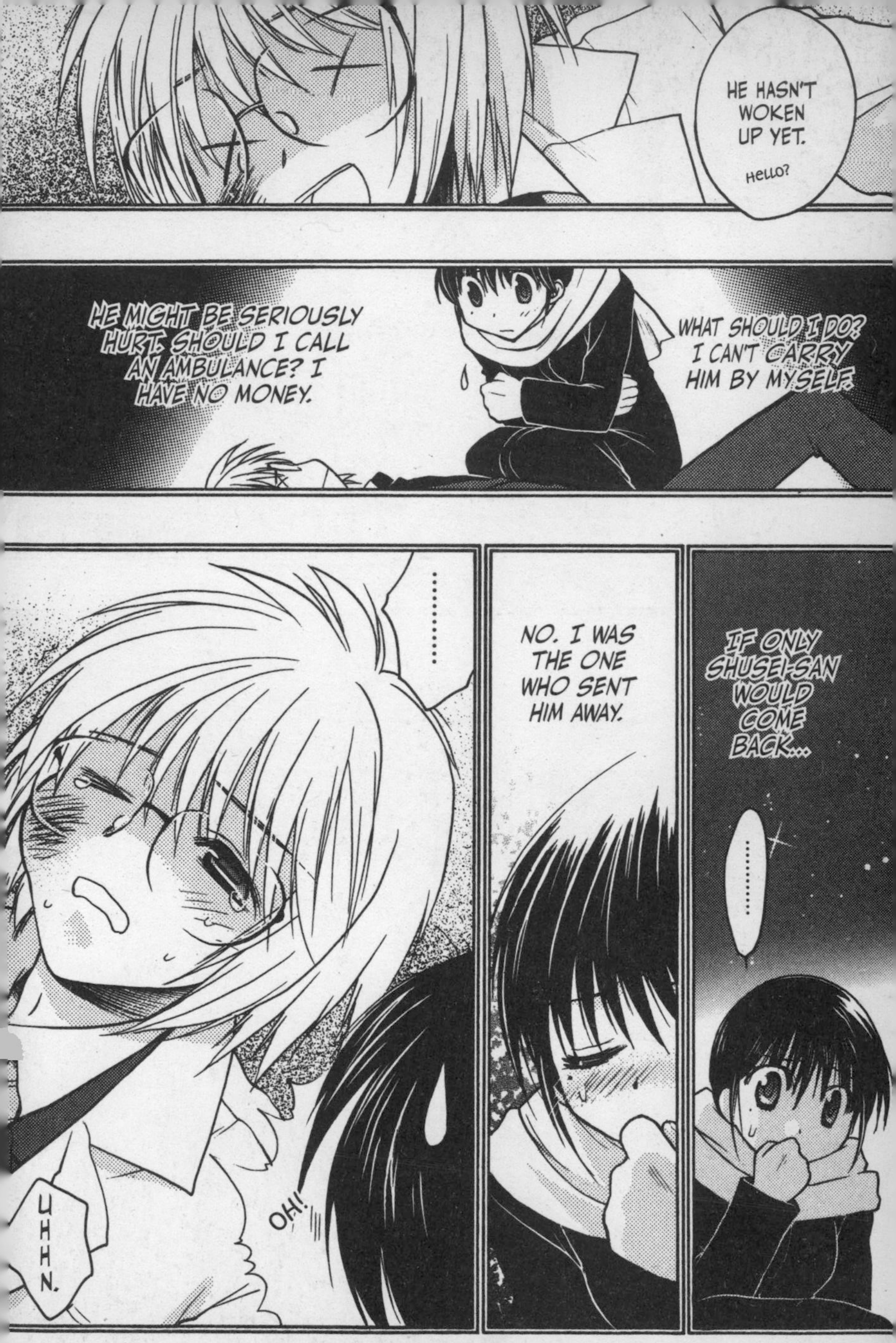
HE HASN'T WOKEN UP YET.
Hello?
WHAT SHOULD I DO? I CAN'T CARRY HIM BY MYSELF.
HE MIGHT BE SERIOUSLY HURT. SHOULD I CALL AN AMBULANCE? I HAVE NO MONEY.
IF ONLY SHUSEI-SAN WOULD COME BACK...
......
NO. I WAS THE ONE WHO SENT HIM AWAY.
......
OH!
UHHN.

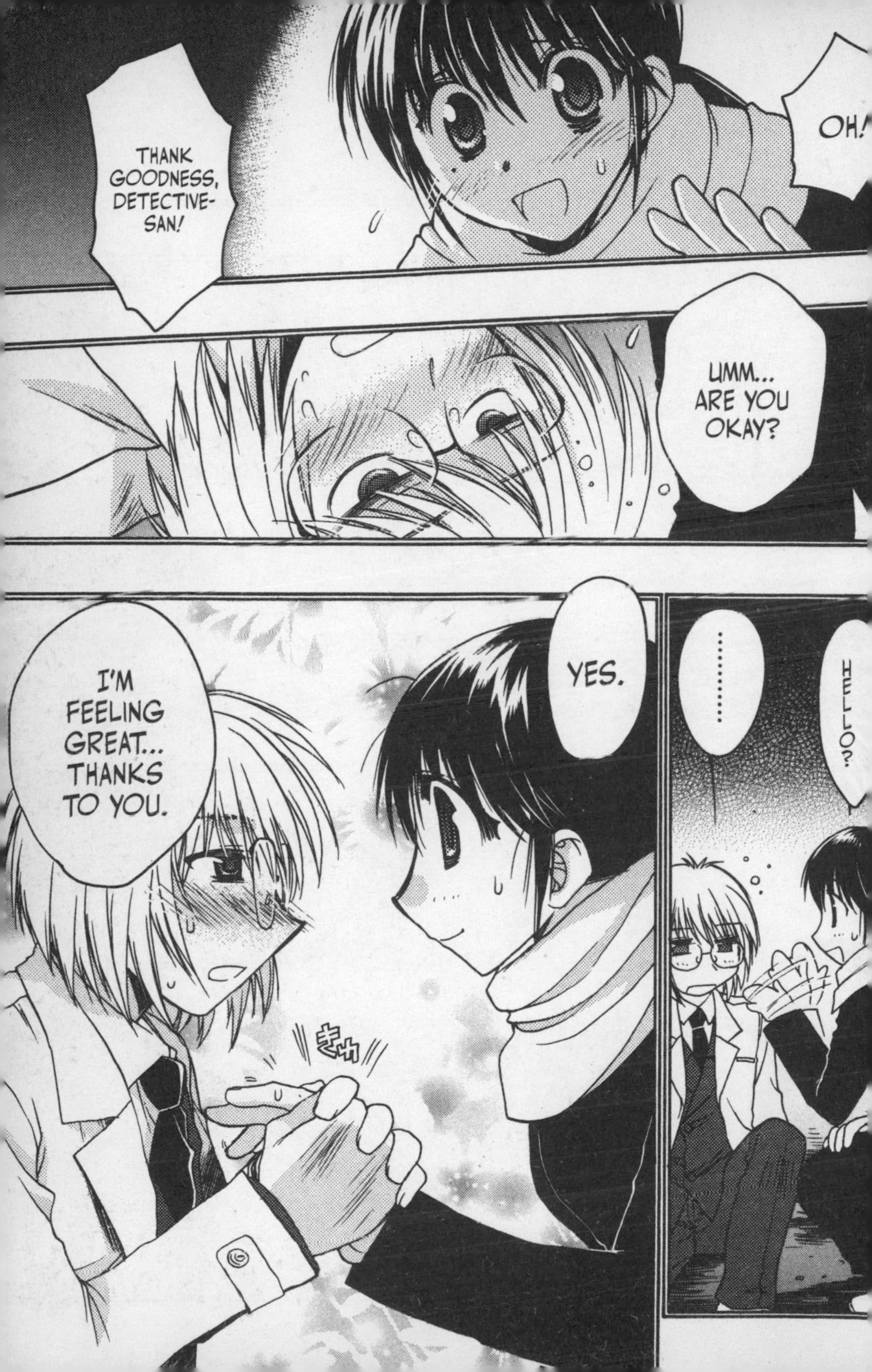
OH!
THANK GOODNESS, DETECTIVE-SAN!
UMM... ARE YOU OKAY?
HELLO?
....
YES.
I'M FEELING GREAT... THANKS TO YOU.
きゅ

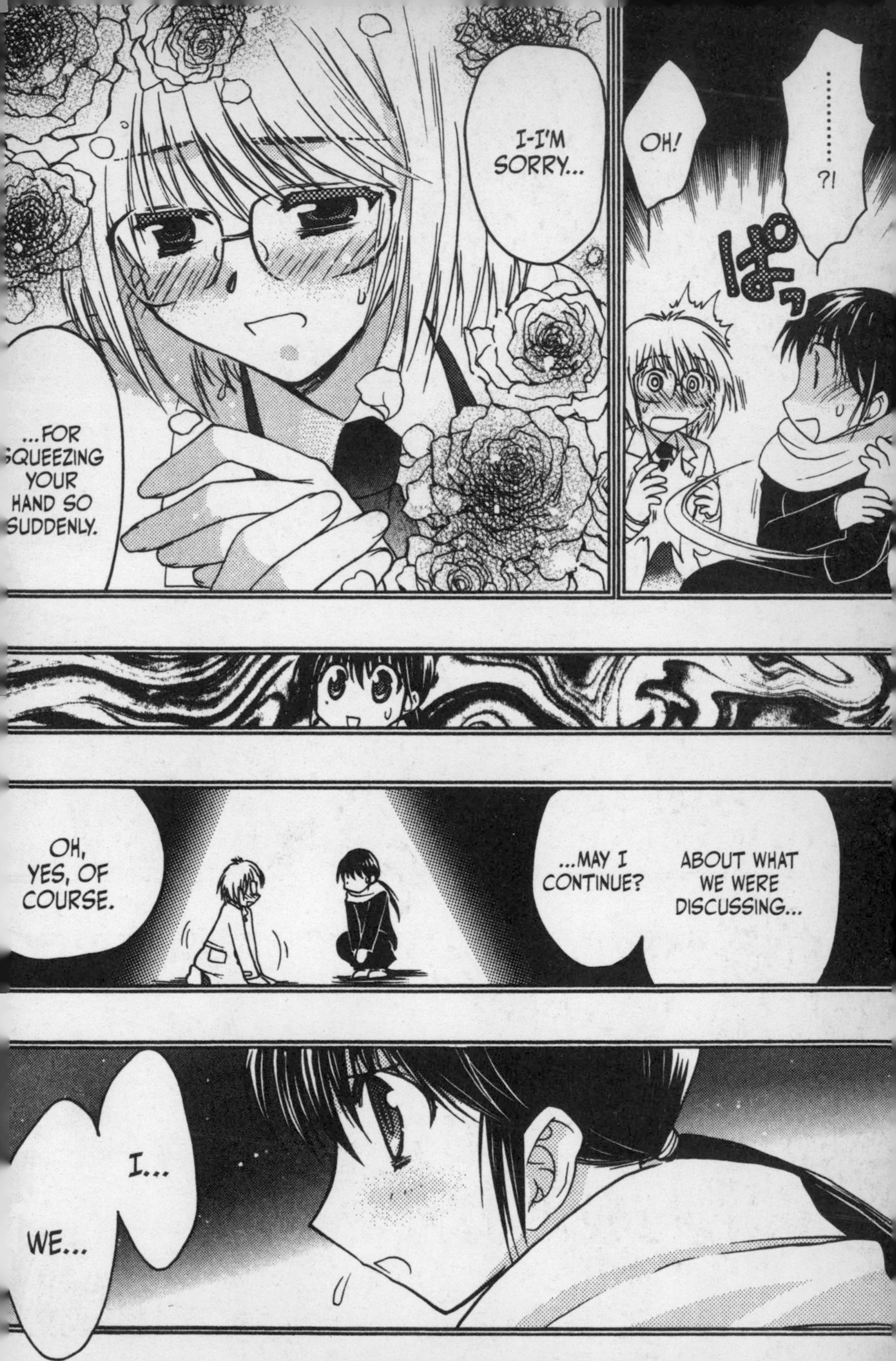
......?!
OH!
ぱっ
I-I'M SORRY...
...FOR SQUEEZING YOUR HAND SO SUDDENLY.
ABOUT WHAT WE WERE DISCUSSING...
...MAY I CONTINUE?
OH, YES, OF COURSE.
I...
WE...

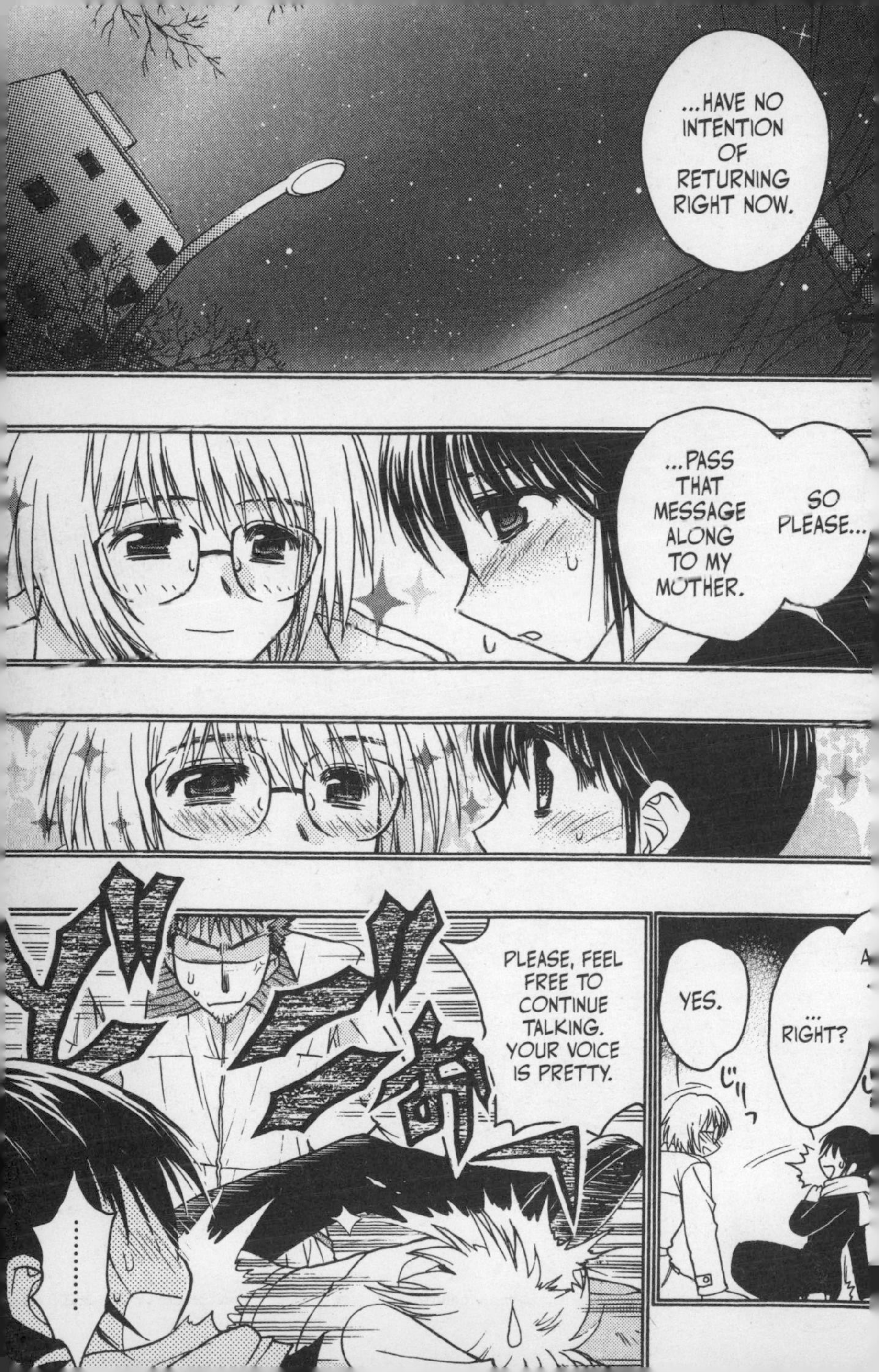
...HAVE NO INTENTION OF RETURNING RIGHT NOW.
SO PLEASE...
...PASS THAT MESSAGE ALONG TO MY MOTHER.
...RIGHT?
YES.
じーっ
PLEASE, FEEL FREE TO CONTINUE TALKING. YOUR VOICE IS PRETTY.
......

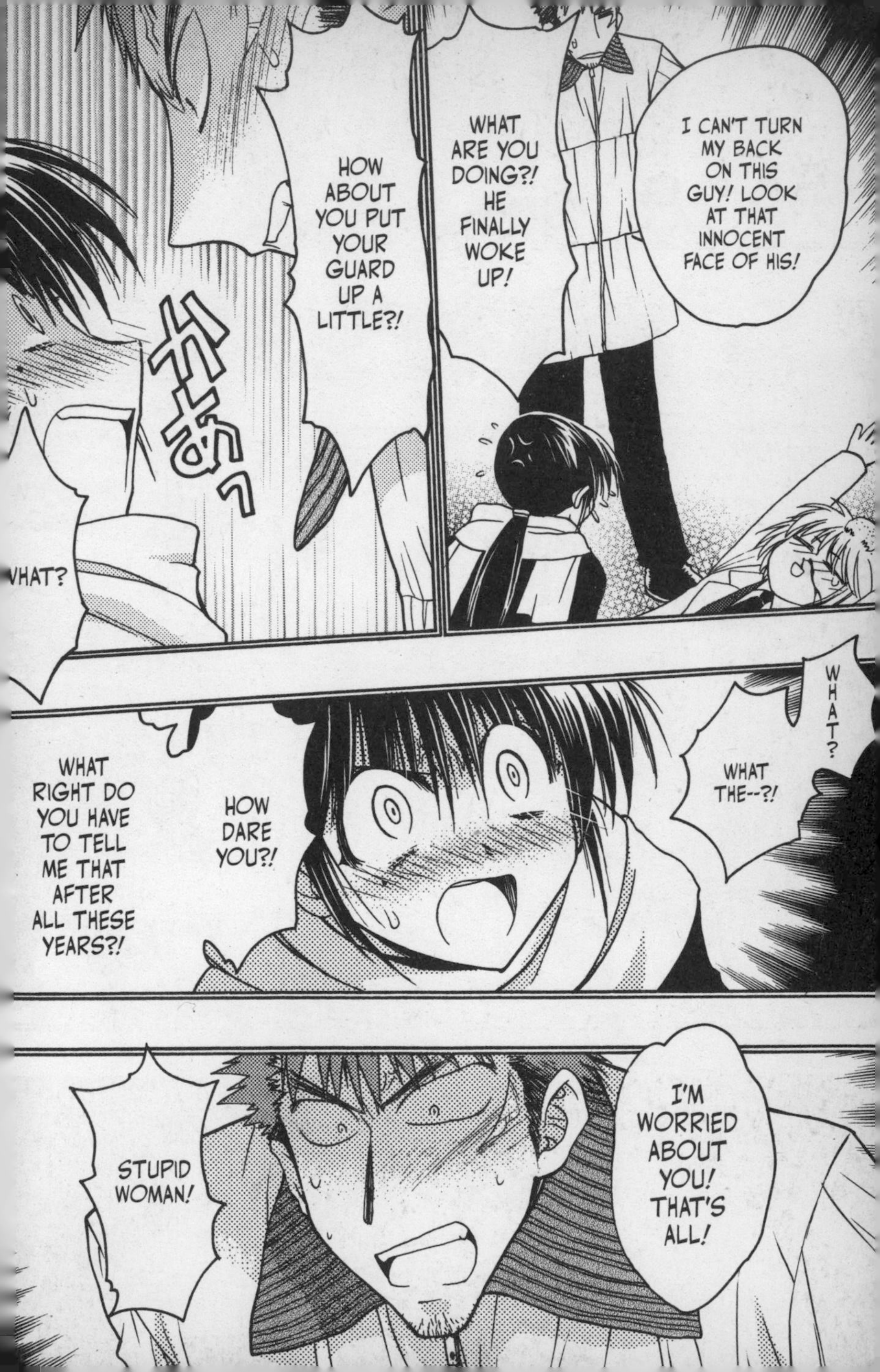
I CAN'T TURN MY BACK ON THIS GUY! LOOK AT THAT INNOCENT FACE OF HIS!
WHAT ARE YOU DOING?! HE FINALLY WOKE UP!
HOW ABOUT YOU PUT YOUR GUARD UP A LITTLE?!
かあっ
WHAT?
WHAT?
WHAT THE--?!
HOW DARE YOU?!
WHAT RIGHT DO YOU HAVE TO TELL ME THAT AFTER ALL THESE YEARS?!
I'M WORRIED ABOUT YOU! THAT'S ALL!
STUPID WOMAN!

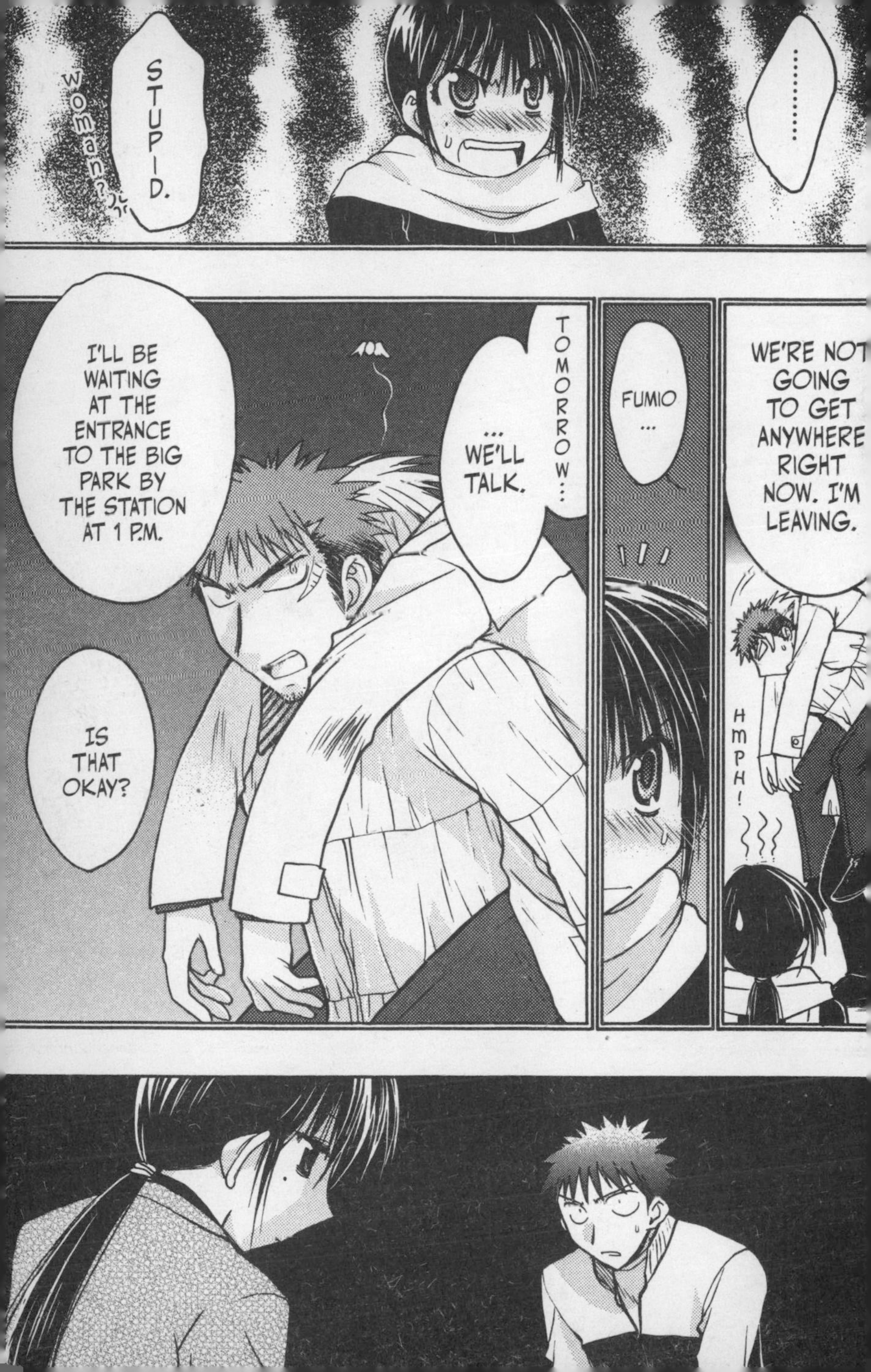
……
STUPID.
woman?
WE'RE NOT GOING TO GET ANYWHERE RIGHT NOW. I'M LEAVING.
HMPH!
FUMIO ...
TOMORROW...
... WE'LL TALK.
I'LL BE WAITING AT THE ENTRANCE TO THE BIG PARK BY THE STATION AT 1 P.M.
IS THAT OKAY?

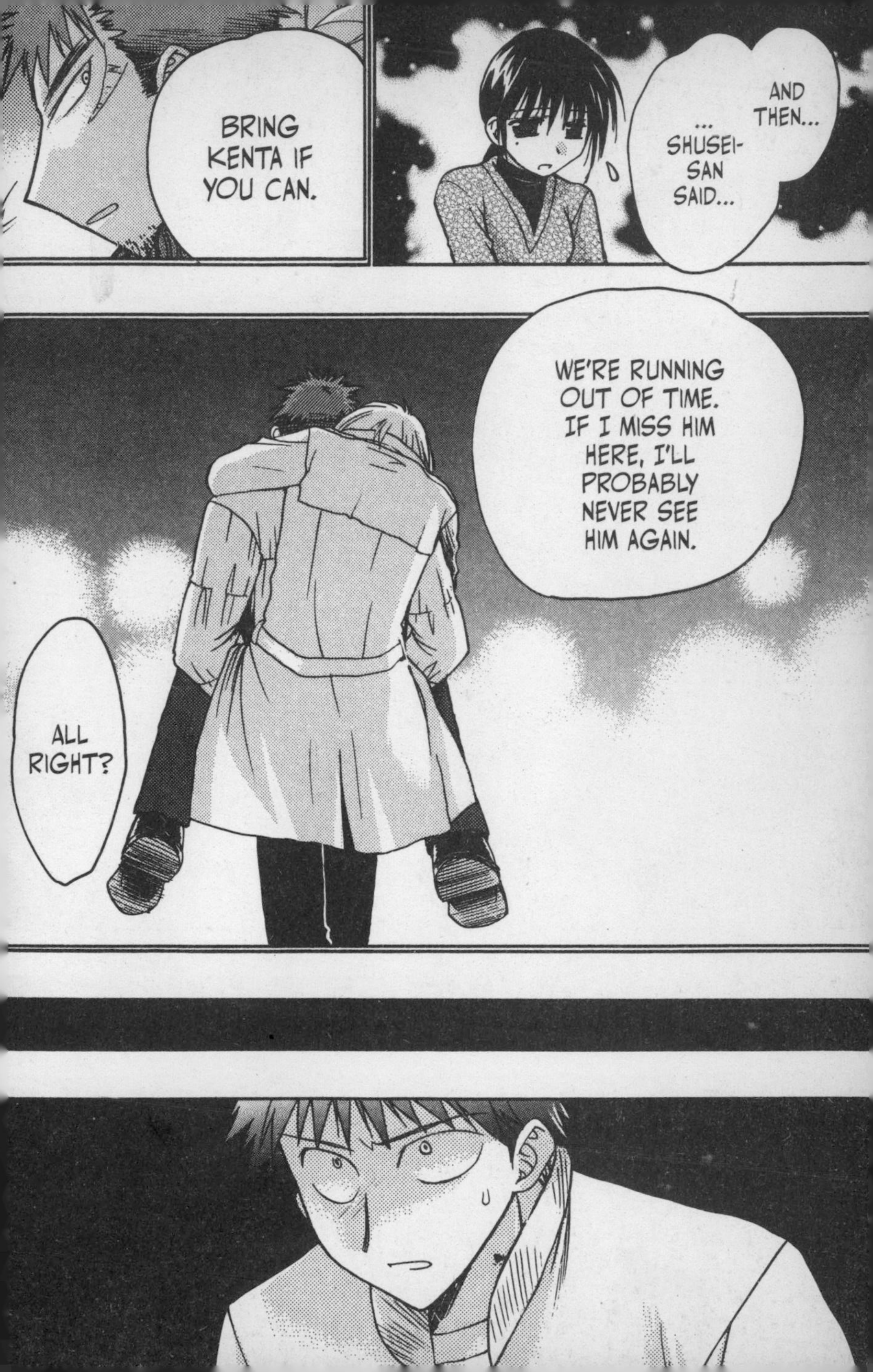
AND THEN... ... SHUSEI-SAN SAID...
BRING KENTA IF YOU CAN.
WE'RE RUNNING OUT OF TIME. IF I MISS HIM HERE, I'LL PROBABLY NEVER SEE HIM AGAIN.
ALL RIGHT?

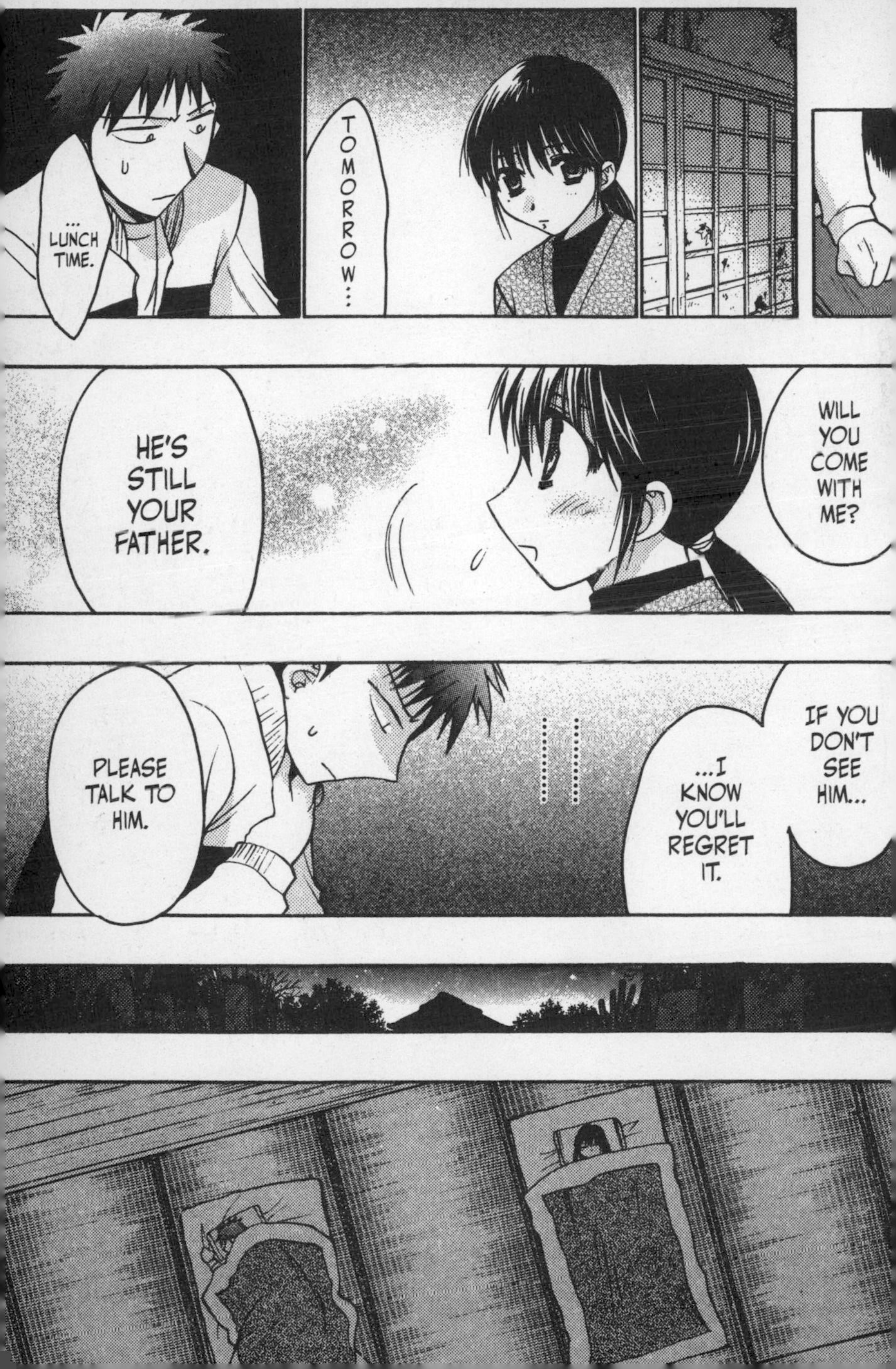
TOMORROW...
...LUNCH TIME.
WILL YOU COME WITH ME?
HE'S STILL YOUR FATHER.
IF YOU DON'T SEE HIM...
...I KNOW YOU'LL REGRET IT.
......
PLEASE TALK TO HIM.

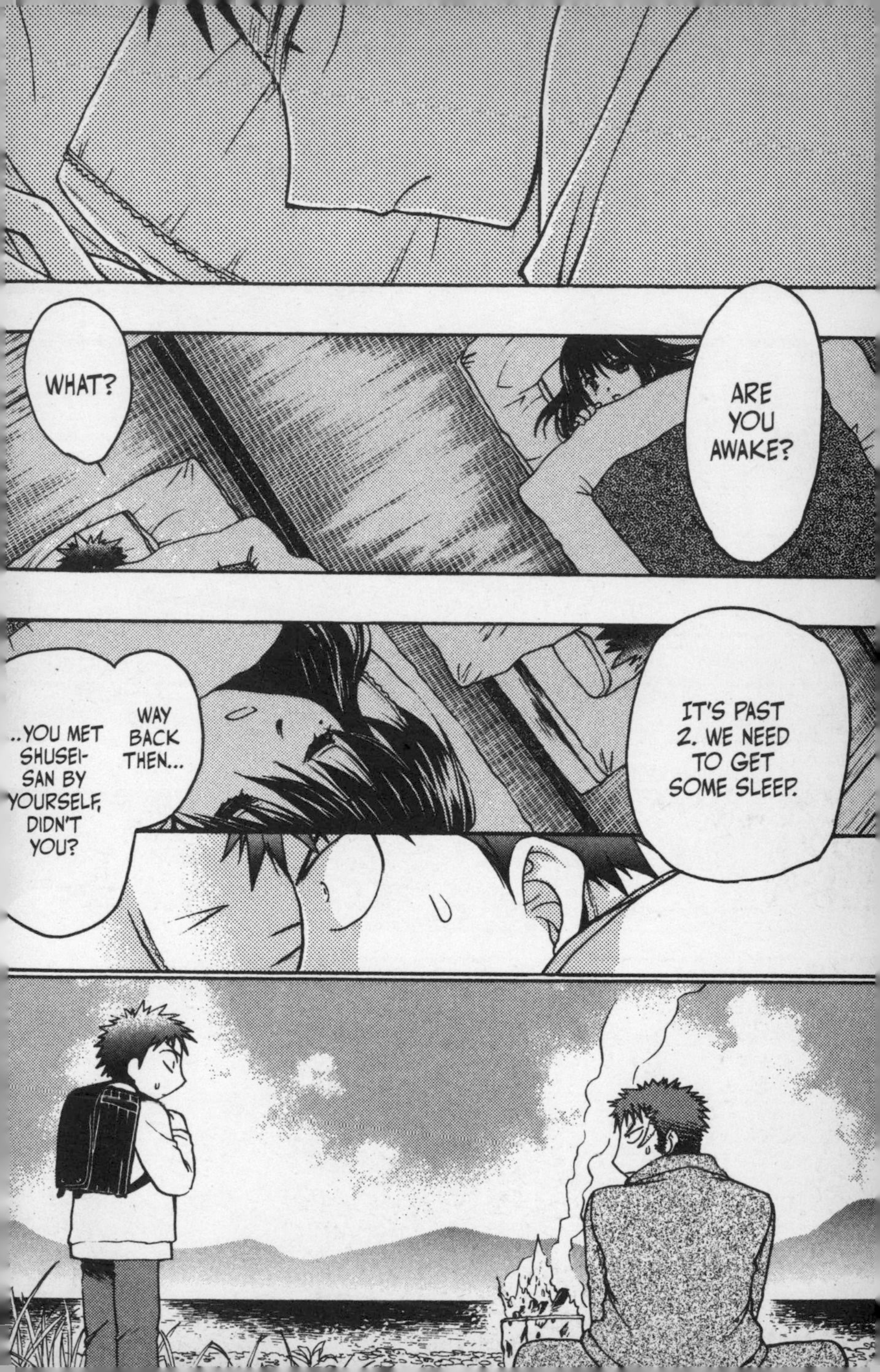
ARE YOU AWAKE?
WHAT?
IT'S PAST 2. WE NEED TO GET SOME SLEEP.
WAY BACK THEN...
..YOU MET SHUSEI-SAN BY YOURSELF, DIDN'T YOU?

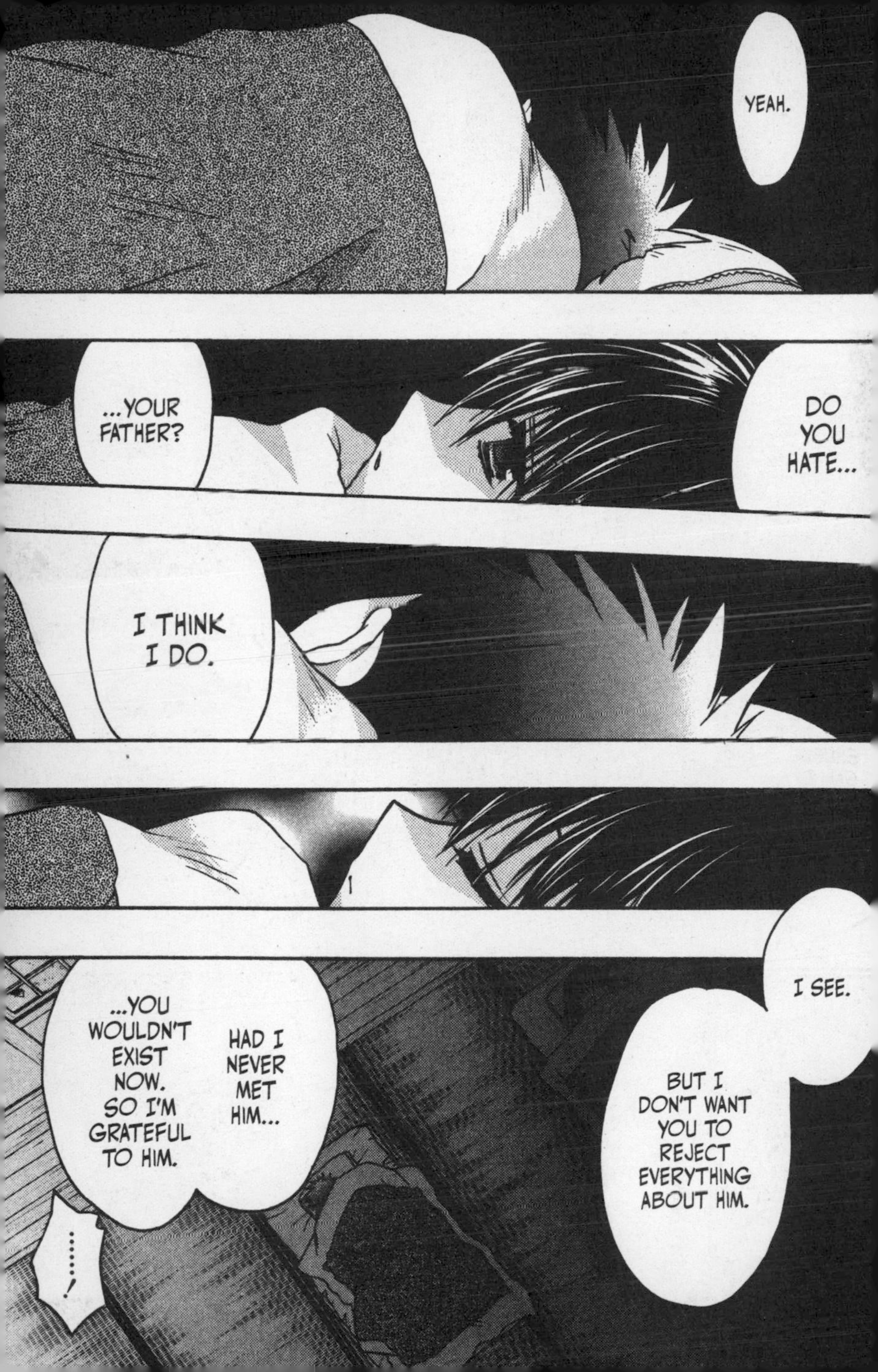
YEAH.
DO YOU HATE...
...YOUR FATHER?
I THINK I DO.
I SEE.
BUT I DON'T WANT YOU TO REJECT EVERYTHING ABOUT HIM.
HAD I NEVER MET HIM...
...YOU WOULDN'T EXIST NOW. SO I'M GRATEFUL TO HIM.
......!

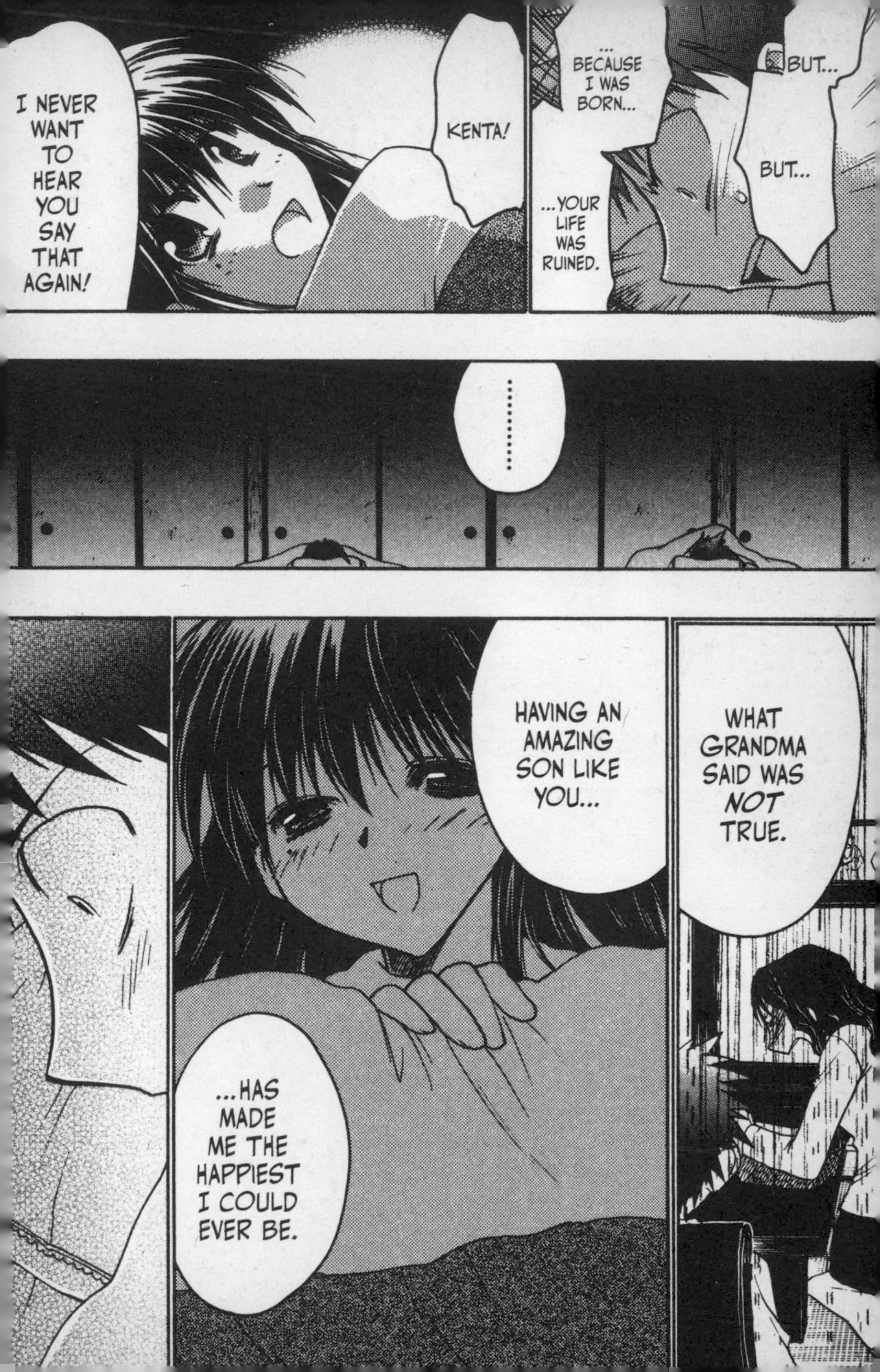
BUT...
BUT...
... BECAUSE I WAS BORN...
...YOUR LIFE WAS RUINED.
KENTA!
I NEVER WANT TO HEAR YOU SAY THAT AGAIN!
......
WHAT GRANDMA SAID WAS *NOT* TRUE.
HAVING AN AMAZING SON LIKE YOU...
...HAS MADE ME THE HAPPIEST I COULD EVER BE.

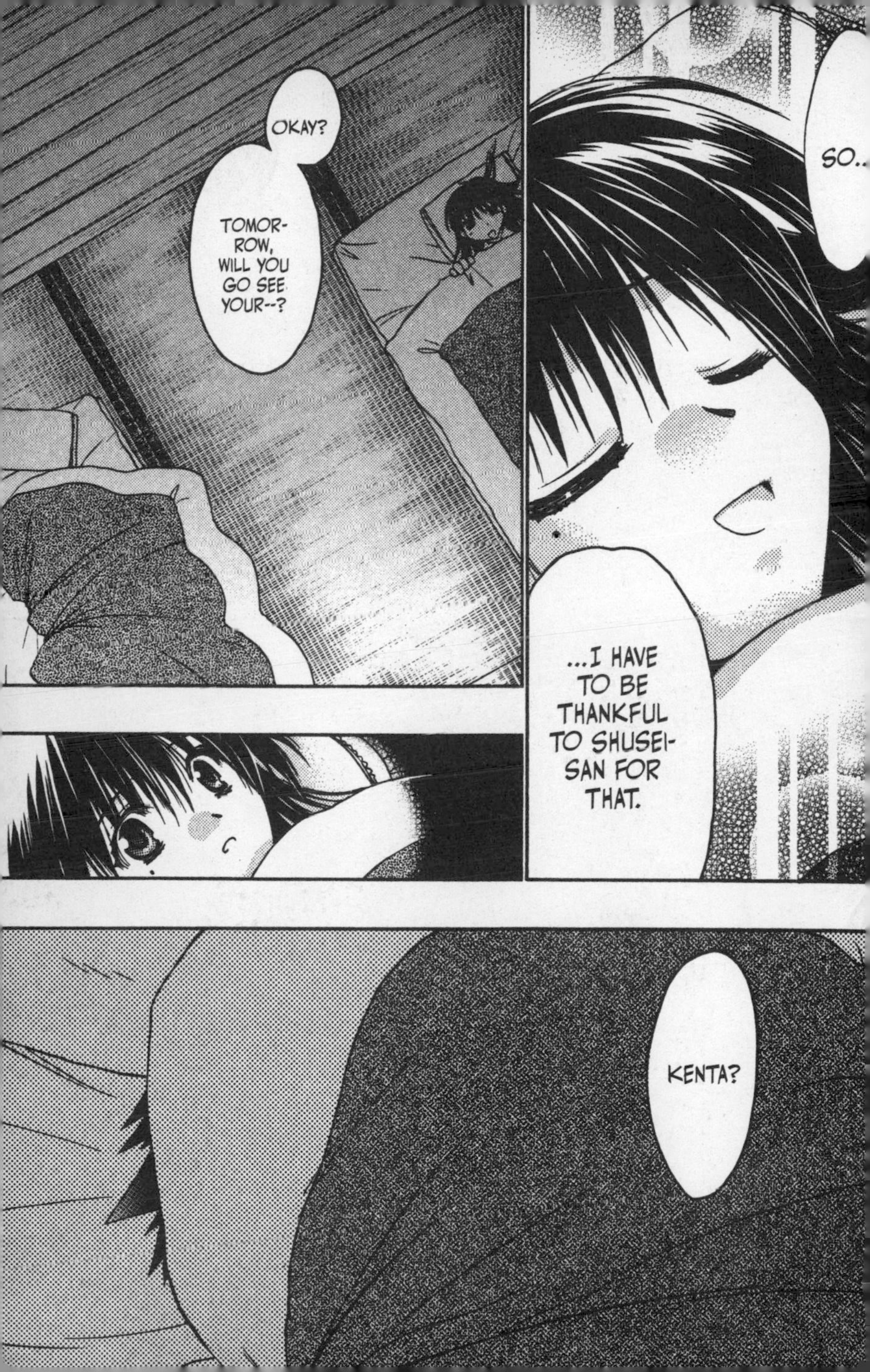
SO..
...I HAVE TO BE THANKFUL TO SHUSEI-SAN FOR THAT.
TOMOR-ROW, WILL YOU GO SEE YOUR--?
OKAY?
KENTA?

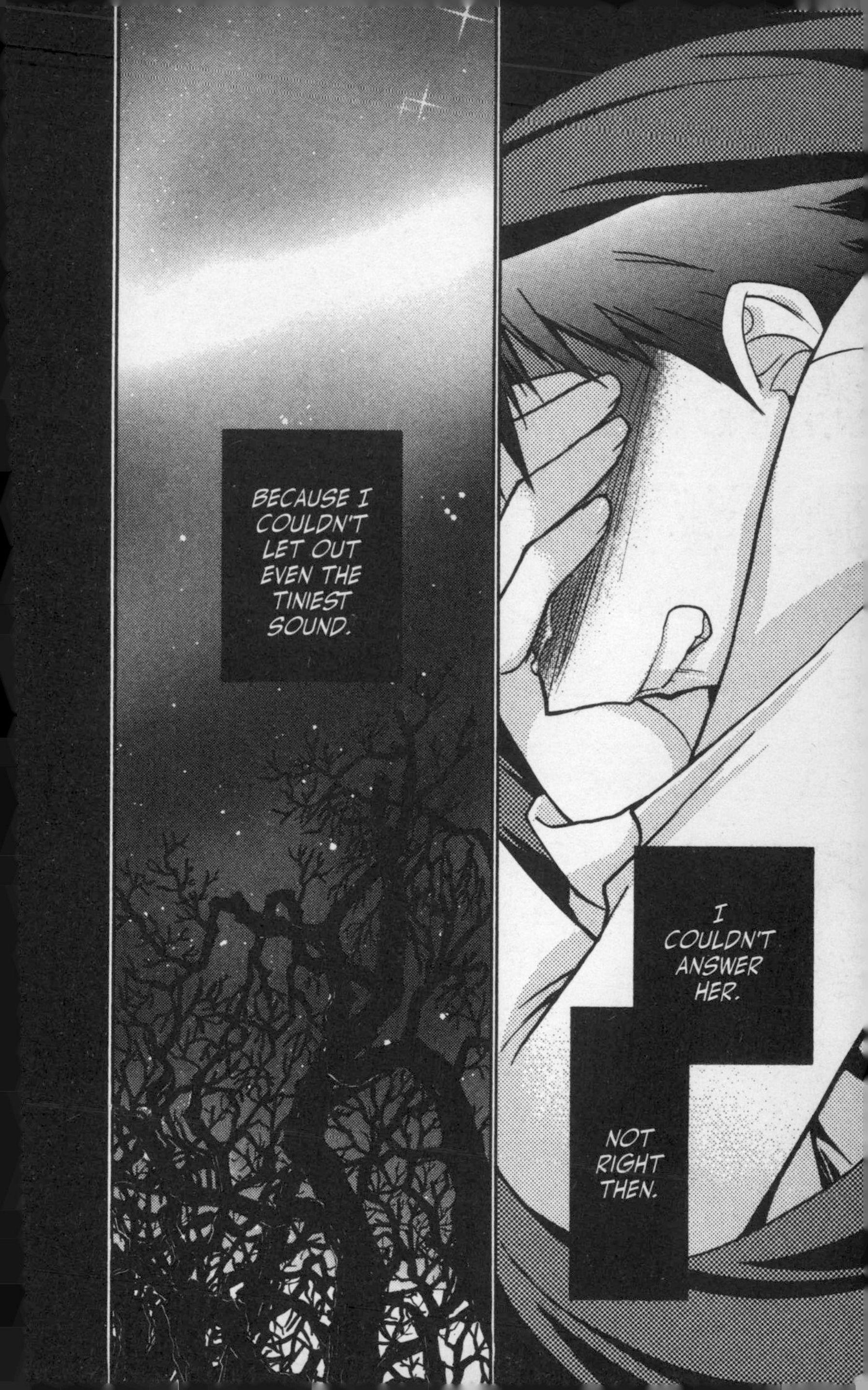
I COULDN'T ANSWER HER.
NOT RIGHT THEN.
BECAUSE I COULDN'T LET OUT EVEN THE TINIEST SOUND.

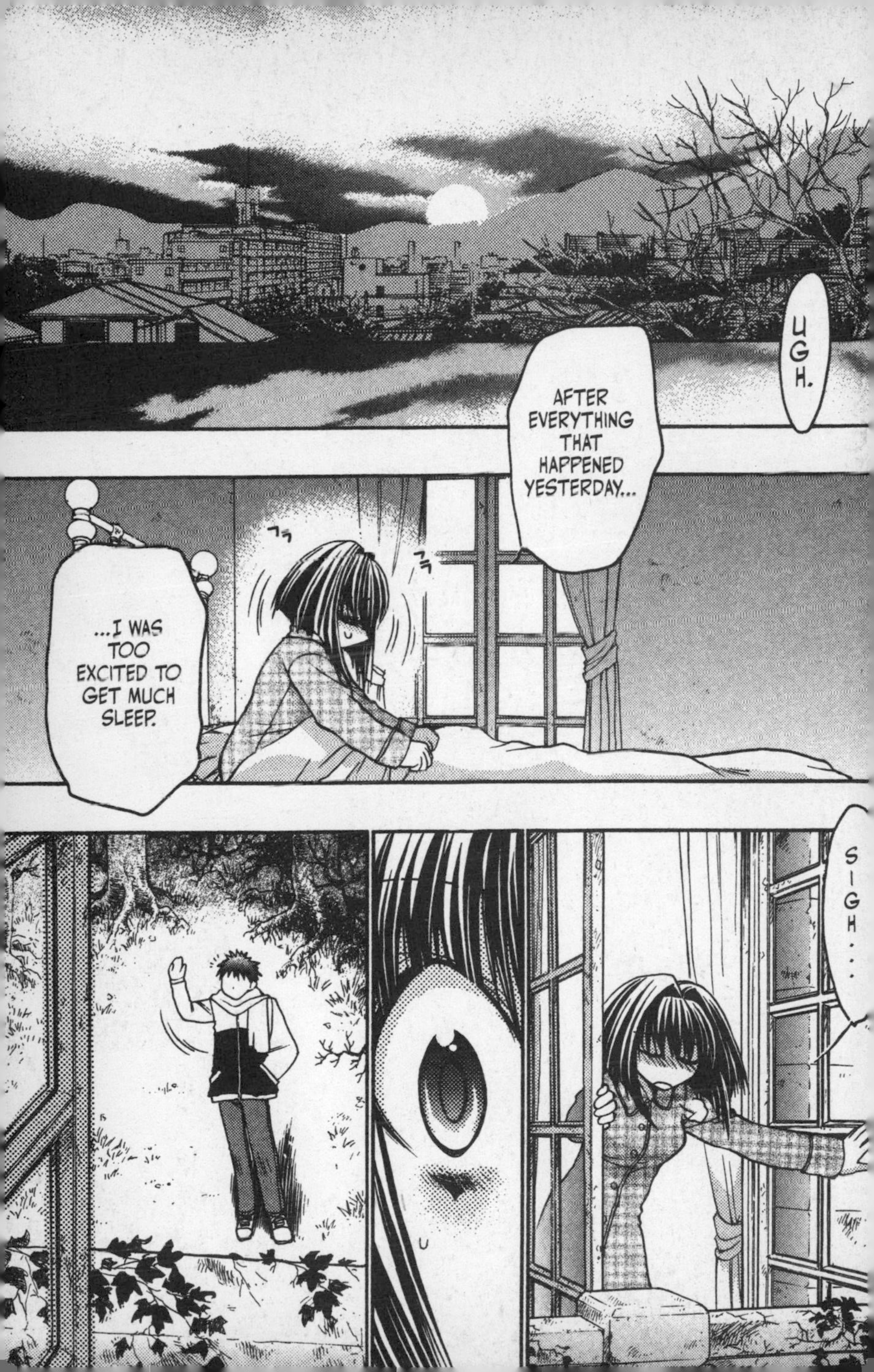
UGH.
AFTER EVERYTHING THAT HAPPENED YESTERDAY...
フラ
フラ
...I WAS TOO EXCITED TO GET MUCH SLEEP.
SIGH...

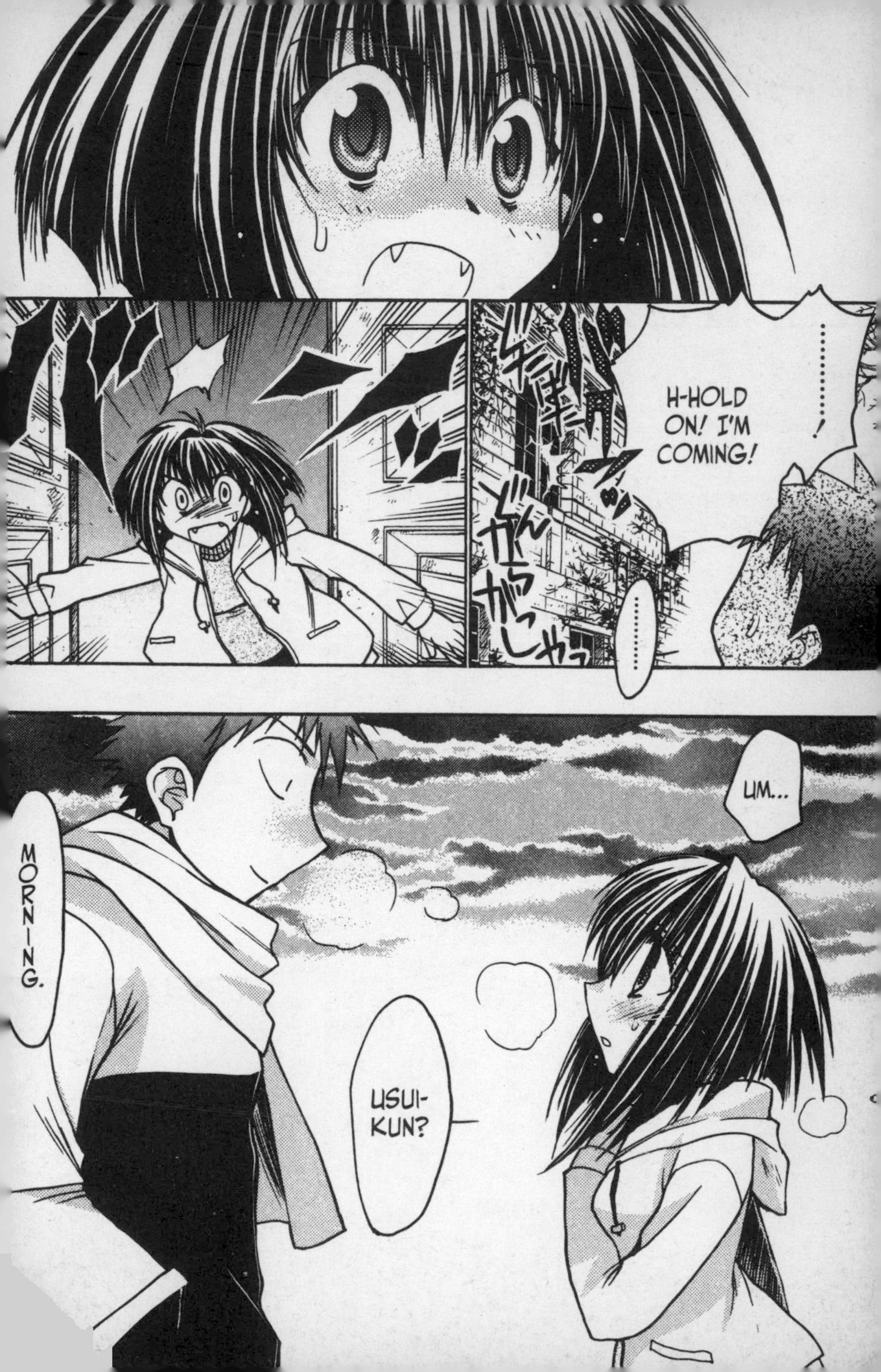
......!
H-HOLD ON! I'M COMING!
......
UM...
USUI-KUN?
MORNING.

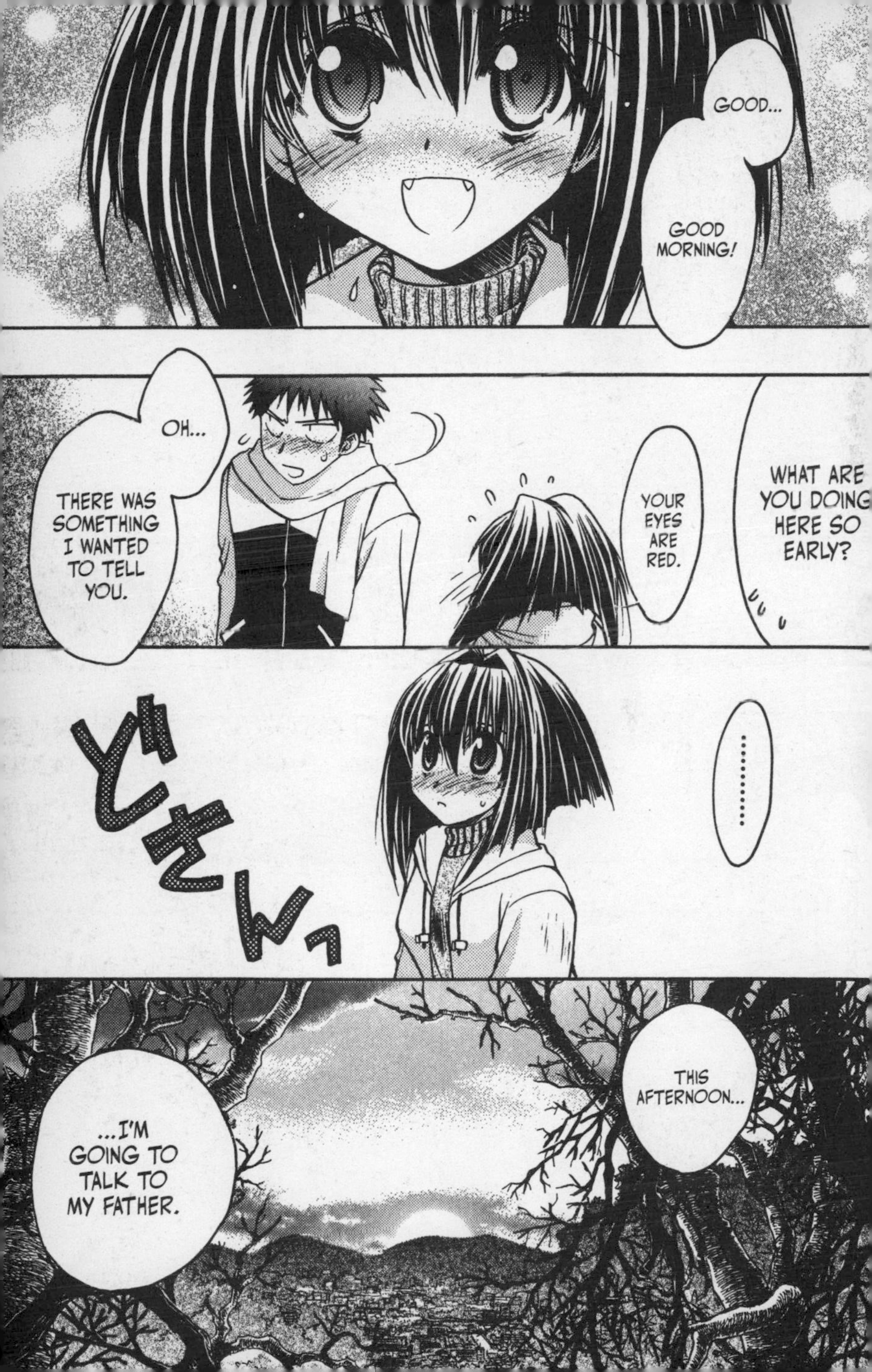

GOOD...
GOOD MORNING!
WHAT ARE YOU DOING HERE SO EARLY?
YOUR EYES ARE RED.
OH...
THERE WAS SOMETHING I WANTED TO TELL YOU.
......
どきんっ
THIS AFTERNOON...
...I'M GOING TO TALK TO MY FATHER.

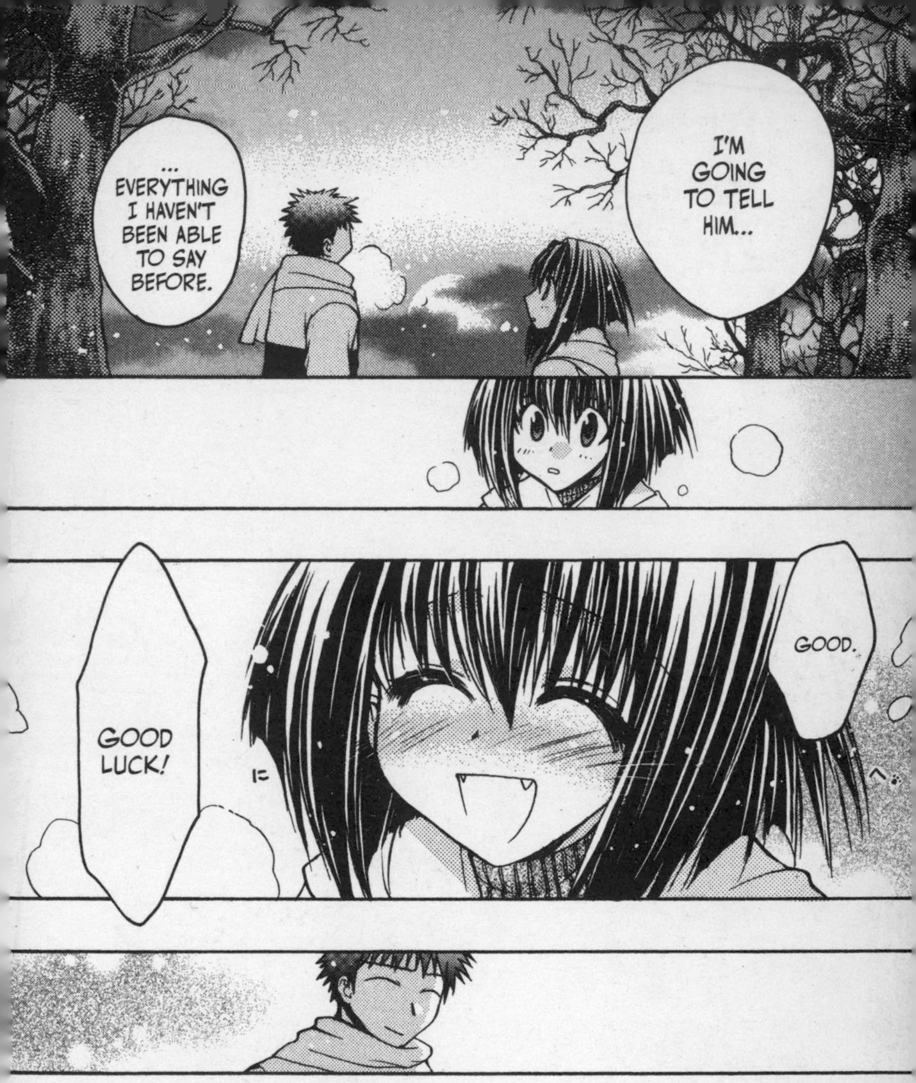
I'M GOING TO TELL HIM...
... EVERYTHING I HAVEN'T BEEN ABLE TO SAY BEFORE.
GOOD.
に
GOOD LUCK!

I WAS SO HAPPY THAT HE HAD COME TO TELL ME THAT.

BUT, OH, USUI-KUN, THIS DOESN'T MEAN I'LL NEVER SEE YOU AGAIN, DOES IT?

9TH EMBARRASSMENT END

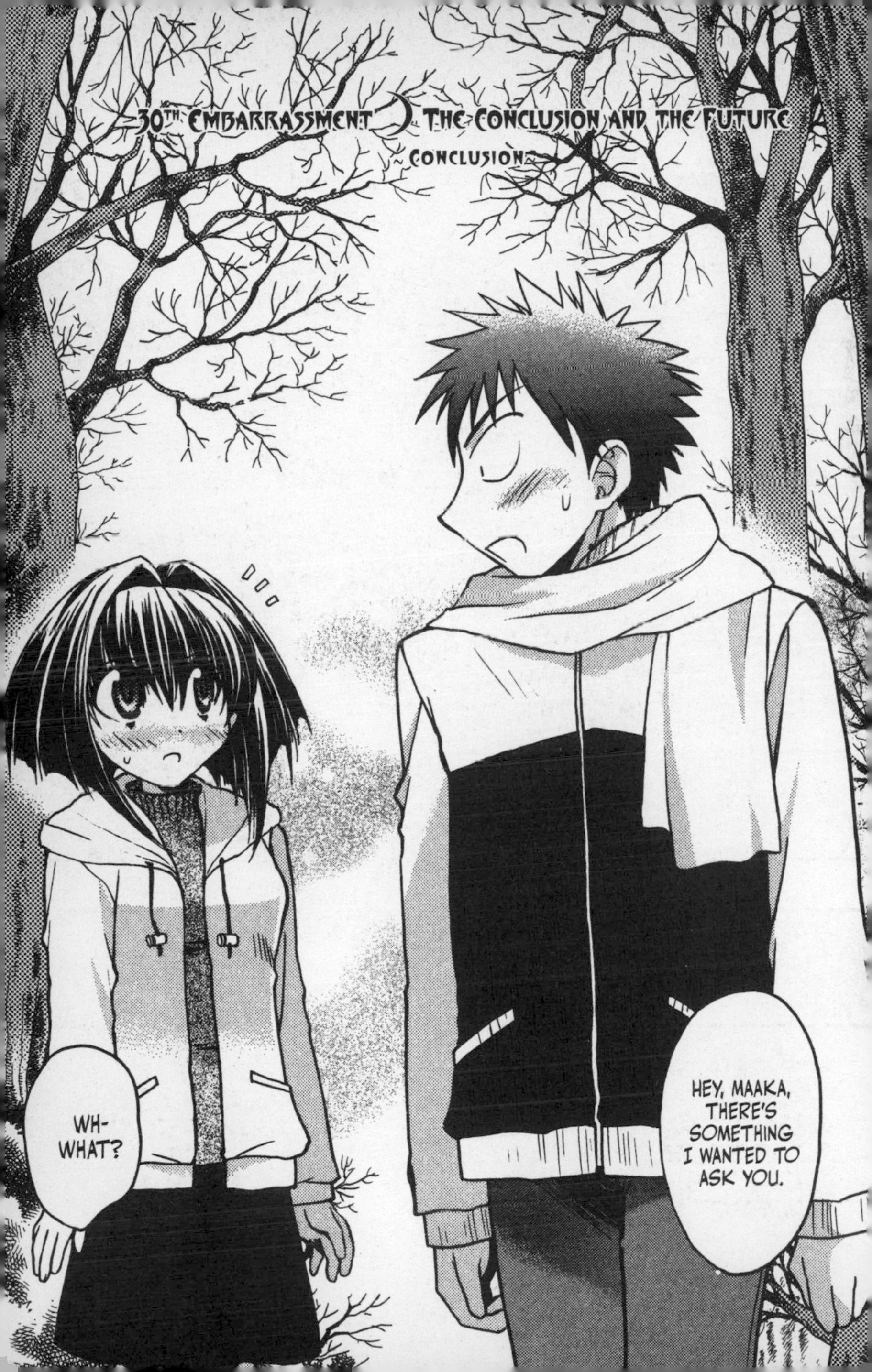
30th Embarrassment: The Conclusion and the Future
~Conclusion~
HEY, MAAKA, THERE'S SOMETHING I WANTED TO ASK YOU.
WH- WHAT?

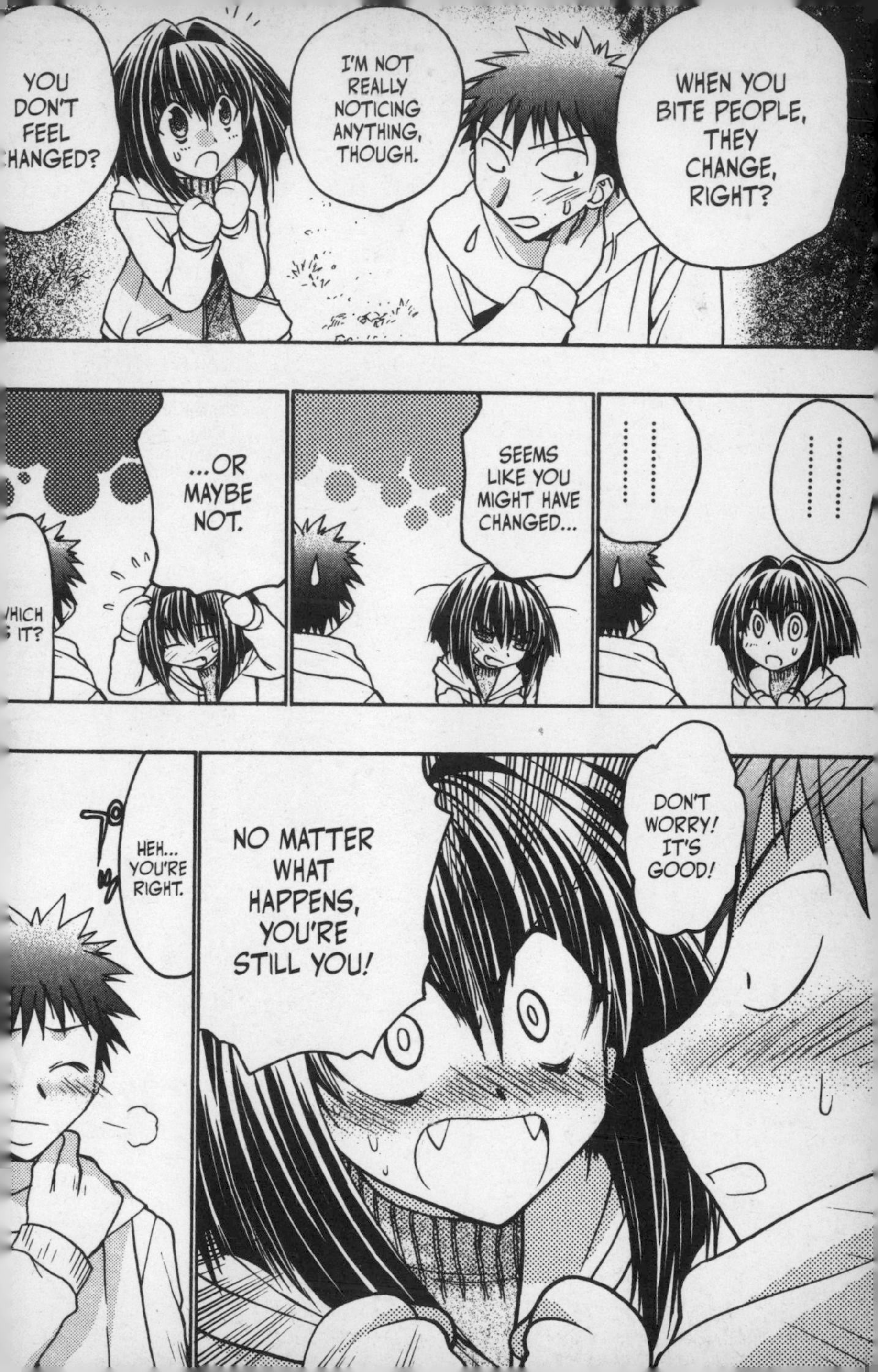
WHEN YOU BITE PEOPLE, THEY CHANGE, RIGHT?
I'M NOT REALLY NOTICING ANYTHING, THOUGH.
YOU DON'T FEEL HANGED?
......
......
SEEMS LIKE YOU MIGHT HAVE CHANGED...
...OR MAYBE NOT.
HICH IT?
DON'T WORRY! IT'S GOOD!
NO MATTER WHAT HAPPENS, YOU'RE STILL YOU!
HEH... YOU'RE RIGHT.

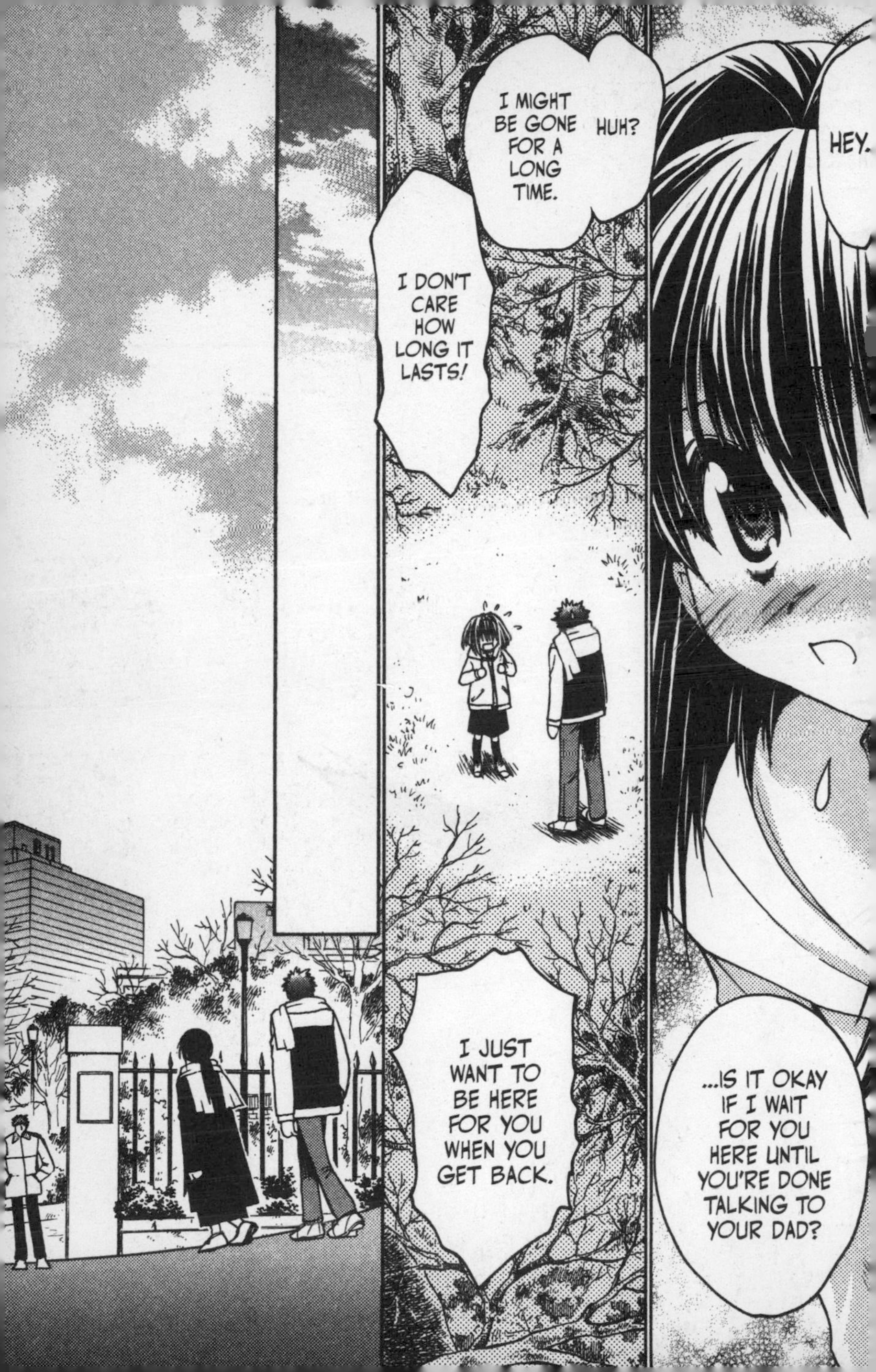
HEY.
...IS IT OKAY IF I WAIT FOR YOU HERE UNTIL YOU'RE DONE TALKING TO YOUR DAD?
HUH?
I MIGHT BE GONE FOR A LONG TIME.
I DON'T CARE HOW LONG IT LASTS!
I JUST WANT TO BE HERE FOR YOU WHEN YOU GET BACK.

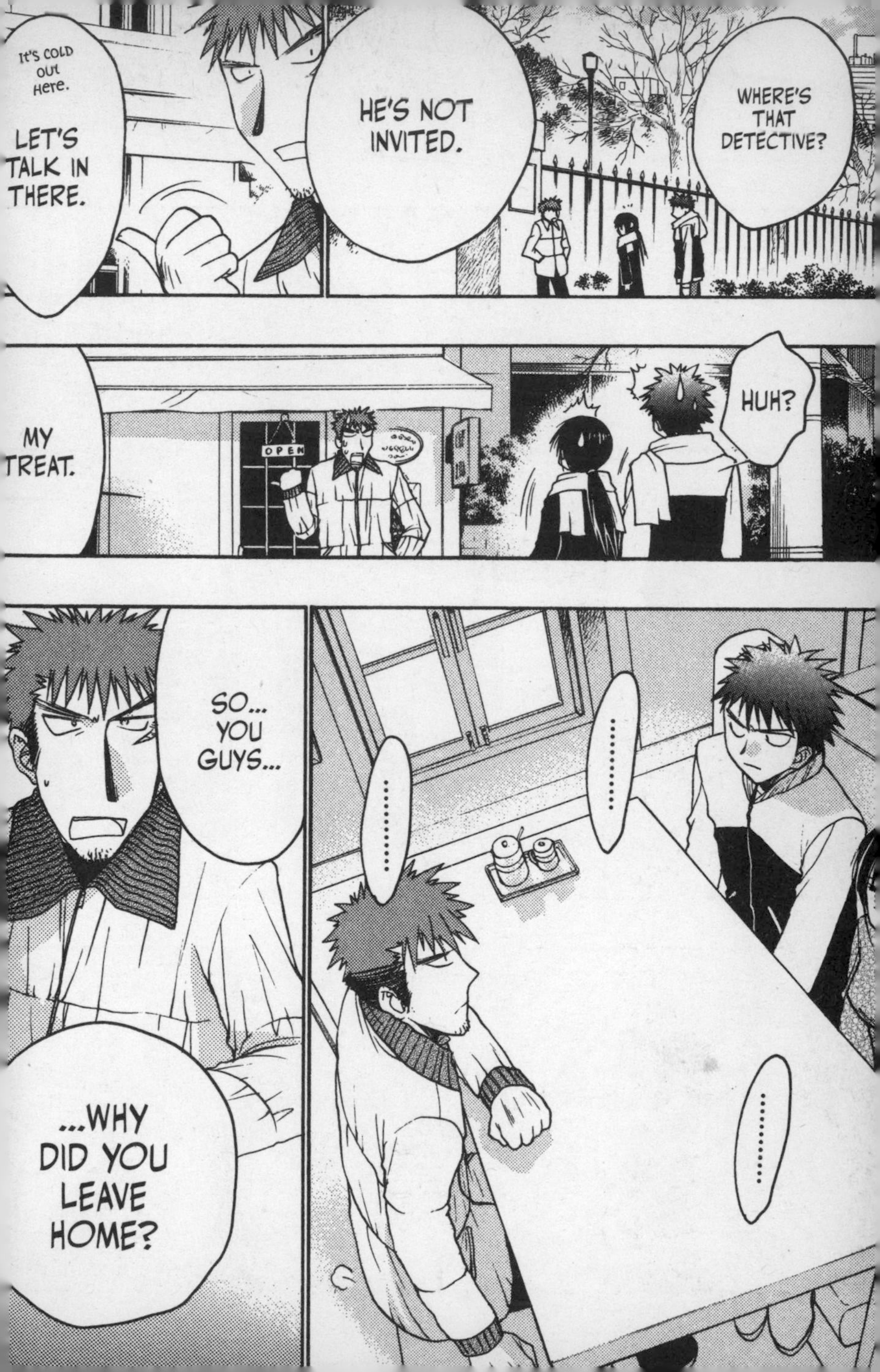
WHERE'S THAT DETECTIVE?
HE'S NOT INVITED.
It's COLD out Here.
LET'S TALK IN THERE.
HUH?
OPEN
MY TREAT.
....
....
....
SO... YOU GUYS...
...WHY DID YOU LEAVE HOME?

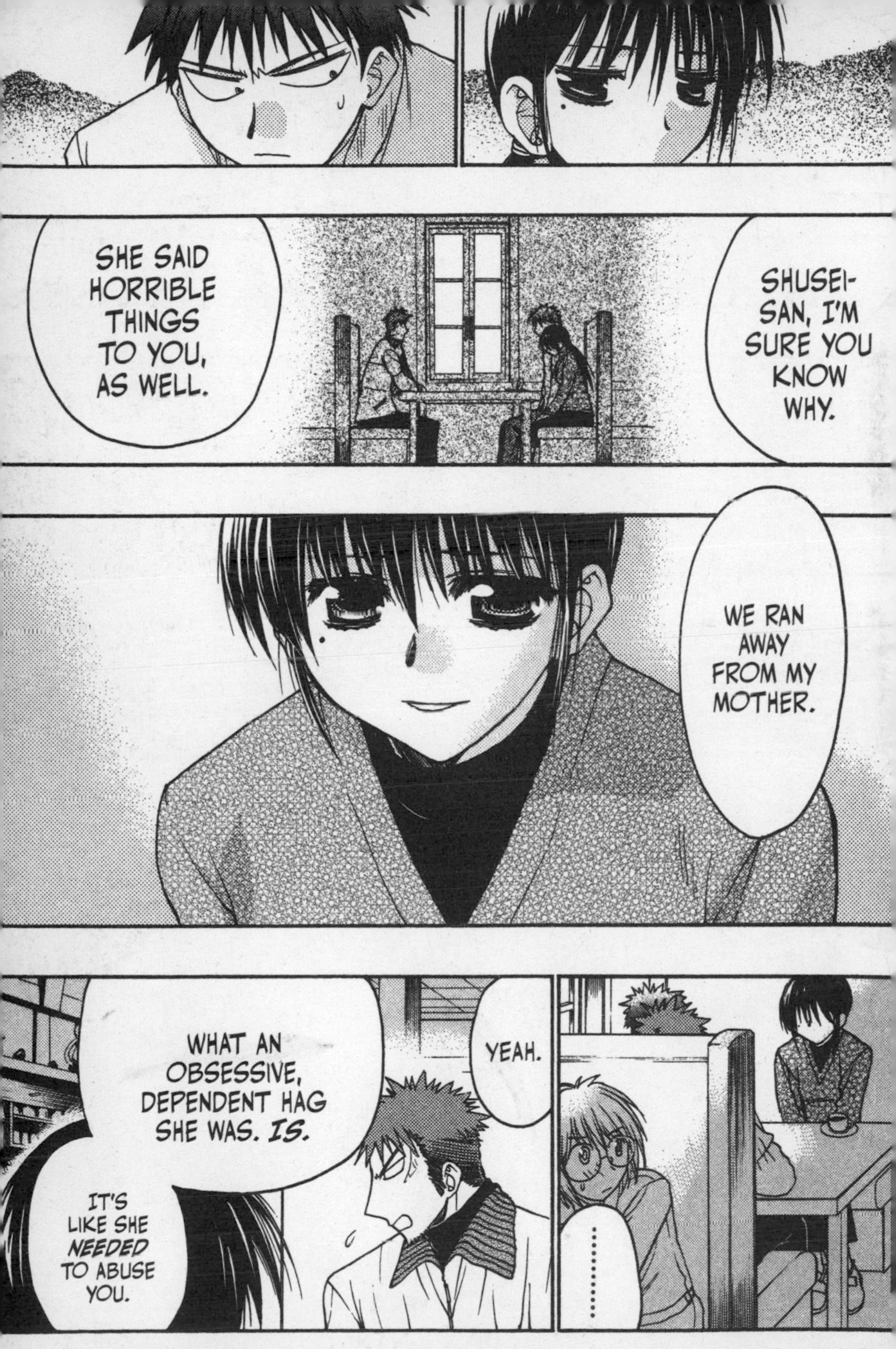
SHUSEI-SAN, I'M SURE YOU KNOW WHY.
SHE SAID HORRIBLE THINGS TO YOU, AS WELL.
WE RAN AWAY FROM MY MOTHER.
......
YEAH.
WHAT AN OBSESSIVE, DEPENDENT HAG SHE WAS. *IS.*
IT'S LIKE SHE *NEEDED* TO ABUSE YOU.

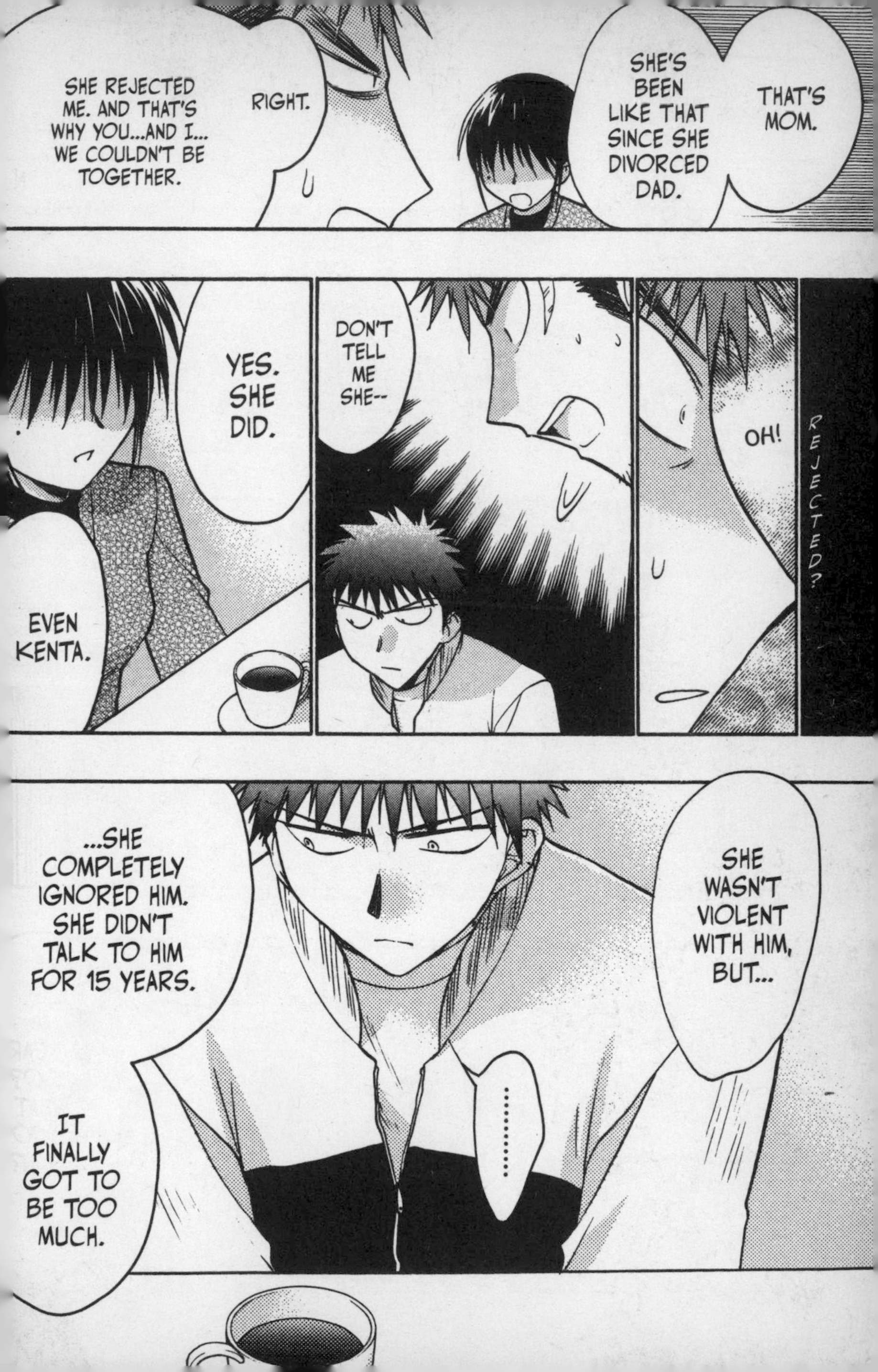
THAT'S MOM.
SHE'S BEEN LIKE THAT SINCE SHE DIVORCED DAD.
RIGHT.
SHE REJECTED ME. AND THAT'S WHY YOU...AND I... WE COULDN'T BE TOGETHER.
REJECTED?
OH!
DON'T TELL ME SHE--
YES. SHE DID.
EVEN KENTA.
SHE WASN'T VIOLENT WITH HIM, BUT...
......
...SHE COMPLETELY IGNORED HIM. SHE DIDN'T TALK TO HIM FOR 15 YEARS.
IT FINALLY GOT TO BE TOO MUCH.

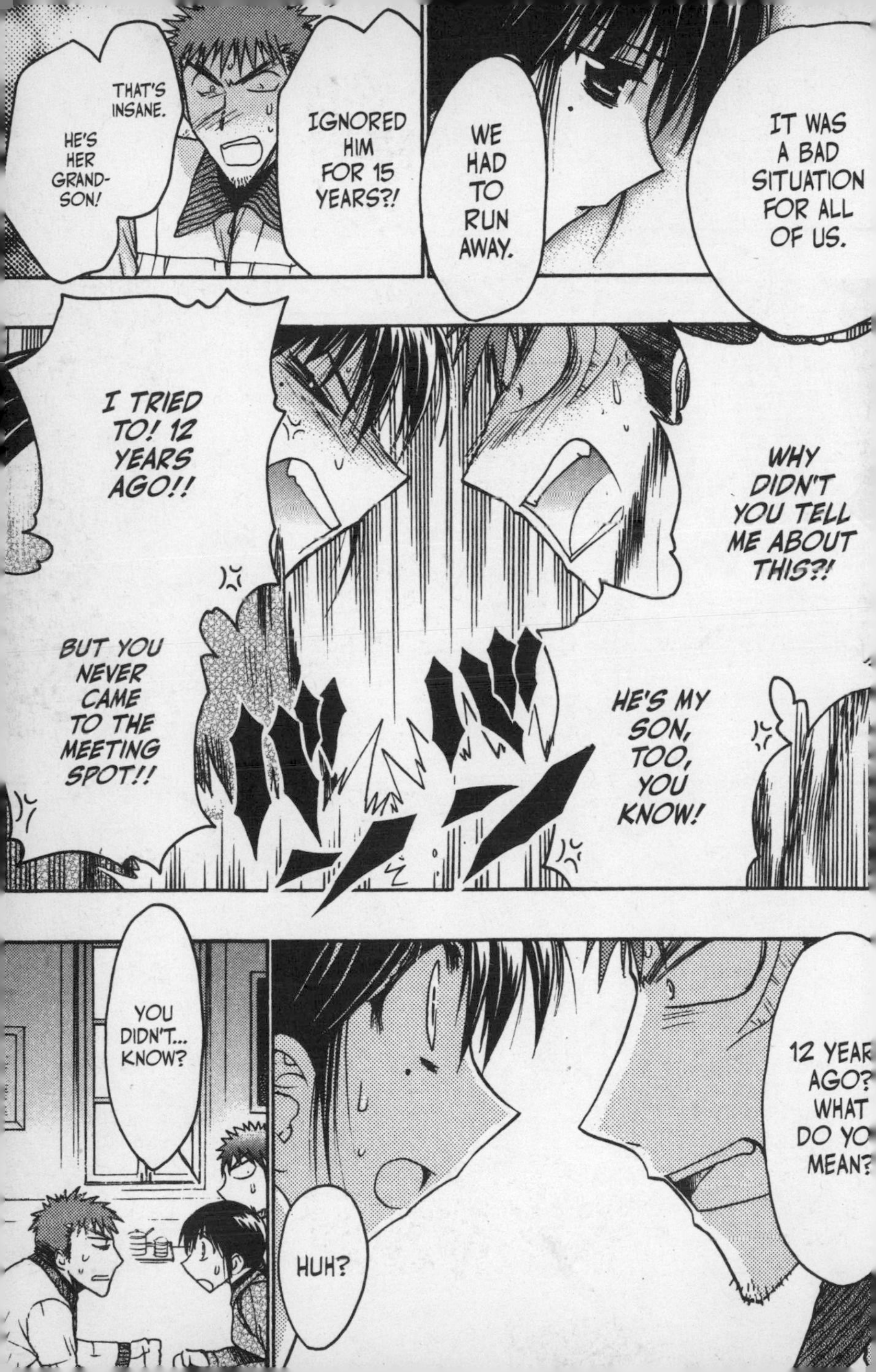
IT WAS A BAD SITUATION FOR ALL OF US.
WE HAD TO RUN AWAY.
IGNORED HIM FOR 15 YEARS?!
THAT'S INSANE.
HE'S HER GRAND-SON!
WHY DIDN'T YOU TELL ME ABOUT THIS?!
HE'S MY SON, TOO, YOU KNOW!
I TRIED TO! 12 YEARS AGO!!
BUT YOU NEVER CAME TO THE MEETING SPOT!!
12 YEAR AGO? WHAT DO YO MEAN?
HUH?
YOU DIDN'T... KNOW?

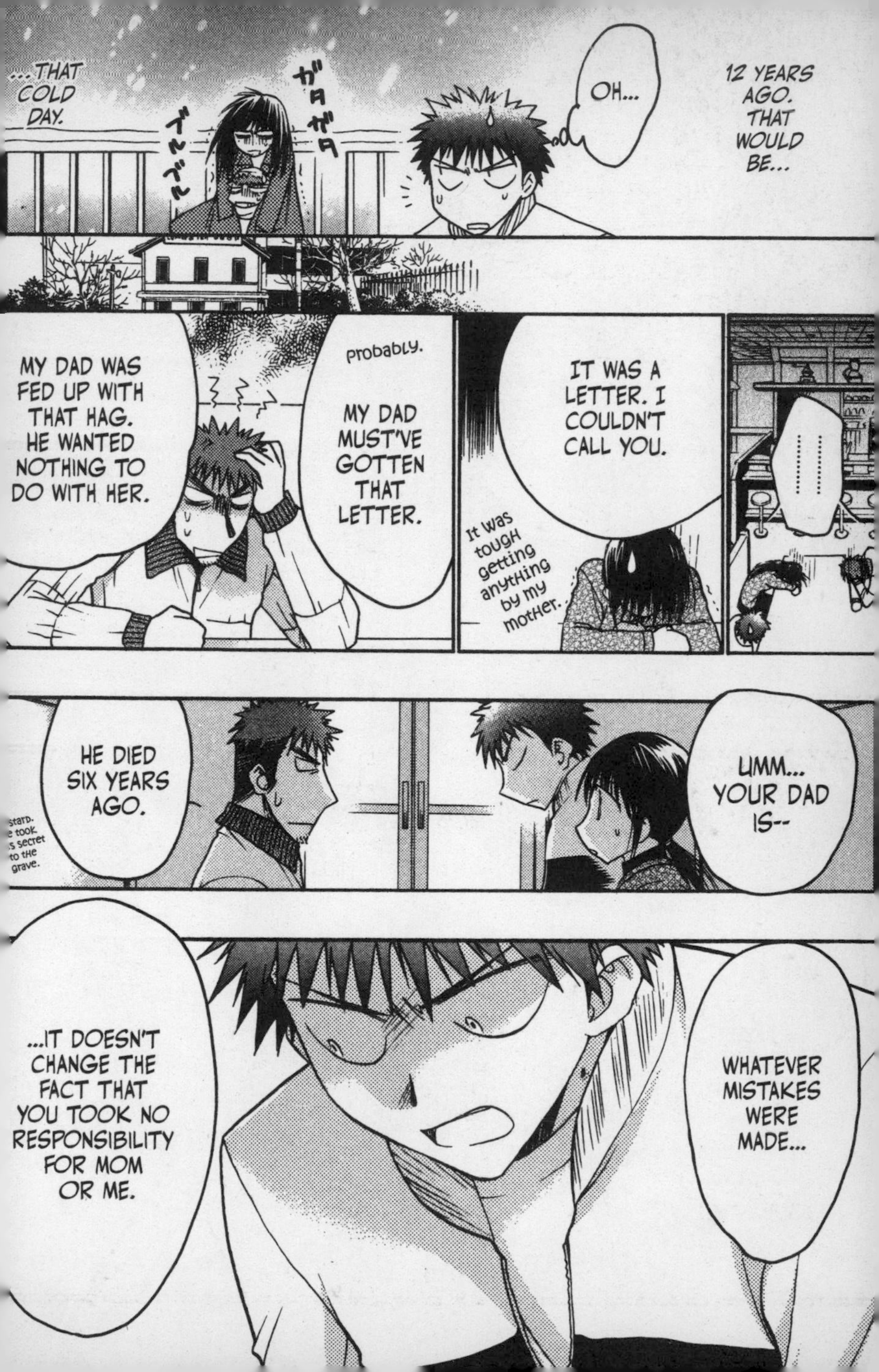
12 YEARS AGO. THAT WOULD BE...
OH...
ガタガタ
ブルブル
...THAT COLD DAY.
......
IT WAS A LETTER. I COULDN'T CALL YOU.
It was tough getting anything by my mother.
Probably.
MY DAD MUST'VE GOTTEN THAT LETTER.
MY DAD WAS FED UP WITH THAT HAG. HE WANTED NOTHING TO DO WITH HER.
UMM... YOUR DAD IS--
HE DIED SIX YEARS AGO.
to the grave.
WHATEVER MISTAKES WERE MADE...
...IT DOESN'T CHANGE THE FACT THAT YOU TOOK NO RESPONSIBILITY FOR MOM OR ME.

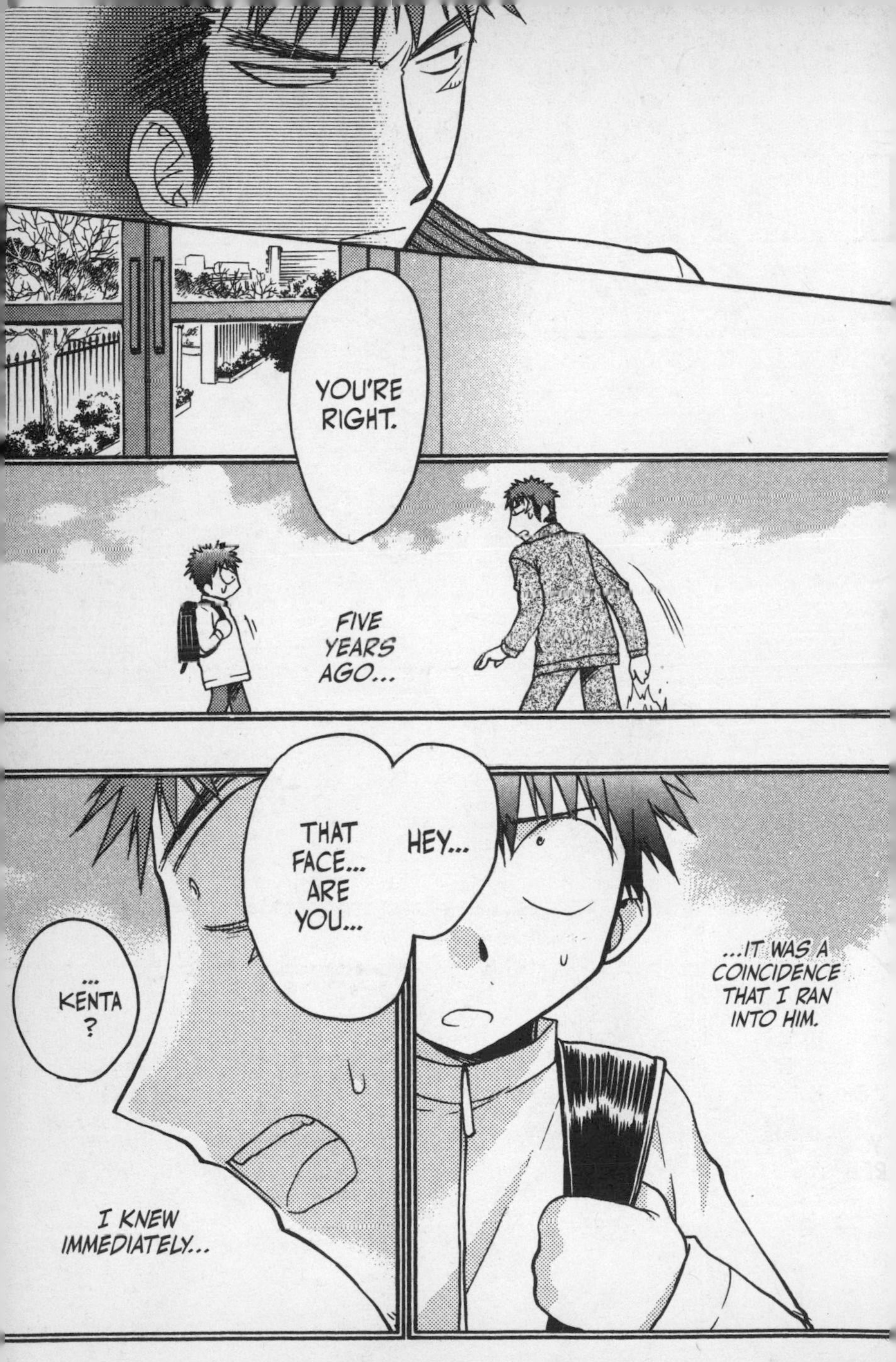
YOU'RE RIGHT.
FIVE YEARS AGO...
...IT WAS A COINCIDENCE THAT I RAN INTO HIM.
HEY...
THAT FACE... ARE YOU...
... KENTA ?
I KNEW IMMEDIATELY...

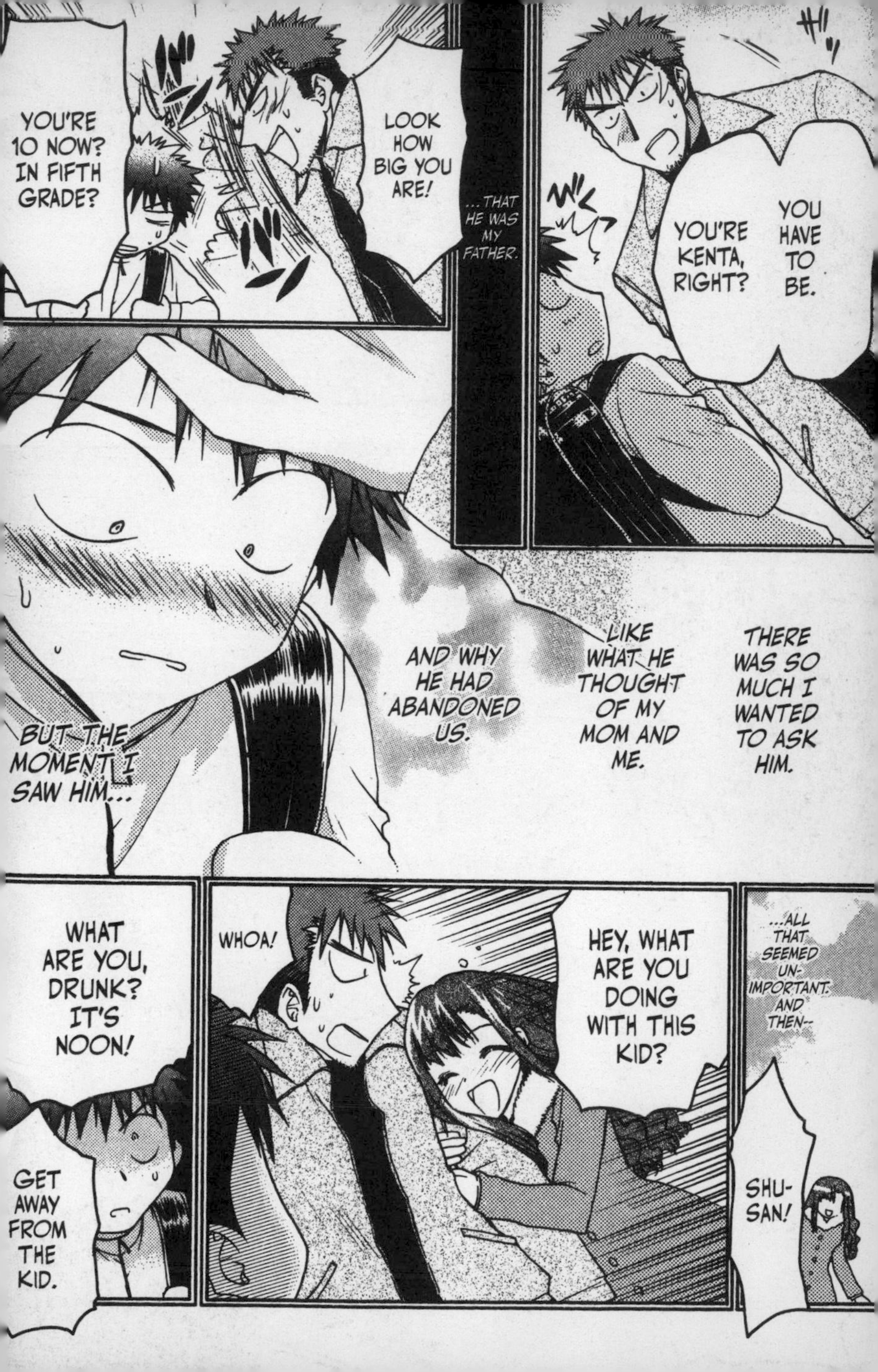
YOU'RE KENTA, RIGHT? YOU HAVE TO BE.
...THAT HE WAS MY FATHER.
LOOK HOW BIG YOU ARE!
YOU'RE 10 NOW? IN FIFTH GRADE?
THERE WAS SO MUCH I WANTED TO ASK HIM.
LIKE WHAT HE THOUGHT OF MY MOM AND ME.
AND WHY HE HAD ABANDONED US.
BUT THE MOMENT I SAW HIM...
...ALL THAT SEEMED UN-IMPORTANT. AND THEN--
SHU-SAN!
HEY, WHAT ARE YOU DOING WITH THIS KID?
WHOA!
WHAT ARE YOU, DRUNK? IT'S NOON!
GET AWAY FROM THE KID.

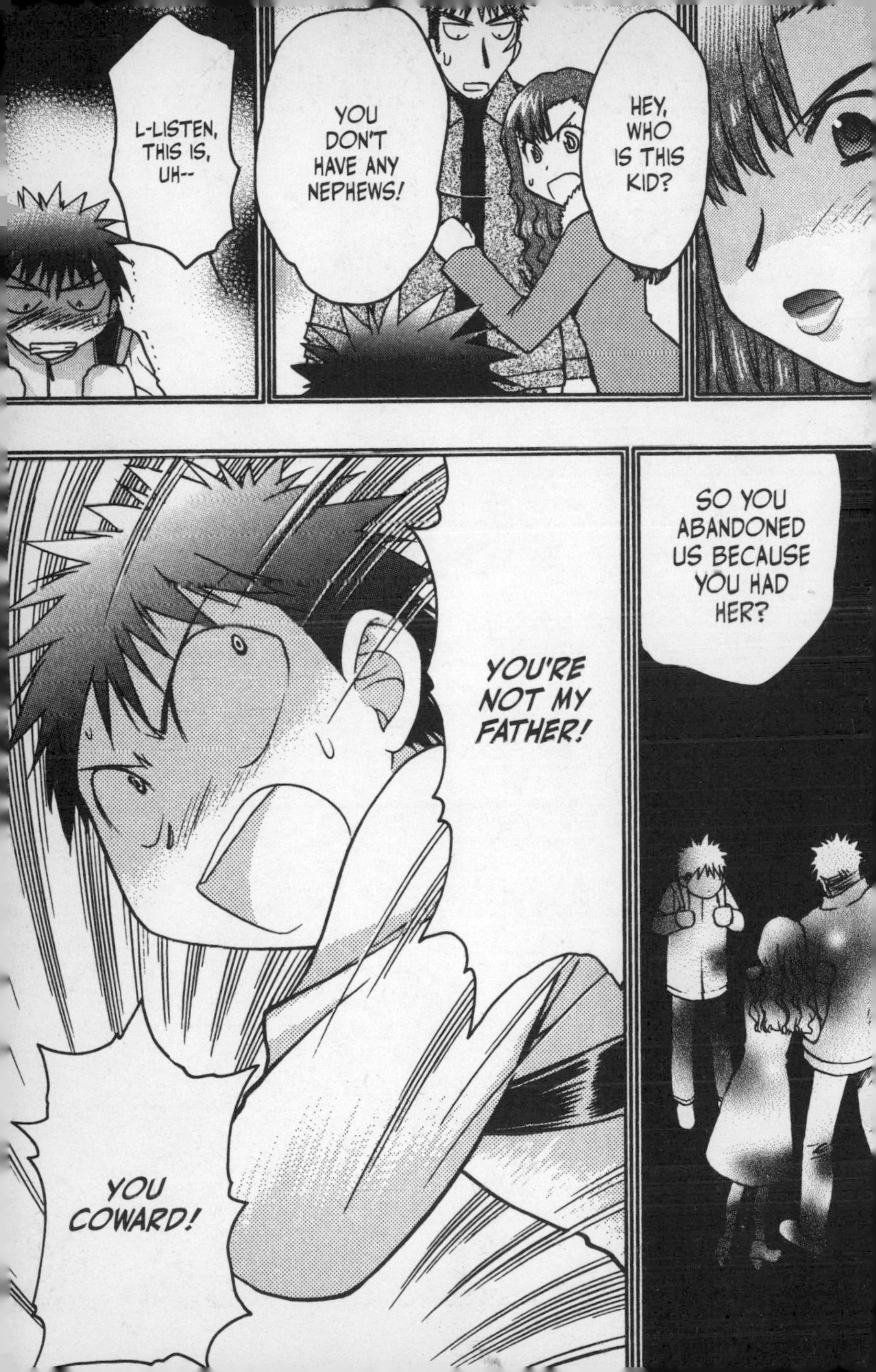
HEY, WHO IS THIS KID?
YOU DON'T HAVE ANY NEPHEWS!
L-LISTEN, THIS IS, UH--
SO YOU ABANDONED US BECAUSE YOU HAD HER?
YOU'RE NOT MY FATHER!
YOU COWARD!

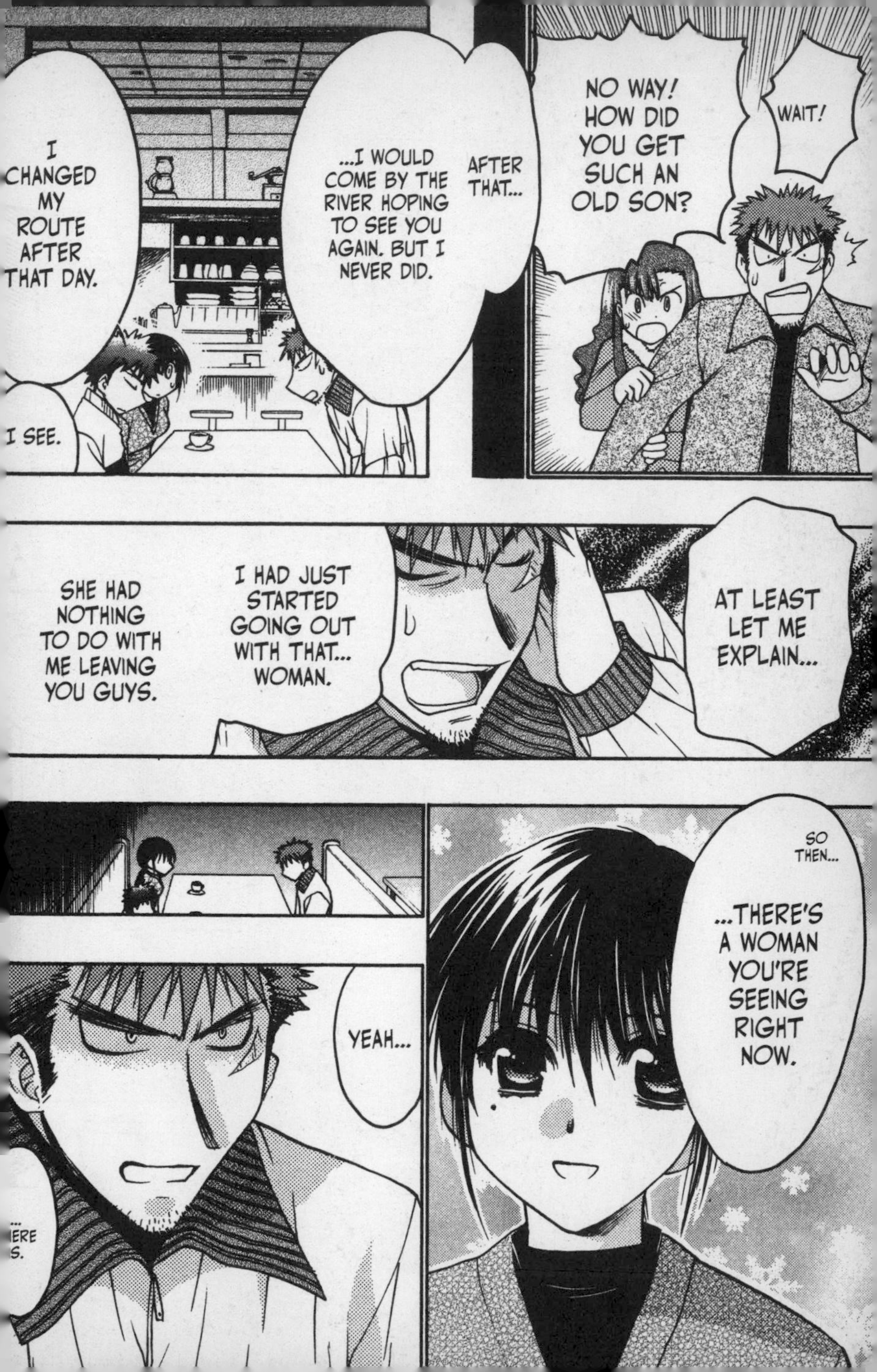
WAIT!
NO WAY! HOW DID YOU GET SUCH AN OLD SON?
AFTER THAT...
...I WOULD COME BY THE RIVER HOPING TO SEE YOU AGAIN. BUT I NEVER DID.
I CHANGED MY ROUTE AFTER THAT DAY.
I SEE.
AT LEAST LET ME EXPLAIN...
I HAD JUST STARTED GOING OUT WITH THAT... WOMAN.
SHE HAD NOTHING TO DO WITH ME LEAVING YOU GUYS.
SO THEN...
...THERE'S A WOMAN YOU'RE SEEING RIGHT NOW.
YEAH...

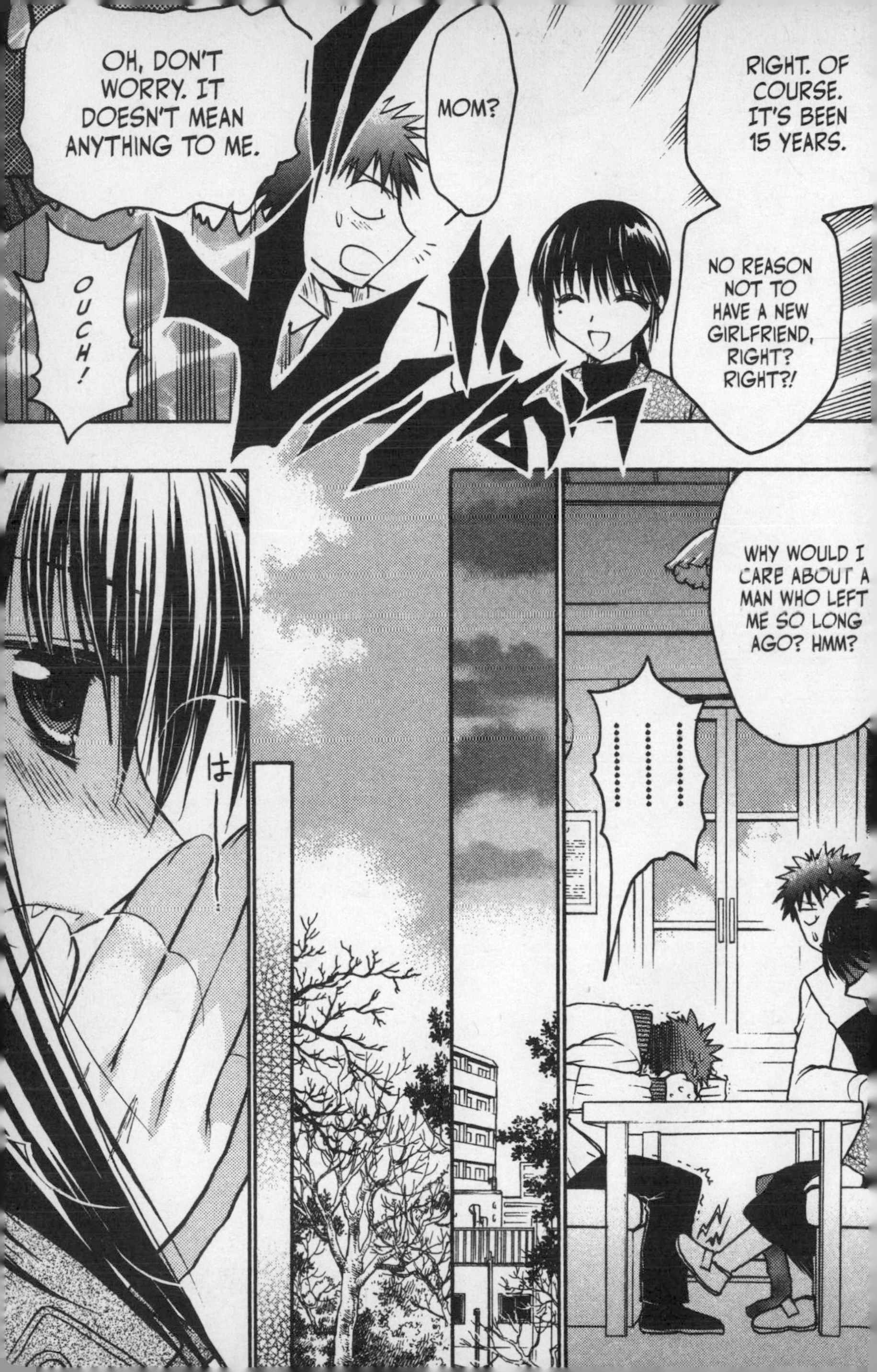
RIGHT. OF COURSE. IT'S BEEN 15 YEARS.
NO REASON NOT TO HAVE A NEW GIRLFRIEND, RIGHT? RIGHT?!
MOM?
OH, DON'T WORRY. IT DOESN'T MEAN ANYTHING TO ME.
OUCH!
WHY WOULD I CARE ABOUT A MAN WHO LEFT ME SO LONG AGO? HMM?
....
は―

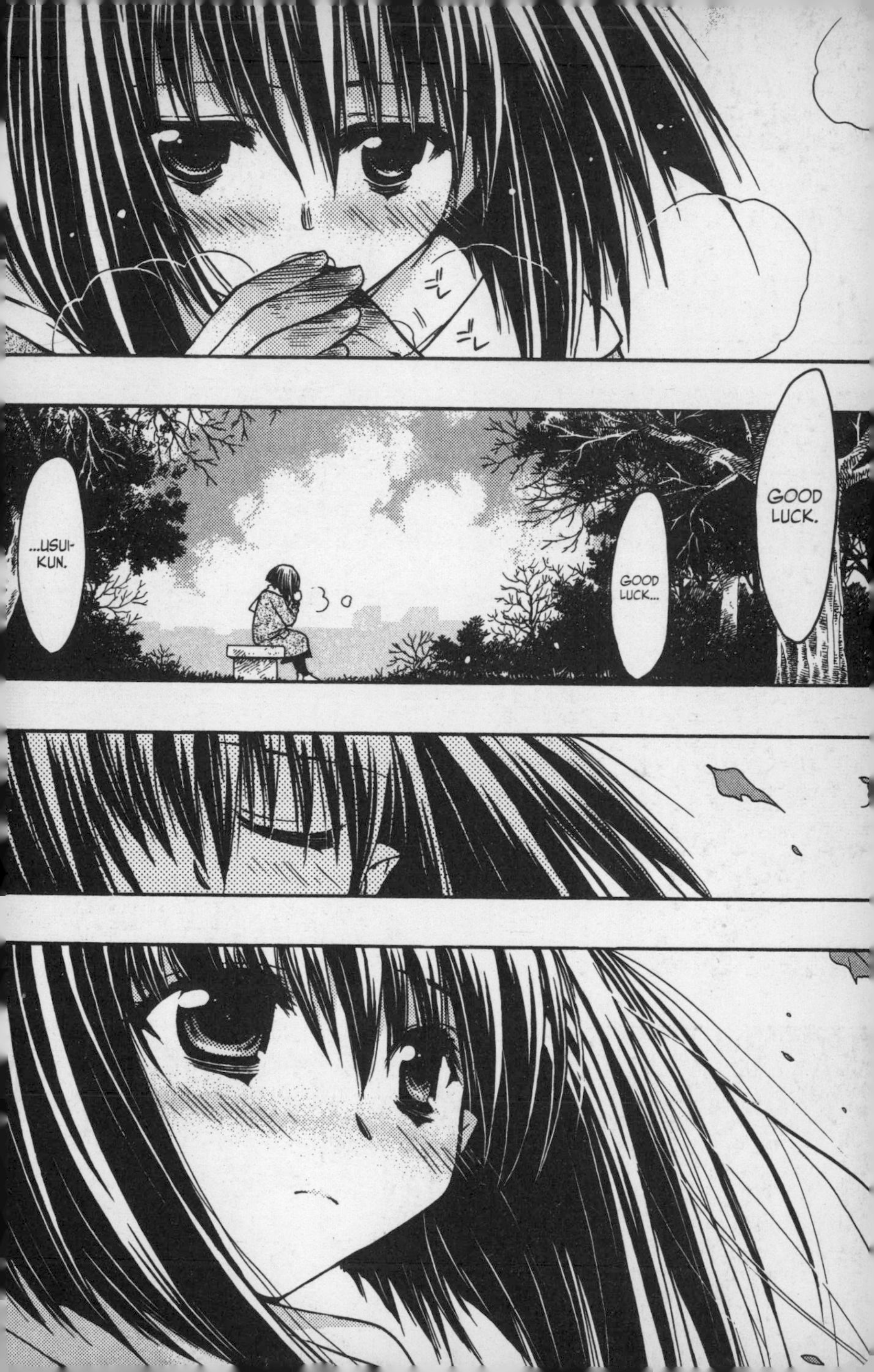
GOOD LUCK.
GOOD LUCK...
...USUI-KUN.

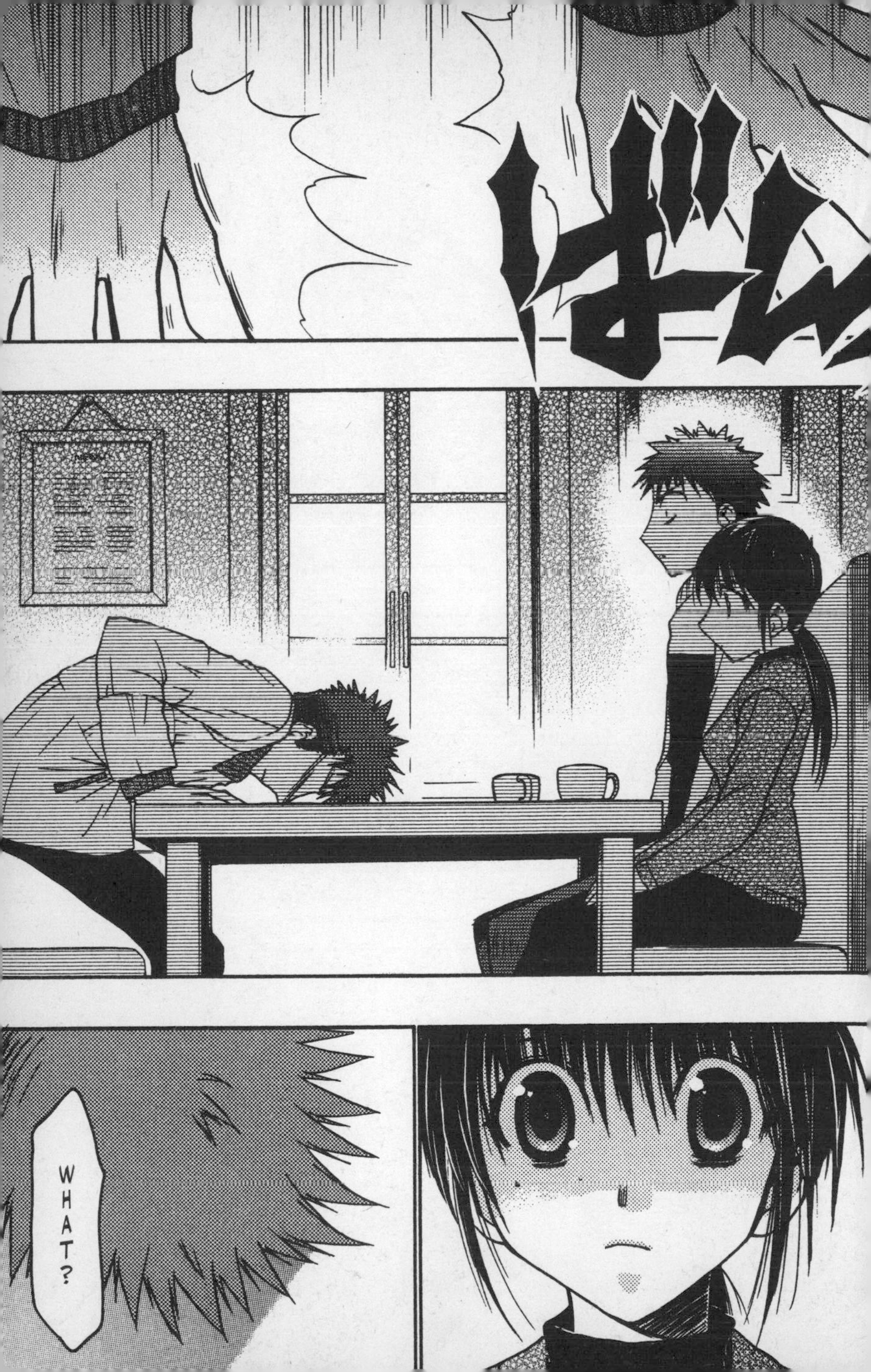
ばん
WHAT?

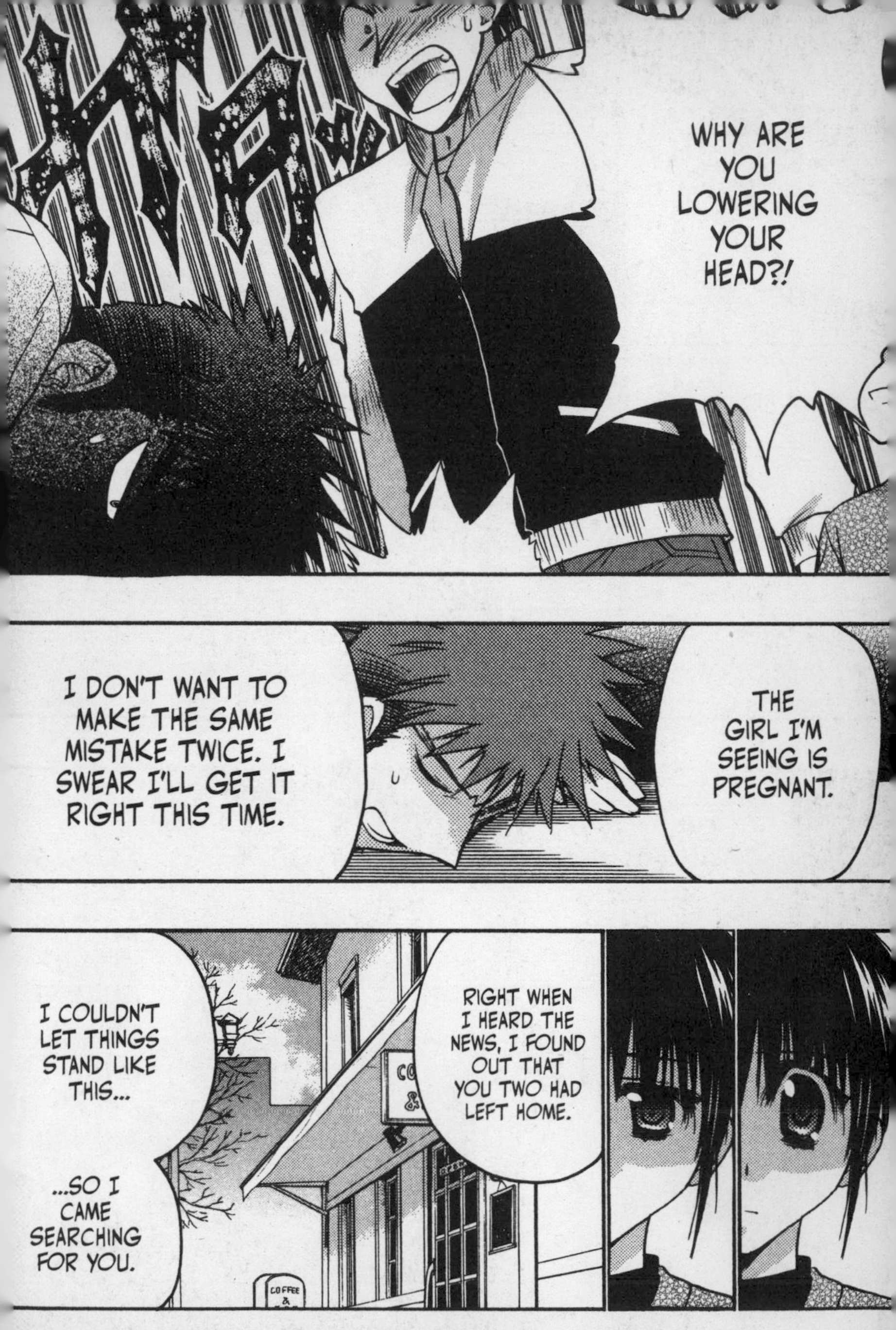
WHY ARE YOU LOWERING YOUR HEAD?!
THE GIRL I'M SEEING IS PREGNANT.
I DON'T WANT TO MAKE THE SAME MISTAKE TWICE. I SWEAR I'LL GET IT RIGHT THIS TIME.
RIGHT WHEN I HEARD THE NEWS, I FOUND OUT THAT YOU TWO HAD LEFT HOME.
I COULDN'T LET THINGS STAND LIKE THIS...
...SO I CAME SEARCHING FOR YOU.

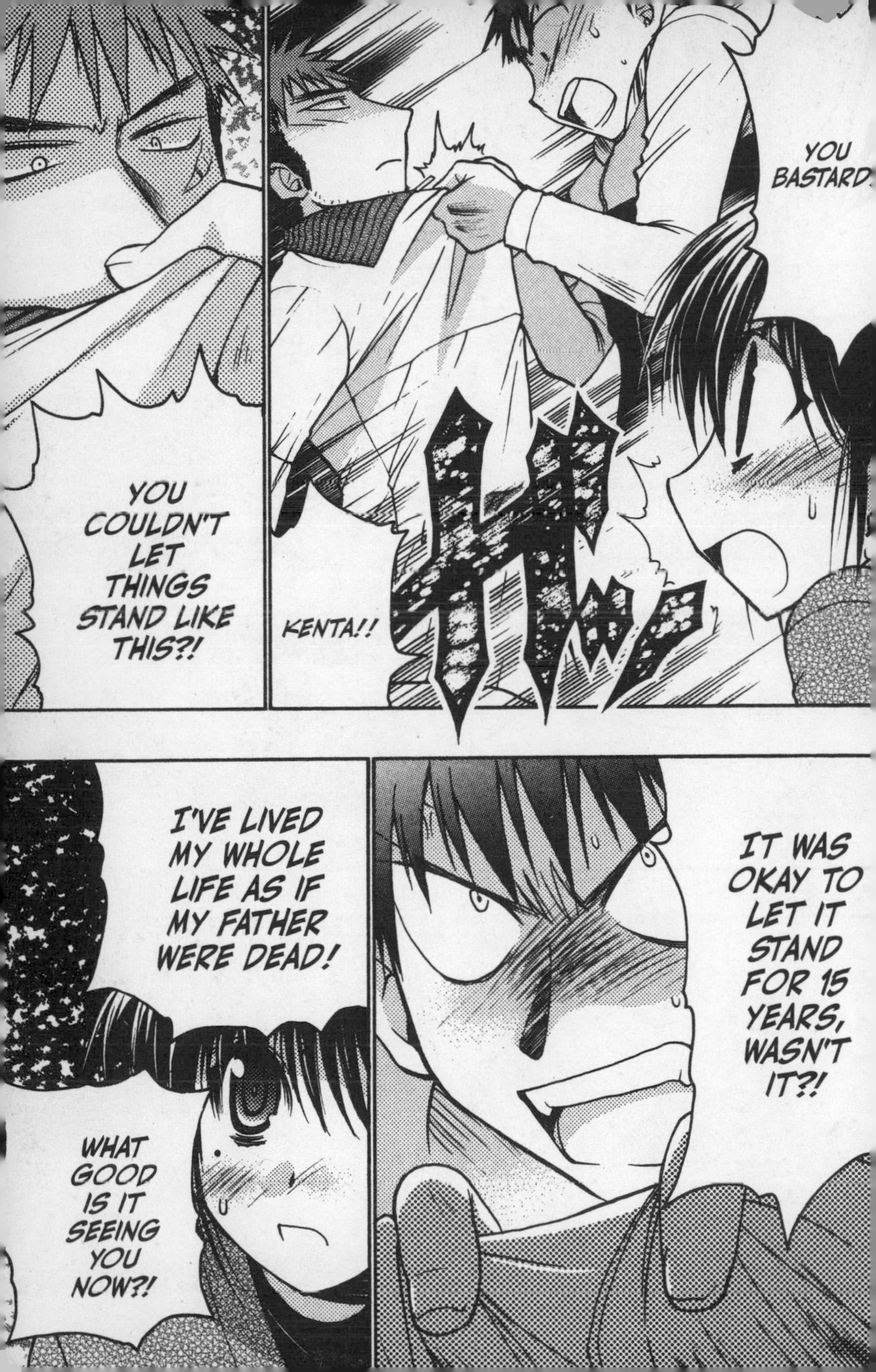
YOU BASTARD
KENTA!!
YOU COULDN'T LET THINGS STAND LIKE THIS?!
IT WAS OKAY TO LET IT STAND FOR 15 YEARS, WASN'T IT?!
I'VE LIVED MY WHOLE LIFE AS IF MY FATHER WERE DEAD!
WHAT GOOD IS IT SEEING YOU NOW?!

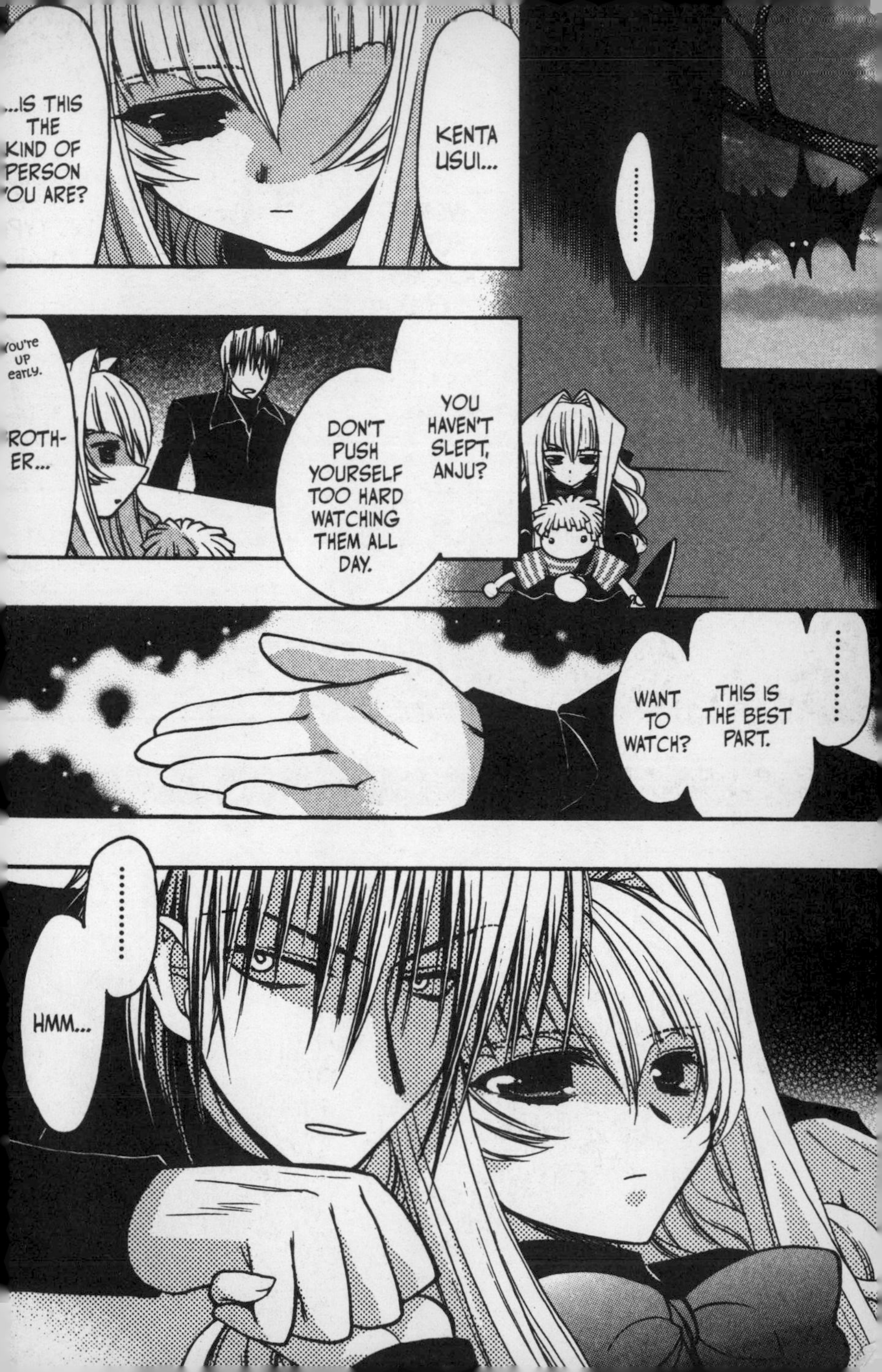
......
KENTA USUI...
...IS THIS THE KIND OF PERSON YOU ARE?
YOU HAVEN'T SLEPT, ANJU?
DON'T PUSH YOURSELF TOO HARD WATCHING THEM ALL DAY.
You're up early.
ROTH-ER...
......
THIS IS THE BEST PART.
WANT TO WATCH?
......
HMM...

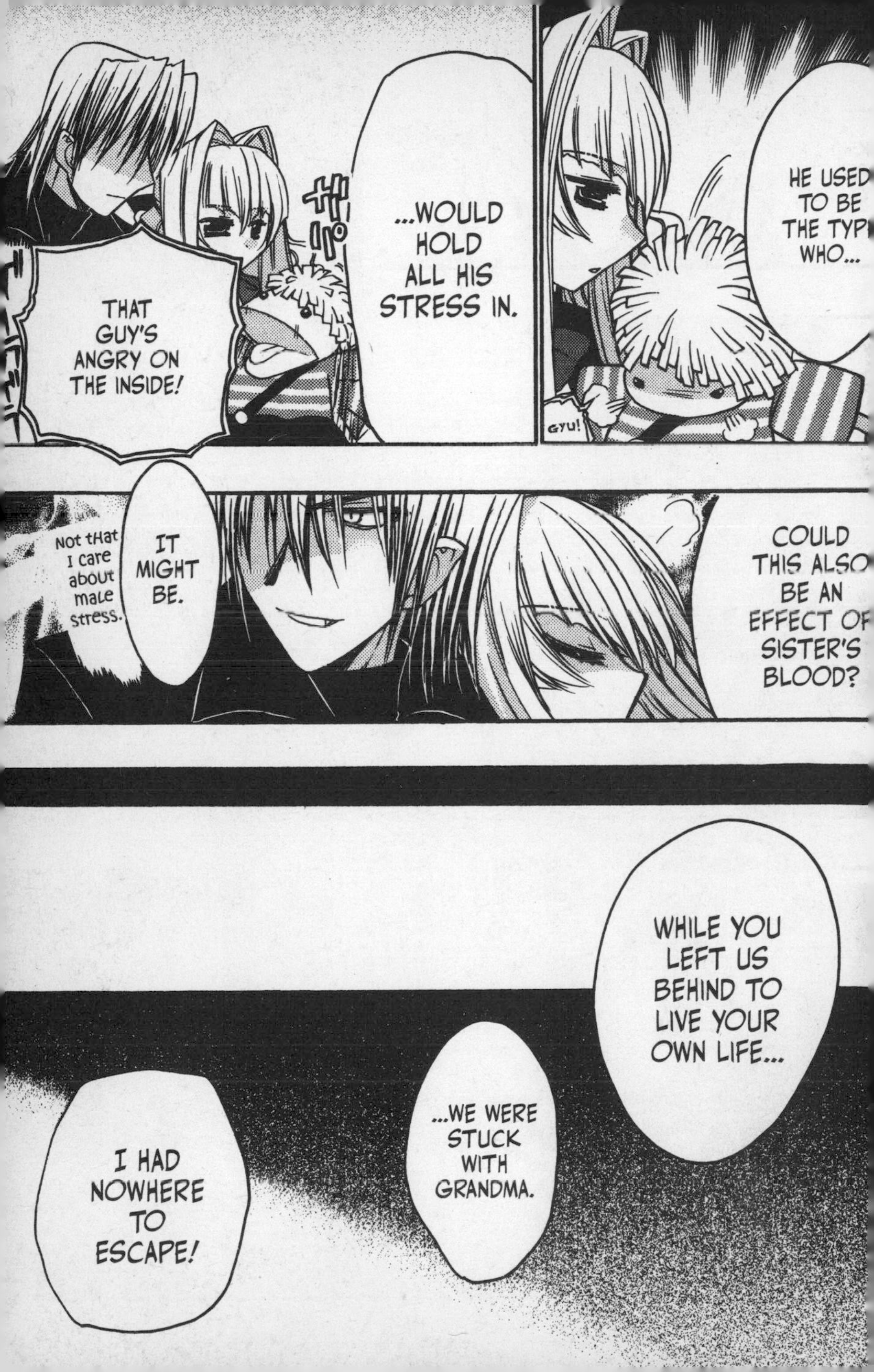
HE USED TO BE THE TYP WHO...
GYU!
...WOULD HOLD ALL HIS STRESS IN.
THAT GUY'S ANGRY ON THE INSIDE!
COULD THIS ALSO BE AN EFFECT OF SISTER'S BLOOD?
IT MIGHT BE.
Not that I care about male stress.
WHILE YOU LEFT US BEHIND TO LIVE YOUR OWN LIFE...
...WE WERE STUCK WITH GRANDMA.
I HAD NOWHERE TO ESCAPE!

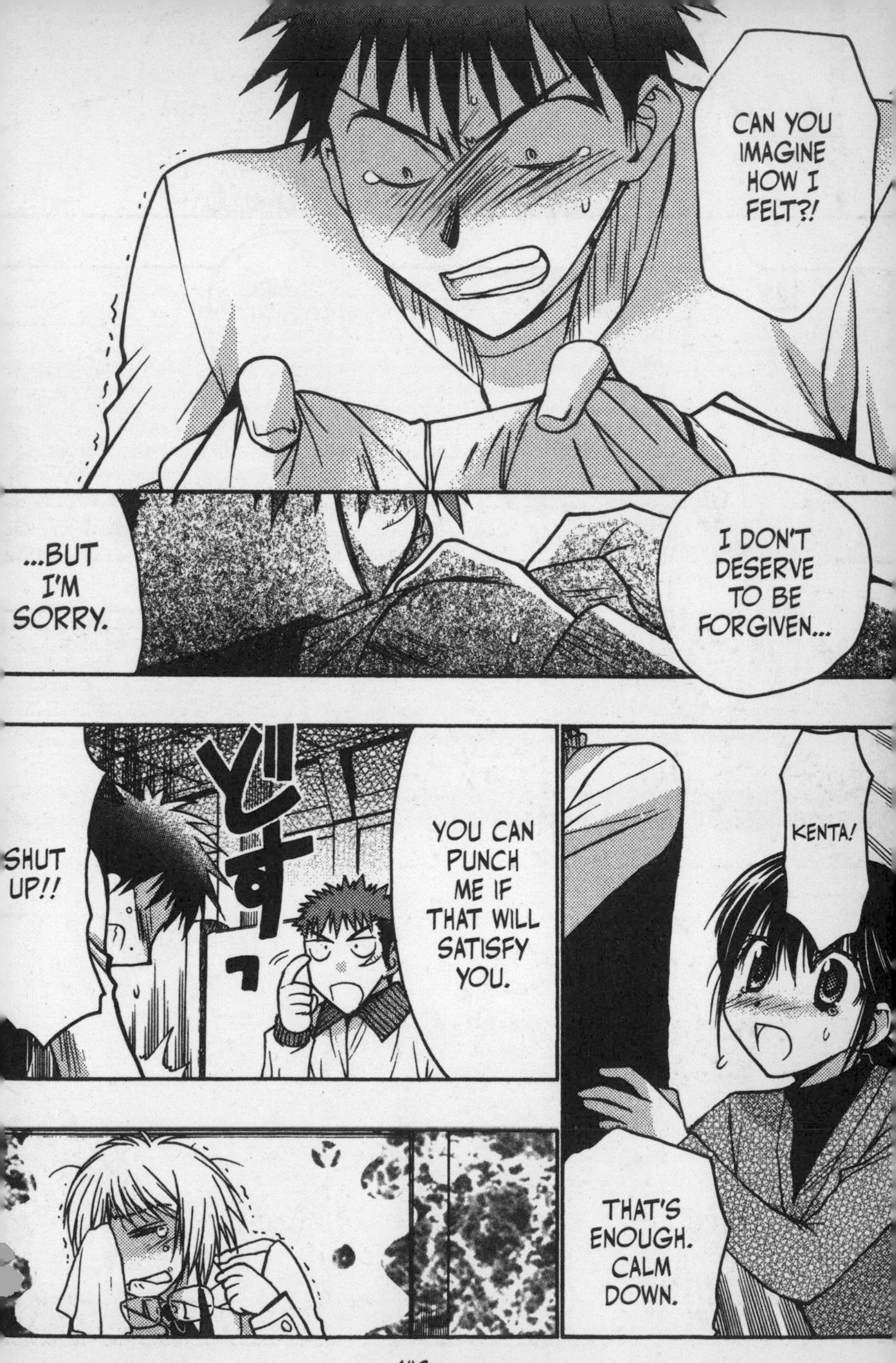
CAN YOU IMAGINE HOW I FELT?!
I DON'T DESERVE TO BE FORGIVEN...
...BUT I'M SORRY.
KENTA!
THAT'S ENOUGH. CALM DOWN.
YOU CAN PUNCH ME IF THAT WILL SATISFY YOU.
どすっ
SHUT UP!!

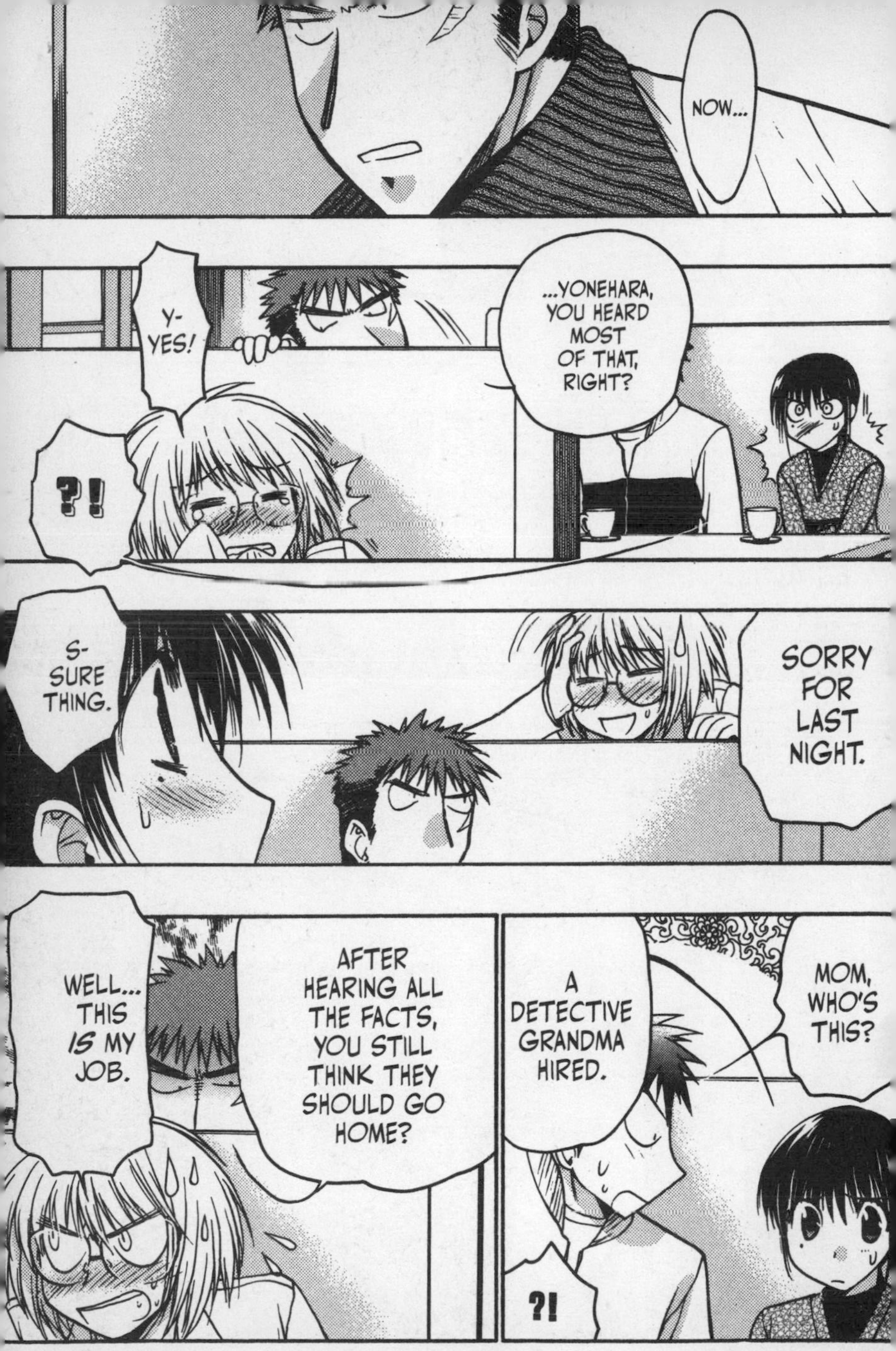
NOW...
...YONEHARA, YOU HEARD MOST OF THAT, RIGHT?
Y- YES!
?!
SORRY FOR LAST NIGHT.
S- SURE THING.
MOM, WHO'S THIS?
A DETECTIVE GRANDMA HIRED.
?!
AFTER HEARING ALL THE FACTS, YOU STILL THINK THEY SHOULD GO HOME?
WELL... THIS *IS* MY JOB.

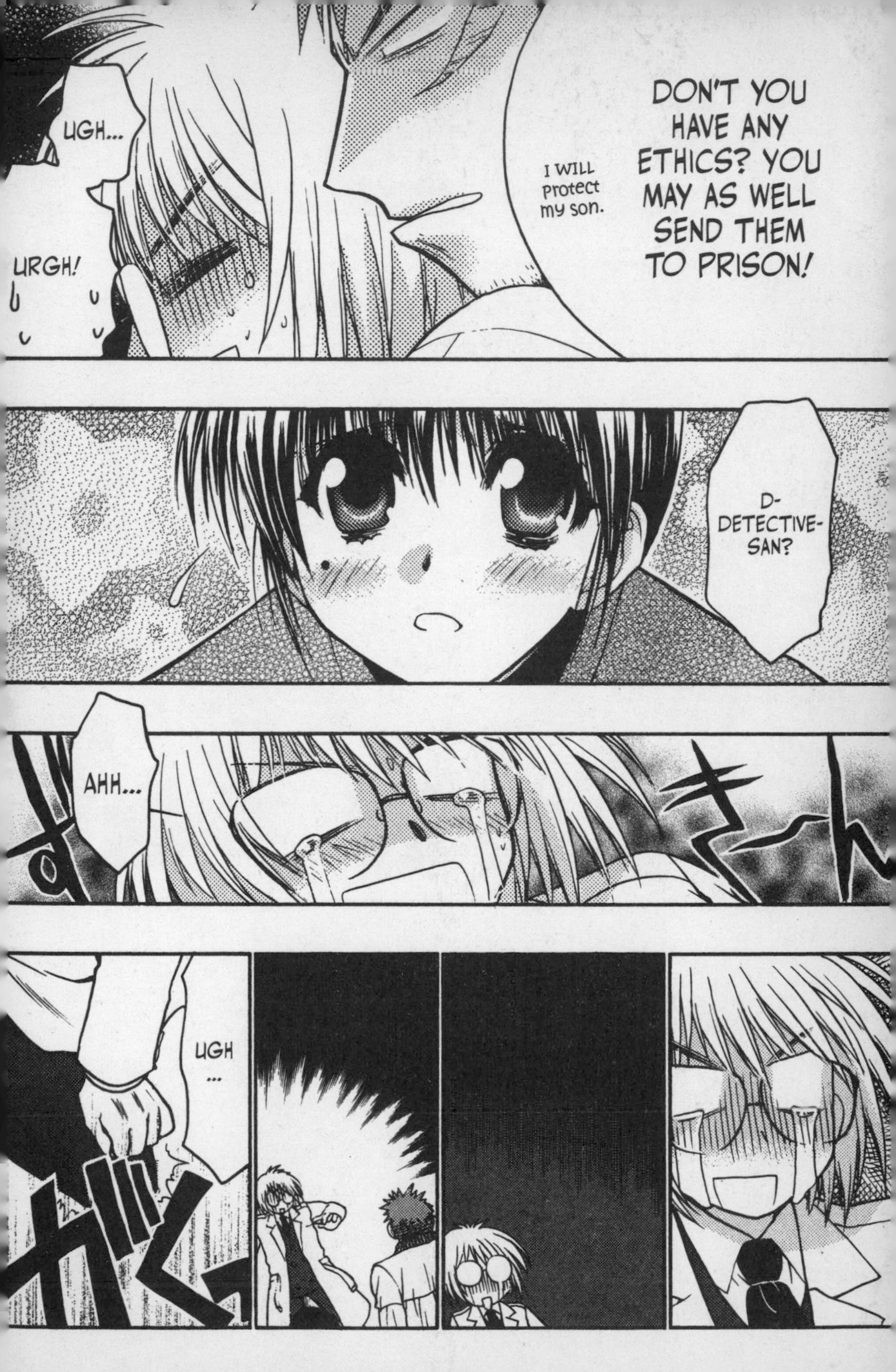
DON'T YOU HAVE ANY ETHICS? YOU MAY AS WELL SEND THEM TO PRISON!
I WILL Protect my son.
UGH...
URGH!
D- DETECTIVE-SAN?
AHH...
UGH ...

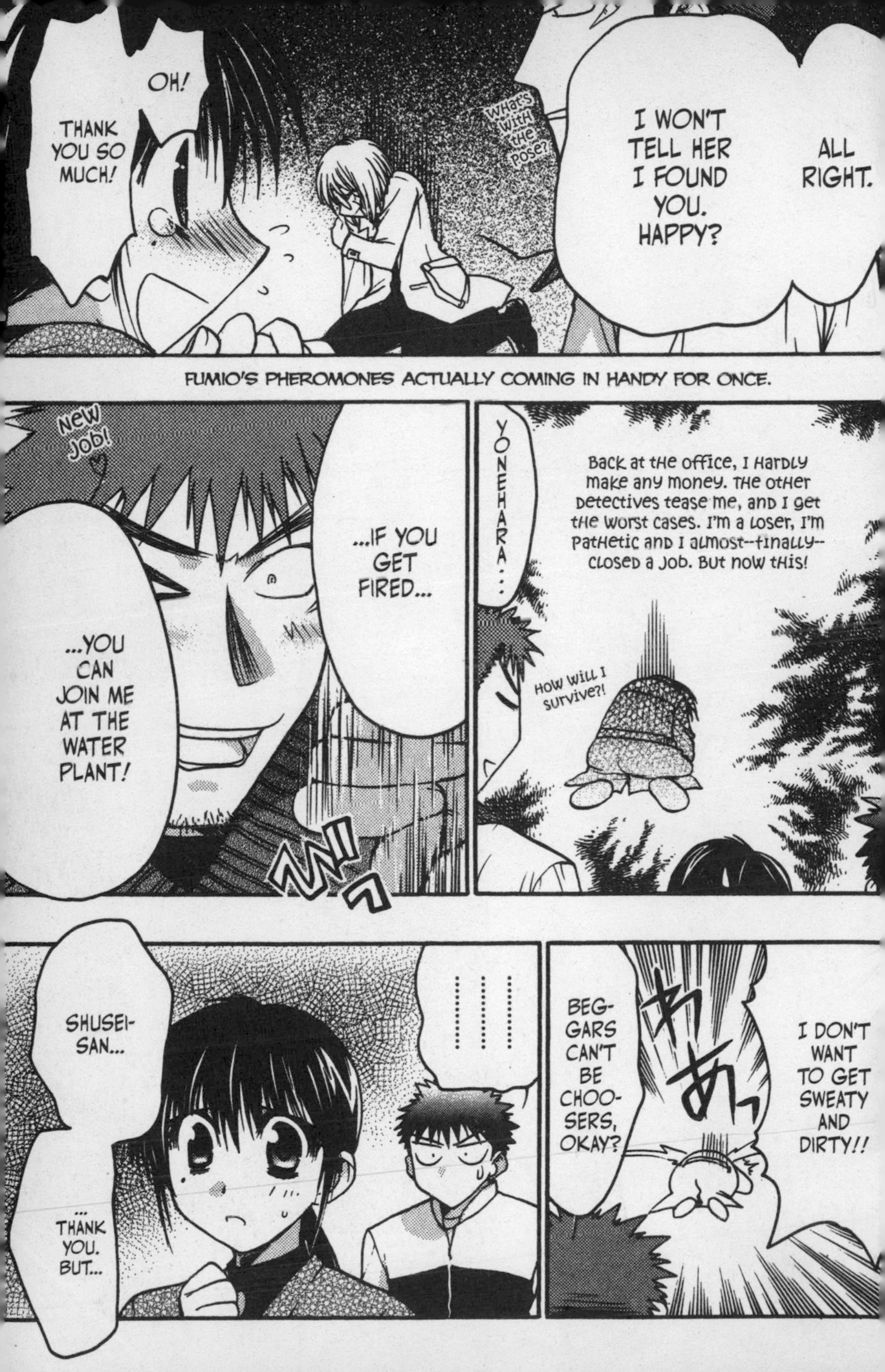
ALL RIGHT.
I WON'T TELL HER I FOUND YOU. HAPPY?
WHAT'S WITH THE POSE?
OH!
THANK YOU SO MUCH!
FUMIO'S PHEROMONES ACTUALLY COMING IN HANDY FOR ONCE.
YONEHARA...
Back at the office, I hardly make any money. The other detectives tease me, and I get the worst cases. I'm a loser, I'm pathetic and I almost--finally--closed a job. But now this!
How will I survive?!
New Job!
...IF YOU GET FIRED...
...YOU CAN JOIN ME AT THE WATER PLANT!
I DON'T WANT TO GET SWEATY AND DIRTY!!
BEG-GARS CAN'T BE CHOO-SERS, OKAY?
......
SHUSEI-SAN...
...THANK YOU. BUT...

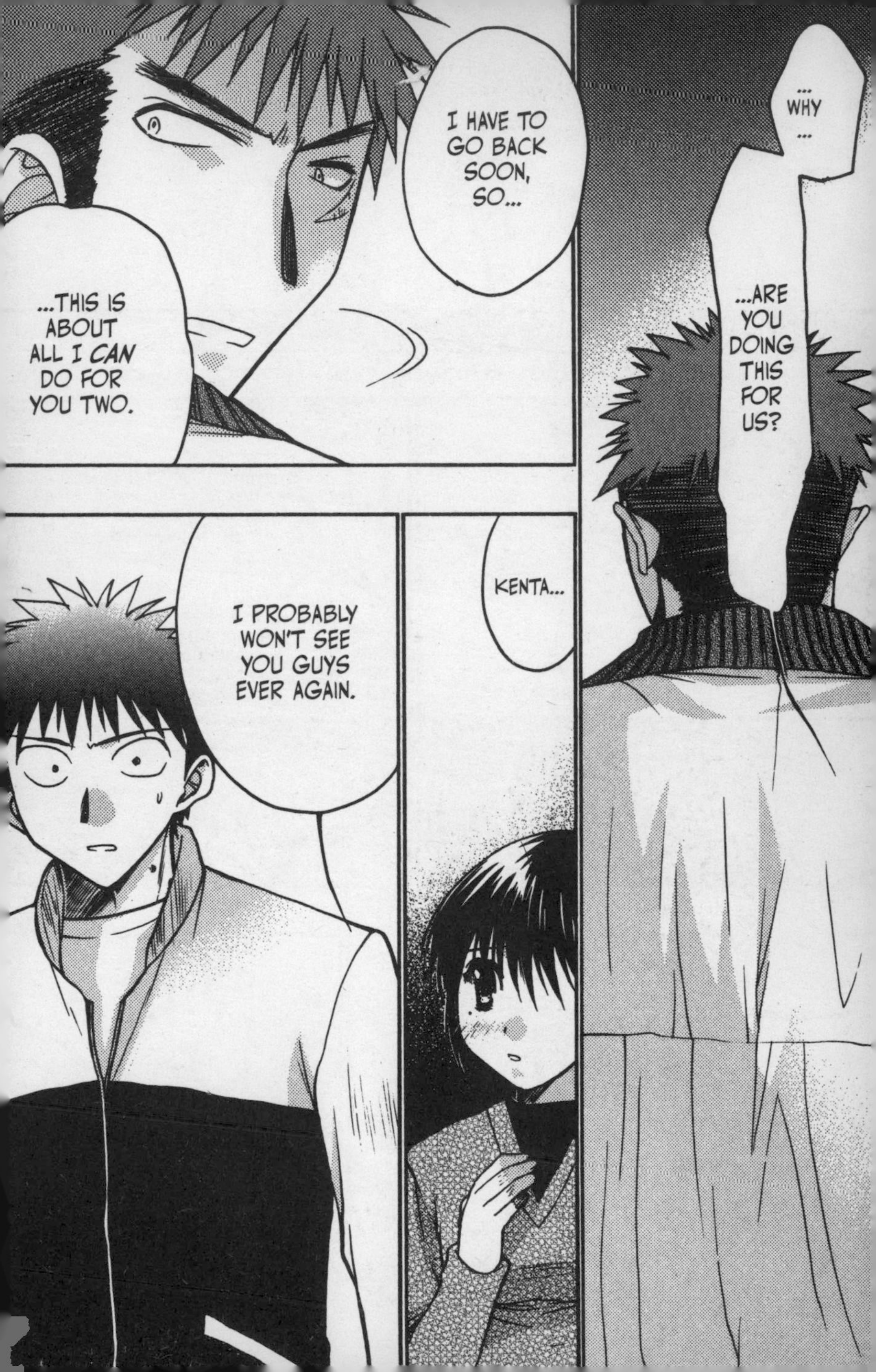
... WHY ...
...ARE YOU DOING THIS FOR US?
I HAVE TO GO BACK SOON, SO...
...THIS IS ABOUT ALL I *CAN* DO FOR YOU TWO.
KENTA...
I PROBABLY WON'T SEE YOU GUYS EVER AGAIN.

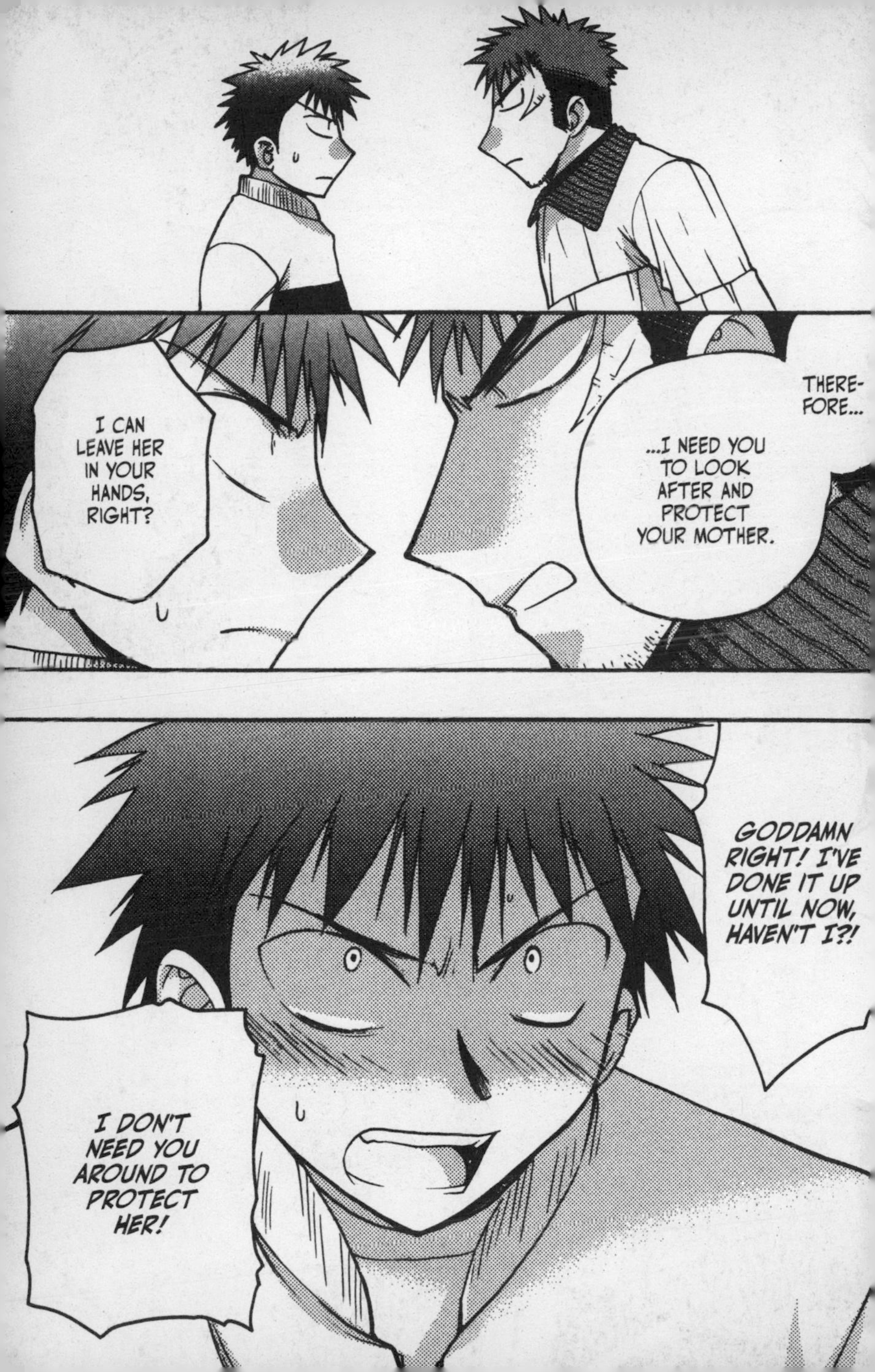
THERE-FORE...
...I NEED YOU TO LOOK AFTER AND PROTECT YOUR MOTHER.
I CAN LEAVE HER IN YOUR HANDS, RIGHT?
GODDAMN RIGHT! I'VE DONE IT UP UNTIL NOW, HAVEN'T I?!
I DON'T NEED YOU AROUND TO PROTECT HER!

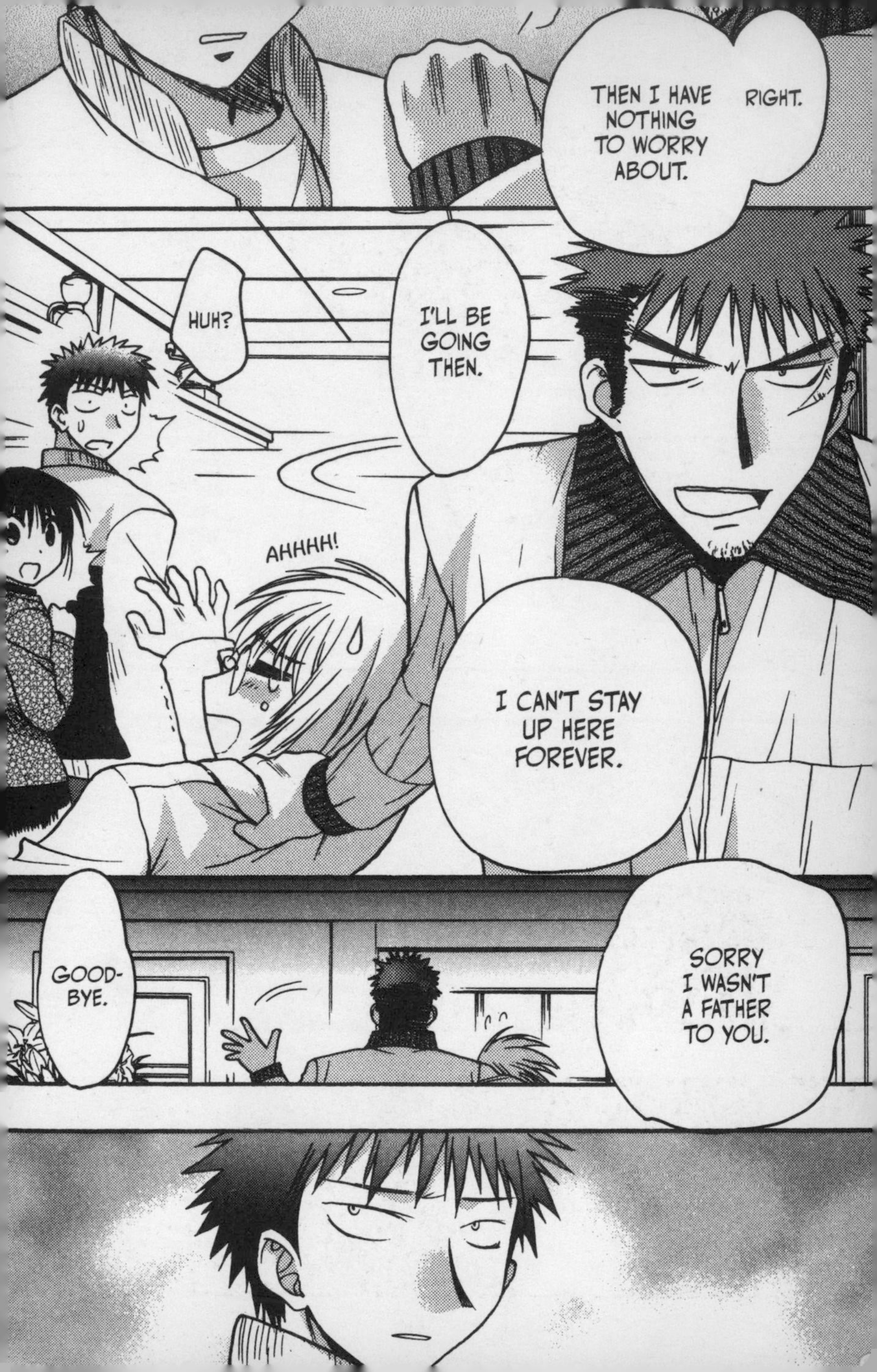
RIGHT.
THEN I HAVE NOTHING TO WORRY ABOUT.
I'LL BE GOING THEN.
HUH?
AHHHH!
I CAN'T STAY UP HERE FOREVER.
SORRY I WASN'T A FATHER TO YOU.
GOOD-BYE.

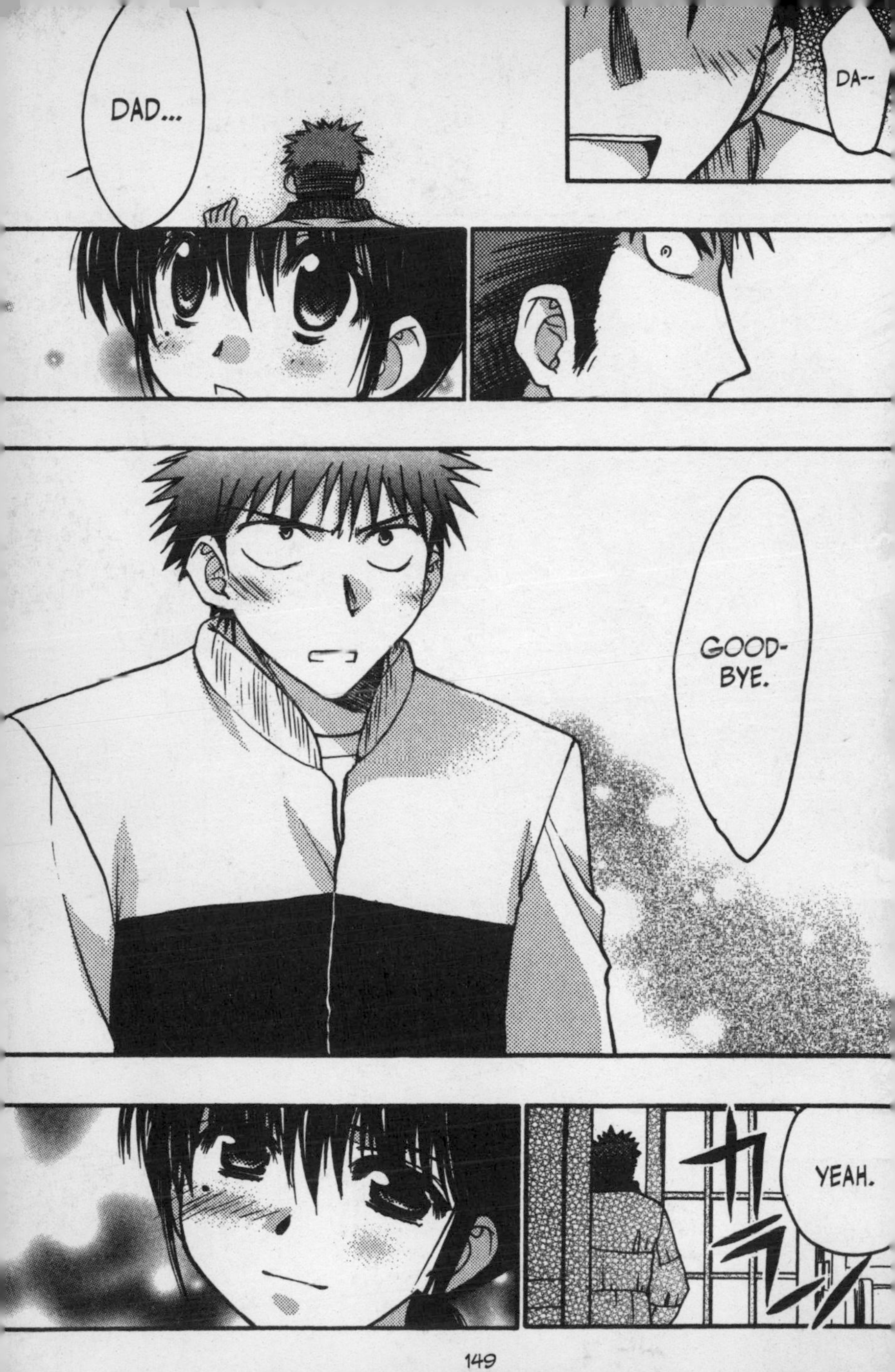
DA--
DAD...
GOOD-BYE.
YEAH.

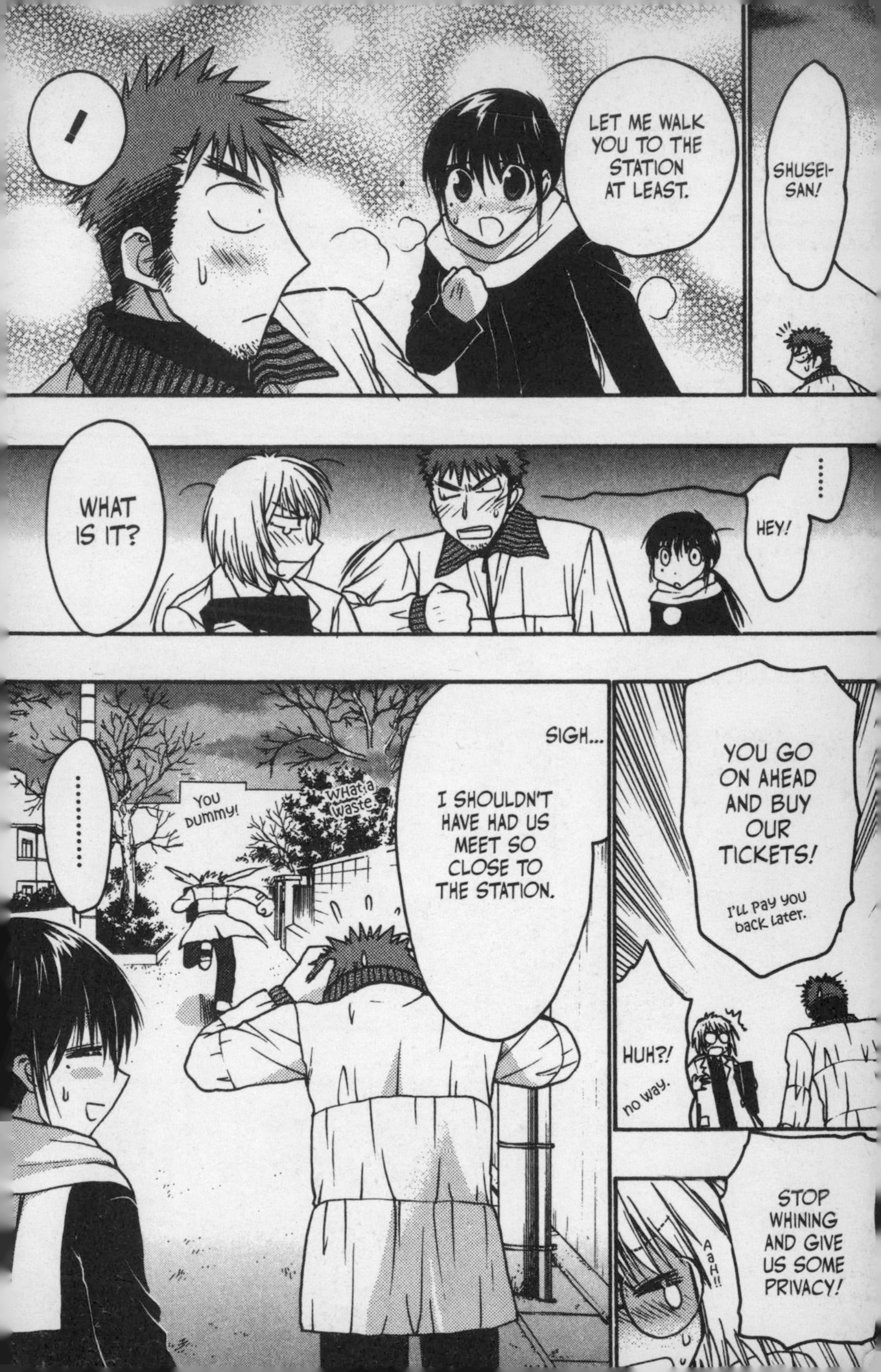
SHUSEI-SAN!
LET ME WALK YOU TO THE STATION AT LEAST.
!
……
HEY!
WHAT IS IT?
YOU GO ON AHEAD AND BUY OUR TICKETS!
I'll pay you back later.
HUH?!
no way.
STOP WHINING AND GIVE US SOME PRIVACY!
AAH!!
SIGH...
I SHOULDN'T HAVE HAD US MEET SO CLOSE TO THE STATION.
What a waste.
You dummy!
……

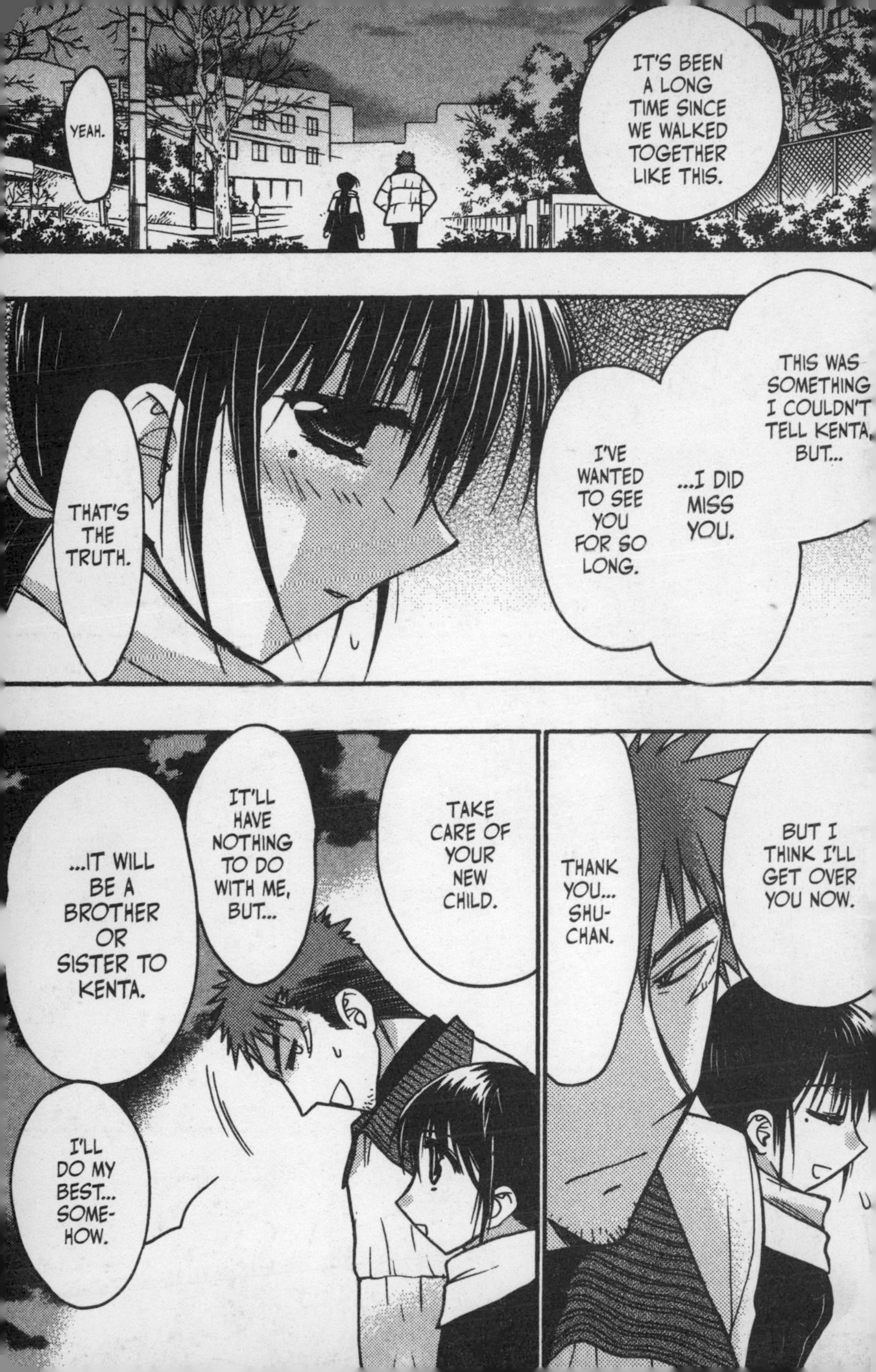
IT'S BEEN A LONG TIME SINCE WE WALKED TOGETHER LIKE THIS.
YEAH.
THIS WAS SOMETHING I COULDN'T TELL KENTA, BUT...
...I DID MISS YOU.
I'VE WANTED TO SEE YOU FOR SO LONG.
THAT'S THE TRUTH.
BUT I THINK I'LL GET OVER YOU NOW.
THANK YOU... SHU-CHAN.
TAKE CARE OF YOUR NEW CHILD.
IT'LL HAVE NOTHING TO DO WITH ME, BUT...
...IT WILL BE A BROTHER OR SISTER TO KENTA.
I'LL DO MY BEST... SOMEHOW.

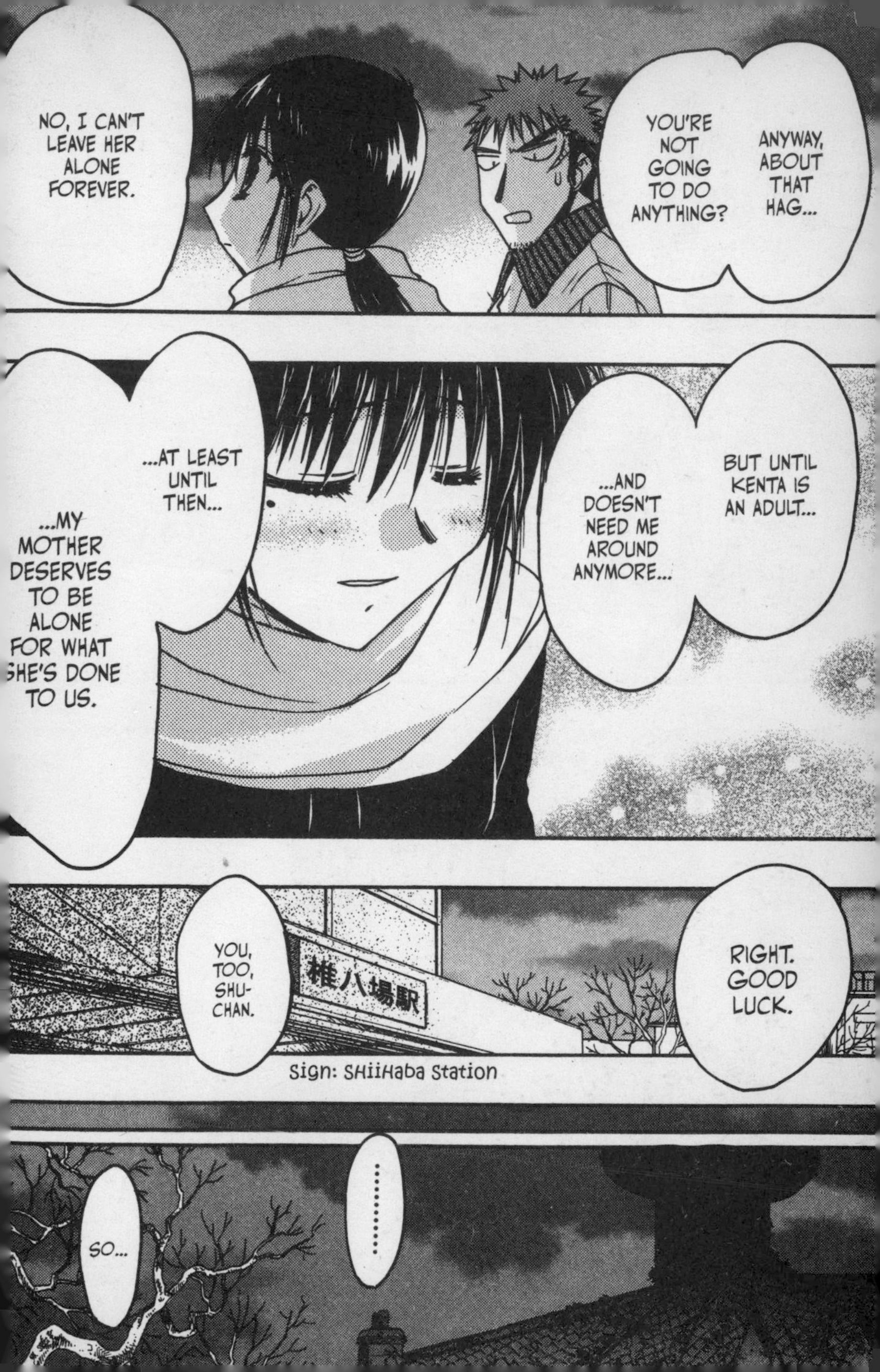

ANYWAY, ABOUT THAT HAG...
YOU'RE NOT GOING TO DO ANYTHING?
NO, I CAN'T LEAVE HER ALONE FOREVER.
BUT UNTIL KENTA IS AN ADULT...
...AND DOESN'T NEED ME AROUND ANYMORE...
...AT LEAST UNTIL THEN...
...MY MOTHER DESERVES TO BE ALONE FOR WHAT SHE'S DONE TO US.
RIGHT. GOOD LUCK.
椎八場駅
YOU, TOO, SHU-CHAN.
Sign: SHiiHaba Station
......
SO...

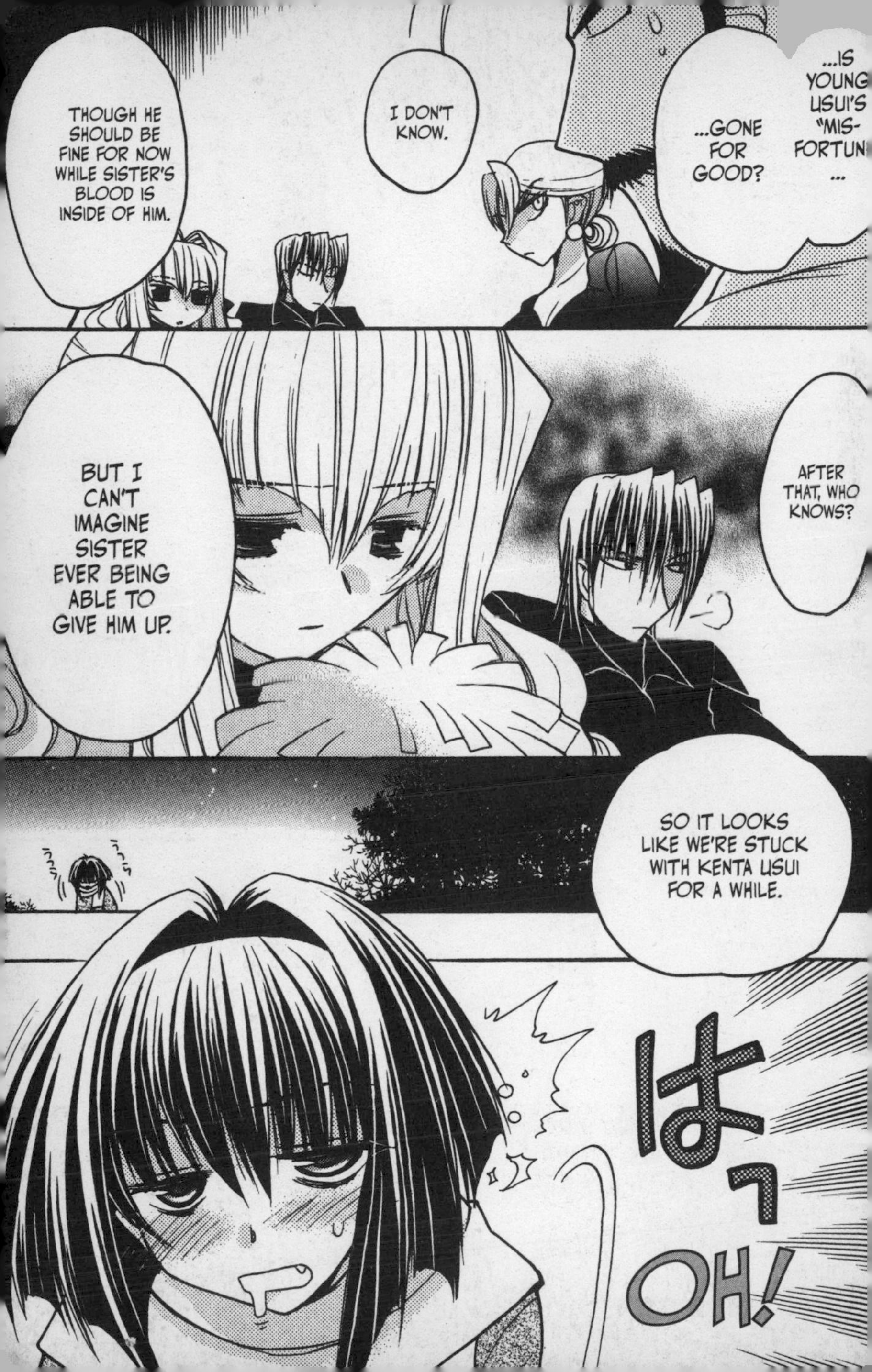
...IS YOUNG USUI'S "MIS-FORTUN ...
...GONE FOR GOOD?
I DON'T KNOW.
THOUGH HE SHOULD BE FINE FOR NOW WHILE SISTER'S BLOOD IS INSIDE OF HIM.
AFTER THAT, WHO KNOWS?
BUT I CAN'T IMAGINE SISTER EVER BEING ABLE TO GIVE HIM UP.
SO IT LOOKS LIKE WE'RE STUCK WITH KENTA USUI FOR A WHILE.
はっ
OH!

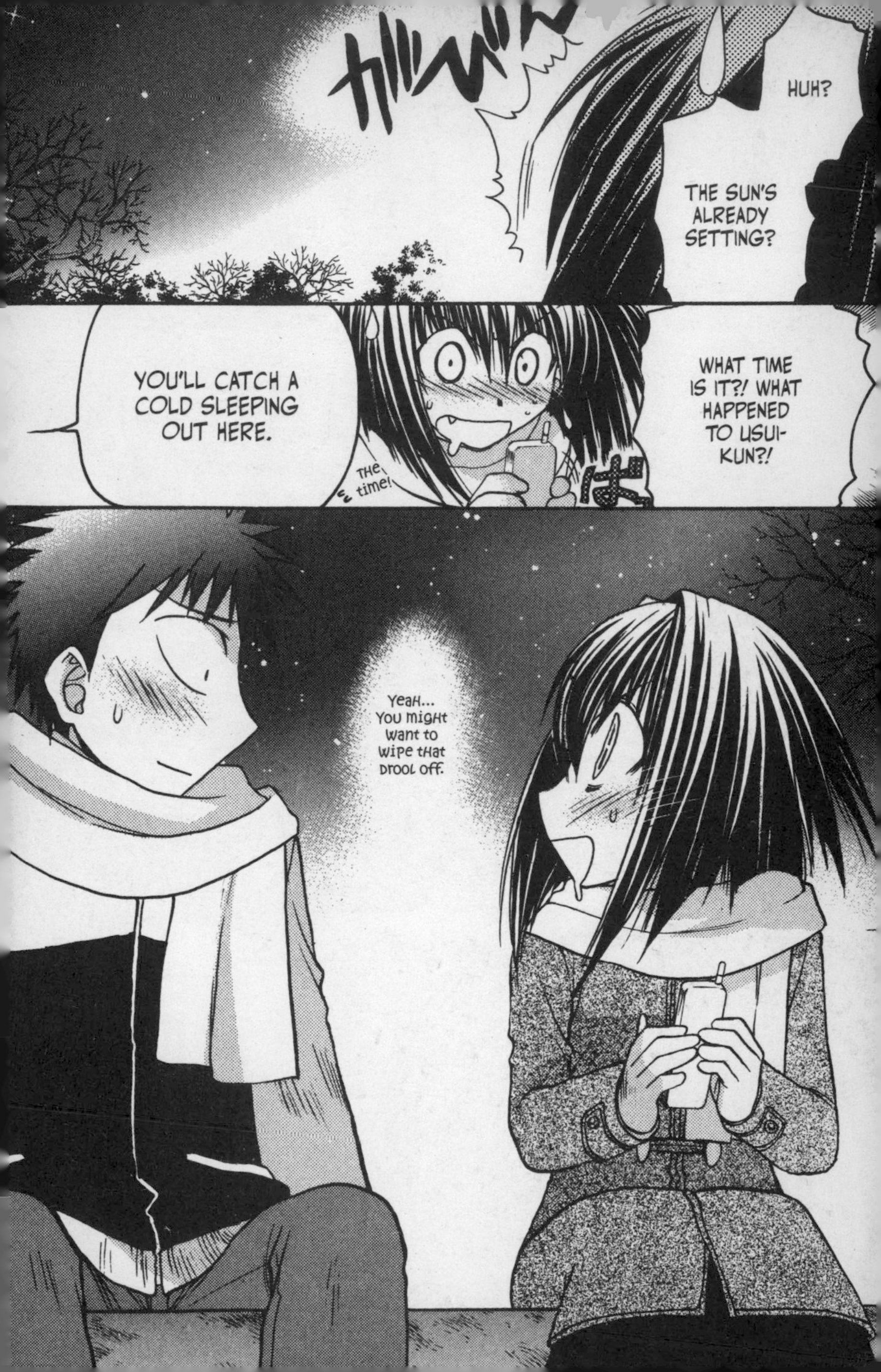
HUH?
THE SUN'S ALREADY SETTING?
WHAT TIME IS IT?! WHAT HAPPENED TO USUI-KUN?!
THE time!
YOU'LL CATCH A COLD SLEEPING OUT HERE.
Yeah... You might want to wipe that drool off.

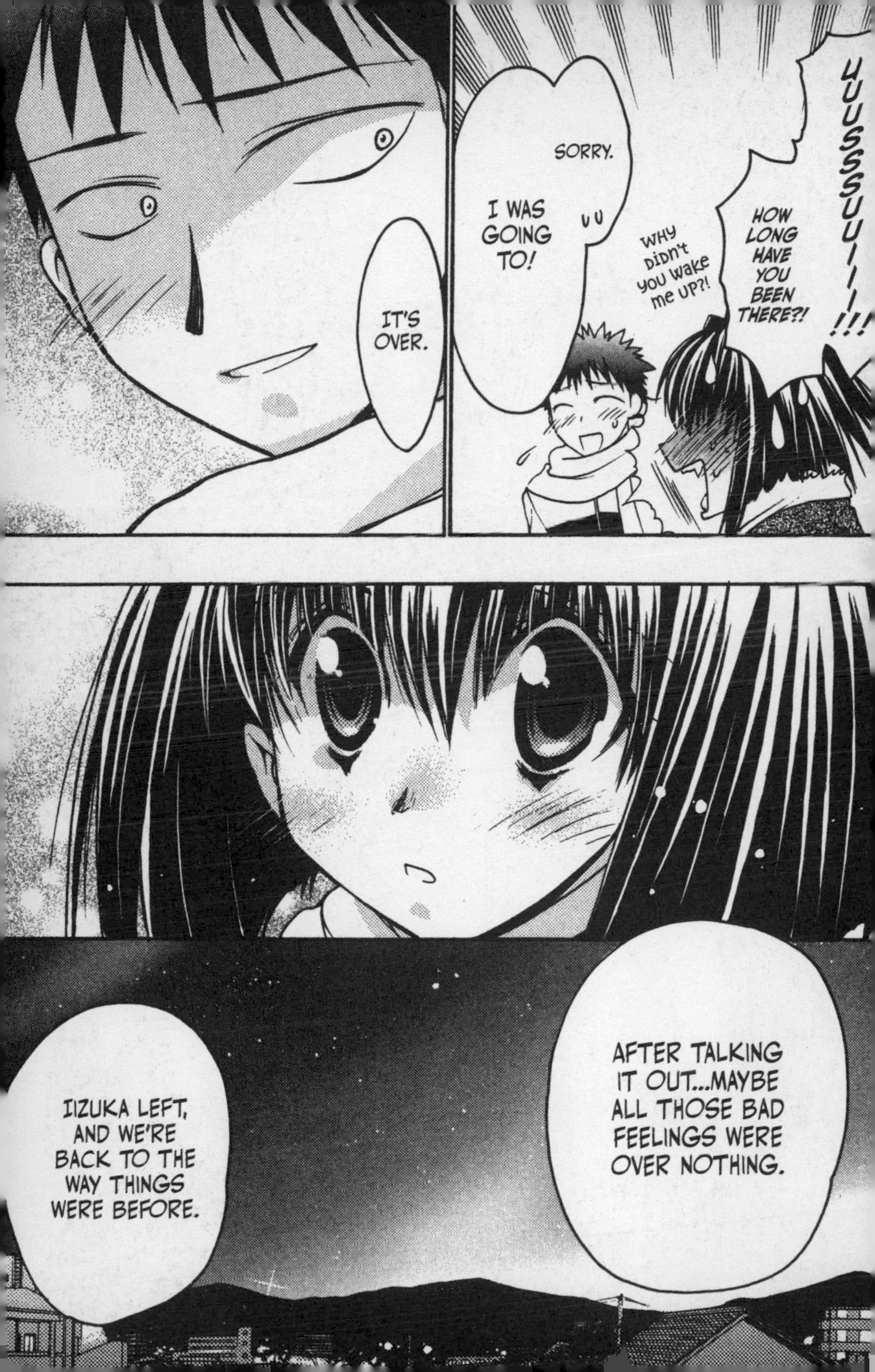
UUUSSSUU———!!!
HOW LONG HAVE YOU BEEN THERE?!
WHY DIDN'T YOU WAKE ME UP?!
SORRY.
I WAS GOING TO!
IT'S OVER.
AFTER TALKING IT OUT...MAYBE ALL THOSE BAD FEELINGS WERE OVER NOTHING.
IIZUKA LEFT, AND WE'RE BACK TO THE WAY THINGS WERE BEFORE.

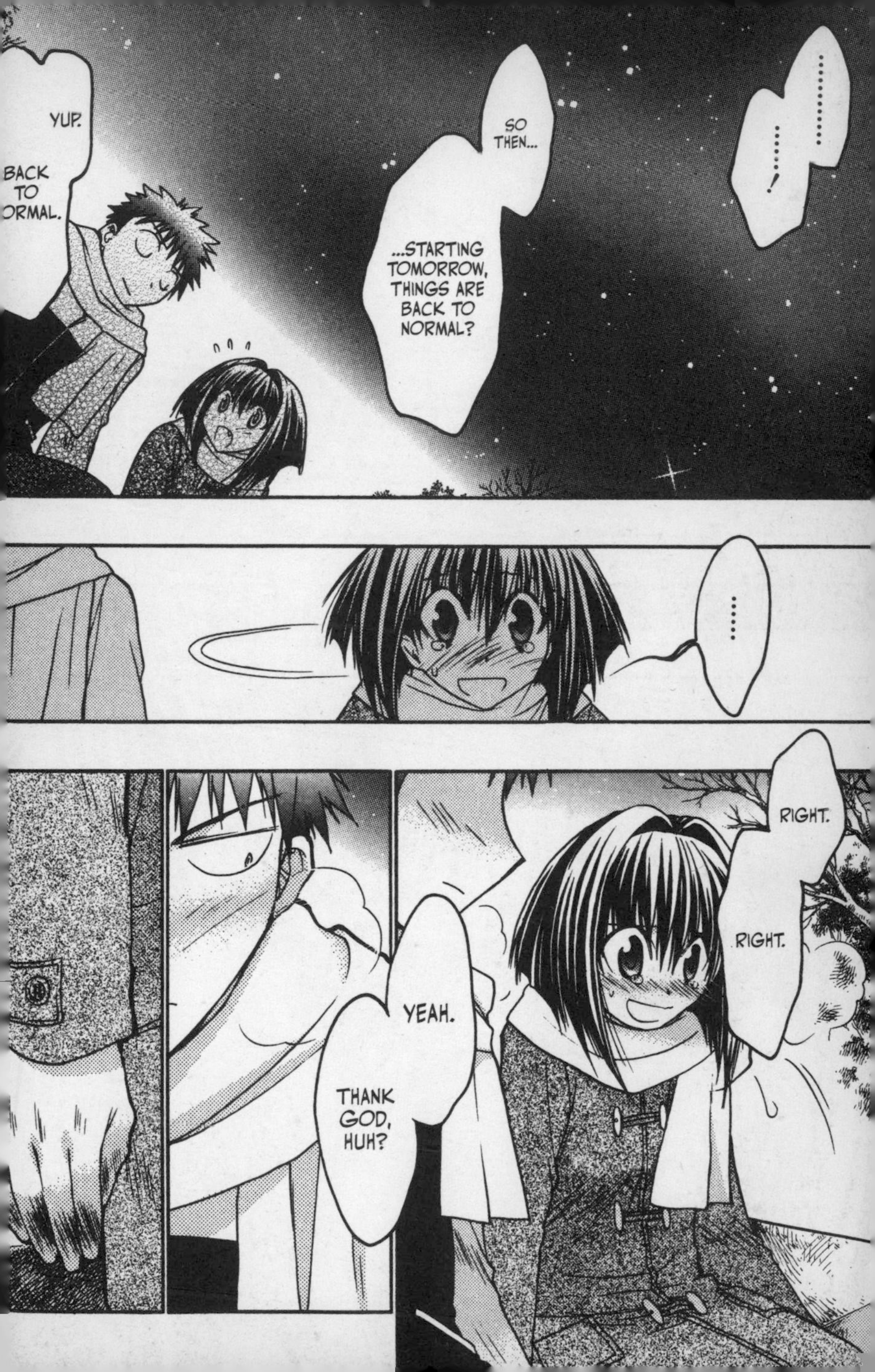
………
……!
SO THEN...
...STARTING TOMORROW, THINGS ARE BACK TO NORMAL?
YUP.
BACK TO ORMAL.
……
RIGHT.
RIGHT.
YEAH.
THANK GOD, HUH?

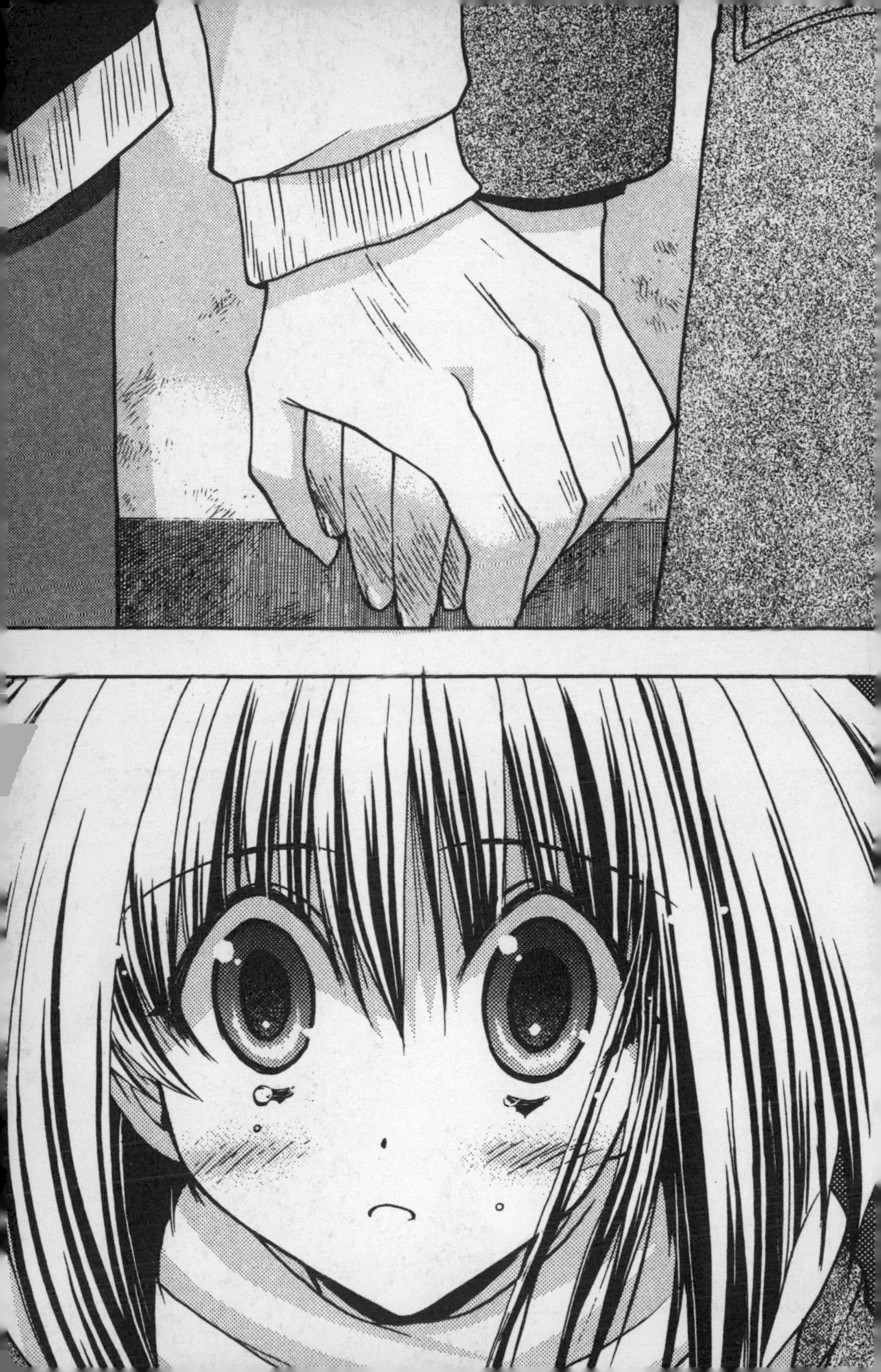

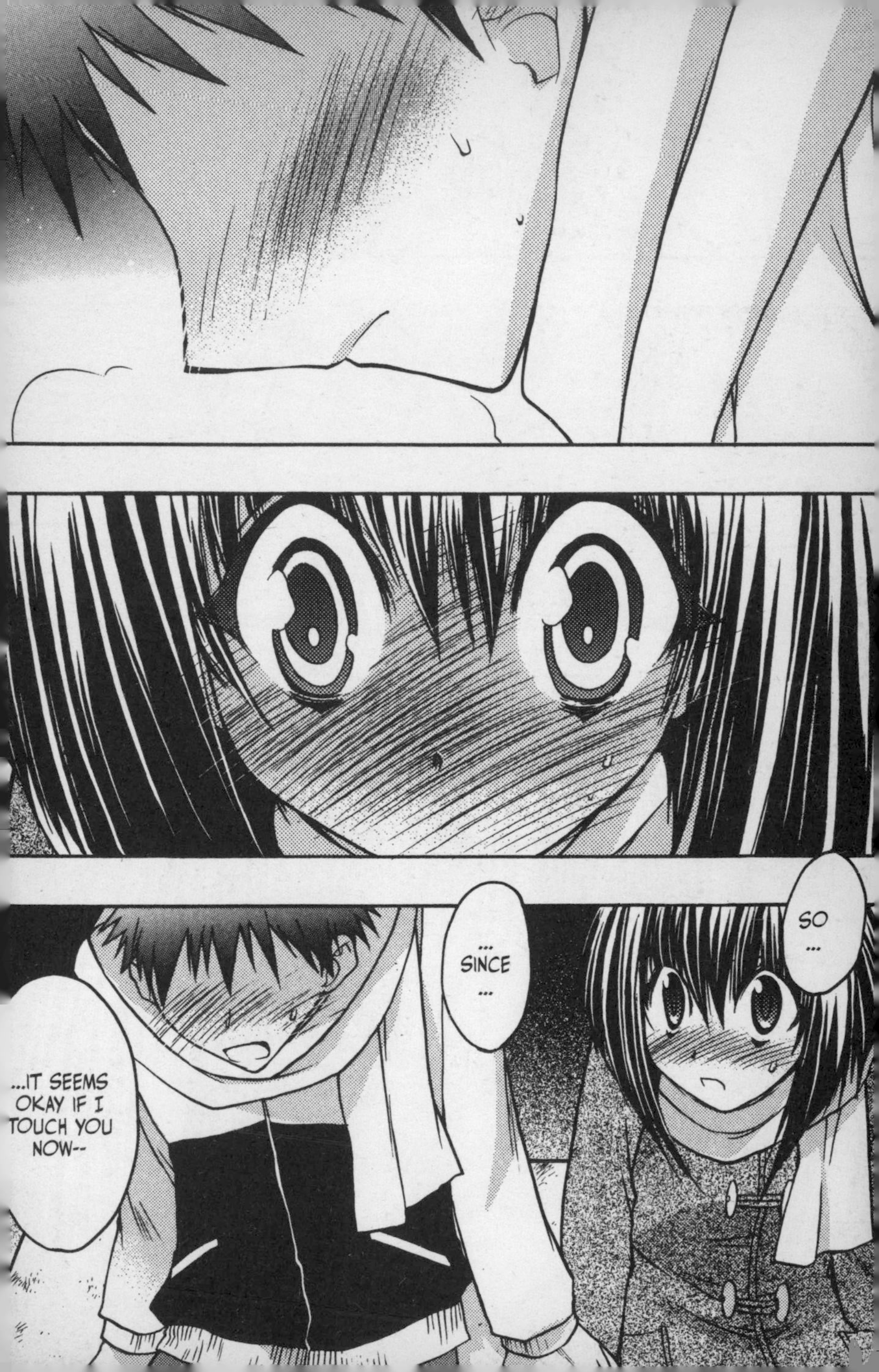
SO ...
... SINCE ...
...IT SEEMS OKAY IF I TOUCH YOU NOW--

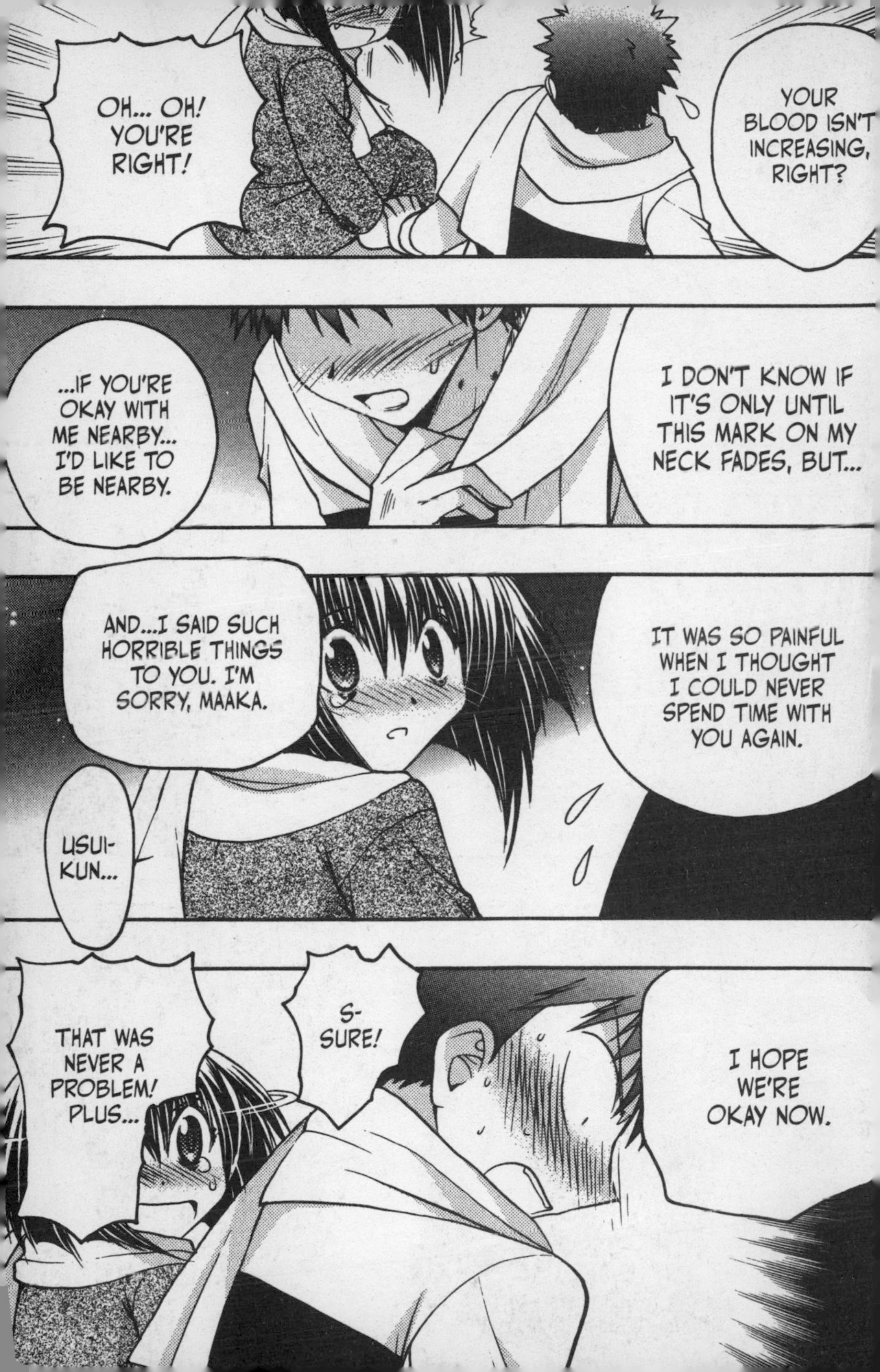
YOUR BLOOD ISN'T INCREASING, RIGHT?
OH... OH! YOU'RE RIGHT!
I DON'T KNOW IF IT'S ONLY UNTIL THIS MARK ON MY NECK FADES, BUT...
...IF YOU'RE OKAY WITH ME NEARBY... I'D LIKE TO BE NEARBY.
IT WAS SO PAINFUL WHEN I THOUGHT I COULD NEVER SPEND TIME WITH YOU AGAIN.
AND...I SAID SUCH HORRIBLE THINGS TO YOU. I'M SORRY, MAAKA.
USUI-KUN...
I HOPE WE'RE OKAY NOW.
S-SURE!
THAT WAS NEVER A PROBLEM! PLUS...

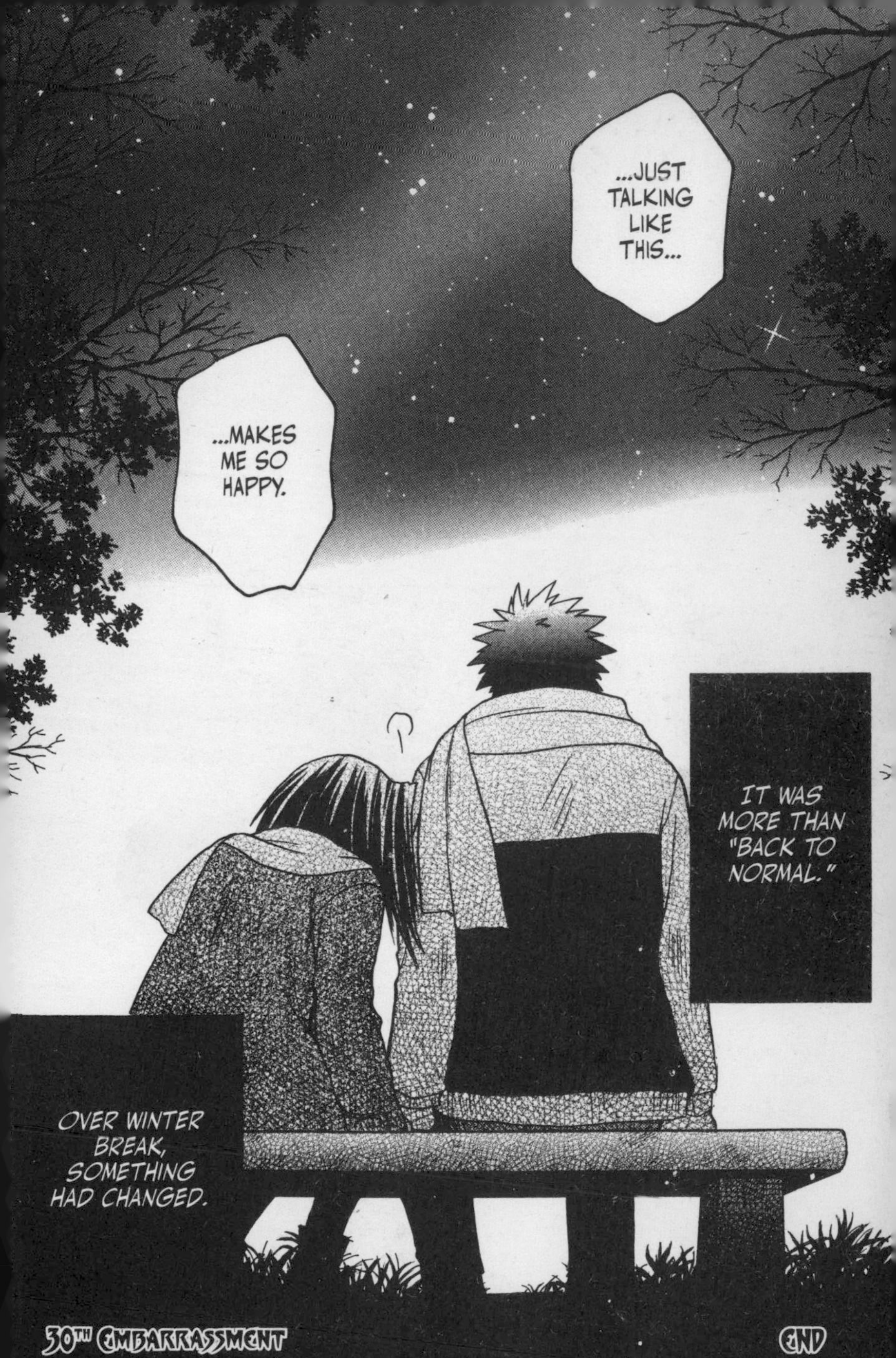
...JUST TALKING LIKE THIS...
...MAKES ME SO HAPPY.
IT WAS MORE THAN "BACK TO NORMAL."
OVER WINTER BREAK, SOMETHING HAD CHANGED.

30TH EMBARRASSMENT END

THE STORY I DIDN'T HAVE ENOUGH PAGES TO INCLUDE!

THE SCAR BELOW SHUSEI'S LEFT EYE WAS PUT THERE BY FUMIO.

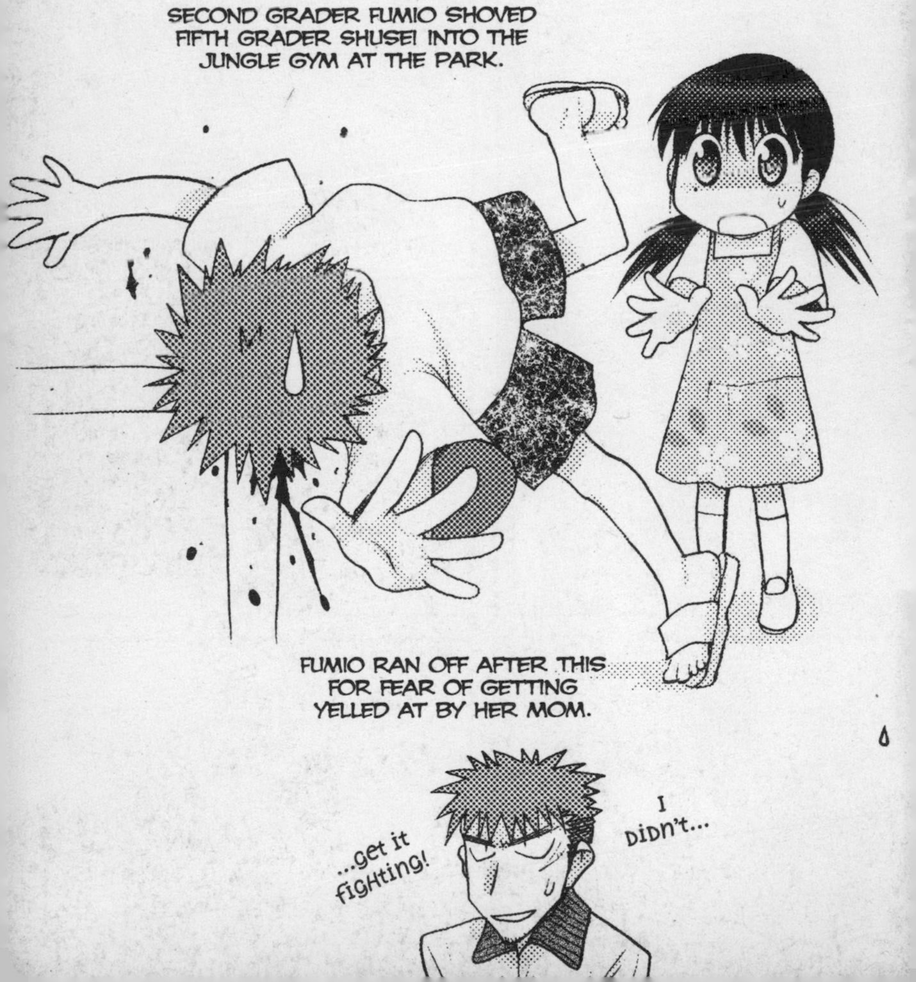
SECOND GRADER FUMIO SHOVED FIFTH GRADER SHUSEI INTO THE JUNGLE GYM AT THE PARK.
FUMIO RAN OFF AFTER THIS FOR FEAR OF GETTING YELLED AT BY HER MOM.
I DIDN'T...
...get it fighting!

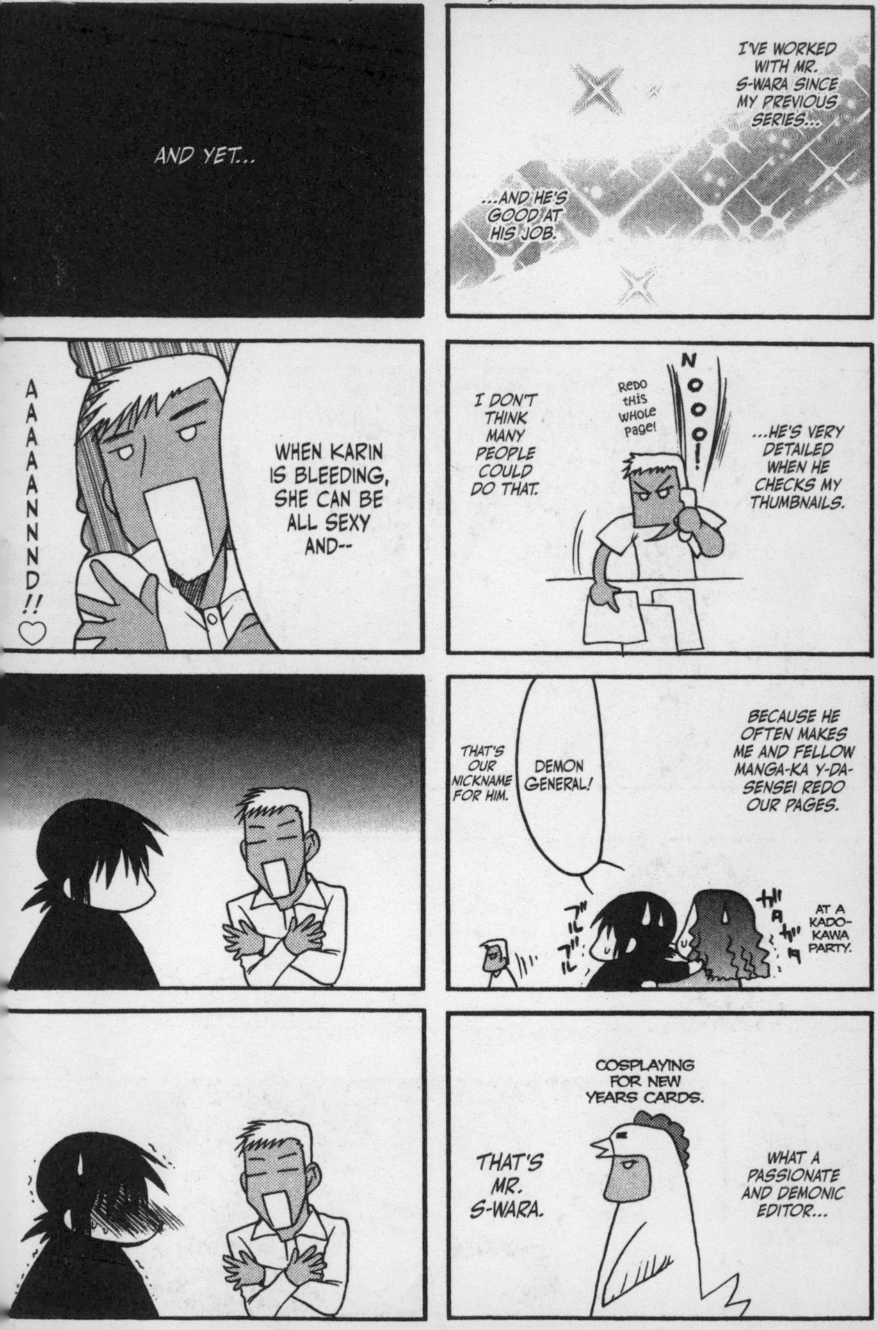
I'VE WORKED WITH MR. S-WARA SINCE MY PREVIOUS SERIES...
...AND HE'S GOOD AT HIS JOB.
AND YET...
...HE'S VERY DETAILED WHEN HE CHECKS MY THUMBNAILS.
NOOO!
Redo this whole Page!
I DON'T THINK MANY PEOPLE COULD DO THAT.
WHEN KARIN IS BLEEDING, SHE CAN BE ALL SEXY AND--
AAAAAAANNND!! ♡
BECAUSE HE OFTEN MAKES ME AND FELLOW MANGA-KA Y-DA-SENSEI REDO OUR PAGES.
DEMON GENERAL!
THAT'S OUR NICKNAME FOR HIM.
AT A KADO-KAWA PARTY.
WHAT A PASSIONATE AND DEMONIC EDITOR...
COSPLAYING FOR NEW YEARS CARDS.
THAT'S MR. S-WARA.

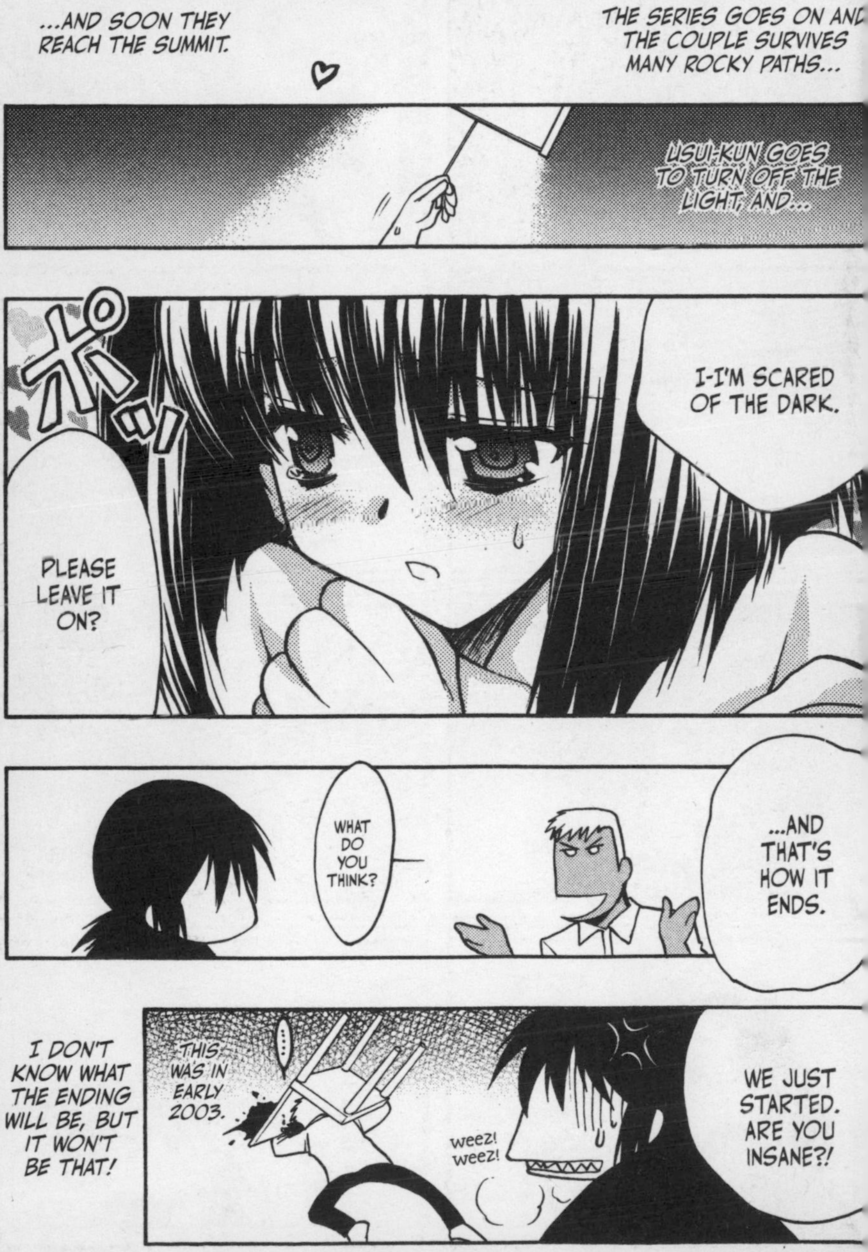
THE SERIES GOES ON AND THE COUPLE SURVIVES MANY ROCKY PATHS...
...AND SOON THEY REACH THE SUMMIT.
USUI-KUN GOES TO TURN OFF THE LIGHT, AND...
ポッ
I-I'M SCARED OF THE DARK.
PLEASE LEAVE IT ON?
...AND THAT'S HOW IT ENDS.
WHAT DO YOU THINK?
WE JUST STARTED. ARE YOU INSANE?!
weez! weez!
THIS WAS IN EARLY 2003.
I DON'T KNOW WHAT THE ENDING WILL BE, BUT IT WON'T BE THAT!

MR. SEXUAL HARRASSMENT

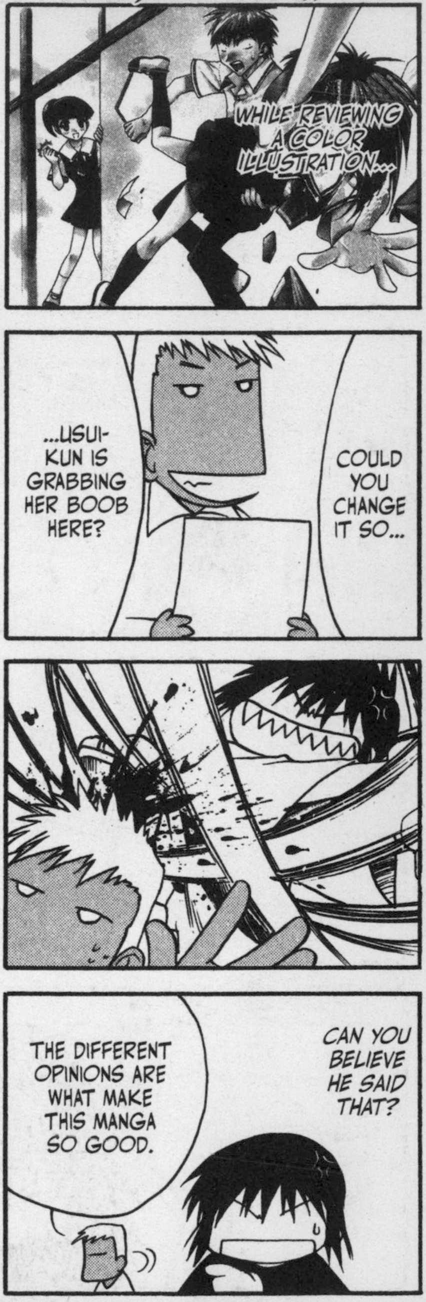
WHILE REVIEWING A COLOR ILLUSTRATION...
COULD YOU CHANGE IT SO...
...USUI-KUN IS GRABBING HER BOOB HERE?
CAN YOU BELIEVE HE SAID THAT?
THE DIFFERENT OPINIONS ARE WHAT MAKE THIS MANGA SO GOOD.

NEWLY WED

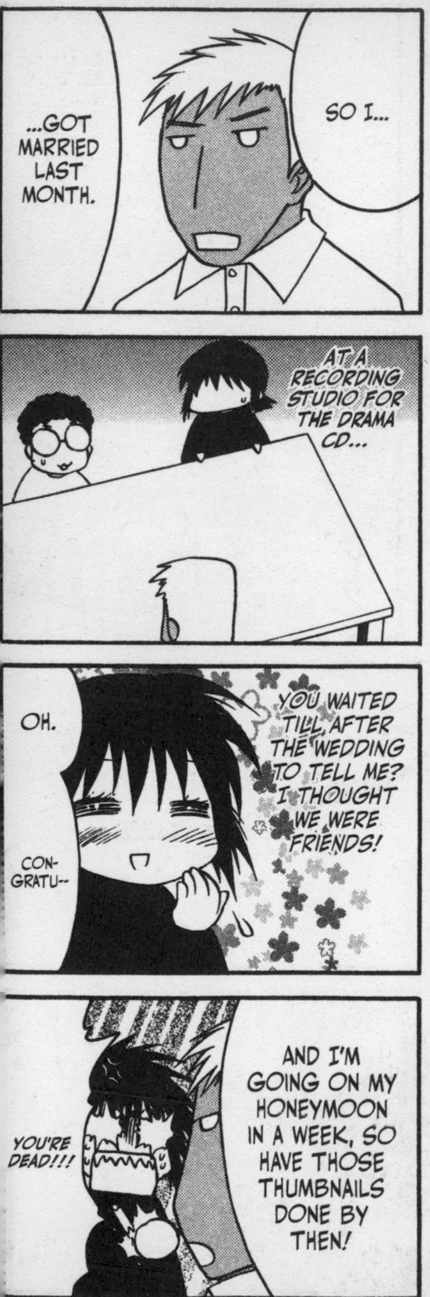
SO I...
...GOT MARRIED LAST MONTH.
AT A RECORDING STUDIO FOR THE DRAMA CD...
YOU WAITED TILL AFTER THE WEDDING TO TELL ME? I THOUGHT WE WERE FRIENDS!
OH.
CON-GRATU--
AND I'M GOING ON MY HONEYMOON IN A WEEK, SO HAVE THOSE THUMBNAILS DONE BY THEN!
YOU'RE DEAD!!!

u made me do all those extra color pages and then this?

Anime Meeting

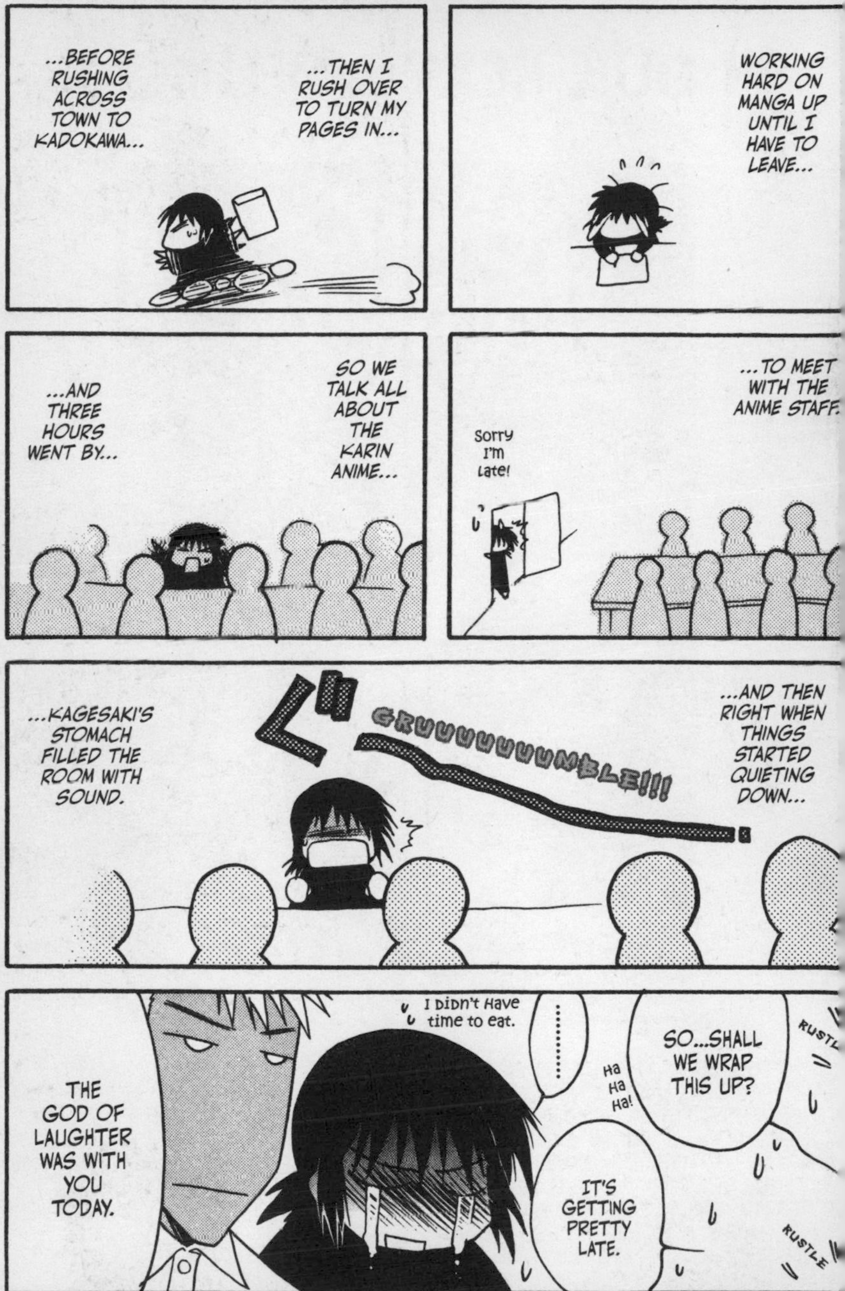

WORKING HARD ON MANGA UP UNTIL I HAVE TO LEAVE...
...THEN I RUSH OVER TO TURN MY PAGES IN...
...BEFORE RUSHING ACROSS TOWN TO KADOKAWA...
...TO MEET WITH THE ANIME STAFF.
Sorry I'm late!
SO WE TALK ALL ABOUT THE KARIN ANIME...
...AND THREE HOURS WENT BY...
...AND THEN RIGHT WHEN THINGS STARTED QUIETING DOWN...
GRUUUUUUUUUMBLE!!!
...KAGESAKI'S STOMACH FILLED THE ROOM WITH SOUND.
RUSTLE
SO...SHALL WE WRAP THIS UP?
Ha Ha Ha!
......
I didn't have time to eat.
IT'S GETTING PRETTY LATE.
RUSTLE
THE GOD OF LAUGHTER WAS WITH YOU TODAY.

Umm... the anime will be starting soon...so please check it out!

IN OUR NEXT VOLUME...

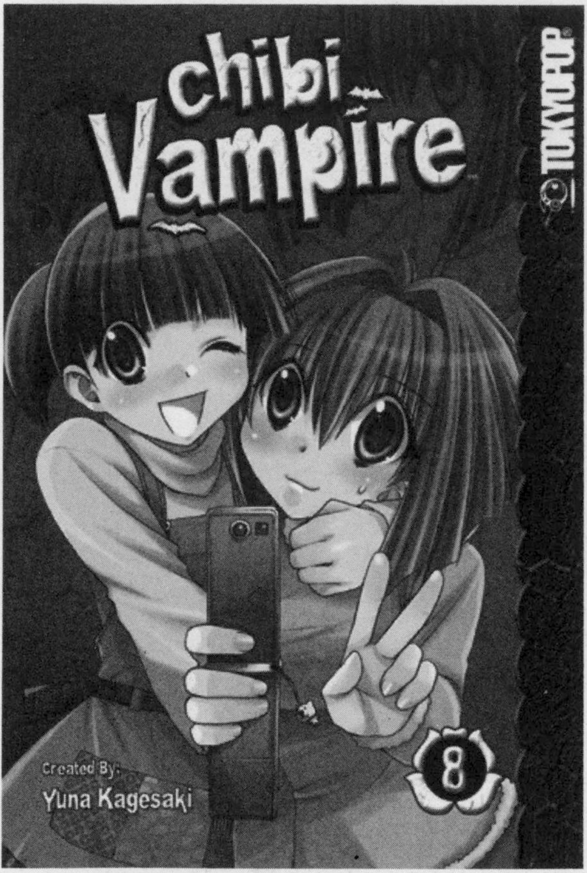
chibi Vampire
TOKYOPOP
8
Created By:
Yuna Kagesaki

AFTER MONTHS OF VERY LITTLE ROMANTIC DEVELOPMENT, ARE KARIN AND KENTA READY TO TAKE A BIG STEP FORWARD IN THEIR RELATIONSHIP? WITH THE YOUNG COUPLE FINALLY STARTING TO HOLD HANDS IN PUBLIC, MAKI FORCES THE ISSUE BY SETTING UP A DATE. WHEN KARIN AND KENTA FIND THEMSELVES ALONE AT THE ZOO, CRAZY MONKEYS AREN'T THE ONLY THING THEY HAVE TO CONTEND WITH. WHAT'S THIS? A ROMANTIC RIVAL? SOMETHING TELLS ME THIS CURVY KOOK COULD BE A MAJOR THORN IN KARIN'S SIDE!

LOST TIME

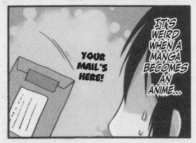

IT'S WEIRD WHEN A MANGA BECOMES AN ANIME...
YOUR MAIL'S HERE!
Here's the script.
Here are the character designs.
I GET SO MANY SILLY DOCUMENTS SENT TO ME...
......
...WHICH MEANS I KEEP LOSING TRACK OF THE IMPORTANT ONES!
AND IT TAKES FOREVER TO FIND THEM!

Especially my approvals for the novel. I always seem to lose those! Yeah, it's my fault, but...

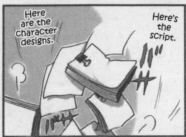

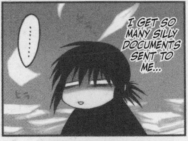

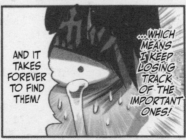

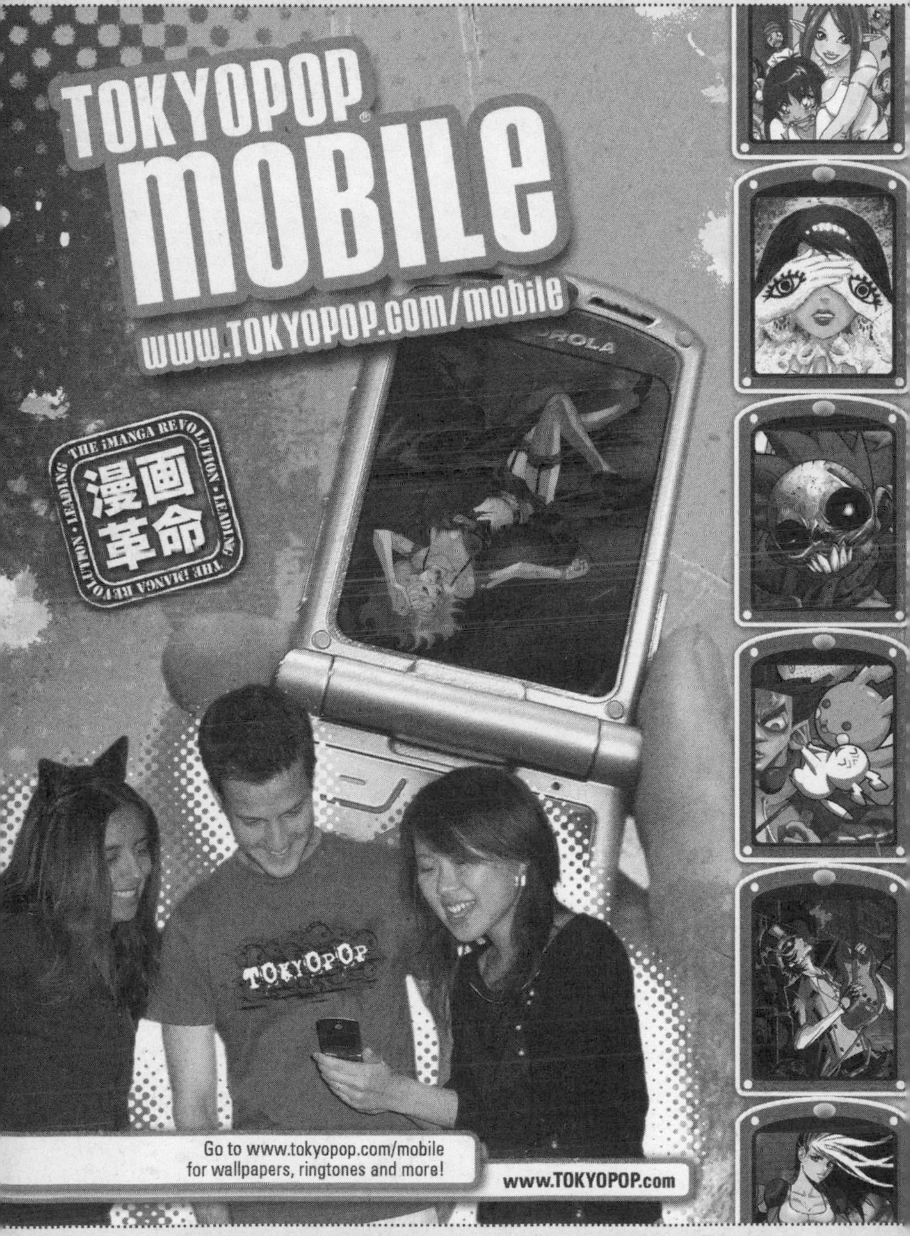
TOKYOPOP®
MOBILE
www.TOKYOPOP.com/mobile
THE iMANGA REVOLUTION · LEADING · THE iMANGA REVOLUTION · LEADING
漫画革命
TOKYOPOP
Go to www.tokyopop.com/mobile
for wallpapers, ringtones and more!
www.TOKYOPOP.com

STOP!

This is the back of the book.
You wouldn't want to spoil a great ending!

This book is printed "manga-style," in the authentic Japanese right-to-left format. Since none of the artwork has been flipped or altered, readers get to experience the story just as the creator intended. You've been asking for it, so TOKYOPOP® delivered: authentic, hot-off-the-press, and far more fun!

DIRECTIONS

If this is your first time reading manga-style, here's a quick guide to help you understand how it works.

It's easy... just start in the top right panel and follow the numbers. Have fun, and look for more 100% authentic manga from TOKYOPOP®!